ARSLAN

A NOVEL

BY

JON KELLY

ISBN: 1-4107-2144-2 (e-book)
ISBN: 1-4107-2145-0 (Paperback)
ISBN: 1-4107-2146-9 (Dust Jacket)

Library of Congress Control Number: 2003091023

This book is printed on acid free paper.

Printed in the United States of America
Bloomington, IN

1stBooks – rev. 03/05/03

INTRODUCTION

"What if a man did not die and experienced life for thousands of years?"

- How could a man or woman survive so many years?
- How would he be different than other men who live for shorter periods of time?
- What would it mean to religion to have someone who defies the rules of mortality?
- What could explain life on earth and the meaning of intelligence under these circumstances?
- Can our developing technology help move religion to another level of understanding of the human situation?
- Does technology hold out hope we can eventually understand what we are and where we are going?
- Are human feelings such as love, curiosity, and hope important in the technological world of the future?

Read and enjoy.

ACKNOWLEDGEMENTS

My sincere thanks to those who assisted or encouraged the writing and publication of this novel. The following people deserve special mention:

Carol Christy, my wife
Cliff Weaver, a friend
Alisha who read it first
Pvt. Shindler, U.S. Army (died 1970)

1.   <u>Amwat, Phrygia 759 B.C.</u>

Truth and common acceptance as true are not the same.

In 759 B.C., a baby boy named Arslan appeared in an unnamed village, too small for a name, within several weeks walk of the city of Gordion in Phrygia, now central Turkey. Gordion was the capital and the home of the great king who had ruled for many years.

Arslan arrived in this unnamed village late one evening when an elderly couple presented themselves, carrying baby Arslan. They approached one of two huts in the village and called out to the occupants, "Oh, esteemed persons, please allow us to enter and hear of our plight."

Amwat, a not too successful farmer, and his wife, Kyla, a kindly woman at the apparent end of her child bearing years, came to the door of the poor hut and asked what the old ones wanted.

The elderly man spoke, "We are very old and will die soon, as we have been driven from our home in the south by soldiers and have no hope for food or shelter. We do not want our only remaining grandson to die with us. Is there no one who will take a healthy young child to raise as their son?"

Amwat looked at the old man and then at the old woman holding the baby. They appeared to be not old, but ancient, as thin as weeds and very pale. However, they projected strength of personality, which belied their obviously frail bodies. Their bodies appeared so weak as to be ready to fail at any moment or be blown away by the slightest wind. Both had eyes glowing like black gold as they stood in the semi-darkness, illuminated only by the moonlight. *"Are these creatures real or are they demons trying to lull us into a sense of safety before they grow sharp claws and fangs and take our lives, and worse our souls?"* thought Amwat.

Amwat's fearful thoughts were interrupted by the voice of his Kyla, who he knew to be the strongest and least fearful of women at important times. She said, "Oh, old ones, do you tell us you are willing to give up the innocent baby you hold, who my intuition tells me you love dearly, so the child can live while you will certainly perish. Is that correct?"

1

The old woman now spoke for the first time, "Gentle lady, you see into our hearts and souls and feel the sorrow we feel as we give up this child, but we must give the child a chance to survive. We can do nothing else."

Amwat and Kyla looked at each other then retreated into their hut with the comment to the old ones, "Wait while we talk."

Inside the hut, Kyla broke the silence," We need a son to care for us when we grow old. Perhaps we should take the child to raise."

Amwat knew to oppose Kyla, who had wanted a child for all their years together but was barren, would be a bigger problem than he was prepared to face. He said, "We will take the child. Perhaps we can get some money from the old ones also."

Going back out of the hut, Amwat spoke, "We will take the child to raise if, in fact, he is healthy, but we are poor people and need some help to protect the future of the child. What can you give us, if anything?"

The elderly man spoke again saying, "We are grateful you will take the child to raise. He is a very special child and as healthy as any you have ever seen. We are also poor but do have this small bag of gold we will give you. You must hide this gold away and tell no one, or others will try to steal it. You must not trust even your closest neighbor and should tell everyone the child is yours. Swear you will do this."

Amwat did not need to think more than a moment since he had never had any gold of his own, although he had seen some in the market at Gordion. He said, "Old ones, we will take your child and the gold to help with his care and swear to tell no one how he or the gold came to us."

And so, the child and the gold, not coin but strange small ingots with markings, came into the hands of Amwat and Kyla. They were told the child's name was Arslan.

Arslan grew into a light brown haired youth, nurtured by Kyla who loved Arslan from the first moment she held him. Amwat was a good father as well. He had no real choice due to Kyla, but he also came to feel Arslan was his hope for being cared for when he became too feeble to work himself.

The gold also made a huge difference in the lives of Amwat, Kyla, and Arslan. They had received some twelve ingots from the old couple and chose to take one to the market in Gordion every year or two to allow the purchase of items they otherwise would never have. The first time they bought two young calves they raised and slaughtered, providing meat and hides, they ate or traded for other things to improve their lives. Neighbors wondered at their good fortune when they returned from the market with two calves, but they explained Amwat's mother had given them a few coins when they married and had saved them many years.

At the age of seventeen Arslan was a handsome young man. He worked the, now better than average, farm of his father, Amwat. He was otherwise not distinguished from other young men of his time and class, except for his intelligence that seemed to be at a bit higher level than his peers. Arslan was a reasonably happy young man who was now interested in finding a woman to be his wife.

In the spring of 743 B.C., Arslan found Amwat keeled over in the fields one day and carried him back to their hut. He lingered but a short time before he died, apparently of heart failure. Both Arslan and his mother, Kyla, the only mother he had ever known, were distressed at the death of Amwat but accepted the fate of all mortal men. Kyla now took Arslan into her confidence concerning how he was brought to them by the elderly couple and told of the gold, of which only three ingots remained. Arslan was surprised but not bothered by the information and began to plan his life taking the existence of the gold into consideration.

2. <u>Mata</u>

the duel

Does the lovely lioness know
the extreme danger of the bull
with horns like sharpened steel
and hooves to break all bone?

She will stalk him in the grass
and think her swifter than his bulk
but she must remember truth
that he's quicker than he looks.

Her pride may risk her skin
with one small slip or misstep,
the game a closer undertaking
than she thought she was making.

If the lioness is a woman
and the bull a mortal man,
and the game, the dance of loving
perhaps the lioness wins in losing
and the bull gains love in winning
and both get more than lost.

Kyla made a point to search the surrounding villages for a suitable wife for Arslan. As his mother, she would not accept a girl who did not have some special qualities to provide to her beloved Arslan. Wealth, in the form of a nice dowry, would be nice, but she also wanted a comely girl who would work hard so Arslan would be pleased. Then one day she found Mata.

Mata was the youngest daughter of a leading family in another village, not too close, that was good so her family would not interfere too much in young lives. Her father had enough to insure a good dowry and she had a reputation as a hard worker. She also was a beautiful girl who turned the heads of most men who saw her. But

Mata was strong willed, born in August, which is common for those born then, and young men generally did not return to court her after being exposed to her biting independence.

Kyla thought, "Mata can be difficult, but Arslan is more intelligent than others, born in May she calculated from his size when brought to her—a birth time common to the intelligent, and if anyone can tame a lioness like Mata, it is a bull like Arslan. So, Kyla arranged for Arslan and Mata to meet.

Sparks flew when Arslan and Mata first met. Sparks of independence clashing with boundaries that could limit or control freedom, even if meant well. And sparks of pure lust between healthy beings who immediately felt physical and emotional attraction.

Mata spoke first as they were introduced under the watchful eye of Mata's kin, "So you are Arslan, the farmer who seeks a wife. Why should I want to share your life and bed? Many others have come who wanted a silent wife who would accept her "place" and never speak. Is that also your dream, a wife with no spine who you can beat into submission and bed for your pleasure alone?

Mata's mother was embarrassed by her outspoken comments; as was usual. Her father, also as usual, was amused by the independence and impertinence of Mata.

Before they had a chance to interject anything into the conversation, Arslan spoke, "Lovely Mata, I have come here to meet you despite the warnings of others you hold yourself in such high self-esteem no man can measure up to your standards. They also say you are so proud even a king would be hard pressed to tame you. Well, I have not come to strip away your self-esteem, and do not want a woman I have to beat to bed. Your pride is a thing of beauty that can make a joining of you and I a meeting and blending of two strong souls. What we make together, who knows but fate, but we can try to go beyond what we are as two souls alone. A king might tame you, but that is the last thing I want. I want to gain the love of the wild and free creature I see before me, not to tame you into submission. This is my truth, believe me or not."

Mata was visibly taken aback by the words of this handsome, young man, as were her kith and kin. Most men want only to dominate women, and make them small in theirs and the world's eyes, so they have dominion over something. In many cases, they would never be strong or intelligent enough to dominate other men so they do the easy thing and dominate their women.

After a long silent pause, Mata spoke," I feel the truth of your words, as only a woman can sense about such subjects. Make your arrangements with my father and I will go with you willingly. No one can predict the outcome of these things between men and women, but at least you seem to believe in your heart of hearts what you are now saying. It is much more than other men who wanted to take me to wife. I will pledge to you I will always give at least as much to our joining as do you, and more when times require, to make as much of our lives as we can."

The kin of Mata were stunned by the exchange they had just heard. This is not the normal way of such matters and the fact Mata had finally accepted a suitor was surprising to those assembled. But as always in the real world, acceptance came.

The father of Mata quickly made arrangements with Arslan, one of his cattle and two sheep as a dowry. It was no time to be cheap; he had a chance to marry off his daughter to a reasonably prosperous young man. If fortune turned bad, he might have to spend his waning years with them and they had good prospects to improve their lot in the world. *"Mata and this young bull, yes, perhaps I should feel sorry for the world,"* he thought.

At their marriage feast, Kyla immediately saw she had been right to bring them together and also saw her part in it was done. Nothing she could do now would alter what fate had already decided—these two would do what they would do—with or without her help now. She would help when she could but would not try to control them.

3.   Amwat—742 B.C.

Education should be the act of learning.

The small village where Arslan returned to with his bride, Mata, was coming to be known as "Amwat" for the father of Arslan. Kyla was pleased with this naming of their living place, as Amwat had been a kind and cooperative husband and was one of the better men she had ever known. It was not surprising when in the surrounding areas; being sent to the "place where Amwat lives" had eventually been shortened to go to "Amwat." Thus the name had stuck.

Upon returning to Amwat, Kyla, Mata, and Arslan decided, as suggested by Kyla, that Arslan should build a smaller hut for Kyla to occupy and Mata and Arslan should take over the larger hut as their home. Kyla explained she wanted to give the young couple the privacy young lovers need, and a chance to learn about each other without the constant presence of another person to influence their perceptions. Kyla said, "There will likely be a short time before children come to impose their presence on your lives. Take the time now to be together as one, without being hindered."

Mata was delighted with the arrangement, and loved Kyla for the suggestion. All three threw themselves into the task of building a new, smaller hut for Kyla and were done within two days. It was not grand but was livable and Kyla was pleased to have a space of her own where she would not bother the pursuits of the young.

The first night in Amwat for Mata, Kyla went to spend the night with neighbors to give the young couple time alone before her new hut was built. Arslan was not totally inexperienced in the act of bedding women as there were girls in the surrounding area that did not choose to wait for a wedding to try out their young bodies and Arslan was young, handsome and willing.

Also, there had also been the hut of a widow about two days walk toward Gordion where he had stopped for a drink of water on his last trip to the city. He had approached the hut and called out, "Can a young traveler find a drink of water here?"

The door opened and out walked a woman some years older than he but not a hag by any means. She was short in stature but walked with a sensual prancing that immediately sensitized his not insignificant sexual awareness. The woman called out, "Who asks for a drink at the house of the widow, Soka."

Arslan said, "I am Arslan of Amwat, two days walk to the north, traveling to Gordion to trade. I am also the son of Amwat for whom my village is named and my mother is the kindly Kyla, who many know as a good woman of our place. Is it enough information to trade for a few sips of water for a weary traveler?"

Soka undressed Arslan with her eyes, or so it seemed, and then said, "You are a comely young man who could do more than give information for your drink of water. Perhaps an offer of a good supper and a warm bed would convince you the home of Soka is a very good place to stop for the night."

Arslan was not totally inexperienced with women but had never, in his short seventeen years, met a woman like Soka. She was not beautiful, her face was pock marked and her hair was unkempt, but her body appeared to be firm, if a little smallish for his tastes, at the time. It was the sexual confidence she projected that made him both uncomfortable and attracted at the same time. Then he thought, "What do I have to lose? She is not a witch, just a mortal woman who seems to want to spend the night with a younger man."

So Arslan said to Soka, "Yes, I would like very much to enjoy your hospitality for tonight and I do have a small skin of wine, made by my mother, which we can use to warm our insides as your hut keeps our outsides warm."

Soka replied, "It is good to see a young man who does not come empty handed when he is invited into my hut. This shows character and a sense of the proper order of things. I think Arslan and Soka will be good friends and perhaps good lovers for the night."

After eating a passable dinner of a stew made from some roots and some small creature which Soka had caught, better not to ask what creature, Soka led Arslan to her fur covered mat on the floor. There was sufficient straw under it to make it softer than the ground and not so cold.

After Arslan was lying on the mat, Soka proceeded to remove his clothing. A small candle provided the only light in the hut with the door drawn closed. Soka quickly completed the task of removing Arslan's clothes until he lay on the mat completely naked. His manhood stood stiff and erect in anticipation, as is common with young men of seventeen. Soka surveyed her prize as though she had caught a young fawn in her snare and was looking forward to a great feast.

Arslan reached for Soka but she said, "Lay back young bull, and Soka will entertain you and teach you those things which a young bull should know about the art of bedding. The things you learn tonight are well remembered, if you want to find pleasure and make pleasure for the lucky women who find their way to your bed in the future. This training is worth more than all the wisdom you will find in the finest schools of Gordion. Even the great king would be happier if he but availed himself of this schooling."

Arslan, more knowing than his years, knew when to agree and laid back and watched Soka. She began to dance slowly in the candlelight and removed her robe and undergarments. Arslan now saw her body was firm for a woman of her age; he guessed about thirty-five. She moved to him and knelt beside him, reaching out with her hand for his manhood. He tensed and felt a wave of desire sweep through him as she caressed his fully rigid part.

He had heard the other young men talk about such things but had never personally participated. He thought, "*I am here to learn and learn I will*" as she moved her body over him. Along with her encouragement and natural instincts they were soon moving well together and became more and more "involved' in the activity until she yelled out with obvious pleasure. Arslan moved under Soka and was quickly brought to the point of spending his load. During the night, the process was repeated several times in various positions.

In the morning, Arslan was tired but felt wonderful and was extremely affectionate toward Soka. She had been right. What he had learned last night was a precious education he would not trade for anything. He promised to stop by again as he departed on his business to Gordion.

Mata had never slept with a man before her first night in the hut of Arslan. She had heard all sorts of stories from other girls and from some older women who sought to educate a young virgin. She had also felt the urges when she saw young men bathing at the river and other times, so she was not totally at a loss when her and Arslan were finally alone.

Jon Kelly

Arslan had two candles burning in the hut and had made a point to go to the river in the morning and bathe to be more pleasing to his bride. Mata stood in the middle of the hut somewhat lost on how to proceed, an unusual circumstance for the normally confident Mata. Arslan put his arms around Mata and held her close for a long time. He kissed her lips and face, then kissed her neck and gradually unfastened her robe. He moved his hands inside her robe and touched her firm, young breasts. He then unfastened, and removed his own clothes, letting his erect manhood appear. He then removed the robe from the still silent Mata and picked her up and carried her to the sleeping mat.

Laying Mata down gently on her back, he straddled her and kissed her face and lips with Mata responding urgently to his kisses. He then moved down to kiss her shoulders, then her right breast, then her left breast, until both nipples were erect and firm. Arslan was amazed at the beautiful firmness and softness of her perfect young body. He continued to apply the lessons learned from Soka. Arslan moved up between Mata's legs and entered her with his manhood. By this time, Mata was more than aware of the presence of Arslan inside her and instinctively started to move under him. Arslan, kissed Mata's face and lips and told her, "You are beautiful, my darling, I love you and want your love." All the while, he continued to move within Mata until the sensations overtook his control and he came within her.

During the night, Arslan passed on more of the knowledge provided by Soka as he acquainted Mata with the pleasures of a man and a woman together in closest physical and emotional intimacy. By morning, both Arslan and Mata were very grateful they had chosen each other and were prepared to build a life together.

4.   <u>Amwat—722 B.C.</u>

Expectations

We anticipate what life will bring,
and are astounded to learn
when we get some other thing,
life has taken a different turn.

Both Arslan and Mata were thirty-seven years old in 722 B.C. Mata was still a good looking woman but the birth of five live children and three miscarriages coupled with the generally hard life of all people in these times left her showing the effect of the years. Her hair showed some graying and she had added weight to her hips. The breasts Arslan loved were not as firm as those of his young bride. Wrinkles showed in her face as years of labor in the sun had its effect. In the overall picture, Mata was aging as well or better than most women of her time.

On the other hand, Arslan showed only a minimal effect of aging. He did not look seventeen but apparently stopped aging at about the age of twenty-eight and showed no gray in his hair, no wrinkles, and absolutely no deterioration in his body—he looked stronger and more lithe if anything. In the course of farm life, he had been injured several times, none of great severity, in retrospect, but his healing ability was nothing short of amazing. Once, he had fallen from a tree trying to get honey from a hive, and had landed on a sharp rock and had cut his thigh to the bone. For many men in these times, infection would mean a lingering death, with such an injury. Arslan walked back to his hut and slept for several hours. By the next day, he was back in the fields with a rapidly healing scar as the only sign of his injury.

Mata counted herself very lucky to have a man such as Arslan who had lived up to every promise he had ever made to her and more. He had never beat her and rarely spoke harshly to her, and then only when under extreme duress from the pressures of life which catch up with all people at times. On the other hand, he treated her with kindness, consideration, and caring which were beyond anything she had heard or seen with other couples. Mata could think of no better man than Arslan.

The children were the great joys of both their lives. The oldest was a girl, Marla, who was now eighteen and ready for marriage. Next came their oldest son, Amwat, named for his grandfather, and now sixteen. Their next son was Brosc, who was twelve; they had had another child, a son, who would now be thirteen who had died of a fever at the age of three. Their youngest daughter was Nyla, who was nine and the sweetheart of her father. Mata had three miscarriages after giving birth to Nyla and now they expected no more children.

The times were good in Amwat at this time, with peace resulting from the power of the great king in Gordion. The hard work of Arslan and Mata making their farm prosperous and their home comfortable added to their good fortune. Kyla had died five years before but not before she had spoiled her grandchildren as best she could, and seen her son was happy with the wife she had found for him. Mata had loved Arslan's mother as if her own mother and also as her best friend. They had shared all things for fifteen years and Kyla had told Mata about Arslan's beginnings, after swearing her to perpetual silence with anyone outside the family.

5.   <u>Amwat—717 B.C.</u>

Troubles started for Arslan in the early summer of 717 B.C. He went to a neighboring village to trade some meat for seed. A man living in the village had known Arslan for many years and was approximately his same age. He was also a man of ill sort who was always looking to find fault with his neighbors. At forty-two years of age, this man was completely gray and wrinkled, and also a bit bent with age and injuries. When the man saw Arslan, he could not believe his eyes. Arslan still looked to be less than thirty years old with no gray, wrinkles or infirmities. The man challenged Arslan, "How can it be you do not age like the rest of us? You are my age, as I well know, but you look like a young man. Are you a demon or have you been bewitched to stay eternally youthful? Answer me, How is this possible?"

Arslan was not so surprised since he had often wondered why he did not show his age but he was now very concerned because accusations of witchcraft or demonology were taken very seriously. Their neighbors sometimes killed people over such things. He decided to retreat from the situation as quickly as possible and said, "I am aging along with the rest of you. I only show it less than you do since I have been lucky to have not had to work as hard as some others. My wife is a very good worker and my sons are now coming of age to help more and more, so I am able to relax more than some men."

The ill-tempered villager was not satisfied but Arslan departed the village without completing his trades to avoid more discussion. Arslan hurried home and went into his hut with Mata. He described the incident in the other village and she too was concerned. These things about demons and witchcraft could get out of hand very quickly. "What could they do?" they thought.

Mata stared at Arslan and observed, "Yes, you are much, much too young looking for your age."

They had discussed this casually before but now it was serious, potentially fatal, if they did not take some action. These kinds of accusations do not easily go away and the ill tempered man from the other village had a reputation for grabbing on and staying with an issue if he saw a sign of weakness. Mata said at last, "Arslan, you must try to make yourself look older so others forget about this."

So, Arslan proceeded to change his appearance by growing out his beard and sideburns more and dyeing them gray using a mixture of herbs. He also started affecting a slight stoop to make him look older. He stayed away from the village of the ill-tempered man and stayed close to home in general. Some neighbors remarked he had aged very quickly but this was soon lost in the passage of time. Quickly, he got used to appearing older in public, but was suddenly restored inside his hut with his family. He warned his children they must never talk about this to anyone outside the family. And so, Arslan became more normal to his neighbors, showing a more acceptable aging pattern to their perception.

6. <u>Amwat—712 B.C.</u>

Measure not a love by years alone.
Fairest beauty of a young girl's face,
The only image my eye is shown,
As she enchants my living space.

The problem of Arslan not showing the effects of aging took another serious turn when the lovely Mata started to become an old woman at the age of forty-seven years. The forty-seven hard years Mata had lived showed in her almost white hair, the plethora of wrinkles, and a stoop at her shoulders that was pronounced. Still, Arslan loved her as the day he had first met her. "Much more than when we were young," he said. Mata had no cause to disbelieve her faithful man of many years, but she knew in her heart it was not the same, nor was it natural.

Mata began to think about the story of Arslan's beginning. He had been brought to Amwat and Kyla by a strange elderly couple. "Maybe they were witches or demons," thought Mata, but "No, Arslan is the kindest most caring man in the world, no demons there." Perhaps, Arslan is the son of a god and he will never age. I would be happy for him, but others will seek to destroy him or try to turn his special power into something they can use for themselves. He must hide all knowledge of this from the world or he will be destroyed by it. Mata would hate to lose Arslan but, perhaps, he should go away to another land. In a few years, she would die and it would become harder and harder to conceal the youthful looks of Arslan. Even their children might encounter problems and be destroyed by the association with their father. She thought, "Yes, he must go away to protect himself and the children."

After long, agonizing discussion between Arslan and Mata, it was decided he would leave and find a new life elsewhere. Arslan would never have agreed but for the terrible truth, his downfall would surely bring the destruction of the lives of his four children if he stayed. He would never risk the lives of Mata and the children. Should he tell the children or just leave without telling the true reason? He finally decided to tell the children the truth, in case, one or all of them should have the same affliction as Arslan. They would need to watch for the signs so they could protect their families.

In the end the act of telling the children, although painful, gave them the chance to understand and grieve over their loss with Arslan still there to guide their thinking into positive channels. When, in preparation for departure, Arslan shaved his beard and washed the gray from his hair, the children were astonished. He truly looked less than thirty years old and had not aged a bit for roughly twenty years. They quickly accepted the decision he must leave or he and they would be at grave risk. As he walked down the road toward Gordion, and left his lifetime home, Arslan was in great distress at the forced upheaval in his life.

7.   <u>Gordion—712 B.C.</u>

Arslan left Amwat, with few possessions, as he knew possessions were anchors, and right now, he needed few anchors to hold him in place. They had decided he should take some coins to provide for his sustenance for a while and he took one of two remaining gold ingots they had saved those many years for emergencies. He might be able to establish himself somewhere with the gold as a resource. In addition, to the coins and gold, he had his clothes, a short sword for bandits on the trails, a blanket for warmth, and a bag with food for two weeks travel.

His trip was uneventful, except when he passed the site where the hut of Soka once stood. It was no longer there and the forest had reclaimed the clearing as another sign to Arslan that nothing in this life is forever. He left the place in tears thinking about what had been lost from his life.

Arriving in Gordion, Arslan went about the city with no real plan. No one showed him any sign of recognition, as he appeared to be a very young man newly arrived in the city. No one here would know him as such a young person, so he saw no reason not to stay for a while. He was in no mood for strangeness at this point and he was slightly familiar with Gordion based on his trips there for trading. He found an inn, one he had never used on other trips, and settled in for his first night as a new person.

He had thought about the need for a name to use and finally decided on his second son's name, Brosc but with a T on the front instead of a B. Trosc of Amwat if anyone asked. He looked close enough in age to his son if anyone made the unlikely connection and he could confuse the issue long enough to make an escape, if necessary. There was not much logic in this plan but Arslan, now Trosc, did not care too much what happened to him now—he had lost all he loved through no fault of his own.

The great king, Mita, still ruled in Gordion as he had for over twenty-five years and appeared ready to rule for another twenty-five. Peace imposed on Phrygia by the great king had made Gordion a city of great wealth and prosperity, as the capital of his kingdom.

Seeing the grand sites of Gordion only deepened the depression of Trosc-Arslan. How could he want to live alone and unloved after having lived in a womb of nurturing his whole life? The change was too much to accept. He wandered the streets of Gordion aimlessly, finding no solace. In front of the palace of the king, he came upon a sergeant of the king's army recruiting young men to serve as soldiers.

Trosc-Arslan thought, "If I join the King's army, perhaps I will go into battle and be killed to end my suffering. Other men have joined armies for less well thought out reasons, I think." He went to the sergeant and enlisted to be a soldier of the great king.

He was escorted immediately to a barracks, fed and assigned a place to sleep. In the morning, he was outfitted with a training uniform and started a grueling training program including swordsmanship, spears, and discipline. The rules were severe and punishments were harsher. Since Trosc-Arslan was in a depression to begin with, the strict discipline did not seem to bother him at all. He excelled at the sword play and training with spears. He was especially strong with the sword because at this time, he had no fear—he would welcome death.

After six weeks, the training was complete and he was a soldier of the king. Transferring to regular barracks, he was put in the normal guard rotation for the city and was now part of the forces to protect the king and kingdom. When paid monthly, most of his fellow soldiers went immediately to the taverns and whorehouses to spend their money, usually lasting a few days at the most. Trosc-Arslan did not follow this pattern and saved his monies and avoided the disciplinary problems that befall drunken soldiers. After several months, the ranking sergeants observed his behavior and marked him as a "responsible" type with potential for advancement.

8.   <u>Gordion—697 B.C.</u>

After fifteen years of service in the great king's guard, Trosc-Arslan was a trusted senior sergeant of the guard who had privilege and honors. He had served honorably and with the maximum bravery a time of relative peace could provide for a soldier. Of course, none knew his bravery was really a death wish. He had been seriously wounded several times, including one abdominal wound which had been diagnosed as fatal but from which he recovered in record time.

Trosc-Arslan now faced the same problem he had faced in Amwat—he was not aging as he should and it would start to become an issue. Again, he started using dyes to make his hair gray to postpone the inevitable problem.

Life had improved as he rose in the ranks and now he had his own house and a woman named Krysia, a soldier's widow, who cared for the house and for his personal needs. He had hired her initially as a housekeeper but the closeness and both their needs led them to share a bed as well as a roof over their heads. It was a good arrangement, but Krysia had already noticed his lack of normal aging. He and Krysia had been together eight years now and were growing closer and closer as the years passed. He would marry her if she really wanted it, since he was sure Mata was dead by now, and would not have objected anyway, or so he rationalized. Krysia had not pressed the issue and he saw no reason to disturb the status quo.

There was another problem facing all of Phyrgia at this time. The Kimmerians, a group of nomadic tribes and fierce fighters were reported to be invading Phyrgia and moving toward Gordion. King Mita had dispatched an army to hurl back the invaders but no word of a victory over the invaders had been received. "Oh well, the great king has defeated all invaders for many years and all bets must go on the great king," thought Trosc-Arslan as he lay in bed with Krysia.

A harsh knocking at his door brought Trosc-Arslan out of his near sleep. He walked to the door of his house with his sword in hand. As he opened the door, he saw a young messenger from the guard captain. The young messenger was frightened and it showed. The messenger immediately said, "A disaster with the army. The Kimmerians destroyed it and the great king has taken poison to end

19

his life. The Kimmerians are one day away from the city and marching quickly for it. The Captain of the Guard has already left the city but sent me to warn his senior sergeants. What will you do?"

Trosc-Arslan only cared about two things in the world, his children in Amwat and Krysia here in Gordion. He would take Krysia and travel swiftly to Amwat and warn his children to take their families to go hide in the hills until the threat passed. He only told the young messenger he would leave the city. No sense in leaving trails.

He told Krysia quickly and they packed lightly but effectively, coins, gold ingot, other small valuables, some food and weaponry, and sleeping blankets. They were out of the city in two hours and moving in the direction of Amwat by morning. They continued pushing on until mid-day then stopped to rest and eat. Looking back at Gordion, they thought they could see smoke rising from the direction of the city. They then ended their rest and moved onward.

By late afternoon they topped a hill and looked back again toward the city. The entire horizon was black with smoke rising from the great city of Gordion. They chose to continue moving until midnight, when they stopped to rest until dawn. It was now a race to get to Amwat before invaders caught up to them.

The trip from Gordion to Amwat, normally taking two weeks walking was completed in only eight days. They were very tired when Trosc-Arslan saw the huts of Amwat and moved toward the hut he had shared with Mata for so many years. He called out to alert those inside of his presence. Amwat his eldest son appeared at the door, somewhat fearful, seeing a soldier of the king.

"Amwat, do you not recognize your father, gone these past fifteen years." said Trosc-Arslan.

Amwat was struck dumb by the sight of the soldier who looked something like his lost father. He finally said, "Yes father, I see you now. Come into the hut, quickly."

After introductions of Krysia and the wife of Amwat, Trosc-Arslan explained the demise of Gordion and the need to warn the rest of the family to flee to the hills for safety. Amwat sent his wife to get other key members of the family. While they waited, Trosc-Arslan observed the ageing of his eldest son and was thankful he did not have the "affliction."

Trosc-Arslan had shared more of his history with Krysia on their journey from Gordion to Amwat but she was still amazed when he washed the gray out of his hair and cut his full beard. He was now a young man, apparently less than thirty years old.

In consultation with his children remaining in Amwat, two sons and youngest daughter, Nyla, it was decided Trosc-Arslan would be introduced to all others, including his grandchildren, as Trosc, a cousin from Gordion who was fleeing the invaders. Krysia would be introduced as his wife. All this made sense under the circumstance, since there was no time to be spent explaining the reality of Trosc-Arslan and dealing with the shock and fear such disclosure would create.

The entire village was now prepared to move everyone into the hills where many caves provided good places to survive for a short time while the nomadic invaders passed through, did their pillaging, and went on. Amwat, retrieved his hoard of monies from their hiding place under the floor of the hut, including the single gold ingot with strange markings which he had guarded for years. Trosc-Arslan observed this and thought, *"I too carry with me one of the gold ingots which has been with me from my beginning. If they could talk, what a story they might be able to tell. Could they tell me why I am as I am?"*

The trip into the hills was difficult for the group now consisting of twelve adults and some twenty-three children of various ages. Children do not usually travel well and these children were not used to traveling so the pace was inexorably slow, or so it seemed to Trosc-Arslan who was used to the fast pace of the great kings guards. He did not think it was likely for the Kimmerian invaders to make a quick transit from Gordion to the region near Amwat. He thought, *"What reason would they have to go in this direction quickly? It is more likely they will enjoy the spoils of Gordion for a time and then come this way if they choose."*

Despite thinking the invaders would not progress in their direction quickly, Trosc-Arslan used his soldier's training and sent some of the older youth out to scout ahead and to the rear to provide warning if invaders were in the area. They had strict instructions to stay out of sight and to be cautious.

Trosc-Arslan was as surprised as anyone when the forward scout came running over the top of a hill and gave them the word a party of strangely dressed soldiers were a short distance ahead on the very path they were taking. Trosc-Arslan asked his oldest grandson, "How many soldiers did you see?"

He retorted, "I counted nine soldiers on foot moving down the trail in our direction."

Trosc-Arslan immediately directed everyone to move off the trail and to take up hiding places as far off the trail as possible. He knew his small party of five adult men was no match for nine soldiers. He was the only one in his party trained in the use of arms. Their best hope was to hide and let them pass. But as a precaution, Trosc-Arslan would take up a position further down the trail and if some problem developed with the hiding of his family, he would show himself and act as decoy to draw the soldiers away from his family.

At this point in the trail there was a large rock formation about twenty feet high which from his past life in Amwat, he knew had a small hidden cave which could only be found with extreme effort of climbing down the back wall of the rock from the top. Trosc-Arslan chose to hide his valuables in this cave so he would be lighter for running from the soldiers if necessary. He put a large rock over the small cave entrance to further protect his valuables.

With everyone hidden, the soldiers appeared, walking steadily over the hill and down the path. All was well until one of the children coughed and the soldiers began searching. Trosc-Arslan knew all was lost unless he could draw the soldiers away. He showed himself on the path some fifty yards ahead of the soldiers and yelled and waved his sword. Immediately the soldiers all started running after him.

Trosc-Arslan was an athlete and well trained. He also knew the trail. He could have easily lost the soldiers if that had been his intent but to do so this close to his family might cause the soldiers to return up the path and find his family. Trosc-Arslan decided to stay just far enough ahead of the soldiers to keep their attention. He kept up this strategy all the way back to Amwat, but was greatly surprised upon breaking into the clearing at Amwat to find his village filled with what he knew were Kimmerian raiders. He was trapped and the Kimmerians formed a large circle around him with swords and spears at the ready.

One of the Kimmerians stepped out of the ranks and spoke in a highly accented version of the Gordion language, "What are you in such a fine uniform, the king of Gordion?"

Trosc-Arslan replied with the truth, "I am but a sergeant of the great king's guard."

The Kimmerian replied, "Well, your great king is dead and so is Gordion. Shall you die also, Sergeant of the Guard."

Trosc-Arslan, as always not fearing death, said, "If it is now my time to die, so be it, but I will die fighting with my sword in my hand."

Again the Kimmerian spoke, "A brave Phrygian, that is rare, perhaps we will let you entertain us with your skill as a fighter."

He signaled to two menacing swordsmen to step forward and said, "Here are two of our best, if you can survive with them, we may let you live and serve us."

Without further discussion, the two soldiers moved toward Trosc-Arslan and tried to flank him so their work would be easy. Neither expected the speed of reaction of Trosc-Arslan as he drew his sword and slashed directly across the neck of the nearest soldier, sending him to the ground gurgling in his own blood. The other fighter, now wary, fought with great effort but was no match for the quickness and skill, developed in fifteen years of training by Trosc-Arslan. In short order, he disarmed the second soldier and the ranks of soldiers prepared to see their comrade in arms struck down. Trosc-Arslan chose to let him live which gained him some support from the crowd.

The Kimmerian spokesman addressed Trosc-Arslan, "Your skill with a sword is great. To kill you would be a great loss. Join us to teach our soldiers to use the sword as you do, and you can live." Trosc-Arslan joined the Army of the Kimmerians.

9. __Atlanta__

history

burning for a moment
only a momentary flash—a brilliance
even all history is
only a megaflash—not a light

So it is—time
the only relevance

Dr. Simon Myers walked quickly to his black Mercedes, clicked open the door locks, opened the driver's door and settled into the seat. It was a cold evening in Atlanta with the temperature hovering just above 45* and a wind blowing across the almost empty parking lot outside the Center for DNA Studies where Simon spent his long days. January could be a cold time in Atlanta and today was one of those times.

As he pulled closed the door and inserted the key to start the car, he thought briefly about his place in the world as one of the four or five "experts" sorting out the human DNA structure and trying to identify what each segment of the DNA puzzle was designed by Mother Nature to accomplish. He was generally pleased with what he had done over the last several years and was proud of some of the promise shown by discoveries, mainly by others, using the information he had developed. They might improve human life dramatically over the next decades.

Simon pulled out of the parking lot and eased onto Peachtree Road for his half hour trip to his apartment in an upscale, but not lavish, complex in the north of Atlanta. Had he been more observant he might have seen the dark colored, late model Chevrolet sedan make the turn out of the parking lot behind his Mercedes, and get into the traffic several cars behind his vehicle.

After an uneventful trip Simon arrived at his apartment complex, punched the entry code in at the gate and clicked open his garage door. Pulling into his garage, he did not take note of the dark sedan pulling through the open security gate and parking on the street several doors away. He clicked closed the garage door and entered his well-kept apartment. Today had been one of the two days per week when the cleaning service applied their efforts to keep his life organized. Simon felt secure in this place. While he was a naturally organized person and did not make a mess out of his living space, he really appreciated the luxury of having the cleaning service "pick up after him" so he could focus energies on more important activities, such as his work, his rest, or the occasional night with high school English teacher, Lisa Mallory.

Perhaps he should call Lisa and see if she "was in the mood" this evening. Their relationship was not close enough that he could ever predict. And he was not planning on it getting much closer than an occasional night of hot sex. He was not sure he even liked Lisa and knew she had been in love with the mutual friend who had introduced them. Unrequited love, since the friend thought of her as a "buddy" but not bedding or long term relationship material. He had moved away from Atlanta for a new job assignment.

"Lisa is not the most attractive woman in the world," he thought, "with a larger than normal nose and a body best described as a bit "clumsy." Her personality was also less than agreeable at times—especially if drinking. She had got them thrown out of several bars for getting into arguments with bartenders or other women.

On the other hand, Lisa had positive points. He had thought this through after bedding Lisa the first time, after both had much, too much to drink. Lisa really appreciated the sexual attention, they screwed—and did other things—all night the first time, and she had some qualities which were real "turn-on's", such as breasts, which sagged a bit, but had nipples like red raspberries, especially when licked and sucked, that got firm and hard.

Some of the comments she made while "in the act", such as "Am I making too much noise?", really warmed a boy's sexual confidence. Her being a redhead capped the decision making process for Simon who had two redheaded sisters as friends in high school. He always wanted to do sexual flashbacks to those days.

The doorbell interrupted Simon's reverie. *"Damn, maybe Lisa is already drinking and decided to stop in unannounced,"* he thought as he moved to the door. Some evenings he would have carefully viewed

25

the doorstep through the peephole before opening the door but "A horny man throws caution to the wind." So, he opened the door before looking.

Simon was annoyed to not see, a somewhat drunken Lisa on his stoop, but instead a well dressed man in a suit with a overcoat open over it. The man was ordinary enough, average height, average weight, hair in a ponytail tucked in the back, not too long, but the eyes were unusual. The piercing look of dark brown, almost black eyes, dominated the face.

The visitor spoke first saying, "Dr. Myers, my name is John Young and I need to speak with you, if possible."

Simon's reply was abrupt, "About what?"

"Dr. Myers, I need a few minutes of your time to describe an important DNA investigation which I am going to ask you to conduct. I realize it is unusual to approach you at this time of the evening about a professional matter but once you have heard what I have to say, I think you will understand." said the visitor.

Unconvinced, Simon mulled over his retort and said, "What organization do you represent?"

Producing a business card from his pocket, the visitor handed it to Simon. It read, "John Young, Adjunct Professor, History Department, The University of Pennsylvania."

Simon asked, "Why can this not be addressed at the office during normal hours?"

"I must explain everything to answer," said the visitor.

"So you're saying I have to listen to your pitch completely before I have enough information to make a decision. Did you ever sell used cars?" Said Simon.

The visitor, who looked to be about 30 years old and was obviously well conditioned athletically from his bearing, did not waver but went on to say, "What I want to describe to you is an extremely serious scientific challenge. Only a few men have the background to pursue this challenge—you being one of them. I could go to others, but you have a solid reputation for doing your work without allowing preconceptions and bias to impede your analysis. Others do not seem to have your open-mindedness."

Thinking about what the visitor had just said, Simon realized he had appealed to the one scientific mind-set Simon held most dear.

Simon knew he thought of himself as more open to new ideas than his peers in the DNA field. The visitor knew him better than most people, even those few who were close to him.

Simon caved in to the determination of his visitor and the appeal to "open-mindedness" which was central to his personal self-image and said, "I will listen, please come in and sit down."

Simon offered the visitor a glass of wine and poured two glasses, then both sat in separate chairs in the living room.

The visitor spoke with an air of reverence and authority that gave Simon pause, "My story will be difficult for you to accept. As a man of science you demand proof—I cannot provide hard proof at this time—in fact, my reason for being here is to develop proof using your help. Let me say what I communicate to you is important, perhaps more important than anything you have done in your professional career—and I know of your accomplishments, I have done my research. Please take the time to listen before you make a decision to make me leave."

Without waiting for a response, the visitor started his story.

In 759 B.C., a male baby by the name of Arslan appeared in the village of Amwat in what is now central Turkey. Arslan grew to manhood in Amwat, married, had children and lived the normal life of a farmer of the period until he was forty-seven years old. In 712 B.C., Arslan moved to Gordion, the capital of the kingdom of Phrygia. In 712 B.C., Arslan joined the army of the great king under the name Trosc, and served, eventually becoming a senior sergeant of the guard, until 697 B.C.

In 697 B.C., the Kimmerians invaded the Phrygian kingdom and all of Gordion was destroyed and the great king took his own life rather than be captured. His guards fled for the most part but Arslan was captured by the Kimmerians and pressed into service with their army as an instructor in swordsmanship. Arslan was 62 years of age at the time.

Arslan traveled with the wandering army of the Kimmerians for some five years. He taught skills related to fighting with a sword and learned their language. He also fought alongside them in various battles and became a respected warrior. Arslan did not learn to accept the harsh brutality of the Kimmerians, especially, their proclivity for slaughtering the populations they conquered. But this was a hard time and there was little one man could do to stop such events without sacrificing his own life.

Arslan was able to save the life of one Canaanite woman, however, by taking her as his woman after his raiding party had captured her. Reba was her name and he was able to keep her under his protection within the Kimmerians' camp.

In 692 B.C., Arslan left the Kimmerians by escaping with Reba from their camp and hiding until the Kimmerians moved on. The two moved south after the Kimmerians had left the area and eventually settled in the Kingdom of Judah, where his skills with weaponry and warfare were more than welcome at this time. Arslan and Reba had twenty-two years of living in Judah until Reba died in 670 B.C.

With the death of Reba, Arslan left Judah and traveled north, wandering for several years from one place to another. He finally stopped in a small village east of Aleppo, in what is now northern Syria. He lived there until 655 B.C. at which time he started wandering again for several years, until he stopped in another small village near Adana, in what is now southern Turkey. He stayed near Adana until 641 B.C. when he moved again and traveled east. He was one hundred eighteen years old at this time.

He settled near Van, which is now near the eastern border of Turkey. As was becoming standard, he lived there for close to twenty years, leaving again in 620 B.C. at the age of one hundred thirty nine. Most of his time was spent in small villages where he used his skills as a farmer to make a living. He usually would find a woman to live with or marry at each of these places.

Simon looked at his watch and saw he had listened to John Young for fifteen minutes. *"Why should I continue to listen?"* he thought. *"The story can have no real basis in fact. It is a fantasy about someone living longer than humanly possible. What could it possibly have to do with important scientific inquiry? I should end it now and throw the guy out."* he almost concluded.

John Young stopped his story, as if sensing a problem with his listener and said, "Dr. Myers, my story is long and your patience is needed. Many times the process of getting information is as important as the information itself. As a scientific man, you are now questioning not only the relevance of the story I am telling but also the source of the information. This is one of those times when you must use your intuition to decide whether the person before you is potentially credible—it takes a "leap of faith" at this point—a hard thing for the scientific mind."

Simon studied John Young, who was now on his feet walking as he talked. The visitor's athleticism became more apparent—he walked with the grace of a lion but with a perfect musculature projecting the strength of a bull. Simon had seen men like this at martial arts schools and a few special operations people while in the army, but none as perfect or as seemingly intelligent. *No, more than intelligent, a combination of wisdom, confidence, knowledge and intelligence so pervasive not believing him did not seem to be a consideration.*

Finally, speaking Simon said, "I should stop you and make you leave. *It had occurred to Simon he probably was not remotely capable of physically making this man leave, but dismissed the thought as moot.* However, you are right, scientific inquiry sometimes requires a "leap of faith" and intuition, which you obviously know I respect, but the story is beyond the believable based on a man living so long."

After saying it, Simon realized something he had not brought to the surface before, *The reason he was still listening to the story told by John Young was he did not tell it as a story, but as a recitation of events; events John Young seemed to have had close personal knowledge about, as though he had experienced them. Of course, it was impossible, but the impact was there.*

John Young stared at Simon and said, "Arslan lived many more years than the story has related so far. He continued to move and change identity approximately every twenty years. Every time his failure to age started to become noticeable or when the unbelievable healing of some dire injury brought unwanted attention to himself."

Simon asked, "How long did Arslan live?"

John Young hesitated before answering but eventually said, "It is the crux of my story. Arslan still lives. I am Arslan."

Simon could not imagine a rational human being claiming to be twenty eight hundred years old but he saw no evidence John Young was anything but rational and truthful.

Simon stammered, "How can you be so absurd? You are obviously a bright, rational person. What makes you make such a weird statement?"

John Young—Arslan did not hesitate this time, "Dr. Myers, my reason for coming to you is to use your knowledge of DNA to test my claim and to prove or disprove it with irrefutable scientific proof. Never before in my history has the means to prove my claim been available. The means is now available and I want to let the testing be done to prove my situation. This is not a casual project being undertaken for no reason other than proving I am special. My DNA must have some differences to cause me not to age as all the rest of humanity does. My ability to heal myself is also far beyond other humans from personal observation. Think about the implications if my DNA can be replicated to join it with the DNA of other humans. Humanity could extend the productive years of individuals dramatically."

Simon was stunned by the total belief of John Young in his claim. *"It cannot be,"* he thought, *"but he believes it beyond a doubt."*

Simon spoke softly, "Mr. Young, I will run an analysis of your DNA. I suggest we go to the lab right now and I will take blood samples. Is that acceptable?"

John Young—Arslan replied, "That will be fine Dr. Myers but you need to take enough samples to send samples to two other of the top DNA labs to run the same analyses and request they provide you with certified reports on the results. I predict at some point we will need to have our proof in very good order to head off attacks on our honesty, credibility, and characters."

Dr. Simon Myers drove back to the Center for DNA Studies followed by John Young—Arslan in his car. Simons head was spinning. He thought, *"Why am I doing this? A strange man with a crazy story enters my life and I am believing him enough to do a thorough DNA study of his genetic information."* Simon thought these thoughts but did not turn the car around, he was hooked.

Arriving at the Center for DNA Studies, the two vehicles were parked in the parking lot. It was after midnight, so Simon took care to locate the security guard before moving away from the building entrance. Security was important in today's difficult world and he did not want the police called by a nervous guard. Fortunately the guard on duty was, Tom Finney, who had worked the building for several years and knew Simon well.

"Good evening Dr. Myers, how are you this evening? I am surprised to see you here so late. Do you have a special project in the works you have to check on?" said Tom.

"Tom, good to see you. I am fine. This is Mr. Young, a scholar from the University of Pennsylvania, and we are working on a project together. Unfortunately it is going to take us most of the night to get it rolling, so we will be around a while." said Simon, giving more information than necessary but seeing no reason to be less than forthcoming.

"I have fresh coffee made in the second floor lounge if you gentlemen would care to try it. It is strong enough to let the spoon sit up in it without falling over, if you do not mind it strong. I have to get a lot of caffeine in my system to keep me awake at night. I have done this shift for years but it does not seem to make any difference. I still get sleepy during the night." said Tom.

Simon and John Young went up to the main DNA study lab on the second floor and prepared to take blood samples from John Young—Arslan.

Simon said, "I will take six sample tubes of blood for testing. Two will be used here and eventually two each will be sent to Johns Hopkins and the University of California labs for testing. Those are the two best labs in the country for this type of study, aside from my own lab here. I do not plan to send the samples to the outside labs until I have preliminary results from my own testing. Initial testing can be started tonight. The testing will not be complete for approximately 56 hours due to the computer analysis required; it is really quite complex. Since it is now late Friday night, No, now it is Saturday morning, it will be Monday afternoon before we have anything to look at in the way of data."

John Young nodded his agreement and said, "I don't blame you for waiting until you complete your own testing before sending the samples to other labs. I understand trust is something that takes time to be developed."

Simon proceeded to take the samples from John Young-Arslan, marked the tubes of blood, put four tubes in the sample storage refrigerator, and started the analysis of the other two samples. The testing procedure was heavily automated since Simon had been able to get federal and private funding far beyond most of his peers based on the excellent reputation his center had developed. The FBI even used his lab as the "final decision maker' when doubts about a DNA study were raised. Simon proceeded with his testing routine leaving John Young-Arslan to his own devices after warning him to not touch any of the equipment.

By 6:30 a.m. on Saturday morning the mechanical part of the testing was done, now the computer would take over the analysis. The computer would completely map the DNA found in the blood samples from John Young-Arslan and would compare it to known human DNA maps to determine unusual characteristics for more intensive study. As a scientist, Simon expected the results to be normal with the DNA showing a standard human DNA structure with appropriate ethnic variations and all the normal sequences all other humans on the planet seemed to display. "How could the results be anything else, despite the convincing story told by his visitor? thought Simon.

"We are done here for the moment." he said to John Young.

"Where are you staying here in Atlanta?" he followed up with the visitor.

John Young replied, "I came into town last night before coming to see you and have not found a hotel yet, any suggestions?"

Simon thought a minute, *"I really do not want to lose track of the guy at this point, until we see what the blood analysis really reveals."*

Simon then said, "Why don't you stay in my guest room at my apartment? We can cover more of your background and satisfy some of my curiosity."

John Young agreed immediately and they headed back to Simon's apartment in their cars.

Back at the apartment, Simon showed his guest to his room with his visitor bringing a small hanging bag from the car. Simon left his visitor to his privacy and went to the kitchen to make some breakfast. He had just gotten some coffee started when the doorbell rang. Going to the door, he was not going to fail to check the peephole this time. So, he looked through it and saw Lisa Mallory, red hair and all, standing on the stoop. *"Well, timing is everything."* he thought.

He opened the door and smiled at Lisa saying, "Good Morning Lisa. Please come in. You look delightful this morning."

Lisa strolled into the apartment then turned and faced Simon. She said, "I know I don't have any claim on you but I was worried about you. I tried calling starting about midnight last night then tried several more times (*eleven times altogether she refused to say*) but got no answer. It was out of character for you to stay out all night, so I decided to stop by. I hope you don't mind my concern."

At this point there was some noise came from the guest room and Lisa's face started turning red. Simon quickly made the connection Lisa thought she had stumbled into a sexual liaison of Simon and another woman. Then John Young walked out of the guest room wearing some walking shorts and a T-shirt. Simon thought, "Oh shit, now Lisa is going to think there is a side to me she didn't know about."

To salvage the situation, Simon quickly made introductions and explained the circumstances that John Young and Simon were working on a project at the Center together and had spent the night there getting it started. Lisa was starting to lose her embarrassment and sensed Simon's potential concern about what she thought. She looked at John Young, saw his extremely attractive athletic build and strong good looks then thought, *"Well, Simon, if you are getting it on with another man, you sure picked a good one, Wow."*

Then John Young-Arslan entered the conversation, "Simon, you are a lucky man indeed to have so lovely a woman calling on you at such an early hour of the morning. I am sorry if my presence is inconvenient. I can still go to a hotel if I am interfering with your social life."

Lisa was warmed by the compliment and the charm of John Young. *"If Simon sends him to a hotel, I might go with him."* She mused.

Simon then said, "No problem, John, let's all have some breakfast together. Lisa is a good friend who was concerned about me being gone all night. If fact, I am touched by her concern and want to thank her."

Simon did some heavy thinking while he prepared breakfast, letting John Young and Lisa talk, *"Lisa may be a bit better friend than I thought and she does not really look bad either. Perhaps I should get a bit closer to her and see where it could go. I had better not be too slow about it either, as he looked over and saw Lisa and John Young in animated conversation."*

Lisa was telling John Young about her work as a high school English teacher and her plans to complete a half finished novel some day. She told about how she had worked as an editor for a book publisher for two years before completing her master's degree and starting to teach. John Young seemed very interested in this and asked several questions about it. She also related that starting next week she was going to be off from school for two months due to a scheduling fiasco within the school system. She was technically junior to a number of other teachers and she had not been placed in a permanent slot. She planned on using the time off to work on her novel. She did not mention she planned to use the time off to get to know Dr. Simon Myers better.

Simon served Denver omelets for breakfast but accompanied them with fresh strawberries, whipped cream and champagne. Coffee was also available. Simon had done the strawberries, whipped cream and champagne thing with Lisa previously but she always appreciated it, more so after a night of good sex. Lisa thought, *"No sexual afterglow this time, but Simon is being very attentive this morning. Must be the competition. Men are so easy to see through."*

John Young-Arslan quickly put all thoughts of sexual politics aside and turned very serious. He announced as they started on coffee after finishing the champagne, "I am always a person to try to seize an opportunity when it is presented."

Speaking directly to Lisa he said, "I have approached Simon to perform a very important DNA study and he has agreed to do so. But I have another project, which needs attention falling into your area of expertise. I have a long manuscript and notes needing to be edited very quickly, so they can be available at the same time as the results of the DNA study become publicly known. Would you be interested in working as an editor for the next two months instead of working on your novel? I can pay very well."

Lisa thought for a few minutes and said, "What is the manuscript about?"

Simon interjected himself into the conversation before John Young-Arslan could answer, "John, do you really want to get Lisa involved in this, at this point. Shouldn't you wait for the results on the testing before getting her involved?"

John Young-Arslan answered thoughtfully, "Lisa seems to be a very intelligent, and beautiful woman, I will add, who can decide for herself if the project is worth her time. At the worst, she can treat the material as a novel for the purposes of editing until the test results are available. You also said you wanted more background on my history and you can sit in on some of the editing to give you the background you need."

John Young-Arslan had sensed Lisa wanted time with Simon and Simon was feeling protective (possessive) of Lisa. Let them work on this together and everything will go better.

Simon sensed Lisa wanted to do the project and any objections he made now would be seen as unreasonable. He also liked the fact he would be spending time with Lisa professionally. It would be a good way to get to know her better and his desire to get to know the person, Lisa, instead of just the sex partner Lisa, was increasing.

Lisa spoke up, "Tell me what the manuscript and the DNA project are about."

Simon and Lisa cleared the remains of breakfast from the table while John Young-Arslan went to his car and returned with a large metal briefcase. He opened the combination locks ad took out seven or eight leather bound manuscript books looking to range from very old to reasonably new. With everyone seated, John started to tell his story again.

John Young-Arslan again told the story he had told Simon the night before. How Arslan had appeared in the village to be named Amwat and had lived there for forty-seven years then moved to Gordion, and the other places he had moved to in his first one hundred and thirty-seven years. As with Simon, he then told Lisa, "I am Arslan of Amwat." He then described the testing Simon had started in process and his intent to prove his claim using the new science of DNA mapping.

Lisa sat thoughtfully mulling over what she had heard. Finally, she said, "Wow, what a story. Obviously Simon is interested enough in the story to do the testing. I think I am a good judge of people lying, based on dealing with high school students and their homework. I do not detect any intentional falsehood from John. But the story is unbelievable, you must admit?"

Simon added, "I feel the same way as you do Lisa but the DNA testing should prove the point, one way or the other."

John Young-Arslan said, "Let's start working through the manuscripts. The level of detail provided in them is far greater than what I have related to you so far. I have worked on these manuscripts for hundreds of years, trying to remember as much detail as possible about the environment and the events of the time. I already know some of the history disagrees with the accepted historical record. Eventually, the impact on the accepted historical record of these manuscripts could be huge. For now, however, treat it in your minds as a novel to be edited, if you choose."

Lisa spoke up at this point, "I accept your proposal. Even if this is a hoax, it has all the makings of a great novel so I am in. But I do need to run to my apartment for a moment to get some supplies and equipment if I am going to do a proper job of editing. I will be back in about fifteen minutes."

Simon walked Lisa out to her car then said, "Are you sure you want to get involved in all this?"

Lisa appreciated Simon's concern and boldly said, "Well, it is an interesting project and I don't have much to lose but some time. It will also give me a chance to spend time with you on a person-to-person level, not just in bed. Isn't it something we both want to do? Is that right?"

Simon was taken aback by the directness of Lisa but recovered and said, "Yes, I did not have it straight in my head until today, but I really do want to know all about Lisa Mallory. If nothing else comes out of this with John Young, I am glad, very glad, I now know I want to be closer to you."

Simon put his hands up to Lisa's face and tilted her head up. He then kissed her on the lips with a long lingering kiss, to which she responded accordingly. They hugged for a long time before Lisa said, "I had better go now unless you want to join me at my apartment."

Simon, who was very tempted, said, "Let's make a date when we have a little more time."

Lisa hurried off to run her errand and returned shortly with writing pads, a laptop computer, and a small recorder. She settled down at the table, set up her equipment and said, "Let's get started." winking at Simon she then said, "Simon and I have a date."

John Young-Arslan, who had been viewing the exchange at Lisa's car from the window said with an amused smile, "I am sorry to be in the way of young love but perhaps I can take your minds off such things with my story."

John Young-Arslan continued, "I have not tried to cover my entire life in these manuscripts. On the average, I had to move on every twenty years to avoid being found out. I had to create a new identity each time and there was tremendous emotional turmoil when I had to give up family and friends. There were times when I thought I had lost my sanity, or wished to.

Some experiences were wonderful; others were horrible. I have been declared dead many times only to recover through my recuperative powers, in a few cases after being entombed or buried. I have been very careful to avoid being mutilated, beheaded, or having a limb cut off. I have had arms or hands severed in battle but have recovered them and rejoined them. I have got so I take extreme care to avoid the situations where these types of injury can easily happen.

I am probably the most complete master of weaponry, especially swords, and martial arts of anyone in the world. I have studied every one of the martial arts extensively as a means to protect myself and have been a soldier in many of my identities. Twenty-eight hundred years of living gives one the time to acquire many skills.

Language is another area of mastery. I have spoken an estimated two hundred languages or major dialects through my history. I have probably forgotten more languages than any other man now speaks. Right now, I can go to almost any country in the world and speak some of the language. Perhaps some of the Eskimo dialects may have escaped me, or some obscure dialects in China. If you want to give me a language test, I think I could prove a mastery that would amaze you and give some credibility to my claims.

You need to understand I have not talked to many people about my true story. Fear of being burned, stoned or otherwise punished as a witch or demon have made me cautious in the past. It is only now, with the advent of scientific means to prove my "case", I feel I can step out of the shadows and speak out.

For hundreds of years, I felt sorry for myself and was depressed. No one else to my knowledge, has felt the repeated losses of family and friends as I have, over twenty-eight hundred years. Try to imagine it? But I met some great people over time, who gave me the insight and strength to see my position was an opportunity, perhaps for all of humankind to learn, understand, and progress. My manuscript concentrates on some of the most important people and times in my life."

Simon and Lisa reflected on the words of John Young-Arslan and wondered how they would react to living such a life where you could always look ahead to cutting yourself off from those you came to love to protect them and yourself. No one could completely understand unless you lived through it.

John Young-Arslan started again, "Assuming the tests are conclusive and this information goes out to the world, be warned the reaction will be severe. My presence in the world will be controversial to some and a direct threat to others. My identities in the world and in history are mostly in the shadows, intentionally. I did not normally allow my identity to become a public figure who might show up on the pages of history. However, this was not always true. So be cautious."

Simon thought about this warning from John Young-Arslan wondering *what enemy would care so much to cause harm if his story were proved true. The historians would be disturbed by major changes in the interpretation of history. Perhaps someone's ancestor would turn out to be a charlatan rather than a hero, but so what. Then it struck him, "religion" The existence of a twenty-eight hundred year old man did not fit into any established religious doctrine. They would come out swinging. Religious differences had caused more death, destruction and misery through history than anything else.*

Simon put voice to his thoughts, "It is the religious people you are worried about, right?"

John Young-Arslan answered quickly, "Yes, the religious people. I have seen the horror of people burning at the stake, and men, women and children being slaughtered in the name of religion. Once seen, you do not forget."

Lisa interjected, "But this is the twenty-first century, people don't do those things today?"

Lisa didn't say more because the image of the twin towers of the World Trade Center in New York City, burning and collapsing, had been visualized in her mind. Lisa then said, "No, I take it back, those things still happen."

John Young-Arslan closed the discussion by saying. "The religious people are part of it but their reaction may be even more than you expect. Anyway, if everyone agrees, let's start with my first manuscript. I will read it to you."

John Young-Arslan then says, "I will start with my manuscript about Athens in 375 B.C.; how did I get to Athens after 300 years of wandering around the Middle East? It was not through any real intent on my part. I simply landed there as part of my extended travels. What was I like by then? Somewhat discouraged, but starting to realize what I was doing might have some purpose in the greater scheme of things. Being in Athens, a center of learning, was part of my mental journey to see if I could become more attuned to what I must do with my life. I will read now."

Jon Kelly

10. <u>Athens 401 B.C.</u>

Arslan arrived in the great city of Athens in the spring of 401 B.C. having come as a mercenary soldier. Since the Peloponnesian War's end three years earlier and the defeat of Athens by the Spartan led alliance, Athens had little reason to turn away any soldier. They had lost huge numbers of their young men in the war, as had all of Ionian Greece.

The war had been long, twenty-seven years, and bitter with Lysander the Spartan General executing 3,000 Athenians captured at the "battle" of Aegospotami in 404 B.C., for example. Arslan had been present for this battle as a crewmember on one of the Spartan ships. Fortunately, he was not required to participate in the slaughter.

Arslan had been welcomed as an addition to their now small military when he made his way to Athens in one of his moves to avoid "discovery." Since Athens was dominated by Sparta at the time, the role of a mercenary soldier was not a bad one as these thing go.

Since Arslan was the most skillful swordsman in Athens, probably in the world based on 350 years of practice, his soldierly peers respected him. His athletic body and good looks was also a subject of some envy by others, and some lust by some others, men and women. Arslan did not partake of excessive drink as was common to most soldiers, so he had time to listen to some of the discourse and scholarly lectures in the streets and schools of Athens. At this time, he tried to understand his place in the world using the principles and methods espoused by these great teachers. He had not had great success in applying their methods to his particular and unique situation.

As was the normal progression with Arslan, he did not begin to really live in Athens until he met a special woman. Eta was only eighteen years old when Arslan met her at a city spring used for drinking water. She was average height but it was the only average thing about her. Her body was one of the sexiest Arslan had ever seen with large, firm breasts, a narrow waist, and athletic hips and legs. Her face was lean with a strong chin and a perfect complexion.

40

Eta was the daughter of a prosperous merchant who traded outside the city and had need of the good will of a respected Athenian soldier. Eta was elated to be allowed the company of the handsome Arslan and soon they were going on long walks in the woods and enjoying each other's bodies. The wealthy merchant soon cemented the arrangement by offering Arslan a sizable dowry for taking his lovely daughter as his wife. Arslan saw no downside to the arrangement since he preferred to act quickly after arriving in a place to establish a stable family circumstance and the two were married.

Arslan spent as much of his free time as possible visiting the various schools in Athens or listening to the great orators or dramatists. Athens at this time had Socrates, Plato, Aristophanes, Antisthenes, Democritus, Diogenes, and others. If a man could not find answers with these minds to help, the answers may not be there. Arslan listened and learned.

Socrates was only two years away from death when Arslan arrived in Athens. Plato was twenty-nine years old and entering his prime. Aristophanes still had thirteen years left to live. Aristophanes was a favorite of Arslan as he had already published many of his works and Arslan has access to the aging playwright through a cousin of Aristophanes who he had befriended.

On one occasion, he was alone with Aristophanes in his garden drinking wine. Arslan asked him, "Esteemed thinker, what would you do if you were an immortal, say the son of a god, but living among mortals who did not know you would continue to live when they would die. How would you deal with the loss of those you love as their lives run their course and you remain?"

Aristophanes pondered then said, "Soldiers do not normally think such thoughts nor ask such questions. Soldiers know too well of death to believe in immortality but in the hypothetical I will try to answer your question. A man who lived for a time then saw all he loved die, not once, but again and again would be too tragic to bear for long. He must surely become despondent and seek ways to end his own life. If he was not able to end his life, it would be the worst hell on earth. Perhaps if he were able to pass along his immortality to his children or some other way transfer it to humanity could give him reason to live. I can think of no other reason for him to want to go on, unless he were a totally selfish cur wanting only carnal pleasure from the world. I hope such men do not exist, but I suspect they do."

Arslan followed with another question, "What if the man could find some other way to use what he learned from living an extended life to help humanity. Perhaps he could find ways for men to please the gods so the lot of mankind would be improved."

Aristophanes said, "Perhaps there would be some way such an immortal could help mankind but I do not think it is through intersession with the gods. There are enough "religious men" already trying to find a way to "help" humankind. I fear them more than any other men because they try to wipe out all ideas different than their own."

Arslan returned to his young bride in the evening no closer to the answer to his questions.

Arslan and Eta lived a good life in Athens, with children soon making them a family. Eta was a good and caring wife and a better mother, totally devoted to her three daughters. This all pleased Arslan as love and closeness to his family was the main thing making his life worth living, despite the lingering knowledge this would be lost at some point.

After sixteen years in Athens, Arslan began the process of gradually ageing himself by growing a beard and coloring it gray along with his hair. He had become very adept at doing this gradually to extend the time he could stay in a place without becoming noticeable. This time he saw his love for Eta and his three daughters was so strong he wanted to make this life go on as long as possible. He also wanted to stay long enough to get his daughters married suitably. He considered this his responsibility.

He had developed ways of changing his posture and way of walking to further add to his ageing, but these were hard practices to continue in intimate circumstances with his wife. Eta finally started questioning his youthful look and Arslan told Eta of his affliction, as he had come to think of it. Eta was incredulous at first but then Arslan washed the gray out of his beard and hair and she was convinced. By this time Eta was thirty-eight years old, still one of the most attractive women in Athens. She said to Arslan, "Darling man, how long do you think you can stay in Athens before you will be forced to move to another place?"

Arslan replied, "Perhaps, ten more years if we are very careful. We will have our daughters married by then and I can leave enough for you to live out your life."

Eta said, "Why leave me behind? Take me with you and I will pretend to be your mother. That way we can extend our lives together, unless you are wanting a younger woman in your bed."

Arslan did not take long to reply, "My sweet Eta, I want no other woman in my bed. We have time to plan for us to go away together after the girls are married. It will keep us together for many more years."

11. <u>Tyre 374 B.C.</u>

Winning the love of that young girl
Hiding in a face etched by time,
Consumes me in a heartfelt swirl,
Making resistance a foolish crime.

In 374 B.C. Eta and Arslan left Athens supposedly on a trip to Corinth to visit with a fictional family of Arslan, but with a real plan to go elsewhere and start a new life as Arslan the young man and Eta his mother. He would have someone write to his daughters their parents were lost at sea or something along those lines after they had gone. They had planned this carefully and had saved monies and converted property to hard currency, some of which they had left for their daughters, who were by now all safely married.

The pair of travelers left the Athens's port of Piraeus in early summer to get the best weather for their long venture along the coast of Asia Minor down to the Phoenician port of Tyre, which was their destination. "Why go to Tyre of all places," asked Eta when Arslan had specified the destination.

Arslan's answer was quick, "We have to go somewhere. Why not Tyre? I have always admired the Phoenicians and especially those from Tyre. They have been colonizing around the known world for hundreds of years. They founded the city of Carthage, you know? It seems like Tyre is a place where the people are not afraid to venture out and do things."

Eta had no more questions. She knew her man had thought about where they could go and had made a decision. Someone had to do it to keep life moving.

The travel by sea was difficult with the ship hugging the coast whenever possible, avoiding pirates, avoiding storms, and trying to avoid any new wars which might pop up. The trip to Tyre took all summer with many adventures and hardships, but basically a good trip because they were together. Both Arslan and Eta had some trouble at first with seasickness but this soon passed.

They stopped in Rhodes and changed ships and identities as far as the age of Arslan was concerned. Arslan was now Eta's son to the

44

rest of the world with his beard shaved and gray dye washed out of his hair. As they sailed out, bound eventually for Tyre, they both had to remember to act like mother and son rather than lovers in public. In fact, there was so little privacy available on board ship they had many weeks where they could not show affection to each other as husband and wife before their arrival in Tyre.

Upon landing in Tyre they immediately began making inquires about houses for sale and located a modest home quickly with enough property for a small garden. They chose not to hire servants for the house so they would have complete privacy in their home but did hire a man to help work their small garden. Arslan sought out the military authorities for Tyre and offered his services as an instructor in sword and spear. After a short test where he easily defeated every challenger; a position was secured so he had a steady income.

Tyre was an island so they had to get used to a new type of living and also bought a small boat so they could travel beyond the island. They settled in as mother and son to the outside world but were something quite different, behind the doors of their home. Yes, his dear Eta, now 49 years old in 370 B.C., was showing gray hair but her body was still exquisite as far as Arslan was concerned and he loved her completely. They missed their children but knew it was for the best they not communicate with them.

They thought life was very good at this time. They could go on walks in the evening or for a short sail in their boat. There was little danger on the island; especially since Arslan was well known as the best swordsman anyone else had ever seen. He was treated with utmost respect. They also enjoyed their time together in their house. Both had healthy sexual appetites and commonly made time for some activity every day, sometimes more than once. They did not make a lot of close friends because they wanted to protect the time at home alone, where they did not have to pretend to be something they were not.

Others around Arslan thought him to be a very strange man but none dared say anything. They thought it strange he did not pursue any of the many women of Tyre who thought the handsome military instructor would be a wonderful addition to their bed. After some years, it was assumed he did not like women and perhaps secretly had some boys he went to for entertainment. After all he was a Greek.

45

No one, no one at all had the courage to say any of this to Arslan's face.

While sailing one evening, Eta said, "My love, what will you do when I am gone?"

Arslan thought then answered, "I have never let that thought enter my head before and I do not want to think of it now."

Eta said quickly, "But you must face reality. One day I will die and you must go on and live and marry and have children somewhere in this world. It is your responsibility to the future and I insist you do it. You must swear to me you will do it for me."

Reluctantly Arslan swore, "To live, marry and have children in remembrance of his love, Eta."

Eta was satisfied. She knew her man very well and he always kept his word to her.

All was well until 359 B.C., Arslan had just turned 400 years old if the truth be known, and Eta was sixty years old. A fever struck Tyre that year and Eta died in Arslan's arms. Arslan was devastated beyond consolation. He had never had so long with a woman, forty-two years, and he did not know how he could go on without her. He had been in Tyre for fifteen years and would soon have to start graying his hair and take other measures to appear to be ageing, if he stayed in Tyre.

He buried his beloved Eta, sold his boat, sold his house, resigned his military instructors position, and booked passage for Egypt. He had never been to Egypt and thought the prospect of learning about a new place and great civilization would take his mind off his loss. He had to do something and be somewhere other than Tyre, memories would haunt him and make him crazy if he stayed.

12. <u>Egypt 297 B.C.</u>

Arslan had lived in Egypt for sixty-two years by 297 B.C. and had just begun his fourth identity there, now as a guard for new construction in Alexandria. On this day he had met a man setting out on a great project, one that could be the greatest attainment of humankind to date in the world. He had met Demetrius, previously Tyrant of Athens, and now advisor to the Macedonian Pharaoh, Ptolemy I, on building a great library to house the knowledge of man brought from the far corners of the world. No activity could be worth more to a world where knowledge was precious.

Learning to read had not been an easy task for Arslan, at first. He had been fortunate to be in the right place at the right time in one of his early identities to get trained in reading by a merchant. This had given him the opportunity to learn and relearn reading as he moved from language to language. He was fairly certain he now read more languages than any other person in the world. *"Some of the languages may no longer exist,"* he thought.

On meeting Demetrius and hearing about his project, he had offered to help if he could. He told Demetrius his ancestry was Greek and his grandfather had known Aristophanes and Plato, among others. He also described the fact he knew a number of languages and could read most of them. He did not show his full command of languages since it would raise suspicion. Demetrius was very interested and immediately acted to get Arslan assigned to the library project.

The library project, inspired by Demetrius was under the control of the Pharaoh and the Egyptian bureaucracy. The naturally bureaucratic Egyptians would have taken much longer to build the library at Alexandria had there not been an Arslan or someone like him finding ways to move the project ahead. Arslan had lived in Egypt for over sixty years and had learned the language, customs, and bureaucratic maneuvering well. His position was not high in the library project but sometimes a lowly out of sight individual can cause problems to disappear more easily than someone shouting from the top.

When stone could not be delivered to the work site because the Supervisor of Barges did not see fit to make barges available, a lowly operative in his organization would find a way to reallocate barges from some other task. Since Arslan made it a point to know many of the people working in these agencies he found ways to use the power of his contacts to succeed. He also knew who could be bribed, who could be threatened, and in some cases who could be blackmailed.

The library was located in the northeast sector of the city near the palace. Classrooms surrounded its Great Hall with many scholars housed there on a permanent basis to categorize and evaluate the acquisitions of the library. The process of bringing scrolls and manuscripts to the library began even before the library was built and many of these items were housed in warehouses under less than ideal conditions. It was a huge project requiring a large staff.

Ptolemy I wanted to possess all known world literature. He and his predecessors took unusual means to accomplish this such as asking the leaders of the world to lend documents to the library to be copied, often returning the copies and keeping the originals or searching all ships stopping in the port of Alexandria, and taking their books to be copied. The cataloging of the works collected was far from perfect but was really the first attempt to systematically list the works of various authors. Even the identity of many of these authors would have disappeared if the library had not taken these steps.

Arslan threw himself into this project because he saw the library as a way to use his background to make something bringing great benefit to mankind. Perhaps, the contribution would be one no ordinary man could make. It would help to offset the tremendous sense of loss and guilt he felt in losing so many loved ones over the years. He thought *"If only my life could have some purpose higher than just repeating endlessly the cycle of loss of loved ones."*

Arslan's involvement with the Library at Alexandria ended rather abruptly in 284 B.C. with the death of Ptolemy I, the first Macedonian ruler of Egypt. A librarian was appointed, Zenodotus of Ephesus, whose efforts to take control of the library and associated construction placed Arslan in conflict with authorities too often. Arslan decided to leave Egypt and find another identity. Arslan's work on the start of the Library at Alexandria was one of the most satisfying times of his life.

13. <u>Atlanta</u>

Lisa turned off her recorder as John Young-Arslan put a marker in his manuscript and closed it. John said, "Let's take a break. We have been at this for over two hours. It is somewhat slow since my manuscript is written in Greek and I am translating as I go. It sometimes takes some thought to find the right word for translation of the true meaning, especially when feelings are involved."

"Do you understand why I chose to include this period in my tale rather than some other time. If not, I will tell you. I loved Eta more than words can express. I have loved others before and after her, especially Mata, but Eta and I were so close and cared so much for each other our relationship has a special place in my life and being. We were together for forty-two of the best years of my life and the world should know it. It is the most important part of me." said John Young-Arslan with hints of tears in his eyes.

Tears welled up in Lisa's eyes as she viewed the bare emotions of Arslan wanting to tell the world first and foremost of his love for Eta. *"Eta now dead for 2,400 years but still loved and remembered by Arslan. For anyone who says love doesn't last, they need to meet Arslan. Maybe it is Arslan's purpose in the world, if his story is true, to show people the eternal nature of love."* thought Lisa.

Simon was also affected by Arslan's show of emotion and Lisa took time to observe this. She was very interested in how Simon reacted to such pure emotion, as she wanted to understand the man he was. Simon said to Arslan, "I have tremendous respect for your need to honor the memory of Eta. She must have been a unique person to have held your love and attention so many years."

John Young-Arslan said, "It is not so much she was so unique but she was my unique person I loved. My experience is that every person I have met in the world is unique. That is the beauty of humankind. We are not ants following in the footsteps and actions of the one before, we all act differently and are unique."

John Young-Arslan then said, "You can see going through these manuscripts is an emotional experience for me. I need to take a long break right now and go out running. Exercise helps me deal with the emotional impact of these memories. I hope you don't mind."

49

Jon Kelly

Simon spoke for both of them when he said "Arslan, take as long as you need. I think we both understand, a little bit at least, what you are going through."

Arslan quickly changed in his room and left the apartment to go for a run. Simon and Lisa looked at each other without saying anything. They were both still sensitized by the emotions shown by Arslan for his memories of Eta. Lisa let some tears come saying, "If what Arslan is saying is true it is one of the most stirring love stories ever."

Simon did not say anything; he just took Lisa's hand and led her to his bedroom. After closing the door behind them, Simon kissed her again as he had outside by the car earlier. Then Simon said, "His story makes you think love is much more important than most people seem to treat it these days. His love for Eta is still there after 2,400 years of struggling to live in the world. It makes you take a completely new look at the importance and permanency of love. Doesn't it?"

Lisa answered as she took off her clothing, "I think I am beginning to like the way you think Simon Myers. Your reaction to Arslan was not a cold, clinical reaction. You bared your emotions and I loved to see it."

Simon meanwhile was taking off his own clothes and when finished he and Lisa slipped into bed. Simon was also thinking about Lisa's reaction to the emotions of Arslan and he thought he was starting to like the way Lisa Malloy thought and felt. He then said, "I want you to know my feelings for you are evolving quickly, meaning I want you more right now than I ever thought possible. The sex is important but I am feeling I want to be close to you for more than gratification. Does it make sense to you?"

Lisa said as their bodies moved together, "It makes all the sense in the world."

Sex was great with each seeming to sense the needs of the other and their emotions, sensitized by the encounter with Arslan, reached heights they had not experienced before. When they were finished with the sex, they remained firmly attached emotionally, and they both knew it.

They were both cleaned up and dressed before Arslan returned from his run. When he said a two-hour run, he had meant it. Arslan

50

went and showered while Lisa and Simon threw some sandwiches together. Everyone needed some fuel after his or her exercise.

Arslan joined them, had some food and a glass of wine, and then said, "Shall we get back to the manuscripts?"

Everyone nodded agreement and Arslan returned to his reading.

14. <u>Rhodes 293 B.C.</u>

Arslan made his way back to Rhodes in 293 B.C. He and Eta had visited there many years earlier when Rhodes was less prosperous. Now Rhodes had thrown off domination after being conquered for a short time by Alexander and was able to grow.

Chares of Lindos, a sculptor, was in the process of starting a great construction project to build a "colossi", a statue of the sun god, Helios looking out over the harbor. The statue was to be 100 feet tall and all would see it as they approached Rhodes by ship.

Arslan, as always admiring men who wanted to make a mark on the world, signed on as a military instructor of swordsmanship for the military forces. A position he expected would give him ample time to monitor the construction.

With funds he brought with him to Rhodes, as he was ever frugal, Arslan bought a small house and settled in to the task of living. Since he had not yet met a "special" woman, he took to going to several taverns in the evening. One night he visited a tavern called "The Torch" and met an unusual woman named, Kari, who frequented the tavern. It was unusual for women to be in taverns unless they worked there serving the clientele or were prostitutes, seeking to find customers. Kari was different. She was a moderately well off widow who just happened to like the tavern atmosphere and did not care what society said about her. She generally sat alone and men usually stayed away since she could be very hostile if someone tried to bother her. Occasionally, she drank too much wine and had to be helped home by the proprietor or his employees.

Kari might have been very attractive at one time but the years had not been especially kind to her. She was not unappealing but she was no longer a beauty. Arslan entered the tavern one evening and all the tables were full. He turned to leave but surprisingly he heard Kari saying, "Sit at my table, quiet soldier. I have seen you before staring at your wine and observing the other people. You will do me no harm."

Arslan moved to the table and sat down saying, "Thank you, kind lady, May I buy you a drink of wine and offer you my conversation."

Kari said, "Of course, wine and conversation are two of the best things in life."

Arslan quickly learned Kari had been the wife of a ship's captain who sailed off and never returned. This was not at all unusual in these times with the state of ships and knowledge of sailing and navigation. Ships often sank in storms or ran onto rocks. The sailor's profession did not have a long life expectancy. She had enough to get by on but was not wealthy and she had few friends. She had some education, very unusual for a woman of her times, as her father had taken the almost unheard of step of having her receive an education, including reading.

As the evening wore on it also became apparent Kari was a drunk. Arslan had always felt pity for those who gave in to their addictions, such as wine, but had never had a relationship with a woman so addicted. As it got late, Arslan offered to see that Kari got home safely, much to the relief of the proprietor.

Kari was able to walk and to show Arslan the way to her home. The home was a modest but comfortable house from the outside. Inside the home was ill kept, not horrible, but not as Arslan would expect his home to be. Arslan turned to go but Kari said, "Kind and quiet soldier, please stay for a while and continue our conversation. If you would like more from me than conversation, that also could be possible."

Arslan said after some thought, "I hesitate because I am not used to laying with a woman who drinks so much. I am sorry to be so direct but it is my way."

Kari said, "An honest man, as well as kind and quiet. Men like you really makes me nervous. Women fall in love with men like you and then do all the foolish things a woman can do when she is in such a state. Stay and have conversation with me even if you do not want me as a woman in my overindulgent state."

Knowing his own appetites, Arslan said, "I will stay for a while, but we will see if it is for conversation only. I did not say I did not want you as a woman, I only said I was not used to lying with a woman who drinks so much. I may decide I want you tonight."

Kari then said, "I see, this reminds me of the saying "A stiff prick has no conscience."

They both laughed with gusto and Arslan stayed.

53

The first night in the arms of Kari was memorable to Arslan. He was pleasantly surprised with the attractiveness of Kari's body with her clothes removed and the tender nature of their lovemaking. He had followed his standard practice, more than a practice by now but part of his personal style of living, he always tried, with extreme consideration and patience, to insure the women he shared a bed with achieved pleasure for themselves before he took his pleasure. This approach to love making had, over the years, given him results, in the form of happy, caring bed partners who always seemed to want to go back to the well for more. This was one of the reasons he steered clear of prostitutes, since such women were generally very difficult to get to experience sexual pleasure. He understood this was not a flaw in them necessarily, but more likely the result of the terrible treatment such women had usually received from men over the years.

Some women took longer than others to bring to pleasure but Arslan had learned persistence was a great virtue; especially in this case, since women who were slow to bring to pleasure were abundantly grateful if their lover were so patient and considerate to take them there. Arslan had found, again based on over four hundred years of "inquiry," a number of women had never slept with a man before who cared enough about their woman reaching pleasure. These women had never had the experience, at least not with a man. He had also learned some women had only experienced sexual pleasure with other women or more often by their own hands. Arslan usually had the delightful experience with women that once bedded by Arslan they would be back for more, and cheerfully so. The downside to this was women tended to fall in love with Arslan quickly, some after one encounter, and they could become very possessive.

With Kari, Arslan used abundant affection and his penchant for oral stimulation to bring her to orgasm several times before Arslan entered her to take his own pleasure. Arslan was pleased Kari was most receptive, with a naturally moist vagina and an interest in having him achieve satisfaction so she encouraged him both with the response of her body and those subtle verbal sounds and comments which men like to hear. The result was, for Arslan and he thought too for Kari, a most pleasant experience. After they were done, Arslan felt the special bonds, which good lovemaking wraps around a male-female relationship.

He left in the morning feeling good about his evening and inclined to return to the arms of Kari soon. Soon to Arslan in this regard normally meant the next night, because his appetite for sex was such he generally wanted release daily and sometimes more than once per day. He often wondered, not too seriously, if he was abnormal because he seemed to need the physical sensation of sex so often, compared to some other men. If he were a woman, he would probably be condemned as "wanton" or worse. He also was concerned his appetites might seem to cheapen the sex act as part of a close loving relationship. He reconciled this problem by remembering he always was faithful, completely faithful, when he was involved in a committed love relationship. Sometimes, this meant he had to compromise his own appetites, when his partner was not "in the mood." He knew this compromise was well worth it to have the emotional relationship with a woman he always needed.

Conversation with Kari during the evening was also fulfilling. She was unusually educated for a woman and had time to think about many subjects over the years with her husband at sea and then as a widow. She did not have to work to make a living, as most were required by circumstances to do, so she had time to use her mind to explore many subjects. Most people in these situations fail to make use of the opportunity to think productively but Kari had not wasted it, although she could have done more if not for her addiction to the "fruit of the vine."

They had fallen into discussions about human nature during the course of the evening. This subject was more to the taste of Arslan than such things as politics, war, fashion, or general gossip. Arslan preferred to think and talk about human nature, poetry, places and the natural world, art, science, and unknown mysteries of the world including magic, for want of a better word.

One subject discussed was how man could be so unkind and unjust to other men. Arslan made clear "man" and "men" in this discussion meant both men and women. Arslan had seen, and even been forced to participate in horrors during his life, which he could not tell Kari about. These had helped to shape his views, at this time, since they were always evolving. Arslan said to begin, "It is my experience some men are born "evil" and simply go through life spreading their evil to the rest of the world. Most of these men are incapable of changing to eliminate the evil from their personalities, even under pressure or to save their very lives."

Kari had a different view, "Men are born and then are shaped by their experiences to become good or evil. Society can provide a good, nurturing environment for raising children so they are guided toward the good rather than evil. Granted there are exceptions of men seeming to turn to evil even if their guidance and environment are good. These apparently evil ones may only have needed "special" guidance at some point in their young lives to counter the apparent inbred evil or perhaps they have an accidental flaw in their personalities which causes the problem. The vast majority of people can be good if the conditions of their environment are correct."

Kari continued "In my life I have seen a few men who seemed to be evil suddenly change and become good. Sometimes the change was the result of some religion or other establishing a foothold in their lives. In other cases, love for a woman seemed to spark the change in "good" or "evil" nature of their conduct. Some men are "hit in the head" and their entire nature changes. Does this not tell us men are not beyond redemption for their evil ways?"

Arslan had not thought about the subject from this perspective before and was grateful for the insight Kari provided. Arslan thought, "From the mouth of someone addicted to wine, I hear new truth which will shape my thinking. How strange is the search for knowledge and philosophy. Tonight I learned two lessons. A lesson about good and evil in men and a lesson, perhaps more important, to look in the least promising places for truth. It may be hiding there."

The next day, after completion of his duties in training Rhodes soldiers, Arslan returned to the tavern where he had met Kari. He waited there for several hours expecting her to enter and join him. He had not set a "date" with Kari but he knew the tavern was her normal routine and he had counted on it. Finally, he decided to go to her home and inquire.

He knocked on the door and was surprised at the sight before him when it was opened. Kari was noticeably cleaned up from the previous night, with her hair combed and braided and an attractive robe versus the older garment she had worn last night. She also had the look of sobriety. He was invited in and was surprised to find the interior had been cleaned, apparently from top to bottom, and was in perfect orderliness.

Kari broke the ice by speaking, "As you can see I was wrong last night and I was right last night. I was wrong when I said, "You will do me no harm." and I was right last night when I said, "Women fall in love with men like you and then do all the foolish things a woman can do when she is in such a state."

Without waiting for a reply Kari continued, "Seriously, one point of our conversation last night was people can change with the right motivation. An evil in my life is my weakness for wine. Addiction will take away my future if I allow it. Today I decided to try to reach out for the future by changing myself. I do not know if I can succeed but I have to try since I am in love with you, kind, quiet, honest soldier."

Arslan was surprised and very concerned. He cared for Kari but was concerned about the huge responsibility he would have if she became dependent on him for her emotional support. His experience with people addicted to drink was they often could not break the cycle of self-pity and depression causing them to return to drink despite their best intentions. He chose caution in his reply, "Kari, last night was wonderful and you know I mean it, women can sense such things. To say it is love, this soon, is dangerous and can lead to harm. I am glad you want to change for the better but you must do it for yourself not just to please me. The underpinnings of such a change must be deeper than a one night relationship, it must be based on a deep need from within yourself."

"Dear, dear soldier, your words of caution are well spoken, but I sense you have extensive experience in the world, and probably know love comes when it comes and we mere mortals have little control over when, where, or with whom. As for your concerns about the depth of my motivation for changing, do you not see this is for me, most selfishly for me? You are just the instrument who has made me see what I need to do. I ask no promise from you, only patience, to give me a chance to pursue my quest to deal with my problem." said Kari.

Feeling Kari had some sense of proportion about their relationship, Arslan said, "For a start I am your friend and a lover, whether it will grow to more, only the fates know. I do promise to be patient with you and caring. That is enough for now, I think."

Kari was satisfied with Arslan's response and their conversation moved to other subjects. They talked for several hours then went to sleep without sex, holding each other and letting the emotions settle in. In the morning, however, Arslan awoke Kari with kisses starting at her neck and going down her exposed back and buttocks, using his experienced hand to explore her thighs and such. Both Arslan and Kari were soon fully involved in the moment and their joining was even more delightful than the other evening, perhaps due to the sobriety Kari brought to the event this time.

The relationship between Kari and Arslan continued for several months with a growing closeness with the most serious problem being the decision as to whose house they would spend the night. Finally, it became clear it was more convenient to spend most of the time at Kari's house since she then had time during the day to clean, do laundry, and fix meals. Arslan took to letting friends or visitors use his house when appropriate since he was seldom there.

On a colder than normal day in February Kari had a problem, however. They had gone to their old tavern for supper, as the food served there was better than many places. The proprietor, upon seeing one of his old, best customers, who had been missing for some time, insisted or buying her wine to celebrate her homecoming. Kari thought she could drink one portion of wine with no problem. Upon drinking one, she insisted upon having another. Arslan did not like the situation and suggested they leave but the wine was in control for the moment. Arslan finally had to use very firm persuading, bordering on force, to get her to leave the tavern and return home. He got her home and put her to bed to sleep off the effects of the wine.

In the morning, they talked very openly about the previous night and agreed upon a lesson learned. Kari could not let any amount of wine or other strong drink pass her lips. She had to stay completely away from drink to avoid restarting her addiction. Kari pledged to do this in the future.

For another five months, Arslan and Kari lived their idyllic life without major problems other than the normal challenges of living. In mid-summer, a messenger sought out Arslan at mid-day as he trained recruits in use of the sword. Kari wanted him to meet her at Arslan's house as soon as possible; the messenger made clear she said it was urgent. Arslan turned the training over to an assistant and went to his house.

Kari was waiting inside the house and was in tears. Arslan asked, "What is wrong, sweet woman?"

Kari poured out her story, "I was at home this morning doing laundry when a knock came at the door. I opened it and there stood a bearded, skinny figure with one arm but who was, without a doubt, my long lost husband, returned after being gone for nine long years. My husband explained he had been shipwrecked on the coast of Africa and had been enslaved for many years. He had eventually escaped and made his way back to Rhodes, the best he could. On his return journey he had lost his left arm in an experience with pirates."

Kari continued, "I told him I had waited for him for eight years then told him about our relationship. He is also a good, kind man, as are you, and he was not angry and understood very well this happens when people are separated for a long time with no knowledge of the circumstances. He is now at my house, really his house, waiting for a decision from me about our future. What am I to do?"

Arslan was surprised but probably less than other men would be due to his special circumstances and experience. Yes, Arslan felt love for Kari. It was not his way to have a close relationship with a woman and not grow into loving strongly. However, it was not a long relationship for Arslan, especially for Arslan, it was not like forty-two years with Eta. He responded to Kari, "It is a decision you alone can make. You once loved your husband very much, to the point you had turned to drink to hide from his loss. He has come back to you and still wants your love. In his circumstances, he probably needs your love more than I, and will be more profoundly damaged if it is withdrawn. I have loved you and do love you but I can survive without you, he may not be able to so easily. You must decide what can bring you happiness, including what will make you feel you have done what is right."

Kari could not speak for a long time then said, "Your thoughtfulness and understanding, even now, are beyond my words to express. I wish I were two people, one who could go with you and one to go with my husband, but that's not possible. It is more than what I want; it is also my responsibility to act in the right manner, not

59

for society but for my self-respect. So the decision makes itself, I must go and care for my husband."

Arslan replied, "Yes, the decision was really made before you asked. I will always be your friend, no longer your lover, but will always love you in a special way. Always treasure the memory of our time together but do not let it stop you from renewing your bonds with your husband."

Arslan then returned to Kari's house with her to meet her long gone husband and to communicate the decision made by Kari. They knocked on the door before entering just to give some notice of their presence. Kari entered first followed by Arslan. In the room stood a taller than normal man, about 6'2", but extremely thin and with no left arm below the elbow. He was bearded and tanned a deep brown. The skin of his face showed the effects of years in the sun.

The man said, "Greetings to you wife and to your friend. Please come and speak with me to understand what we are to do about our futures."

Arslan spoke, "Greetings to you kind sir. Welcome back to your home after such a long and arduous journey. You have my regrets your homecoming is less than what you might have expected. If there are no objections from Kari, I will leave the two of you alone here and take a walk to a nearby tavern, have one drink of wine then return to this place. This will give Kari time to tell you her decision concerning this situation and for you to say what needs to be said. We can talk further upon my return."

Arslan left the house and walked to the tavern thinking, "It is better this way to let husband and wife resolve their situation between themselves. I know when I am the outsider."

Arslan drank a cup of wine and walked back to Kari's house. He knocked, the door was opened and he was bade to enter. There stood Kari and her husband, introduced as Julian, of Roman extraction. They now stood side by side facing Arslan, *"As husband and wife should be,"* thought Arslan.

Kari spoke first, "I have told my good husband my decision and we are reconciled."

Arslan said, "I wish you the best things for your lives together. Anything I can do to help either of you in the future, please call upon me. I will gather my things from the house and be leaving."

Julian said, "Arslan, Kari has told me of your great kindness to her and the rescue from her addiction to wine. I owe you more than I can say. Thank you."

Kari approached Arslan and gave him a very firm hug while she cried. Arslan broke away after a time, gathered his possessions and left the house of Kari.

15. <u>Kos 291 B.C.</u>

After ending the relationship with Kari, Arslan threw himself into his work for a period of time then volunteered for a military mission which involved hunting down pirates who were harassing merchant ships transiting from Rhodes to various trading locations to the north, along the coast of what is now Turkey. In the spring of 291 B.C. ten ships loaded with soldiers left Rhodes and made their way first to the island of Kos. Using Kos as a staging base they attacked pirates operating from small villages along the coast of the mainland.

In the first action, five of their ships landed by surprise at a small unnamed village catching three pirate ships moored in the small natural harbor unawares. Arslan was second in command of the landing party assigned to search the village and to capture and kill all pirates found. He had the rank of sergeant under a commanding officer. There was little resistance as their party of sixty soldiers took over the small village and assembled all the people in the village on the seashore. Women, children, youths, and the aged men were sorted out but held on the shore. The officer from Rhodes ordered the men questioned individually. The first man was selected and tied to a pole with his hands over his head tied to the pole. He was asked if he was a pirate and of course he said, "No."

Without further questioning a sword stroke severed his right leg at the ankle. A preheated piece of iron was then used to sear his wound closed so he did not bleed to death. He passed out at this point but was revived. He was then asked if he was a pirate again. He said, "No, but I can say who are pirates." The men of the village were then brought before the man one at a time and he said who was a pirate and who was not.

The first man had identified twelve men as pirates. Twenty-five other men were in the other group supposedly not pirates. After some discussion it was decided only twelve men could not man the three pirate ships. They would require at least twenty-five or more men to man those ships. First, logic said the man who had already lost his right foot was a liar. Second, the non-pirate group included at least another dozen pirates.

Their mission was to end piracy so their next step was to execute the twelve identified pirates and the man who had lied. This was done quickly with no option to appeal. Next it was decided to cut off the right hand of each of the twenty-five men in the non-pirate group. They may be maiming some innocents but had no other way to stop the piracy than to make these men unable to participate effectively. The men were taken one by one to a block set up for the purpose and their right hand held in place by soldiers until the task was done.

Arslan did not like the violence but recognized the pirates had killed many innocents as they raided shipping. Even the potentially innocent who were maimed had undoubtedly helped the pirates or benefited from their spoils. Word of the severe treatment of pirates and villages harboring pirates would spread along the coast and act as a permanent warning to those engaged in piracy. One-handed men would also be a lasting reminder.

Returning to Kos, Arslan saw the work on this mission would be brutal and dangerous. Their party was not so large they could not be challenged by an alliance of pirates and they would get no aid if this happened. He knew one thing; he did not want to be caught at sea by a larger force of pirates who would have the advantage of being in their element. He would prefer a land fight where his soldiers, and especially himself, would have a great advantage over sea-trained pirates. He voiced his concern to his commanding officer, but as a sailor, he did not share Arslan view.

For about two months, their party attacked small villages with results similar to the first attack. They had not seen serious opposition and began to become somewhat casual about what they were doing, except for Arslan. Arslan was on edge and extremely alert to any sudden change in their circumstances.

Early one morning seven of their ships sailed out to attack a somewhat larger village with approximately seventy soldiers and thirty-five sailors on board. Their commanding officer left three ships back at their base for security. As the fleet neared the selected village ten ships appeared from the north. The commander ordered his seven ships to attack the ten pirate ships. They sailed toward the pirates and were almost within bow range when eight more pirate ships appeared from the south. Arslan now saw the potential for a disaster.

The Rhodian commander finally asked Arslan for his advice. Arslan suggested they make for land and set up for a land battle. The pirates would not be prepared for this and the advantage of numbers of ships would be negated since the total number of fighters on the Rhodian ships was probably about the same as the smaller pirate ships. The commander showed wisdom by accepting this advice and ordering his ship to head for shore. The pirates were initially surprised but then followed toward the shore.

Once to shore Arslan had the ships beached and then used as protection as they had their archers send fire arrows at the pirate ships as they came to shore. The pirates were off balance due to the unfamiliar tactics being used by the soldiers and sailors from Rhodes.

Three of the pirate ships were set afire before they could reach shore and the pirates on board either died by fire or drowned in the sea. Arslan knew in a sword and spear fight, his trained troops would provide a very difficult opponent for the pirates. Arslan's biggest concern now was the pirates running away before they could be dispatched by his troops. His next tactic was to have about half of his troops hide behind the beached ships while the rest of his force formed on the beach to attract an attack from the pirates. This worked well.

The pirates landed on the beach and saw they considerably outnumbered the party from Rhodes visible on the beach. They launched a full-scale attack with their entire force. As they engaged the Rhodes' soldiers and sailors on the beach they were suddenly attacked from their flank by the hidden second contingent of troops. A small party of troops headed for the beached pirate ships with torches to set them afire and cut off escape.

The pirates were no match for the trained sword and spear fighters from Rhodes. The best swordsman in the world had trained all these men. They cut through the pirates like a red-hot knife through butter. Pirates started to flee but their ships were afire and rocks and cliffs blocked their retreat inland. Afterwards, Arslan counted 76 dead pirates on the beach and forty-six captives.

The captives immediately became an issue for discussion. The commander initially thought to execute them on the spot. Arslan wanted to avoid more death at the time and suggested the captives would have a major impact on trading and the confidence of merchants using Rhodes for trade if they were taken back to Rhodes for justice to be done there in public view, rather than on an isolated seashore.   After a little thought about the advantageous politics of Arslan's suggestion, the commander agreed.

They sailed back to their base with the captives on board then set sail for Rhodes via several stopping points along the coast.   Arriving in Rhodes in early August, word spread quickly of the huge success of the mission and the now forty-three captives, three had died or been killed during the return trip.   The captives were marched through the city and imprisoned in the palace prison.

16. <u>Rhodes 291 B.C.</u>

The mission commander and his second in command were called before the leaders of Rhodes and given gifts and bonuses to recognize their success. The fact Arslan was the true hero and author of the strategy converting the mission from potential disaster to great victory was made know through word of mouth from the troops. The commander was wise enough to join in praising Arslan since he would have lost much favor if he had tried to claim the credit he was not due. As it was there was plenty of honor to go around to everyone and the mission commander got his share for being wise enough to listen to Arslan. Arslan saw this was an excellent lesson for any leader.

The discussion of what to do with the pirate captives gave Arslan an opportunity to accomplish two things. He suggested the captives not be executed but be put to work as slave labor for the construction of the Colossi being built. This suggestion, coming from Arslan, was approved almost unanimously by the leadership. The warning to pirates a life of slavery awaited them if caught by the military of Rhodes would be effective. For Arslan, this solution avoided more slaughter and provided a boost to the construction of a great gift to mankind, the soon to be great Colossus at Rhodes. As proof of the suggested policy, piracy along the coast dropped off significantly for many years.

Arslan was surprised at being called to an audience with the leaders of Rhodes. They had recognized Arslan was the best swordsman in Rhodes, a clever military tactician, and the most popular military man on the island with the soldiers. They offered Arslan a position as an officer so his skills could be best utilized.

Arslan saw an opportunity and spoke up, "Eminent leaders, I am proud to accept your offer but would like to offer my skills for a particular duty. I would like my assignment to be the security and organization of the project to build the colossi. You may not be aware my past includes some training in Egypt on construction engineering as well as my military skills. The use of the pirate captives for the construction will require additional security and my engineering background can be put to use. The leaders saw no reason not to agree and placed Arslan in a liaison role between the architect, Chares of Lindos, and the military with responsibility for security.

Elevation to officer status meant significant responsibility and money to Arslan but also placed him on a new level of society. The immediate expectation was he would use his position to enrich himself as was the normal course. His resistance to being bribed and general honesty quickly became known.

Women from a higher level of society now wanted the company of the handsome, young officer who was the hero of the day on Rhodes. Arslan recognized the danger to himself of this situation, but the combination of his love for the colossi project and the fact he could probably last fifteen to twenty years before his lack of ageing would force him to move along, made him dismiss the danger. He began to socialize with women of the higher social levels in Rhodes. The beautiful young daughters of the rich and powerful made their attempts to lure the handsome officer, but Arslan did not find one who made him want to make a commitment.

17. <u>Rhodes 289 B.C.</u>

In the spring of 289 B.C., Arslan met the thirty-year-old widow of a wealthy merchant at a social function. He immediately was attracted by her beauty and sensuality. After talking with her for some hours, he saw she was reasonably intelligent but not educated to the extent of Keri. He missed the deep conversations with Keri but saw no way to find a woman who could give him that as well as other womanly companionship. There simply were very few educated females in the world at this time.

Her name was Maria and she showed enough interest in Arslan he began to call on her. After several visits, she demonstrated the force of her personality by suggesting to Arslan he visit her private apartment, alone. Once alone in her apartment, she made clear she wanted Arslan in her bed and he was more than willing. Their coupling followed Arslan's normal pattern with the lady quite satisfied and wanting to continue to see Arslan. He was not yet sure about a permanent relationship with this lady and chose to be somewhat hard to get at this point. It was not a strategy, he simply was not sure.

For Maria, a lady used to having her own way in all things, the fact Arslan did not ask, "How high?" when she said, "Jump!" increased her desire to have his company. She sent gifts and invited him constantly to attend her, privately and publicly. Arslan accepted a few invitations but was unavailable for many. This only increased her ardor.

Finally, Arslan accepted an invitation to her private apartment and suggested they talk openly about their relationship. She agreed quickly but waited for Arslan to speak first. Arslan began, "Dear Maria, I care for you and certainly find you a most attractive woman but you must understand I am an independent person. I must have you respect me as a man and not expect me to be impressed by your wealth or position. Your attitude seems to be you should be able to tell me what I should do. I cannot be in a relationship with a woman who continues with such an attitude. Do you understand?"

Maria was crushed by the comments of Arslan. "Dear Arslan, I never meant to treat with anything less than respect but I am a product of my upbringing. I was taught by my parents and husband to act this way. Please give me a chance to change. I want you more than you understand," she said.

Arslan replied, "At times, the most difficult behavior to change is your own. I believe your sincerity at this moment but time will tell."

Arslan left the ladies apartment then after promising to give her an opportunity to change. The number of invitations now dropped to a reasonable number of request to attend some public functions with her. At the first of these, Maria told Arslan she would wait for him to ask to come to her apartment or she to his house. She had lost her imperial air in dealing with Arslan and was much more open and close in their conversation.

Maria and Arslan were married before the end of the year. Arslan had found Maria had profoundly changed in her attitude toward him and others as well. She was now much more approachable by everyone and she and Arslan became close in many ways. She wanted children and Arslan did not object. He was quite willing to be a participant, in fact. Time passed and the colossi grew as their family grew with six children over twelve years. Arslan did not worry too much in this case about providing for his children since Maria had vast wealth. He was free to focus on the colossi project, which was his passion.

Arslan's talents at organization and finding ways around obstacles served well the building of the Colossus at Rhodes, and it was for the most part completed by 277 B.C.

Arslan looked at the towering statue when completed then turned away and started planning his next move. Sixteen years in Rhodes meant he was now approaching the point where he would have to start ageing or face discovery. He had never attained the type of relationship with Maria he wanted. She was happy enough, especially with her children, but Arslan was a romantic and she never was prone to the degree of emotional intimacy he needed. This further made the need to make a change more attractive. Arslan felt some guilt at this situation, but real feelings are real feelings, he had to be the person he was.

18. <u>Rome 147 B.C.</u>

Arslan arrived in Rome in the fall of 146 B.C. The Romans had conquered Macedonia in 168 B.C. and in 147 B.C. the Romans had made it a province of Rome. Arslan had been in Macedonia for twenty years serving as a mercenary soldier in the now Roman controlled military. He had reached the point again his lack of ageing was becoming conspicuous and he had to move on. This time he signed on with the Romans as a mercenary adjunct to the Roman legion returning to Rome. This legion had just participated in the destruction of Corinth after a revolt in Greece.

As a student of military matters, Arslan was very interested in the reason why the Romans could defeat the Macedonians whose military methods had worked so well in Asia. The armies of Macedon had won their wars under Alexander the Great using the phalanx as their key military formation. As Polybius points out in *The Histories* the phalanx works well on perfectly level ground but not on rough terrain. The Roman formations do not require smooth terrain so the Romans could battle anywhere.

Rome was the greatest power in the world at this time but not without contest. They had the reputation as brutal conquerors using their discipline, arms and tactics to destroy their enemies. They were still in the process of subjugating the most of the western world, but Arslan had seen enough to want to see where this powerful force emanated from, and who the Romans were.

Arslan entered Rome quietly, not part of a triumph or such. The Romans of the republic were very concerned about soldiers entering Rome in large numbers as the military was not trusted to avoid involvement in politics. As a non-Roman citizen at this point he did not want to attract attention to himself. He wanted to learn the lessons about what to do to make his way in Rome. Therefore, Arslan was keeping a low profile.

He found sleeping quarters in a public house and set out to explore the city. He had long since learned the Latin language and written word working with the Romans in Macedon. He had no fear as he set out to find out what he could about the great city of Rome. The buildings were certainly impressive and the city was huge.

People were everywhere and with a wide variety including people obviously visiting from the far corners of the empire based on their strange looks and dress.

Arslan was not so interested in the political institutions of Rome as he was in the people and social systems. He set out to find a tavern to find some people to have conversation. He found a tavern which looked promising and entered. He found an empty bench and ordered wine. He sat for a while and observed the other customers in the tavern. Two soldiers from a legion; he did not recognize their markings, sat at one table entertaining one of the serving girls. Several men at another table appeared to be merchants of some kind. There was an older woman, probably early thirties, who seemed to be in charge of the tavern at the moment. Possibly her husband owned the tavern. The serving girls were younger.

Business was slow in the tavern in mid-afternoon. Arslan was hungry despite the time of day so he asked the older woman if he could get some food. She said she had some stew that was reasonably fresh and tasty, and fresh bread just brought from the bakery.

Arslan said, "It sounds very good to me. And could I get some stronger wine, this seems to be watered a bit much."

The older woman said, "I am sorry soldier, my brother tends to put more water in than necessary to increase his profit. I will pour you some of the stronger wine."

Arslan said, "Thank you, but I do not want to get you in trouble with your brother."

The woman replied, "Thank you for your concern but I can take care of my brother. He only owns half the tavern, I own the other half. He does not tell me what to do. In fact I tell him what to do in most things, but don't tell him I said it."

Arslan said, "Well, you seem to be an independent lady. What is your name?"

She replied with a smile showing the beauty of her face, "I am Sylvia. What is your name, gentle soldier?"

"I am Arslan, just arrived in Rome from Macedonia as a auxiliary to the legion." said Arslan, smiling at Sylvia.

"Welcome to Rome then, have you found a place to stay or will you stay with the legion? We have rooms to rent above the tavern if you are looking?" said Sylvia.

"I stopped at a place across the street and said I would be back but have not paid so I could change to here if the quarters are good." said Arslan.

Sylvia said, "Let me show you the room and you decide. If I know the place across the street you visited, it will be an easy choice and you won't get so many bed bugs with your room here."

Arslan followed Sylvia upstairs to see the room. It was a small room but neat and clean and much better than what he had seen across the street. He asked the price and a deal was made. He agreed to pay by the week to get a lower rate and Sylvia seemed pleased he was going to be a tenant.

Returning to the tavern Sylvia saw her brother had returned and introduced him to Arslan. "Brother, this is our new tenant for the upstairs room, his name is Arslan and he has paid for a week but may stay longer, I think. Arslan, this is my brother, Paulus."

Sylvia then remembered Arslan's food and wine, "Arslan I will get your food. Brother, in the future, please make sure the wine for Arslan is not watered too much."

Arslan returned to his table and down. Sylvia returned quickly with a large plate of stew with plenty of bread. She also brought a fresh goblet of wine. "Please let me know if there is anything else you would like." she said smiling.

Arslan decided to be bold since he had already decided he liked this lady, and said, "Sylvia, the only other thing I need is someone to answer some of my questions about Rome. Can you help me?"

Without comment Sylvia sat down across from Arslan and then said, "Ask away, Arslan."

Arslan asked many questions and Sylvia helped him on many subjects, especially about the customs and good manners in Rome. When asked about places to see and where to find things it became obvious, someone needed to take Arslan to these places until he learned the city. Arslan spoke up, "Sylvia, I have no right to impose on your time as you are obviously a busy woman but if you could make some time available to show me around I would be most grateful and perhaps we could become friends."

Sylvia looked at Arslan with a glowing smile and said, "I think we will soon be good friends and I will show you some of Rome when you have time."

They agreed to meet the next day at mid-morning and would go for a tour of the city with Sylvia as guide. Arslan retired to his upstairs room for the night but not without finding out Sylvia also lived upstairs.

Their trip around the city was very informative for Arslan but also very enjoyable due to the company of the attractive and cheerful Sylvia. Arslan liked happy women who did not make a habit of complaining about things just to be complaining. It is a bad habit some women get into and it makes those around them suffer. Arslan bought them a nice afternoon meal from a street vendor and a bottle of wine from a shop. They went to a public park to eat and enjoyed a beautiful day with Sylvia telling Arslan about Rome and Arslan telling Sylvia about Macedonia. He could have told her about many other places but it might give away too much.

They returned to the tavern before dark drawing a glance from Paulus. Arslan decided to have a goblet of wine before retiring for the night and sat down. He saw Sylvia in conversation with her brother; it did not seem to be an agreeable conversation. After a few minutes Silvia came to Arslan table and sat down then said, "My brother is being protective. He said to me that the soldier probably has a wife back in Macedonia, or perhaps several; that's how soldiers live. I told him it was none of his business anyway and besides I was just showing you where to find things in Rome not being betrothed."

Arslan thought a moment and said, "First of all I have no wives in Macedonia or elsewhere. Second, You are a beautiful woman with great charm and intelligence; your brother has every reason to worry about you. You should thank him for his concern. Third, the man you spent today with is already thinking, no thinking and feeling, he wants to have the opportunity to spend much more time with you and get to know you better."

Sylvia blushed, then smiled and said, "You are right, I will thank my brother, for his concern and for causing this conversation so we could get these things said. I am a direct woman, sometimes overly so perhaps, but being direct seems to be your way also. I too want to spend time with you and want to learn more about you. There, we have both said what we feel right now. That's good, very good."

Arslan looked into Sylvia's eyes and said, "I like you better with every word you say, Sylvia."

Arslan and Sylvia began spending as much time together as possible, taking long walks whenever their schedules allowed it and generally becoming good friends, and more. On a Saturday after about two weeks, they planned a short trip out of the city for a picnic. Arslan rented a horse and Sylvia rode behind him with her arms around him holding on. Their picnic was in bags tied across the neck of the horse.

Sylvia knew a spot that was normally quiet and they rode there. It was a beautiful fall day with the sun shining. They laid out their picnic and ate then shook out the crumbs from the blanket and sat on the blanket. Sylvia was her direct self, "Arslan I want you and I think you want me. Let's move this blanket to a more secluded spot and do what we both want."

Arslan kissed Sylvia then said, "My beautiful lady, I have wanted you since the first moment I saw you. Now, I know what a kind, intelligent person you are in addition to being beautiful, I want you much more."

Sylvia and Arslan, moved the blanket and proceeded to enjoy each other's bodies with joy and feeling.

As they rode back to Rome, Arslan could feel the breasts of Sylvia against his back and he felt the feeling of closeness and caring he always sought. He knew he wanted Sylvia to be with him as long as possible.

Sylvia and Arslan were married before the New Year and chose to stay in a larger room above the tavern as their home.

The legion was now permanently assigned to the defense of Rome so unless something unusual happened Arslan would be able to stay in Rome indefinitely. As it was Arslan stayed in Rome for over ten years with only minor forays out to other parts of Italy for the legion to deal with problems close to Rome. These problems were largely the result of economic disparities brought on by the success of empire building. The large tax revenue coming from the provinces, especially in the West, was going mainly to the benefit already wealthy patricians and some other city dwellers. The plebeian small farmers were getting no benefit and had been devastated by the invasion of Hannibal meanwhile Arslan and Sylvia had their own issues to deal with. Sylvia was pregnant with their first child due in the spring of 144 B.C.

One room above the tavern would not be a good place for a baby and the crying of a child would not be good for business.

Sylvia had all her wealth tied up in the tavern. Arslan on the other hand had an amount of gold hidden away. He never was a wild spender and had secretly brought a sizable stash of gold with him to Rome. Arslan had Sylvia keep her eyes open for a property to serve them as a home. After some wait, Sylvia took Arslan to visit a residential sector about one-half hour's walk from the tavern.

Once there, Arslan liked what he saw. There was a moderately sized house with three rooms and a kitchen with a large enclosed garden and patio. There were fruit trees in the garden and lots of room for children to play or adults to enjoy the outdoors. Sylvia thought she would shock Arslan with the high price but Arslan knew value when he saw it, and those born in his birth month spend money like water, or so they say. They decided to buy.

Arslan surprised Sylvia by putting the property in her name. He did this he said because he could go off with the legion and not return. It would make it difficult to get the property transferred to Sylvia or children without great delays and expense. In reality he was planning for the time when he would need to leave.

By 133 B.C. Arslan and Sylvia had two children, boys, and were happy with their lives. A civil war started in 133 B.C. with the election of Tiberius Gracchus as tribune. He made proposals to limit land ownership and to seize land from those who owned too much, which was strongly opposed by the wealthy property owners in the Senate. Implementation of his proposals was blocked but when he tried to be elected for a second term there was a riot and Tiberius Gracchus was killed.

Arslan had been very careful to watch what was happening in Rome and to stay away from becoming aligned with the wrong element. He knew from experience in many lands politics was a dangerous game. He saw there was a struggle going on between the rich of Rome and the poorer elements for a share of the wealth being generated by the empire. The political structure of Rome was changing to a situation where politicians would appeal directly to the masses, as with Tiberius Gracchus.

Arslan had already started his artificial ageing process by 131 B.C. by adding some gray to his hair and growing a beard. He gradually grayed more and more over the years to provide the appearance of ageing. He knew he probably had only another five years, ten at the maximum, before he would have to leave this identity. He had to make plans.

His first step was to decide whether or not he should tell Sylvia. Throughout his many identity changes this was always one of the hardest decisions to make. Was his woman at the time strong enough to understand and accept the strange fate of Arslan? Did he tell her or simply disappear, never to be heard from again.? Through the many identities, he had made the decision to tell his spouse at least eight times. He had not regretted any of these decisions, but each decision was made based on the individual not on any general rule. His own sense of what was best and right with each person was his guide.

He decided to tell Sylvia. She was surprised but not surprised. She had noticed Arslan did not seem to age but had liked it too much to make an issue about it. She was amazed at the story he told about his past identities but was not panicked by the knowledge. She had always known Arslan was unusual; he seemed to know so much and be able to do so many things. She thought about the news he would have to leave within the next few years and, although sad, she immediately thought about what kind of plan they should make.

The boys were fourteen and twelve. If Arslan could wait seven years until they were 21 and 19 they should be old enough to take care of themselves. Arslan and Sylvia would see they had the best start possible. Arslan agreed.

Should Sylvia go with Arslan wherever he chose to go? Sylvia was inclined to say, yes, but Arslan cautioned her to think about it. In Rome she had the comfort of owning a home and being part owner of a profitable tavern. She also had a good brother who could help her and the boys. If she stayed she could act as advisor to the boys and to continue to provide a home for them to return to when needed. Sylvia was now 48 years old and she was beginning to show age in the form of graying hair, which she dyed. If they left together in seven years she would be 55 years old. It was an old age to be starting out on a new adventure to start a new life. Arslan remembered the last years with Eta and how much they meant to him, but also remembered the searing pain when she died. They did not have to decide now but had to keep the need to decide in mind.

By 123 B.C. Rome was in turmoil again with Giaus Gracchus of the same family elected tribune and the politics of Rome boiling over into the streets. Giaus was extremely popular with the people and tried to fix the price of grain at low levels and proposed citizenship for all Italians to expand his base of power. The patricians in the Senate were livid. Arslan took his boys aside and made it very clear to them they were forbidden to get involved in politics. It was very dangerous, even if they sympathized with the people over the Senate; they were small pawns and would be the first to be destroyed. They would heed the instructions of their father.

Arslan decided he would go to the east within two years on the pretext he was going to visit family in Macedonia, then send word back he had been killed by bandits. He also made the decision Sylvia must stay in Rome. When he told her this decision she cried but agreed it was probably for the best. The boys needed someone to provide guidance in dangerous times. Leaving them alone completely would not be responsible.

19. <u>Rhodes 49 B.C.</u>

Arslan had returned to Rhodes in 51 B.C. after an absence of 226 years. He had been dismayed on hearing of the destruction of the Colossus at Rhodes by an earthquake in 224 B.C. He had been instrumental in the construction of the Colossus and felt great loss when an attempt by men to make something larger than themselves, which was supposed to last through the centuries had been destroyed so soon. "Well, at least the great library at Alexandria is still there and growing; it is much more important than a statue." thought Arslan. Nevertheless, Arslan still looked at the emptiness of the sky where the Colossus once stood with remorse.

Arslan had again offered himself to the military leaders of Rhodes as an instructor in weaponry and was again accepted after giving a demonstration of his skills. *"It is strange some things never change through the ages. If you offer the powerful a skill to enhance their power, they will be your friend and support you."* thought Arslan.

Arslan changed his name to the Romanized form, Arslanus, upon landing in Rhodes, to make his claim to Roman citizenship more valid.

He had now lived on the earth 700 years in close to 50 different identities. He had been a farmer, a soldier, an engineer, a merchant, a leather worker, a silversmith, a fisherman, and other professions, some less noble. The skills he had developed over so many years included weapons, especially the sword, military tactics, farming, construction, trades such as leather and silver work, fishing and hunting, and languages, so many languages. He could read and speak more languages than anyone else in the world.

Arslanus had been in some of his identities for as short a time as a few days, a rare thing, and as long as 47 years, his original identity as Arslan. Normally he could stay in an identity for twenty years before suspicion about his inability to age became a problem.

He had been the husband of many wives and the lover of many more women. He was also the father of many children but each time he went back to check on the life of one of his offspring, all seemed to be ageing normally. They did not inherit his condition. He had also seen so many wives and children die from disease, violence, famine and old age. The sense of loss was overwhelming, if he allowed it.

His personal character had evolved from a good man who did not understand why he was different to still a basically good man but somewhat jaded by his long past. He had been forced by circumstances to do things he considered to be wrong even evil at times. The number of lives he had taken by violence was much more than he cared to remember. He did try to avoid killing his fellow man but it was a violent world and often he had no choice except to die himself and curiously his instinct for self preservation was extremely strong. He let his skill with weapons become known whenever he chose an identity as a military person so he would discourage people from forcing him to use his weapons to kill. The problem was his "leaders" would want to use his skills to kill.

He had been exposed to many of the religious beliefs of the day and was not overly impressed any truly captured the essence of truth as he came to know it. His existence in many cases belied the tenets of many religious beliefs, centered on belief in an afterlife. These beliefs seemed irrelevant to someone who did not age or die. If the religious belief does not have implications for the conduct of men in this world then he had trouble looking ahead to a next life. He was certainly no closer to understanding his place in the world than he had been at the beginning.

On the other hand, Arslan tried to do good in the world whenever possible. He always tried to help men, women and children survive if possible. He never used people for his own personal gratification without giving in return. He sincerely loved the people he loved and would do anything to keep and protect them. Moreover, he hoped he could do something in the world to improve mankind.

What kept Arslan going through the many lives, changes and losses? Perhaps it was instinct but he always thought it was more than that. He was still seeking an answer as to why he was on the earth. It could not be just chance he was so different. Where had he come from—the old couple claiming him, as their grandson left no answers? They had only left Arslan and some gold ingots. The gold ingots are gone and only Arslan remains. *"Well one gold ingot was buried near Amwat in a cave. Perhaps some day I will return to Amwat and try to find it,"* thought Arslan, now Arslanus.

79

Jon Kelly

Julius Caesar arrived in Rhodes in 48 B.C. in the middle of a great civil war in the empire with Pompey. In the course of his visit he had an occasion to be introduced to a reputed great swordsman who was a mercenary in the service of Rhodes, a Roman citizen named Arslanus. A demonstration was ordered with Arslanus to fight the best from the Roman legion with Caesar.

Arslanus had not volunteered for this demonstration but he had no choice. His opponent was a man named Titus who had a considerable reputation. Betting was heavy with the military men of Rhodes, who had trained with Arslanus or even seen him fight, willing to bet every piece of gold or silver on the island on his success. The Romans, somewhat out of pride, were sure no one could be that good and their man was a great swordsman. Therefore, the betting was considerable.

Caesar told them to proceed and offered a considerable gift of gold to the winner. The Romans were speechless when their man was disarmed in seconds, with most, literally unable to follow the sword speed of Arslanus. Caesar beckoned Arslanus to approach him. Caesar said, "Roman, you are the best swordsman in the empire, perhaps, the world. I would have you join my legion for my current venture to Egypt and teach swordsmanship."

Arslanus knew a request from Caesar was the equivalent of a command so it was better to appear to be enthusiastic rather than reluctant. He said, "As you wish my Caesar, I will gladly accompany the legion and teach what I can."

Caesar had his staff make arrangements for Arslanus to be attached to the legion as an honored instructor. The status of Arslanus in this situation was quite advantageous. He was highly respected by the legions because of the skill he showed them every day but lived with the officers and was well taken care of with no other duties or personal tasks to occupy his time. He had the opportunity to discuss military tactics with the officers and even with Caesar on several occasions. Seven hundred years of experience on the battlefield gave Arslanus a unique grasp of tactics. The added element of having participated in some of the battles they would discuss gave Arslanus an advantage. Arslanus, of course, had to hold back most of the knowledge he had but in the end, everyone was quite impressed with his grasp of battlefield tactics. He also learned more about Roman tactics and methods.

80

Landing in Egypt, Arslanus did not realize he was about to see one of the great accidents in history, resulting in the destruction of a huge amount of irreplaceable knowledge. The legions and navy of Caesar were pursuing his war against the forces of Pompey including ships of the brother of Cleopatra. Caesar ordered the ships to be burned. Arslanus only learned of the order some hours after it was issued and too late to do anything, even if he had been able. He immediately saw the implications of the order. He knew the direction of the river currents and the fact the grain warehouses along the river would be caught on fire by the burning ships. Arslanus also had been told the warehouses were being used to store a large quantity of scrolls, not yet fully cataloged for inclusion in the library. Forty thousand scrolls were destroyed in the fire, an accident for which neither history nor Arslanus could ever completely forgive Julius Caesar, even though he did not intend it.

After Caesar completed his mission in Egypt and returned to Rome, Arslanus, feeling depressed by the destruction of so much human knowledge, chose to travel east and not return to Rhodes. When he heard about the murder of Julius Caesar in 44 B.C., Arslanus wondered if his death was somehow punishment for the burning of the scrolls.

20. <u>Sidon June 29 A.D.</u>

Arslan, in the identity of a graying merchant of 40 plus years, named Lucas, was passing through Phoenicia in 29 A.D. after spending time in the east. As such thing happen he was staying at the home of a woman of some wealth he had met in the market place of the city when he arrived. This woman was a widow named Zeloa. She was a friendly woman who had many friends in the neighborhood around where she lived.

One afternoon while Lucas was there, the neighbor, named Karuska, came to her and said she had very important guests at her house but had an emergency with her sister outside the city and had to leave. Her problem was she would not be there to fix an evening meal for the main guest, a religious teacher, and his chief disciple. The others in the party had made other arrangements but these two were ones she wanted to treat extremely well. Could Zeloa help? The kind-hearted Zeloa of course agreed.

In the evening, the two strangers appeared at the door and introduced themselves as Jesus of Nazareth and his disciple, Peter. Zeloa bade the men to come in and introduced them to her guest, the merchant Lucas. Lucas had a thick gray beard and longish gray hair and had a slight stoop to project an aged look.

Jesus and Lucas looked at each other for a longer time than expected. They seemed to be locked together by some force. Peter said, "Do the two of you know each other?"

Jesus said," All men are brothers."

Lucas said, "Brothers in the flesh or brothers in the spirit?"

Jesus said," Sometimes both, sometimes both."

Lucas felt a connection with this religious teacher. *'Why?"* he thought.

Jesus said, "Do you too feel a connection between us, Lucas?"

Lucas said, "Yes, but I do not understand it. Do you?"

Jesus said, "No, but the universe is wholly and ever law-abiding and unfailingly dependable. Eventually it will be revealed why we are drawn together. However, there is something more, Lucas, I sense you are younger than you look and at the same time much older than you look. Such contradictions are not of this world."

Lucas said, "Perhaps there are elements of this world no man understands. What seem contradictions to men are not to the universe. Might not the gods understand more than men?"

Jesus said, "The one god, the father, understands all it is true, and men do not. But you, Lucas, speak of gods, and there is only one true god in the universe. God may take on many manifestations, however."

Lucas said, "It is difficult for some men, such as me, who grew up in the context of many gods, gods we can see as wind, and sun, and trees, to believe in one unseen god as the answer."

Jesus said, "Faith is the answer. If you believe, all will be clear."

Lucas said, "The argument is flawed. To ask men to believe without demonstration does not convince me. I could just as well ask you to have faith I am seven hundred years old, and would you believe without thinking or testing the truth of it?"

Jesus looked at Lucas with a burning intensity and curiosity, "If I were to believe, by faith, you were seven hundred years old might it make it so in my eyes? Or if you were to believe, by faith, I am seven hundred years old or older might not make it so in your eyes? If we both believe, by faith, something is so, might it not be so?"

Lucas said, "Just because the individual deludes himself into believing, by faith, something is true does not make it true in the eyes of the gods. There is a difference between perceived truth and absolute truth."

Jesus said, "Whose truth is the perceived and the absolute? Only the one god sees the complete truth."

Lucas said, "It seems to me the argument of "faith" is a circle invented by men who cannot find logic to prove their case."

At this point Peter suggested they proceed to eat the food prepared by Zeloa before it cooled. During the meal Lucas said, "We have not determined why there is a connection between us. What explains the feeling we share?"

Jesus said, "I must pray to the father for the answer."

After the meal, Jesus and Peter had to leave to take their message to others. Lucas bade goodbye to Jesus and Peter saying to Jesus, "I hope the one god gives you the answer. Please let me know if he does."

Jesus did not respond.

Jon Kelly

21. Jerusalem 31 A.D.

Grove City College Chapel (Spring 1967)

Dimmer now the chapel's glowing
Darkened by the truth of knowing,
The world he shaped is losing form,
And found not guiltless in the storm,
A good man, yes, I say perhaps,
But who can tell such time elapse.
A good man but not the great divine,
Not great enough to be our shrine.

Perhaps the tale was pure invention,
Made by men with cold intention,
Spread swiftly by an evil thief,
To cheat the world through false belief.

Arslanus walked through the gates of Jerusalem on a bright, sunny
day in 31 A.D. He had no special reason to be in this city at this time
but he was curious about the city and had not been there for over 600
years. He could travel in this part of the world with some ease due to
his Roman citizenship which he took pains to maintain even as he
changed identities. It was not always easy but he found ways to be in
an identity on the citizenship lists.

Jerusalem had a turbulent past and the current times were not any
less so. The Romans were not loved in this part of the world but
Rome had subjugated the region as only Rome could do—with brute
force. Now Roman officials did their best to maintain the peace
without having to call upon major military actions that were
expensive to the empire.

Arslanus was using the identity of a merchant looking to buy fine
rugs and other high-end art objects to be shipped back to Rome
eventually. He had suitable contacts in Rhodes and other places to
make such a business work quite well. One side benefit was he did
not have such a great problem with his lack of ageing because he

84

moved so much as a merchant no one really remembered how he looked or when he was last in a place.

He was somewhat unusual as a merchant since he carried a sword and was not reluctant to show he could use it. His Roman citizenship was also another deterrent to mistreatment by locals. The Roman legions in the area were there specifically due to the unrest caused by local groups opposed to Roman domination for political, social, and religious reasons.

Arslanus plan for a life here was to set up a central store house in Jerusalem then to travel about the surrounding small cities buying up such fine items as he thought would sell well in Rome. He would consolidate purchased items at his storehouse then make bulk shipments to Rome where his agents would sell the goods and send his share of the profits back to Arslanus. This process called for a long term view of trading since from the time he bought goods from locals to the time he got money back from Rome for the items could be a year, if he was lucky. If he was not lucky, bandits could get his goods, or the ship could sink, or there could be a war, or there could be hard economic times in Rome and the goods would not sell at a profit. Such were some of the pitfalls of being a merchant.

Arslanus' first step was to find a house with suitable street access and storage for his business. He then put out word he was open for business to buy fine goods and hired a young man to act as his on site agent in Jerusalem while he traveled around the area outside the great city. These were dangerous times in Galilee and many men, especially Romans, would think twice about traveling alone outside the city. Robbers and worse stalked the roads to take what they could and did not care too much if they hurt people in the process. Arslanus saw this situation as a business advantage to him. With a sword in his skilled hand, he could take on a large group of robbers by himself with little danger, except to the robbers. Since other men were afraid to do the same, Arslanus could go places to buy goods with little competition.

There was a large mark-up from the price Arslanus paid for goods and the price they sold for in Rome, fifty times or more in some cases. This may seem like Arslanus was taking advantage of the poor souls he bought from but Arslanus was the one who had to front the funds to buy the goods, risk the shipment of the goods, and risk his agents in

Jon Kelly

Rome being honest. He saw himself as providing a service to the makers of the goods who could not find a local market for the goods, but could sell them to Arslanus for a fair price. Some men would see Arslanus as a rich man, and he was at times, when his goods made it to their destination and the funds came back to him, but he could also starve when the process failed.

Arslanus hoped to establish relationships with makers of fine goods in the smaller cities and to then have them eventually send goods to him on consignment. This would reduce his outlay and risk. Even if he could not get it to the point of being on consignment, he at least wanted to have a group of trusted vendors he could buy from without searching for the goods he needed. Since trust is a two way street, he would take pains to be honest and fair with his vendors.

After Arslanus had set up his storehouse, with adjacent living quarters in the city, he set out to travel to the smaller cities. His travels were extensive and he had many opportunities to meet people and find out what was happening in the region. On one of his early trips, he had stopped at a well for water and was approached by a man. The man said, "Esteemed teacher, it is good to see you."

Arslanus replied, "I am sorry sir but I do not know you and I am not a teacher, I am a merchant."

The man continued, "But you look very much like the great teacher, a man called Jesus of Nazareth, who comes by this way from time to time."

Arslanus replied, "I am sorry but I am not the teacher. I am a Roman merchant called Arslanus."

The man departed with apologies but did not seem totally convinced.

Arslanus thought about the incident and realized his gray hair and gray beard in Sidon had kept his resemblance from being obvious. He had noticed Jesus bore some resemblance to him but had not had anyone else make the connection, until now. He thought no more about the incident and completed his trip and returned to Jerusalem bringing a substantial amount of trade goods back with him. As he and his hired agent, a man called Ruben, sorted through the goods and got them ready to ship to Rome, Arslanus casually asked about a great teacher named Jesus of Nazareth. Ruben reacted strongly, "Be careful about that man, he preaches to the people and some say he is a rebel. The religious ones in the city do not like him and will arrest him soon. I suggest you not mention his name around the high Jews."

Arslanus thought it good advice and thought no more about it.

Over the next year Arslanus made several more trips out of the city to buy goods and had good success. His first load had reached Rome and sold at excellent prices so now he had a substantial amount of capital to work with. In the summer of 32 A.D. Arslanus set out on another buying trip. In one medium sized village he was approached one day as he entered the village by a man running up to him and saying, "Master, why are you dressed so strangely, and you have cut your beard, and are wearing a sword? What has happened to you?"

Arslanus replied quickly, "I am Arslanus, a Roman merchant, you mistake me for someone else."

The man responded, "Sir, you bear strong resemblance to my master, Jesus of Nazareth; I am Thomas. He is due to preach near here tomorrow, near the olive grove to the north of the village. I am here to make arrangements. You are welcome to attend. He will be here tonight and teach in the morning."

Arslanus said, "That will be good, I have business in the village today and will stay tonight and hear your teacher in the morning. But I would like to learn something about your teacher before hearing him speak. Do you have some time to talk with me?"

Arslanus was thinking *he did not know if he remembered all Jesus has said on Sidon and wanted to be prepared if he did see him. He knew he was playing with fire, seeking out a man who knew him in another identity but his feeling of a bond with this Jesus of Nazareth was too much to pass up.*

Thomas said, "I have some time until my master arrives tonight. We can talk."

Arslanus suggested he purchase some wine and food which they could enjoy while they talked under a shade tree. Thomas agreed and off they went.

Once settled with their wine and food, Arslanus said, "What are the basic ideas of your teacher?"

"He teaches men should love one another. He has said he will be killed and arise again from the dead. I know these ideas may seem strange but when you hear him, it is like a light shines with truth." said Thomas.

Arslanus thought about what Thomas had said, *"If Jesus says he will rise from the dead, how is it unlike my own situation, I have done this several times. What is the strange connection between us?"*

Thomas continued, "I have seen him heal men with grave afflictions and restore sight to the blind. His miracles are truly awesome."

Arslanus read into the words of Thomas he was not a great thinker himself; he was a follower and Arslanus would not be able to discuss the ideas of Jesus with him in any depth. Thomas had to go meet with Jesus and so took his leave of Arslanus after a while.

Arslanus reflected on these strange teachings and prepared to attend the teaching of Jesus in the morning.

In the morning, Arslanus went to the olive orchard and found a small crowd of about fifty people there. After a time, Thomas and several other men arrived, one of them apparently this Jesus of Nazareth. Jesus of Nazareth did bear a striking resemblance to Arslanus, except for the beard, his rustic clothing, and no sword.

Arslanus listened to teachings revolving around treating your fellow man as you wished to be treated.

After the teacher spoke, Arslanus stayed at the back of the crowd and waited while others went to the teacher and spoke personally with him or some just touched his robes. After most of the crowd cleared away Arslanus approached Thomas. He said, "Thomas, may I speak to your teacher?"

Thomas said, "Of course, Arslanus, this is Jesus of Nazareth. Teacher, this is Arslanus, a Roman merchant who befriended me yesterday. He also bears a striking physical resemblance to yourself."

Jesus looked at Arslanus and Arslanus looked at Jesus. Arslanus thought there might be a spark of recognition but Jesus did not say anything about it. These two did look very much alike except for Jesus being thinner, wearing a beard, his clothes being rustic and no sword. Their eyes locked for several moments before anything was said.

Jesus spoke first, "What does a Roman think of my teachings? Especially a Roman who looks like me and has eyes which seem to look inside me?"

Arslanus thought for a moment and said, "My opinion may not be truly a Roman opinion since my background is not Roman from birth.

Your teachings may not translate well to a non-Jew. A persons background and experience has much to do with what he can and will believe."

Jesus said, "There is one truth, however, which is the same for all men."

Arslanus said, "I have read some writings from the east, far to the east, one said, "There are ways, but the way is uncharted. There is truth but not nature in words. Nameless indeed is the source of creation, but things have a mother and she has a name." You seem to say you have the only way to God. This is hard to accept as true."

Jesus said, "You must have faith and believe to have everlasting life."

Arslanus thought then replied, "Great teacher, what if a man already was immortal living on this earth and never dying? What would the promise of an afterlife mean to such a man? Would the promise of an afterlife be an attraction to him or simply a sham?"

Jesus said, "If such a man existed he would no doubt be puzzled by the quest for an afterlife, but does such a man exist in this world?"

Jesus looked at Arslanus with puzzlement. Arslanus continued to look into the eyes of Jesus. Arslanus felt a connection like he had felt in Sidon. Arslanus thought, *"If this Jesus can identify me as what I am, he must be as he says. If not, it would seem he is not what he says. But then what is he?"*

Arslanus spoke, "There is a connection between you and I. Do you also feel this?"

Jesus said, "I also feel the connection. I have felt the same connection once before, several years ago in Sidon with a man, older than you, but similar in looks and eyes. Do you have a father or uncle there?"

Arslanus said, "Men have relatives in many places. I could have one there. How long has Jesus of Nazareth lived on this earth?"

Jesus said, "My mother says I was born thirty five years ago. I could be that old, as you could have relatives in Sidon."

Arslanus said," But is it how old you think you are?

Jesus said, "I think I am much older but perhaps not of this world."

Thomas interrupted at this point and said Jesus had to depart.

Jesus seemed ready to say more but apparently thought better of it, and walked away. Arslanus was disappointed in not receiving an answer. He felt something unusual about Jesus and Jesus seemed uncomfortable or confused with something about Arslanus. The physical resemblance between the two also made Arslanus think, *"What if they were more alike than just the physical resemblance? What if there was more than one person walking the earth who had the same affliction as Arslanus? I will try to learn more about this Jesus of Nazareth and try to see him again."*

Arslanus continued on his travels to buy trade goods then returned to Jerusalem. He had no more opportunities to cross paths with Jesus of Nazareth but did ask a few people about what they knew of this teacher. Most answers were not too enlightening with people having only surface information about his teachings and little was known about his background. The lack of information on his background was not too surprising but it gave rise to speculation on Arslanus' part.

In the spring of 33 A.D., Arslanus heard the Jews were getting ready for a local holiday called Passover, celebrating their supposed deliverance from captivity in Egypt. All religions have these special stories which they place great emphasis upon but which usually have little basis in fact. Arslanus heard from Ruben that the great teacher, Jesus of Nazareth, was coming to Jerusalem for the event. This increased Arslanus' interest in the event and he asked Ruben to keep him informed.

Ruben said one day, "Jesus of Nazareth is supposed to arrive in the city tomorrow based on the word on the street. He is very popular with the poor who see what he preaches as their hope for a better life; they don't understand he talks about a kingdom in an afterlife. On the other hand, the Jewish temple leaders hate him and call him a blasphemer and worse they say he preaches revolt against the Romans. The situation will be very tense while he is in the city."

I have heard Caiaphas, the high priest of the Jews, has predicted Jesus will die for the nation. Obviously, Caiaphas intends to do everything he can to see he does die. Most of the hatred of Jesus seems to come from Caiaphas. On the other hand, the Romans, who may not hate him for any reason, are in a predicament. Tiberius, the Emperor, is looking at the current governor under a magnifying glass since the man who appointed Pilate as governor has been condemned as a traitor. Pilate now considers everything he does in the context of how Tiberius will view it.

Arslan reflected on this information. Blasphemy could get you in trouble some places but revolt is a sure way to get the attention of the Roman officials; if true. *"Watch out Jesus of Nazareth, Rome will crush anyone preaching revolt."*

The next day Arslan watched Jesus of Nazareth enter the city riding a donkey and receiving the cheers of the poor. Arslanus had seen triumphs in Rome and celebrations in other cities honoring people. Many times he had seen how quickly fortune can turn and the cheers turn to shouts of hatred. *Public figures attract attention, good and bad, good fortune, Jesus of Nazareth.*

Arslanus asked Ruben to try to set up a meeting with Jesus through Thomas, if he could be located. Ruben tried but everyone was very busy and nothing could be done.

When Arslanus heard Jesus of Nazareth had been arrested and was to be put on trial, he was concerned but not surprised. The words of Jesus had predicted this and more. He hoped Jesus would escape the fate his words had predicted but he also felt Jesus would do little to help himself. He still wondered what Jesus really was?

Upon hearing, Jesus was condemned to death by crucifixion Arslanus considered what this would mean. Such a death would be an agony. *He thought about what would happen if he were sentenced to be crucified. Arslanus knew from past experience his body would shut down after his body reached a certain point and he would appear to be dead. He had been confirmed as dead several times, even being buried, fortunately in shallow graves. After several hours to several days his body would have healed enough to start back up and would do so. He wondered again about Jesus of Nazareth.*

The prediction by Jesus of arising from the dead swirled through the mind of Arslanus. If he is what he claims, he could do it, or even if he were "only" like Arslanus, he could do it. Arslanus thought about somehow switching places with Jesus to save his life. He was the one person he knew of in the world who could do it. But pulling off such a switch was almost impossible and the agony of crucifixion was not something to volunteer for. Jesus of Nazareth had driven his life toward this moment; he would not want to lose the opportunity. It was better to let this Jesus live and die with what he had set in motion.

Arslanus did not attend the crucifixion. He had seen enough death and it was possibly not safe to be hanging around looking so much like Jesus. He might become someone's target. Ruben reported to Arslanus the act was done and they had taken his body to be entombed. He also reported the words of Jesus at the end, "My God, My God, Why hast thou forsaken me?" Arslanus took these words to mean Jesus may not have found what he expected at the door to death.

Arslanus heard Roman soldiers had been assigned to guard the tomb of Jesus due to the prediction he would rise from the dead. The concern was the followers of Jesus would rob the grave and fake his resurrection. Arslanus waited to see what would happen, perhaps with a different view than anyone else in the world.

When Arslanus heard the news the body of Jesus was missing from the tomb he was filled with wonder, but not surprised. He had felt a special connection with the man. Perhaps he did rise. Later he heard rumors Jesus had appeared to some of his followers several times and the followers were very excited. Since the witnesses had a stake in the subject he did not seek them out for more information, except for Thomas. On one of his buying trips he crossed paths with Thomas in a small city of Galilee and asked if he remembered him.

Thomas said, "Roman who looks like Jesus, the Christ, I remember you. My master won his contest with death, did you know. I saw him after he was resurrected and placed my hand in the wound on his side. He lives."

Arslanus said, "I believe you may be right. Where is he now?"

Thomas said, "He has gone into heaven to prepare a place for the rest of the believers."

Arslanus said, "Did you see this happen yourself."

Thomas said, "No, but it was reported to me to be so."

Arslanus did not question Thomas more closely, because he knew Thomas was a believer, *but Arslanus wondered where Jesus really went.*

22. <u>Atlanta</u>

It was 1:00 a.m. Sunday morning when Arslan said he was tired and needed to sleep, they had covered a long span of history and the last section involving Jesus of Nazareth was particularly interesting and emotional to both Lisa and Simon. Neither were strongly religious people, but Arslan understood the context of their upbringing made this subject emotional. Arslan had been raised as a "pagan" in the Christian concept of the word and he had a very different starting point than Lisa and Simon.

Arslan's "pagan" background meant he had been raised to believe in natural gods, plural, who were factors influencing human lives. When the wind blew, Arslan talked to the wind. When he saw the sea, he talked to the sea. The Christians defined everything coming before Christianity as pagan, including Rome's many gods. Arslan thought this was unfair and a way to put down beliefs when they were not part of Christianity. Arslan was not sure what he believed now but paganism was just as believable as Christianity, Judaism, Islam, Hindu, or any of the other religions of the world. Arslan was amused the Romans often referred to the Christians as "atheists" because they did not believe in the gods of Rome.

Lisa and Simon retired to Simon's room without any comment or concern about who thought what about it. Both Simon and Lisa, had heard enough about Arslan's sex life to be sure he would not be offended by their sleeping together. Arslan for his part would have been disappointed in them if they chose some other, socially acceptable, solution. Sex wasn't the issue tonight; they were both tired as hell and went off to sleep holding each other.

In the morning, Arslan was up first, went for a one-hour run, returned and was cleaned up, and made a nice breakfast for everyone before 8:30 a.m. He roused Simon and Lisa who showered and ate so they were ready to go back to work by 9:30 a.m. Before they started Lisa had a question, "In your discussion of Jesus of Nazareth, you seemed to think he might be someone like yourself. Why?"

Arslan did not have to think, he had thought about this for almost two thousand years. There are several reasons. First, he looked so much like me, it must be more than coincidence. Two, it is the easiest explanation to accept for his rising from the dead, it fits. Three, He did not seem to know what I was when we spoke, if he was part of God he would be all knowing and would not have been confused by me. Four, the connection I made with him was special but, in my mind, not a connection with a divine being. These are my reasons, I am not asking anyone else to accept these, they are personal.

Simon then asked, "Where do you think Jesus went after he appeared to the disciples? He supposedly went up to heaven but what is your take on it?"

Arslan replied, "I have no idea. Perhaps he was a divine being and went to heaven, I personally think not, but you decide for yourselves. He may have hidden in the mass of humanity like I have for twenty eight hundred years. He may still be out there waiting for something."

Arslan then said, "Before we start again, I want to see about booking a flight to Ankara, Turkey for Lisa and myself, leaving Tuesday."

Simon and Lisa both did a double take. Simon said, "What is this all about?"

"I want to take a trip back to Amwat and try to find the gold ingot I buried over twenty seven hundred years ago. It is the only connection to my origins, aside from myself. Perhaps there is some clue there. It is our only relic." said Arslan.

Simon asked, "Why is Lisa going?"

"Lisa is going because we need a witness and you will need to stay here to handle the analysis of the DNA data, because once you get the information on Monday, all hell will break loose in your DNA world. I mean in the world of Dr. Simon Myers. The data will change everything, I believe." said Arslan.

Lisa called the airlines; fortunately she had a valid passport, and booked them on a Delta flight from Atlanta to Paris then to Ankara for Tuesday evening. She used Arslan's credit card in the name of John Young. When she finished she said to Arslan, "The name John Young is your little joke, isn't it."

Arslan nodded then started reading again.

23. <u>Rhodes 56 A.D.</u>

Arslanus moved from Jerusalem to Rhodes in 56 A.D. after twenty-six years in Galilee. He stayed in the same identity as Arslanus because he knew no one in Rhodes anymore who would challenge his ageing. He maintained his older persona by keeping his hair and beard gray as a safety measure. He did not plan to stay in Rhodes for long but he needed some time to get a new identity with Roman citizenship set up before he made a change. He was also waiting for some monies from his last shipments to Rome to reach him before he made a move. He had done quite well financially in Jerusalem and did not want to lose what he had worked to put aside.

He thought about where he would go now. Nero was the new emperor for two years now and he thought being as far away from Rome as possible was a good idea. He could go to Egypt, Tyre was still too painful, Damascus was possible, or far to the east.

These decisions were important, but in the end, they were a roll of the dice, at best.

Arslanus had been in Rhodes for over six months and the New Year had started when he heard a Paul of Tarsus was visiting the island, recruiting converts to a new belief based on the teachings of Jesus of Nazareth. Arslanus was curious and made arrangements for this Paul to have dinner at his house.

Paul came to the house and was introduced by an acquaintance of Arslanus who had already met the visitor. Paul spoke to Arslanus, "Sir, I was surprised someone on this island would request to meet me and offer the hospitality of their home. I have not met you before in my travels, have I?"

"No, we have not met. But I just came to Rhodes from Jerusalem less than a year ago, after living in Jerusalem for many years as a merchant. During the time, I traveled throughout Galilee and met many people including your Jesus of Nazareth and his disciple, Thomas. I am interested in the purpose of your trip and the beliefs you are talking about." said Arslanus.

Paul was a little wary but did not detect danger from Arslanus. "Arslanus, I teach the same message Jesus taught in his life. Men should treat other men as they wish to be treated. The way to God is through Jesus Christ who died for our sins. We can be forgiven of our sins through Jesus Christ. Spreading this message is the purpose of my visit to Rhodes."

Paul continued, "You said you met Jesus, our Savior, can you tell me about it?"

Arslanus told Paul about his being mistaken for Jesus twice, the second time by Thomas, and his desire to see Jesus. He related the teachings he had heard from Jesus, as he remembered them. He told Paul about Jesus asking for a Roman's reaction to his teachings and of Arslanus replying he was not truly Roman in background and he thought some of the teachings were foreign to his background. He did not relate the rest of his discussion with Jesus.

Paul was very interested and asked Arslanus if he still had trouble believing after Jesus arose from the dead. Arslanus responded he knew Jesus had lived and he thought it was possible; even likely, he arose and left the tomb. He had trouble with the part where he ascended into heaven to sit on the on the right hand of God. This was unusual for Paul, he was used to people not believing Jesus had arose from the dead, but once they believed they usually accepted Jesus becoming one with God.

Paul saw Arslanus was a reasonably wealthy Roman merchant who could do much to help spread the word about Jesus if he believed, and even better since he had actually met Jesus. This man could be a wonderful convert. Arslanus immediately saw what Paul wanted but Arslanus was not going to be the convert Paul wanted. Paul was not aware of Arslanus' special background. Paul continued to talk to no avail. Eventually Arslanus bid farewell to Paul and reflected, *Paul would do well spreading the new religion since he was intelligent and persistent. Arslanus was not sure Paul was honest. He would say what it took to sell his product. Arslanus had met many merchants and vendors of that ilk.*

Paul left Rhodes after a few days and Arslanus never saw him again but heard about his death in Rome years later. Arslanus left Rhodes some months later.

24. <u>Britain 80 A.D.</u>

Arslanus had decided to go somewhere far from Rome so finally he chose Britain. He had never been there and thought, *"Why not."* This attitude was influenced by the fact he continued not to age and he was now looking for new experiences and places.

It took Arslanus approximately twenty years to work his way from Rhodes to a position in Britain appealing to him. During this time, he explored the German provinces and Gaul, as he made arrangements to be a military trainer in swordsmanship assigned to a legion in Britain. By 80 A.D., Arslanus, a name he still managed to retain, was assigned to a legion under the governor of Britain. The legion eventually came under the command of Cnaeus Julius Agricola, Governor, who was campaigning against the Picts.

Arslanus was, as usual, a respected member of the legion due to his weaponry skill and his tactical expertise. He occupied the equivalent of a senior centurion's spot in the legion but was a staff person due to his special training responsibilities.

One day in the summer of 82 A.D., he received an assignment he did not like. Due to illness in the legion, there was a shortage of centurions to lead patrols into Pict areas. Arslanus was pulled from his normal training role and assigned to take fifty men to attack and destroy a Pict village some four or five days march away. The term "destroy" was not defined precisely but Arslanus sensed the implication was he was to kill everyone; men, women, and children. He specifically did not ask since it would have taken away any option he might have to spare lives.

As they marched toward the village, Arslanus talked with the men of the legion whenever possible and made clear his intention they should take the women and children prisoners so they could be sold as slaves, implying the soldiers might get a share of the proceeds. This tactic would tend to insure there was an incentive for the soldiers to act to save as many as possible. They approached the village with as much stealth as fifty legion soldiers could muster.

Jon Kelly

Arslanus sent squads out to cover both sides and the rear of the village to cut off escape then sent the main element at the front gate of the compound. The "wall" around the compound was basically a pile of intertwined thorn branches with several openings for entry and escape.

As soon as the main party was spotted by the villagers, with the total population of the village at approximately 100 persons including about 20 to 25 men of fighting age, the alarm was sounded and the men formed up to meet the attack. These untrained villagers were generally no match for the trained and well-armed legion soldiers. Several of the best fighters from the village immediately threw themselves at Arslanus as the leader of the Romans. Arslanus sword made quick work of these assailants. The action did not last long as the experienced legion soldiers cut down the village men with little problem. All the men who had come out to fight were dead or dying within 20 minutes of the start of the action with one legion soldier seriously injured with a stomach wound and all other legion injuries minor.

The squads sent to stop the escape from the sides and rear had been successful in keeping everyone else in the enclosure. The non-combatants were then flushed out of the enclosure and grouped by women with children, women with no children, and old men and women. As a kindness the old men and women were summarily dispatched, marching them through the forest would probably kill them anyway and this way they suffered less.

The women with children in arms had a rope tied around their necks and tied to each other in a long line. Their children were expected to stay with them and keep up on the march or they would be left in the forest to fend for themselves. The younger women with no children were also tied with ropes around their necks and had their hands tied behind their backs. These ones were more likely to try to run away. The younger women with no children were the targets of some attention from the legion soldiers. Normally, if the village was destroyed and all were being put to the sword, the legion soldiers would have the opportunity to rape the women before killing them. In this case, Arslanus made it clear they were not to be raped since they would bring higher prices as slaves if they were "intact." There was some grumbling but orders were followed in the legion. The fifty legion soldiers then started the march back with about sixty prisoners, ten younger women, twenty or so women with children and the rest, children of various ages.

Travel was much slower with the prisoners but the pace was still fast and several children were in fact left in the forest because they could not keep up. At the end of the first day's march they had lost five prisoners, three children and two adult women who had fallen from exhaustion. There was no room for mercy in these circumstances. The second day they lost only one child and the third day they lost none. Arslanus calculated they had two more days march at this pace to return to the fortified Roman base camp.

On the morning of the fourth day, they discovered one more child had died during the night, apparently from exhaustion. Arslanus did not cut back on the pace as he was getting close to the goal and did not want to extend this ordeal any more than possible. They lost one more child and all the prisoners were worn out as they started the final day's march. Just after mid-day they reached the fortified Roman town.

Arslanus' superiors were surprised at the sight of prisoners being brought in to the compound. After explaining he had thought the prisoners had value as slaves and estimating the value in silver, his superiors were happy with the outcome. In fact, they were pleased enough they said Arslanus could chose one of the younger women for himself, personally, as a bonus for his good effort.

Arslanus had to chose one of the women. It turned out to be an easy selection. He had noticed earlier a girl of about seventeen years was by far the most attractive and most spirited of the young women prisoners. She had very dark hair, a firm young body, and a face with large eyes. Arslanus had her removed from the others and taken to his quarters and tied there. A little later, he made his way to his quarters amid some comments from the legion soldiers he was on his way to "get some."

Arslanus had never, in over eight hundred years, taken a woman against her will. He was not about to start now. He walked into his quarters and closed the door. Light through the rough window, which could be closed with a skin covering, showed the girl tied to a post looking at Arslanus with hatred and fear. Arslanus, who had learned some of the Pict tongue, said calmly, "What is your name? I mean you no harm."

The girl spat out, "Why not kill me now." I will never submit to you. I will try to kill you the first chance I get."

Arslanus said, "I mean what I say, I will not harm you. If it had not been for me, all of you, including the children would be dead by now. A life as a slave is better than being dead. Slaves often live well and may get their freedom. It happens often under us Romans."

The girl thought a bit and said, "My name is Cloe, I am the daughter of a king, so you had better not harm me."

"Cloe, do not say that again in this camp. If you truly are the daughter of a king, my superiors will use you ill. If you are not, they will punish you, perhaps, kill you when they find out. Keep you tongue in your head by keeping your mouth shut." said Arslanus.

Cloe said, "You are a strange Roman, you lead the legion against my village, kill my people, then save the women and children, then try to help me. You are a contradiction, but thank you for your advice, it sounds correct. I will do as you say. What is your name?"

Arslanus answered looking into the large dark eyes of Cloe, "I am Arslanus, Arslanus of Amwat to be precise."

Cloe said, "I have never heard of Amwat, is it near Rome?"

Arslanus said, "No it is in Phrygia, far to the east of the famous city of Troy."

Cloe said, "You have come far to fight my people. Why do you Romans come so far to try to take land and freedom from people?"

Arslanus answered, "I cannot defend the Roman need to expand and grow their empire except to say in many lands the force of Rome is the way peace is achieved. Rome brings many of the material goods and knowledge of civilization to these lands, albeit usually without the consent of the residents of the land."

Cloe asked then, "What happens to me now? Am I your slave? Will you force me to be your woman?"

Arslanus thought briefly, "Cloe, I do not know what will happen to you. I will try to see you are not harmed until we come up with a plan to get you back to your people. You are my slave in name only, for the others in this town to believe. I have never forced a woman to lay with me and do not plan to ever do so. Does that answer your questions?"

Cloe said with a bemused smile, "You are a strange Roman indeed, Arslanus."

"You must make an appearance of being my slave and my woman to protect yourself here. You must prepare meals, do laundry, clean my quarters, and do other tasks to give the appearance of being my slave. For my part, I will give others the impression I am laying with you and am very jealous anyone else would try to have you. Since I am the best swordsman here, it should be enough to keep anyone from bothering you." said Arslanus.

"Are you still going to try to kill me the first chance you get? If not I will untie you." said Arslanus as he cut her bonds.

Arslanus made up a separate sleeping pallet for Cloe on the opposite side of the room from his and took her around the camp to show her where to find things. He also made a show of being like an affectionate lover. He made comments such as, "The little dove has found a real Roman man to lie with rather than a dirty Pict, and is now a happy bird." All seemed to think Arslanus now had a slave woman to entertain him.

Cleo explained in the evening, still a little nervous at being alone with Arslanus in his quarters she was the daughter of a sub-chief of her people and was visiting the village the Romans attacked and destroyed. Her home was in a very large village where her father was the equivalent of king. This village was over three weeks walk from the Roman fortified town they now occupied. Arslanus asked, "Will your father look for you?"

Cloe said, "I am sure he will but it will be difficult for him to find me here, perhaps."

The fortified town only had about 250 legion soldiers stationed there when all were present, which was not often. Typically, groups of fifty went out to attack Pict villages for five to fifteen days at a time. This normally left about 100 soldiers at the fortified town and perhaps another 100 to 150 camp followers.

Cloe had been in camp about one month when a warning went up that Picts were surrounding the town. Looking out of the town a large number of Picts surrounded the town with Arslanus counting about 700, perhaps 1000. Not good odds even with the advantage of fortifications. If all the troops stationed there were on hand it might be possible to survive but with only 100 against 1000 it was not likely. Surrender was not a option, too many dead Picts and destroyed villages for that.

When the attack came it was fierce. The legion soldiers held their places on the fortifications and made the Picts pay for every inch. The legion trained their soldiers to live and die like Romans. Sheer numbers and the attrition of the defenders soon forced the few remaining defenders back against the huts used as quarters. Arslanus was one of these. The attackers were amazed at the swordsmanship skill of this one man. He had killed at least twenty-five Picts before a dozen or so Picts got him backed up against a wall and were prepared to skewer him with a dozen spears. Suddenly, there was a loud scream of a woman's voice, "Stop, I am Cloe, daughter of Harnish, do not hurt this Roman. Obey my command."

The Picts threatening Arslanus froze at the name of Harnish, the great warrior chief. No one wanted to challenge Harnish or the daughter of Harnish for that matter. Cloe strode through them and took the sword from Arslanus, then told the Pict fighters to tie his hands behind him with a rope attached, which Cloe took as a leash. She led him through the crowd of Picts until she found the chief in charge of the attacking forces.

He asked her, "Why have you saved a Roman? All should die."

Cloe knew this chief, Garnard, not too bright but brave. She said, "Garnard, this Roman saved the lives of many of our people and protected me from death and dishonor. My father, Harnish, will not want him to die or be harmed."

Garnard blanched at the mention of Harnish. He would not challenge the words of the daughter of Harnish. Let Harnish decide if his daughter was correct. This was not a decision Garnard would make over the objections of Cloe.

Cloe asked, "Where is my father?"

Garnard said flatly, "He is attacking the Romans at another camp to the west and should now be on his way back to your village."

Cloe said, "Give me ten men as guards and we will take this prisoner to my village to meet with Harnish."

Garnard knew better than to argue. He assigned the men and Cloe and Arslanus set off.

This was the situation Arslanus, the survivor, was always concerned about. At the village, the Picts might decide to dismember Arslanus. It was a death he would not survive. With his skill with the sword, he could take the ten Picts if he could get free with a sword. He would then make a run for a Roman camp.

Arslanus spoke to Cloe, "What will happen to me at the village?"

Cleo, thinking turnabout was fair play said, "I do not know but I will try to protect you and will not let the women take you against your will."

Even in the dire circumstances, Arslanus laughed heartily at the humor.

After two weeks of travel at a very fast pace they reached the Pict village, really a small city. Arslanus had not had an opportunity to escape. When they entered the village there were cheers when Cloe was recognized. She had been reported as dead or enslaved. Arslanus was subject to some ill treatment including being hit and excrement being thrown at him.

Cloe guided him up to the largest structure in the village. In front stood a man of larger than normal size and fierce countenance. His ferocity softened when he saw Cloe.

He said, "Sweet daughter, it is so good to see you alive and apparently well, and with a Roman puppy as a pet on a leash." He gave Cloe a robust hug.

"Daughter, have you brought this dog of a Roman as a gift so I can see if a Roman can die well?" said Harnish.

"No Father, this is an unusual Roman. He saved fifty of our women and children from being slaughtered at the village where I was captured. They were released when Garnard captured the Roman town. The Roman also protected me and kept me from death and dishonor for these past thirty days of captivity." said Cloe.

Harnish said, "Daughter, what would you have me do with this Roman?"

Cloe said, "Perhaps we can trade him back to the Romans for some captives or other thing. Even if we are not ready to do this right now, it could pay in the future to keep him unharmed and have him available to trade."

Harnish said, "I will do as you suggest but you are assigned responsibility for the captive."

Cloe said, "Thank you father."

Arslanus was taken to quarters adjacent to those for Cloe with two guards placed in front of the only door. He was still tied and was also tied to a pole. After a while Cloe entered. She said, "I am sorry for the bonds but to some extent it is for your own safety. If you gave your word you would not try to flee, I may be able to get security reduced."

Arslanus said, "Thanks for the offer, but I do not think I would like to be tied by such bonds."

Cloe said, "It is interesting, you refuse because if you gave your word you would feel bound to keep it. A man of honor as well as merciful and kind."

Arslanus said, "Some among your people probably think me much less than kind and merciful. The widows of the twenty or so men I killed defending the fortified town, for example"

"Those were death's in battle, it is respected. We respect warriors who kill in battle." said Cloe.

The men who traveled with Cloe and Arslanus had seen Arslanus in battle and word quickly went around the Pict Village of the skill with a sword the captive Roman had displayed. They said they had never seen a man move with such speed and skill. When word reached Harnish, he summoned his daughter, "Daughter, you did not mention the Roman is a master swordsman. Perhaps he can teach our fighters how to fight better?"

Cloe said, "I fear he will refuse to teach our men to kill so they can better kill Romans. He is a man of honor. He already refused to give his word he would not try to escape if I took off his bonds."

Harnish said, "I will try." And called for Arslanus to be brought to him.

Arslanus stood before Harnish not knowing what to expect. Harnish began, "Roman called Arslanus, I thank you for your care for my daughter; she tells me you protected her from many dangers and treated her well. She also says you are a man of honor; perhaps it will help us both some day. But today we must discuss your skill with a sword. Men say you are the best they have ever seen. How did you develop such skill?"

Arslanus said, "Years and years of practice with many dead instructors."

Harnish said, "I would like to see a demonstration, but not to the death, only a demonstration. Will you do it?"

"Yes." said Arslanus.

So an area was cleared for a demonstration and the best swordsman among the Picts came forward to challenge Arslanus. Harnish gave the signal to begin. The Pict champion, named Rolf, attacked, in less than five seconds flashing sword strokes from Arslanus disarmed him. As usual most could not even follow the speed of Arslanus' sword. Another Pict then sought to challenge. Arslanus nodded his agreement and another match started with a similar result.

Harnish was stunned, "I was told you were good but not faster than the eye. You have an amazing skill. Will you teach some of your skill to my men?"

"That is a difficult thing for me, if I teach you to kill better, you may kill my comrades. It might make me a traitor in some men's eyes. Do you understand my problem?" said Arslan.

Harnish said, "If you do not teach my men I may kill you, that would make you a fool."

Arslanus said, "Perhaps a compromise is possible. I will train your men in some skills of swordsmanship and in return I will be allowed to be in your camp without being tied. I do not promise not to try to escape but you may use what other methods you chose to prevent my escape."

Harnish thought for a while then agreed. He assigned two spearmen to stay with Arslanus at all times with orders to kill him if he tried to run away.

Arslanus trained Harnish's men in some of the fundamentals of sword fighting which improved them considerably but were not up to the skills of the Romans Arslanus had trained. Meanwhile, Cloe watched Arslanus go about his work and spent what other time with him she could. Arslanus learned more of the Picts language from Cleo and they spent many hours talking. Arslanus was attracted to Cloe as a woman but circumstance did not permit him to act on the attraction. He also felt Cloe was very attracted to him but also was holding back because of circumstances.

Finally Cloe said to him one day when they were alone, "Arslanus, You are the most interesting man I have ever met. If you were a man of the Picts I would have my father order you to be my man."

Arslanus said, "Cloe, I would not take well to being ordered to take you as my woman but in fact I would not need to be ordered. You are beautiful, intelligent, kind and honest, I would be proud to be your man. However, our circumstances here are such any hint we harbor such thoughts will probably result in my death. Do you understand? You, as the daughter of Harnish, cannot take a Roman as your man, not while we are at war."

Cloe said with a sad look, "I understand all too well, dear Arslanus."

Several days later, Arslanus was practicing sword with several Picts near the edge of the forest. The Picts also had spears with them in addition to their swords but laid them down on the ground during sword practice. The two spearmen assigned to kill Arslanus were nearby watching. Arslanus maneuvered near the spears and in a clean motion sent one spear into one spearman and before the other spearman could move a second spear was in his chest. Arslanus dispatched the men he was training, with the sword, then ran into the woods and started on his escape. They had not known Arslanus was also the best spearman in the world.

It took some time for the alarm to be raised and Arslanus had a head start. Harnish sent his fastest men after Arslanus but Arslanus was fast also. He made good time but knew his knowledge of the country was much less than his pursuers. He decided he would not just try to rely on speed, he would use some craft to slow down those behind him. He set up some traps to cause a man to twist or break his ankle if he tried to follow Arslanus too quickly. This would also make the followers very cautious and slow them down.

After eight days they had not caught Arslanus but were very close behind him. He had to choose which of the Roman fortified towns he would try to reach. Had the Romans rebuilt and reinforced the town captured when Cloe was with him or had the Romans left it to the Picts? He chose to go for his old camp since it was closest and he knew the way.

When Arslanus burst out of the forest near the town and saw many legion soldiers he was happy. He was quickly recognized by some of the soldiers he had trained in swordsmanship and was taken to the commander, Cnaeus Julius Agricola, the Governor. There was an entire Legion camped at the fortified town, with the governor in command. Arslanus explained about his capture and escape, and the location of the large village.

The governor wanted to attack the village but was concerned the Picts might be able to field a larger force than he had, or several forces would fall on the Legion and cut it to pieces in the forest. He asked Arslan what he thought since he had been there. Arslan agreed it would not be a good idea to try to take the legion into the forest without finding out how many Picts were in the area. They needed some good scouting done to understand what forces they might be up against. Arslanus also suggested some mapping needed to be done to insure this and future commands would be able to find their way through these lands. Sentry outposts to provide an early warning of large bands of Picts were also needed.

Agricola then commended Arslanus for his adventure and promoted him to his staff. Agricola recognized talent and initiative when he saw it. Arslanus was given responsibility for the scouting and mapping projects.

25. <u>Atlanta</u>

It was now mid-Sunday afternoon in Atlanta. Simon and Lisa were amazed by the level of detail in the stories being read and told by Arslan. How could they not be true? Some of this just could not be made up. In addition, some cross checking on the Internet had not found a single flaw not be explained by an error in the accepted history.

Arslan asked, "Are you getting tired?

Lisa, who was doing most of the work taking notes and keeping the recorder working answered, "No, I am ok. I think it is important we get through as much of this as possible before we get the test results tomorrow and we have to leave for Turkey on Tuesday. Besides, I find the story to be the most interesting thing I have ever heard. How much more of this do you have Arslan?"

Arslan thought a minute and said, "I don't really think you want to know Lisa. What I am giving you right now is just the short version. These are the sections I have finished, there are other stories for time periods, some of which we have already skipped, which have yet to be written in prose, I have notes. Right now we are just going through the times I have finished, and there is about 1900 years to go. To get through all the prose I have written now should take about two more weeks."

I am going to turn the tapes over to a transcription person to get started so I will be able to start editing when we get back from Turkey. I know a person I trust very well. I will tell her it is a novel but no sense in taking chances.

Simon asked, "What is the rush with getting this done now? It has waited hundred of years."

Arslan replied, "Simon, It is true it has waited hundreds of years but once we have the test data things will get crazy. If the information leaks out, there will be a tremendous demand for more information.

Let's go back to work." said Arslan.

26. <u>Britain 82 A.D.</u>

In the summer of 82 A.D. Governor Agricola felt comfortable enough with intelligence about the Picts to make an attack on the large village where Arslanus had been held by Harnish. Arslanus had mapped the area and had sent scouting parties many places to get a good handle on what forces were pitted against the Romans.

Arslanus was not happy, however. He had not seen Cloe for eight months, since he had made his escape. Now he was leading the Romans back to attack her home and, perhaps, put her in grave danger. *"What could he do to reduce the risk to Cloe?"* he thought.

Arslanus went to Governor Agricola, who had come to rely on his judgment. Arslanus said it would be wise, if they could, to avoid a major battle with the forces of Harnish. Harnish was mainly looking to protect his people. Agricola could not afford the huge losses in manpower a major battle with Harnish could mean. Could a peace be brokered so Agricola could then use his forces against the rest of the Picts and bring Roman rule to almost all of Britain. Agricola was delighted with the strategy, if this was done right it would play very well in Rome.

Arslanus suggested he approach Harnish, first through an agent then personally. The Romans had captured Rolf, the swordsman Arslanus had defeated in a demonstration at the Pict village. Arslanus had made sure Rolf had been saved and cared for better than others. He would send Rolf to Harnish to set up a meeting to discuss a truce or treaty. Agricola agreed and Arslanus talked with Rolf and sent him on his way.

Rolf had reacted well to the mission given him by Arslanus. Arslanus had spent some time with Rolf while he was captive and Rolf had heard from other Romans Arslanus could be trusted. Arslanus could not help sending a message to Cloe saying he wished her well and hoped to see her again.

Arslanus had set with Rolf to be at a particular clearing about six days march from the fortified town four weeks from the day Rolf left. This would give Rolf time to get there and for Rolf and Harnish's party to get to the meeting site. Arslanus would go with guidelines from Agricola as to what kind of truce or treaty could be negotiated.

He would have some room to improvise as long as he followed the general guidelines.

Two weeks later Arslanus set out with a party of fifty legion solders, the number told to Rolf, as security for the meeting. Rolf knew Harnish's scouts would tell him exactly how many men he brought so there was no reason to do anything different. Harnish was supposed to bring no more than one hundred men. Arslanus had no way to confirm exactly how many Harnish brought but his own scouts were now good enough to give him an inkling if a much larger force was coming.

Arslanus arrived at the clearing on the morning of the appointed day but saw nothing of Harnish's forces. Suddenly, at noon, Harnish walked out into the clearing accompanied by Rolf and Cloe. Arslanus felt his heart skip several beats when he saw Cloe. She had only gotten more beautiful in the last nine months. Arslanus walked to the center of the clearing accompanied by his second-in-command, a centurion named Osal. Arslanus said, "Hail Harnish, king of the Picts." He wasn't really king of the Picts but it sounded good.

Harnish said, "Hail Arslanus, honorable Roman."

Arslanus then said hello to Rolf and then Cloe. He looked into Cloe's eyes for more than a moment. Harnish's voice brought him back to the business at hand. Harnish said, "Rolf says you would make a truce or treaty with me to spare deaths on each side. You told him you would come with a proposal. I am willing to listen to the proposal of Arslanus. I would probably not listen to another Roman but you have always shown yourself to be honorable."

Arslanus spoke, "I try to be an honorable man. The Roman Governor I speak for here is also an honorable man, I believe. I cannot guarantee his honor in these matters, however. A man can only be responsible for his own honor. You would think I was a fool or worse if I said I could guarantee another man's honor. But I say again, I believe he is also an honorable man who you can trust."

Arslanus continued, "I do have a proposal for you. I have thought about what is good for the Romans and what is good for your people. In the end we must come up with a framework which will allow both parties to coexist, otherwise, I fear the power of Rome will crush and destroy your people. The key points of the proposed treaty are: First, Rome will be permitted to set up fortified towns at key points to exert

Roman protection over this land. Second, Your chiefs will agree to pay a reasonable tax to Rome to support the protection provided. Third, You will agree to provide soldiers to fight side by side with Rome when outside forces attack Roman forces. Fourth, Administration of all other matters will be left to your laws when the question is between Picts, Rome does not want to be involved. These four items are the heart of the treaty proposal. We can negotiate the details."

Harnish thought for several minutes then said, "Your proposal is well thought out. Some details need to be discussed but the basic concept can work if we are all honorable. Let us sit together and take the time to discuss the details, such as where the fortified towns will be, how much the tax will be, how many soldiers will be provided and who will pay them, and exactly how the Roman law and Pict law will coexist."

Arslanus agreed and they proceeded to discuss all issues and completed a draft treaty. At this point Harnish spoke up, "There is one other issue we must agree about if the treaty is to be made. It is not negotiable."

Arslanus was stunned, *"What could he possibly ask for now that was not negotiable?"*

Harnish smiled, "The fifth item in the treaty will be Arslanus, honorable Roman soldier, will take to wife, Cloe, daughter of Harnish, chief of the Picts. This will seal the validity of the treaty. Do you agree, Arslanus?"

Arslanus was happily surprised and quickly said, "Wise Harnish, you have looked into my heart and of your daughter. The treaty will be sealed by our marriage."

Arslanus looked at Cloe whose eyes were filling with tears of happiness. Harnish stood and spoke to his men, "We have agreed on a treaty to bring peace to our peoples." A cheer went up from the Picts and was soon echoed by the Romans. Arslanus then moved to Cloe and hugged her to another cheer from all assembled.

Arslanus and Harnish finalized all items of treaty language and each signed a preliminary copy. It was agreed the final treaty would be signed and a marriage performed at the Pict village in another month.

Arslanus traveled back to the fortified town bearing the good news for Agricola and a heart filled with joy. Agricola was very pleased with the treaty and promoted Arslanus on the spot. He would be deputy governor to implement the treaty. Agricola was amazed at the fifth clause of the treaty and asked Arslanus if it was what he wanted to do. Arslanus said it was.

Arslanus went to the Pict village at the appointed day with an honor guard of fifty, very nervous, legion solders. The Pict village had about one thousand men at arms assembled for the signing of the treaty and the marriage. The treaty signing was done with little ceremony as everyone wanted to get to the marriage and the celebrating. Harnish formally approved the marriage and a Pict elder blessed the union and then the celebration began. Meanwhile, Arslanus and Cloe were escorted to the marriage house set aside for their first night together.

Both Arslanus and Cloe were deliriously happy. They had wanted each other for so long and it had seemed so unlikely they would ever end up together. They clung to each other inside the hut for a long time without words then Cloe said, "Arslanus, I have wanted to be with you from the moment you entered your quarters back in the Roman town after making me your "slave." I truly love you."

Arslanus said, "And I have wanted you just as long. I also love you."

They then spent a long, beautiful night of discovering each other's bodies. In the morning they were ready to face the world together.

Cloe and Arslanus went to set up their new home in the fortified town. Their lives were filled with Arslanus working to implement the treaty terms and Cloe learning to be a Roman wife as best she could in a rustic fortified town. For the first three years life was very good. Governor Agricola made significant progress in bringing Roman order to Britain and was close to completing the task when he was recalled to Rome in 85 A.D. Agricola did his best to support Arslanus from Rome and even tried to get him appointed Governor, but to no avail.

Arslanus continued in his role of implementing the treaty with the Picts and furthering the relationship so Britain would be stabilized, at least in the area where Harnish had power. He continued to work at this through 93 A.D. when Agricola died in Rome, rumored to be by poison from Emperor Domitian. Harnish died a year later and Cloe and Arslanus went to a huge funeral to honor the great man. Arslanus retired for the legion in 101 A.D. to start farming on land he and Cloe had bought over the years. He had over twenty years in this identity as Arslanus the Roman soldier and could no longer age enough to prevent problems.

Cloe and Arslanus had four children by this time and their wealth had reached the point they had six workers tending their lands. Their farm was really a fortified farm with a protective wall around their dwellings and their workers were all trained fighters; the times demanded it. Their children now aged between eighteen and twelve.

Cloe and Arslanus had a relationship of equals. Cloe had always been a powerful woman, even as a young woman, and Arslanus did nothing to discourage her from continuing as she grew older. He loved women in general, and had true friends as women, not lovers, who he enjoyed talking to and being around. Cloe had no problem with this and saw Arslanus was always faithful; he just liked the company of women. Both Arslanus and Cloe thought their relationship was the central thing in their lives.

At this time, Arslanus felt it was time to tell Cloe the truth about his "affliction." He knew she already thought he was very unusual to not show ageing and she had become aware he was dyeing his hair gray. Arslanus told Cloe the truth one evening when they were alone together. Cloe did not know what to say, she was dumbfounded.

After a while she had to ask, "What is to become of us? I will become old and you will remain young? Will you stop loving me? Will you not want to make love to me and go to others? What is our future?"

Arslanus knew the shock would wear off but he had to answer the questions and make her feel better. He told Cloe the story of Eta, how he had lived with her for forty-two years until she had died at the age of sixty. How he had loved her the same way he now loved Cloe and still loved her. He asked, "Do you understand how much it means to me to remember Eta and the love we had. I feel the same about you as I did about Eta. I will always love you. Let's go on and have as many years as we can have together. I cannot help being what I am just as you cannot help ageing."

113

Cloe started to feel better. She saw the brutal sincerity of Arslanus as he talked about Eta. She did want Arslanus to love her the same way. She started to think about the numbers. She married Arslanus at eighteen. They had been married nineteen years; she was now thirty-seven. If Arslanus could stay in Britain another seven or eight years, the children would be old enough to take over their lands and care for themselves and each other. Arslanus and Cloe could then do what Arslan and Eta had done. Go away and pretends to be mother and son. She told Arslanus what she wanted to do. He agreed.

Four years later at the age of 41, Cloe was struck by the kick of a plow horse that had just been stung by a bee. The kick hit her on the right side of her head and fractured her skull. She died within minutes.

Arslanus had again lost the person he was most closely tied to in the world. *"How could he face it again?"* he thought. *"Only the need to protect his children, kept him from going insane."* he saw in retrospect.

Two years later, he told his children, all now eighteen or older he was returning to his home in the eastern part of the Roman Empire. He did not think he would return. He had done some preparation of the children for such a thing so the effect was not as dramatic as it might have been as a surprise. They were left with substantial properties and wealth so they were on a good start for their futures. They were sorry to have their father go but were basically reconciled. He had been a wonderful father and they wanted him to do what he needed to do.

It was 107 A.D. when Arslanus left Britain, and set out for some new place, he was not sure what his final destination was going to be.

27. <u>Atlanta</u>

It was after eight p.m. on Sunday evening, Arslan was sobbing at the table after he finished talking about the unexpected death of Cloe. His emotions were spent on the last story. He said he had to take a run, dressed quickly, and left.

Lisa said to Simon, "If his story is true, and I think it is, the definition of "love story" will have to be rewritten. He has lived and loved and lost his love so many times, it breaks your heart."

Simon said, "But he has been able to live out wonderful times with women he loved for more years than anyone else in history. Don't feel too sorry for him, he has had so much more than the rest of us get a chance to have. He has to take the sorrow of loss along with the good parts."

Lisa said, "That is another side of it."

"Now as for us, how are we doing?" said Simon.

"What do you mean?" Lisa said.

"I think I'm beginning to think like Arslan. He moves ahead so quickly in falling in love with his women. His feelings start and grow quickly but have tremendous depth. Once he finds the right woman he is like a moving train or a bull. There is no hesitation. I am starting to think about you and I that way. The more time I spend with you the more convinced I am, I want you for the long term. How does this happen to conservative Dr. Simon Myers in two days? It must have something to do with the emotional stimulus of the Arslan saga. I just hope I am not alone in this," said Simon.

Lisa smiled and said, "You are not alone. I was way ahead of you about two days ago but it sure is nice to see you catching up. And I agree with you, the impact of Arslan's story is causing my emotions to move ahead quickly as well. You didn't say anything like "I love you. Do I have to be the one who says that too?"

"Let's move this conversation into the bedroom where those words seem to pop out so much easier." said Simon as they both got up and headed for the bedroom. They agreed to leave Arslan a note they would continue his story in the morning.

In the morning, Simon and Lisa found Arslan sitting at the table with breakfast already made when they came out at seven a.m.

Arslan had gotten up early. Arslan's first words were, "Well gang, today is the day for my report card. I hope I get an "A.""

Simon's first order of business was to place a call to the Center for DNA Studies and to tell his assistant he would not be in until 3:00 p.m. He also asked her to check on the computer program running an analysis of the blood samples coded as "Arslan." She inquired in the system and indicated the program was running properly. Simon thanked her and asked her if she might be able to leave early today, about 10:00 a.m. then return at 3:00 p.m. to work about five more hours helping with the results from the Arslan samples.

The assistant's name was Carrie and she was a graduate student working on her doctorate at Emory University in Atlanta, DNA analysis was the topic of her studies. Simon knew Carrie's schedule was light on Mondays so he did not feel too bad about asking her to rearrange her day. She happened to be unattached, which was strange since she was drop dead gorgeous, so it added another element to her flexibility in scheduling. He had thought several times about breaking the unwritten rule at the center of keeping social lives separate from professional lives but had never decided to cross the line. She immediately agreed to the schedule change.

Arslan then said, "Eat up guys, we have about eight hours before the report cards are handed out, and we have work to do." Then Arslan started with his story, again.

28. <u>Ctesiphon (Persia) 227 A.D.</u>

Arslan arrived in Ctesiphon in August of 229 A.D. as part of a large caravan of trade goods which had started out in Damascus. Arslan was at a point where he had to leave the identity he had established in Damascus and go somewhere else. He had been in Damascus for eighteen years as Arslanus, the Roman, and now reverted to Arslan for his travels to the east.

His goal in going to Ctesiphon was to learn more about one of the world's oldest religions, the Zoroastrians. A new leader, Ardashir I, coming out of the southern Persian province of Fars (Pars) had overthrown the Parthian Empire and was now ruling Persia. He was an adherent of the Zoroastrian religion that had been made the state religion. Arslan had heard much of this religion over the years, with some saying it went back as far as 1500 B.C. or earlier. Arslan was still searching for his place in the world. Since he had to be somewhere in the world, he might as well be where he could learn something.

The new ruling powers in Persia had their roots in the priesthood of the Zoroastrians. Starting from the temple of Anahita in Istakhr, near the ruins of Persepolis, a city destroyed by Alexander the Great, a movement to restore rule of Persia by native Persians grew. From 180 A.D. until 224 A.D., when Ardashir defeated the Parthians, the momentum toward revolution grew and eventually won the day.

Arslan sensed immediately upon arriving in Ctesiphon, if he stayed, he would be required to show a conversion to Zoroastrian religious practices. He did not have to believe but he had to show respect for their practices and rituals to gain acceptance. He offered himself to the military as an instructor in weaponry who was familiar with Roman military tactics and weapons after making a show conversion to their religion. They were pleased to accept his offer and gave him a junior officer's position after demonstrating his proficiency with weapons and tactics.

Shortly after Arslan was established with the army of Ardashir, war with Rome broke out over moves by the Persians against Mesopotamia, Armenia and Cappadocia. Arslan's knowledge of the Roman war machinery was greatly valued and immediately put to use.

Arslan advised Ardashir's generals to make changes in tactics and weaponry to be more effective against the Roman legions. For three years subtle changes were introduced which had their payoff in 232 A.D. when the Roman emperor, Alexander Severus, led the Romans against Ardashir's forces in a great battle.

The changes Arslan had introduced were enough to allow Ardashir's forces to fight the Romans to a draw in this battle with huge losses on both sides. This was essentially a victory since the Romans were forced to withdraw and Ardashir took Armenia. During the battle Arslan coordinated the fighting of archers as light cavalry to harass the Roman legions constantly during the battle. Arslan had promoted this tactic and it was one of the key factors in the battle helping to turn the tide for the Persians.

Upon returning to Ctesiphon, Arslan was given rewards and honors for his efforts, including an opportunity to spend time in Ardashir's home province of Fars where Persepolis, the ancient capital of Persia is located. While visiting near Persepolis, Arslan met a young woman of the Ghashghai tribe named Shira.

Shira was from a highly placed family in the tribe. Arslan was introduced to her as he toured the ruins at Persepolis with other officers. She lived not far from the ruins and offered her knowledge to help educate Arslan about the great history of the region. Shira, as with other women of her tribe were not as subservient to men as would be expected. In fact, Shira was like a wild force of nature seeming free and natural to Arslan. He wanted to see more of this woman.

Through another officer, Arslan approached the father of Shira requesting his permission to call on his daughter. The father was hesitant, Arslan was not from a local family, and they knew nothing about him. The officer friend of Arslan told the father Arslan was the hero of the great battle with the Romans and was highly favored by Ardashir. At the mention of Ardashir, the father immediately changed his mind and gave his permission, if Shira agreed.

The first time Arslan visited Shira's home he was surprised at the richness of her father's farm. Their home was large and comfortable and Arslan was shown to a large patio where several members of the family were gathered. Arslan was shown to a bench and was asked to sit. Shira then came walking out of the house dressed in a colorful native dress showing off her nineteen-year-old figure perfectly.

Shira sat next to Arslan and they started their conversation. Shira said, "Arslan, my father told me things you did not mention when we first met. He said you were a great hero of the battle with the Romans and now most favored by our king. You are also apparently a modest man to not mention such things."

Arslan said, "From my experience, when a man meets a beautiful woman like you, he should focus his attention on her, rather than talking about himself."

Shira responded, "You also know how to flatter a woman as well as being modest. But some women want to be respected for things other than their beauty. Beauty does not last forever but what is inside the beauty is more important in the long run."

"Shira, men and women must balance many factors when they consider people to be wives or husbands. No single factor, beauty, intelligence, kindness, independence, honesty or other characteristic can be the only reason for a good decision. Each person must weigh all the items in the package before making a decision. The decision must eventually be made by the heart not the mind." said Arslan.

"A hero who is modest, flattering and philosophical." said Shira.

"Not a hero, just a man, with all the faults, inconsistencies, and bad habits most men have. I do not want to start out with you as more than I am, in your mind." said Arslan.

Shira blushed and said, "Arslan, a woman wants to see her man as more than he may be. Much of love is in the mind and emotions. Women want the romance of their men being princes. Women are grounded in the real world enough with having and raising children. They want their men to be larger than life, if their men don't always live up to it they still try to believe it anyway."

"Shira, the lives of a military man and his wife are not always easy. There are long separations and the constant possibility of death in battle or being taken captive. It is a dangerous occupation. Do you want to face that kind of life?" said Arslan.

"With the right man, and I think I have met the right man." Shira said boldly.

Arslan hesitated but then spoke, "I must return to Ctesiphon in a few days. There is little time in this life to waste. Decisions must be made and then we must live with them. If I leave without you, fate may separate us forever. Come with me as my wife and we will learn to share our lives."

Shira spoke through tears of joy, "Arslan, I will be honored to be your wife."

Arslan made arrangements with Shira's father and they were married the next day. Then they left for Ctesiphon to find a home. Arslan had been living in military quarters and had to find suitable quarters for a married man and his wife quickly.

Upon hearing of the return of a married Arslan to Ctesiphon, Ardashir summoned Arslan to see him. The king said to Arslan, "I have heard you married well. I know your bride's father and he is a great source of strength for the kingdom, as are many farmers. As thanks for your services, there is a small farm close to the city which is the king's to dispose of, since the former owner is dead, it is now yours by my command."

Arslan thanked the king for his generosity.

The farm gave Shira and Arslan a home close enough to the city for Arslan to be available but gave Shira a home more similar to where she had lived. Shira loved their new home and her new husband. Arslan returned the growing love of Shira and spent as much time with her as possible.

The next eight years went well for Arslan and Shira. Two children were born and the favor of Ardashir made for a good life in Ctesiphon. Then Ardashir died and was replaced by Shapur I who had already been regent. Another war with Rome was started in 241 A.D.

One change for the better with Shapur I on the throne was a significant reduction in the emphasis on the Zoroastrian religion as the state religion. Arslan had felt somewhat stifled by the extreme influence of the priesthood under Ardashir. He was used to more religious freedom with the Romans. Unfortunately, Shari, coming from a background of strict adherence to Zoroastrian religious practices did not share Arslan's views on the new religious freedom. They began to argue about this frequently.

Arslan had continued to implement improvements in the Persian military to counter the power of Rome. In 244 A.D. a great battle was fought against the Romans near the city of Edessa. This was a complete victory for the Persian forces with the Roman Emperor Valerian captured along with 70,000 Roman legionaries. Arslan could do nothing to prevent the killing of Valerian, nor did he see any reason to, but he did try to influence merciful treatment for the legions. Most were either sold into slavery or ransomed back to Rome. The Persians now dominated.

Despite the success of the Persian armies, Arslan's life at home deteriorated. Shari had a religious fervor she would not even try to control. All other aspects of their lives together were wonderful but religion drove a widening wedge between them. Finally, in 246 A.D. Arslan decided they could no longer live together. It was decided they would sell the farm at Ctesiphon and Shari and the children would move back to her family farm in Fars, taking with her two thirds of the proceeds from the farm. This was not a divorce but a permanent separation.

Arslan had now been in Ctesiphon for seventeen years and knew he had to start artificially ageing himself to extend his time there. Fortunately this was now easier with Shari and the children not around to observe him. It was time to start thinking about where to go next. This time his break from this identity had to be well planned because he was a public figure in the empire and could not come or go without attracting attention.

In May of 248 A.D. Arslan decided to throw off his current identity in Ctesiphon and travel to Egypt. He gathered as much gold, as possible, to take with him, washed the dye from his hair and shaved his beard. He assumed the identity of a merchant and set out for Egypt.

29. <u>Atlanta</u>

Arslan, Simon and Lisa wrapped up their last session about 1:00 p.m. and started getting ready to go to the Center for DNA Studies. They all knew they were early but all were anxious to see the results spit out by the computer. They arrived at the center about 2:00 p.m. all riding there in Arslan's rental car.

Simon was surprised to see Carrie's car was still in the parking lot. If she had not taken a break this could stretch into a thirteen-hour day for her. When they reached Simon's office, Carrie was already at his conference table with reams of data spread out on the table. Simon asked, "What is happening Carrie, didn't you take a break?" Then Simon remembered his manners and introduced Arslan and Lisa to Carrie. He introduced Arslan as John Young from the University of Pennsylvania and Lisa as an editor friend working with John Young. He introduced Carrie as Carrie Sloan, ABD (all but dissertation.)

When Arslan looked into Carrie's eyes and vice versa, Simon detected a major connection. Simon thought, *"Oh no, Arslan is loose in my laboratory. Not my business but I know a little about his effect on women. Well, Carrie should be able to take care of herself."*

Carrie recovered from the introduction and said, "When I rechecked the program before I left at eleven, I found it would finish earlier than we estimated, about 1:30 p.m. so I came back earlier and have had the data for about one half hour. But something appears to be wrong with the data; it is unlike anything I have ever seen.

Simon asked, now the DNA wizard, "What kind of problems do you see?"

Carrie said, "There are no telltale ethnic markers we would normally see. It is like the DNA predates most of the ethnic adaptations over the last ten to twenty thousand years. It is like an archaic form of DNA, but it's not the biggest problem."

Carrie continued, "There is a whole branch of DNA attached which is unlike anything we have ever mapped for a human, or animal for that matter. See this print out? Ever see this before? It has to be a program glitch."

Carrie was very surprised when Simon just said, "I see," rather than agreeing.

Simon closed the door to his office. Simon began speaking to Carrie, "Carrie, I have to ask you to hold this information as absolutely confidential. The implications of what we have here is beyond anything we have ever dealt with. Since you know this much, with the permission of Mr. Young who is not really Mr. Young, I will tell you the story."

Arslan nodded his agreement and Simon took about a half hour to go through the Arslan saga. At the end he reintroduced John Young, "Carrie, this is Arslan."

Carrie was amazed at what she had just heard coming from the mouth of her boss, a noted scientist, and friend. *"How could this be? A man exists who has walked this earth for almost 2,800 years, never ageing, healing rapidly from all injuries?"* she thought.

Arslan spoke, "I am sorry we have to hit you with this concept out of the blue but there was no easy way to break it. We do need to control this information until we are prepared for the storm when it goes public. Am I correct, Simon, this changes our thought about sending this out to another lab until we are ready? Another analyst will come up with the same information and the cat will be out of the bag? You should probably take some additional blood samples then rerun the analysis several times to reconfirm the results but do it here with Carrie or yourself analyzing the data?"

Simon nodded agreement then said, 'Some implications of this information are first, you have fathered many children over 2,800 years yet none of the extra branch of DNA has ever shown up before. We must conclude it does not pass to your children. Second, your DNA without the ethnic adaptations apparently has been masked in your children because your mate's characteristics were passed along to your children. Both of these need additional research."

Thinking ahead Simon said, "It will be interesting research. We may have to ask for volunteers to mate with you so we can study the results. Of course, it can be done in the lab but isn't as much fun?"

Carrie blushed noticeably at this comment and Simon thought, but did not say, *"Well, I think we just identified the first volunteer."*

Simon got serious and said, "Based on this first pass data, I am convinced of the truth of Arslan's information. I do not know how but my mind and emotions convinced me before, now the data supports it. As a man of science, I will check and recheck but right now, we must assume it is correct. As responsible human beings what are the implications of this information? If we can somehow take the DNA traits in Arslan's extra branch of DNA and make them transferable to the rest of mankind, the result would be the greatest achievement in history and would forever change mankind. But let's recognize this will not be a change, which everyone will like or support."

Simon continued, "Some men may want to limit the impact to themselves or some small select group. If widely done, overpopulation could destabilize the world. And don't underestimate the religious implications of this information. Again, the implications are enormous and our responsibility right now, I think, is to treat the information as so secret it is almost a moral imperative to keep it quiet. Does everyone agree?"

Everyone immediately nodded his or her assent.

Simon continued, "I am not comfortable working on this data here at the center. There are too many people here who could interpret the data or conversations we might have and get wind of what we are about. I suggest we put the highest possible security encryption on the data already run on the computer and do the same with a new test series we will start on the system. Then we should go to my apartment and continue to work there until tomorrow afternoon when Arslan and Lisa are leaving for Turkey. We can log into the center's system from our laptops or my home computer to do our research and check on the program. I have a three-bedroom apartment, Carrie, Arslan is in the guest room and I have a computer room set up with a foldout sofa bed. You can take the sofa-bed and Lisa and I are in my bedroom."

Carrie said, "Ok," taking a quick glance at Lisa who smiled.

Simon said, "I think it is important we work on this as a team, especially since we don't want to bring others into it right now. Carrie is behind the rest of the team in access to information about Arslan. She needs to spend time with us to get up to speed."

"Arslan, we need to take more blood samples from you and have Lisa and Carrie witness them formally, along with me. We will use one of the new samples for the test we start today and have two more to send to outside labs eventually. I will take the samples we already have in the lab and lock them in a secure freezer as back up." Said Simon.

Carrie brought in the equipment to draw more samples of Arslan's blood, took samples, had everyone witness and sign the samples, then took them to get the analysis started.

Simon asked Carrie while she was taking the samples, "Do you need to go by your apartment to get a change of clothes or anything."

Carrie answered, "No. I keep a bag and a couple of changes of clothes in my trunk all the time in case I get stuck at the lab all night, so I am good to go."

Simon said, "Good, very efficient as always."

Arslan was very quiet. Simon noticed it and asked, "Arslan, is there something wrong?"

Arslan rose from his chair and spoke, "Something Carrie said earlier is nagging at me. My DNA does not show ethnic variations going back ten to twenty thousand years, correct?"

Carrie spoke, "Yes, Arslan, it is most likely the twenty thousand number or more."

Arslan followed, "How can it be? If I was born in May of 759 B.C. shouldn't I have the ethnic variations before that time not be an "archaic DNA" with no such variations. I don't understand."

"Another interesting question raised for us to study in addition to other questions. I don't understand either." said Simon.

It was about 5:30 p.m. before they were ready to leave the center for Simon's apartment. Carrie wanted to bring her car so Lisa volunteered to ride with her, and Arslan and Simon left in the rental car.

In the car Lisa said to Carrie, "I saw you pick up on the sleeping arrangements with Simon and I. We have been friends for a while but not close except for sleeping together. I had wanted to be closer but Simon was not going there. It changed Saturday. Since then our relationship has hit warp speed. He can't believe it himself. He is talking about long term and everything. After you are exposed to some of the stuff Arslan has lived through, you may understand why. The sheer emotion of living and loving as Arslan has, then losing the loved ones over and over again is probably more than most people could handle. He is an amazing man. There has been a dramatic impact on Simon and I emotionally."

Lisa continued, "I think I can select a few sections we have already recorded for you to listen to first to help get you caught up. I know you must hear the section on Eta. He lived with her for 42 years as his wife and he broke down when he talked about her. She died 2,400 years ago and he still loves her. The story is beyond any other love story in the world, I think. It really makes you believe in love."

Carrie thought for a while, "How well do you know Arslan from what you have heard so far?"

Lisa said, "As I said, he is amazing. He is almost everything anyone could want in a man. I have no reason to doubt any of this, he isn't just talking, he is reciting events. If I wasn't involved with Simon, there isn't a question, I would be madly in love with him. Almost any woman would be. So, you had better be careful with your emotions around him. Did I forget to tell you—he falls in love quickly and deeply—and once in love he is relentlessly faithful. It takes major, major problems, to break him away from the women he chooses to love. Scary, isn't it?"

They arrived at Simon's apartment and went inside carrying some of the information from the office, Carrie's clothes and bag, and her laptop. After settling in, getting Simon's home computer on line, and the laptops hooked up, they all sat down at the table for some "Steak Out" carry out the men had picked up on the way to the apartment.

Carrie asked, "Why the trip to Turkey?"

Arslan explained in short form the circumstances of his appearance in Amwat and the burial of the gold ingot as the only artifact of Arslan before his arrival. Arslan mentioned the ingot had some inscriptions on it.

Carrie asked, "Do you remember what they said or looked like?"

Arslan thought a moment, "Well it has been over 2,700 years since I saw them so the image doesn't just jump right out at me but I remember they were not in any language I had seen up to that time, which wasn't many. I just can't remember more."

"Lets start with another section of the manuscript if everyone is ready." said Arslan.

He started speaking…

30. <u>Sidon 301 A.D.</u>

Returning to his Arslanus name even before he came to Sidon, he was now military advisor to the Republic of Sidon. Sidon was a beautiful city on the east coast of the Mediterranean Sea not far north of the city of Tyre where Arslan had lived with Eta almost 600 years ago. Part of the Roman Empire, Sidon was still a seafaring power but not at the level of previous times. Not as many pirates were allowed to use the seaport for protection as there had been in previous years.

The weather was wonderful here and all manner of interesting people and things moved through the port. On a given day, you might see slaves from any part of the world being brought to the market to sell, or spices arriving from the east by caravan, or a Roman general on his way to fight a war against Persia, or pirates bringing their stolen goods to sell. Arslanus did not like the slavery but he could not make the rules in the world where men treat other men as animals or worse. Arslanus still hated the brutality and barbarism of pirates and would kill them all if he had the option, but people in power protected these people because of the monies they brought with them.

On this fine day in 301 B.C. he saw something unusual. Passing by the slave market he saw three young females aged about fifteen years dressed in the dress normal to the mountains of Phrygia. They were tied together and were being led toward the slave auction. The man who led them was a horrible looking man with dirty clothes and dark complexion. He was a slave trader, perhaps a slave catcher who stole young girls from the places where they lived and sold them elsewhere. To be correct some of these slaves were sold into slavery by their parents or others with power over them for economic reasons. The cruelty of this was unbelievable. These young Phrygian girls were now going to be sold into a life of bondage. For all he knew, they could be his descendents. Today he would not let it happen.

Arslanus approached the slave trader. He said, "Trader, how much do you ask for these girls."

The trader looked at Arslanus, the military uniform, the sword, and his bearing. He decided to be polite to this one and said, "No less than 100 gold Denari for each one. They are virgins, you can check for yourself, and are pretty and strong. Of course, they need a little beating to get the wildness out of them, these mountain girls are always that way until you train them."

Arslanus said, "I offer fifty in gold for all and won't ask where you got them or how. There are people in the Roman Empire who do not like slave traders who steal young girls from citizens under the protection of the empire. I am military officer of the Republic of Sidon and a Roman citizen and can ask such questions if I am provoked."

The trader blanched and said, "Esteemed officer, I will lose money if I only get fifty in gold for all of them. I paid my bribe to the officials here to be protected from such things. Perhaps I should go to the officials to solve this question."

Arslanus did not know if he could win in a dispute with the port officials who collected the bribes and did not want to find out. Arslanus spoke, "We both take a risk if we take this dispute to the officials. I may be overruled by those who got money from your bribe. In which case I will lose the girls or have to pay a higher price. Not too much danger for me. But if you lose, I will take you to the Roman governor and he will have you strangled. And perhaps you should know, I have friends among the port officials. So who is risking the most?"

The trader decided the logic of Arslanus was greater than his greed and sold Arslanus the girls for fifty in gold. Arslanus led the girls down the street and made his way to his house. There were several comments along the way he heard such as, "Three at a time." or "Morning, Noon and Night." Arslanus led the girls into his three-room house and had them sit down.

Arslanus looked at them then spoke in one of the languages he knew from Phrygia. After several tries, he found a language in which they could converse. They were frightened but were very glad to find someone who knew the language. First Arslanus said, "Girls, I bought you because I did not want to see the three of you go into slavery. You would be badly treated. I will not hurt you. I will not force myself on you nor will I let others. I also will not beat you. So, for now, get the fear out of your eyes."

Arslanus then took a knife and cut their bonds. He asked, "Do any of you know how to cook? There is food in the other room but it needs to be prepared and I have other things to do. At the mention of food all three girls brightened up. He sent them to the other room to find what they could find to eat.

When they returned they were eating but not stuffing themselves. At least they had manners. Arslanus asked after they sat down, "Please answers some questions. What are your names and how old are you?"

A girl who looked to be the oldest and was probably the prettiest answered first, "I am Islasa and I am sixteen years old. My sister Sheea is the girl over there." indicating the smallest girl, also pretty but with darker hair, "She is fourteen. The other girl is Tira, our friend, she is fifteen." pointing to a black haired girl the same height as Islasa but thinner and less pretty than the others.

Arslanus asked, "How did you get taken to be sold into slavery."

Islasa answered, "Our village was raided by bandits. The men were away working and we had no protection. They killed many of the older women but took all the younger ones. They raped all the others but kept us because they said pretty ones could get a high price if we were still virgins. We were beaten several times for not walking fast enough but nothing worse. The bandits sold us to the slave trader you bought us from; he is a beast. He did not rape us but he did make us undress for him and had us put his manhood in our mouths and put his hands on us."

What was the name of your village and what city is it near?

Again Islasa answered, "Our village was Racj, with the nearest city, Gordion.

Arslanus said, "I know Gordion." He almost said he had lived there but thought better of it. Islasa looked surprised.

Arslanus continued, "How far from Gordion is Racj and in what direction?

Islasa again responded, "Racj is about ten days walking south of Gordion."

Arslanus asked, "Have you ever heard of a village call Amwat, about two weeks walking north west of Gordion."

Islasa said, "I have not heard of Amwat but I have heard of a village called Amnoc located near there."

Arslanus said, "It does not matter. By the way, my name is Arslanus."

Islasa asked with concern in her eyes, "Kind Arslanus, what will become of us now? We are very afraid, especially my sister who is youngest."

Arslanus thought for a few minutes, "I will do the best I can to find a way to get you back to your people near Gordion. Until then, you can live here, under my protection. The three of you will take the room I have been using as a bedroom and I will move my sleeping place to the kitchen room. With this many people living here, each one of you will have to do work in the house to keep it clean and neat. You will also have to shop at the market, get water, wash clothes, and cook meals."

"Does that sound fair? Are there any other questions which need to be answered right now?" said Arslanus.

Islasa said, "Yes it is very fair and we thank you so much Arslanus, you have probably saved our lives. We owe you much. One question more, where can we bathe, we are very dirty."

The other girls also agreed with Islasa and thanked Arslanus.

Arslanus said, "I will show you where to bathe and other things you need to know."

By the end of the day the girls had been to the public baths, the market to buy some clothes more in the style of Sidon, and to the food market to stock up the house. He also bought a dagger for each one of the girls and gave some instruction on how to use it for protection. They were to carry the daggers on their persons at all times. As they moved about the city, Arslanus made it a point to make clear to people he recognized, and some he did not, these three girls were under the protection of Arslanus, military advisor to the republic, and by reputation the best swordsman on the island. People who knew this would go out of their way to see the girls were not harmed in any circumstances where they might be blamed. All feared Arslanus steel.

The girls were beginning to understand they did not have an ordinary protector when they saw tough looking men turn into mice when Arslanus was around.

Back at the house in the evening, Arslanus poured a cup of wine and went to sit in his garden with a view of the sea. Islasa came out to join him. She was quite beautiful being cleaned up, new clothes, and her hair fixed in a style obviously copied from what she had observed the women of Sidon wearing.

Islasa said, "Master Arslanus, may I join you in the garden?"

Arslanus said, "You may, if you never call me master again. You are a lovely, young, free woman and have no master in this house."

Islasa blushed then sat down across from Arslanus and said, "You are a powerful and respected man here in Sidon. You have done more for us than we could have possibly dreamed about at the beginning of the day. We wonder why you have done the things most men would not do or would do for their own personal advantage? What can we do to thank you?"

Arslanus thought and answered, "There is much you do not know about Arslanus, and much you will probably never know. You can thank me by helping your sister and friend adapt to this situation since they look to you to lead them. This will make my responsibility in protecting the three of you easier and will be a great service to me."

Islasa said, "Arslanus, few men would act as you have. Thank you, from my heart."

"Islasa, you are very well spoken, have you been educated." said Arslanus.

"My father was educated in Gordion before he became a farmer and has taught my sister and I to read and write. We had little to read but did have a few scrolls." said Islasa.

"I have some books and scrolls here, some in Greek and some in Latin, and a few in other languages. I will try to teach you to read and speak these languages while you are here if you want. It could serve you well in the future." said Arslanus.

Islasa said, "I would love to do it, and I think the others would also.

So Arslanus started to have a school every evening, teaching three girls to speak, read and write Latin and Greek. It became a time everyone loved to spend together. Arslanus made up games to help them learn and after several months they would alternate speaking Latin or Greek in the evenings. Arslanus found Islasa was the brightest and quickest to learn. They all became good friends.

Arslanus was telling them stories one night, the girls were young and loved this, especially when it gave them more time with their favorite man, Arslanus. He decided to tell a story, perhaps an unwise choice, of a man who lived forever and the choices and problems he faced. It was just a story and did not last long. He forgot all about it.

Some months later, he was sitting in the garden late at night and Tira walked out and sat across from him. Arslanus said, "Why are you up so late child?"

Tira said, "First I am not a child, I am now sixteen years. I am a woman."

Arslanus, realizing his great mistake with a sixteen year old said, "Dear Tira, I am sorry, I know you are a lovely young lady and I should never have called you a child. Forgive me."

Tira said, "No need for you to ask forgiveness, all three of us owe you so much, you could call us anything and we would be happy. Actually, I must ask you to forgive me for something I have done."

Tira then explained she was cleaning the room the girls slept in and found a hiding place under the floor where Arslanus hid his manuscripts. She was by herself at the time with the other girls at the market. She read a manuscript telling the story of Eta, It was in Latin and she knew enough by now to understand the story. Tira then said, "You told us the story of the man who was immortal. The story of Eta tells me you are such a man. I am sorry to have done this thing to learn your secret but know I have told no one and will never tell. You know I love you, as do the others, and would never hurt you."

Arslanus saw there was little he could do but agree and said, "Tira, your actions are nothing needing forgiveness. I do ask you tell no one, it will be our secret forever. You should know I also love the three of you. Now go to bed and sleep, young lady."

Arslanus still had not found a good way to get the girls to Gordion safely. Sending three pretty young girls with someone he could not trust could easily land them back in slavery. It was the truth of the cruel world of these times. He could go himself but owed service to the republic and would have to wait at least a year before he could go. The girls were safer here in Sidon than crossing strange lands without adequate protection. They would have to be patient, which was not too great a problem, since they seemed to like their lives in Sidon.

After about six months, Arslanus and Islasa were sitting in the garden one evening after language class while the other girls were sleeping. Islasa said with some apparent difficulty, "Arslanus, I need to speak to you about a matter. I don't know how to say it but as you know by now I am one to speak out if something is important. We have become good friends, close friends I think. In two months, I will be seventeen. In my village, I would probably be married by now. I think you know this to be true. Here, I have no dowry to offer since my father is back in Phrygia. What am I to do?"

Arslanus surprised said, "Have you met someone here you want to marry, Islasa?"

Islasa smiled and said, "Yes, dear Arslanus, you."

Arslanus hesitated several minutes before he answered, "Dear Islasa, are you sure you understand the reason to marry is not to show gratitude but because you want to spend your life living with someone."

"Arslanus, I think I understand gratitude and it is not the reason I want to be your wife. I have observed Arslanus, the man, and know your are a kind, generous, honest man who makes me want to share my person and body with you." said Islasa.

"Islasa, I too have come to have strong feelings for you, beyond friendship, but have said nothing because of the sense of responsibility I feel for your welfare. Before I let you leave Sidon, I was going to speak out and ask you to stay with me. If you are sure about your feelings, we will get married, perhaps on your birthday." said Arslanus before taking Islasa in his arms and kissing her.

Just then Sheea and Tira came into the garden from the house and asked what was going on. Islasa answered immediately, "Arslanus and I are going to be married on my birthday." Everyone hugged, kissed and in the case of the girls, giggled, for several minutes.

Islasa and Arslanus were married in April of 302 A.D. with military honors of the Republic of Sidon. Islasa and Arslanus, moved into the bedroom now and the other two girls found places in the kitchen. Since they had become such good friends before being married their physical union was joyful and without tension. They loved each other from the start and it grew daily.

In August, by a stroke of luck, a Roman ambassador, headed for Gordion passed through Sidon. Arslanus talked to him about taking Sheea and Tira to Gordion under his protection. He agreed, thinking it would be nice to have two pretty young women who spoke and read Latin and Greek with his party. Since he was a widower, who knows, he might marry one of them, he acknowledged.

133

When the two girls got ready to depart, Arslanus gifted them each with sizable sums of gold, enough for several dowries each, and even greater treasures, two scrolls each, one in Latin another in Greek. They would be able to demonstrate their abilities to read and speak the languages. Islasa told Arslanus after they left, "I will never in my life forget your kindness to my sister and friend. I love you more than you can ever imagine, my kind Arslanus."

Three months later, two letters in Latin came to Arslanus and Islasa. The letters were from Sheea and Tira telling they had gotten to Gordion safely. Sheea's and Islasa's father had thought they were dead or worse. He was so happy to see Sheea safely back and to hear Islasa was well and married to the man who saved them from a life of slavery. Their mother had been killed in the bandit raid but their safety had made their father happy to be alive.

Tira wrote with great news also, as the Roman ambassador had predicted, he fell in love with her and they were married when they reached Gordion. Her family was also delighted she was alive and Tira thanked Arslanus repeatedly for what he had done. She promised to write again.

After reading the letters several times, Islasa put them away and pulled Arslanus into the bedroom where she made love to him with an urgency he had never seen before. She just said, "Arslanus, you are the best man in this world." Arslanus was delighted.

In August of 303 A.D. Islasa was nine months pregnant with their first child. She went into labor in the bedroom and the midwife was called. Arslan waited in the garden. The midwife and a neighbor woman attended Islasa. Arslan heard an baby cry but then heard the midwife call out for him to come. Arslan met the midwife in the center room of the house and she said, "You have a strong son but your wife is not well. She is bleeding and it will not stop. I fear she will die."

Arslanus said, "Is there nothing else to be done?"

The midwife said, "I have done all I can do, it is in the hands of the gods. Go in to her now."

Arslanus went in and saw the weakened condition of Islasa. She was conscious but seemed to know she was dying. Arslanus held her gently as she said, "Arslanus, my protector, my man, love our child as you have loved me. Do not feel bad for me, I have had more love and wonder in the last two years than most people ever have. Remember me as the living, loving person who had this time with the man she loved more than anything in the world." Slowly she sank into coma and died.

Arslanus asked the midwife to find a wet nurse to come and care for the child and the neighbor offered to help also. Arslanus then went out to the fortifications along the sea and cried until nothing was left in him.

31. <u>Atlanta</u>

Arslan had tears rolling down his cheeks when he finished at about 9 p.m. "I am in no condition to go on right now, I need to take a run." he said. He changed quickly and left. Everyone else also had tears in their eyes.

Carrie spoke first, "Now I understand what you meant about the emotions. May I take the tape about Eta you suggested and listen to it while Arslan is gone. I saw a stereo in the computer room."

Lisa gave her the tape and Carrie went to the computer room and closed the door. About an hour and one half later she came out in tears. She said, "I'm sure listening to the tape is nothing like seeing the emotions of Arslan relating it, but you were right, it might be the greatest love story ever." Carrie then said, "I'm serious about the next thing I'm going to say. I think it could be important. Do you think Arslan can hold up emotionally to going back through these events in a short period of time? We are concentrating the emotional devastation he is feeling into a short time frame. Do we want to slow down and give him some time to rebuild? I am not a shrink but this is potentially damaging to Arslan. Any thoughts?"

Simon and Lisa were both thoughtful for a while then Simon said, "I agree with Carrie, we need to slow down, we could hurt Arslan. Do we need to talk to Arslan about this?"

Everyone agreed they needed to discuss it with Arslan when he returned.

When Arslan came back in the door, he went to his room to shower then came back out in about twenty minutes. Before they had a chance to speak as they agreed, he said, "After some thought, while I was running, I have decided I have to slow down on how quickly we go through the story. My emotions can't take this pace. It is too concentrated."

Carrie then said, "We had just decided to talk to you about the same thing, so it looks like the team is really in tune here."

Simon and Lisa were tired and wanted to go to sleep but Arslan wanted to go out to get something to eat and Carrie was not going to let him go alone. Off they went to a little Italian bistro in a shopping center that had good food but was overpriced as many of these places tend to be. They ordered a bottle of Merlot and pasta with clam sauce.

After a glass of wine the food arrived and they started to feel better.

Carrie said, "It has to be hard on you to go back through these events, more than events, lives you have lived. How can you stand it?"

Arslan said, "It is not easy but I believe it is important. The people I loved deserve to be remembered. They were wonderful, caring, courageous people who lived with me and gave me so much. I am just trying to get their stories out so they can be remembered and maybe help some other people by their examples."

"It makes more sense than anything I have heard in years." said Carrie and added, "You should know I listened to the tape about Eta while you were running. You can't imagine how moved I was."

"Well, at least you are learning something more about me. You might as well know I have a weakness for women. I never make such close friends with men as I do with women. Even when it's women I don't have a physical relationship with, I still make deep friendships." said Arslan.

"You can call it a weakness if you want, but I think it is natural and right. I don't make the same quality of relationships with women as I do men." said Carrie."

"The way you look, Miss Carrie Sloan, ABD, men don't have a chance." said Arslan.

"Thank you for the compliment, Arslan, you are not so bad yourself. I haven't seen any women chasing you away in the stories so far." said Carrie.

"I just don't tell any of those stories. I can't handle the rejection." said Arslan.

"Likely story, Arslan" said Carrie.

"You know, Lisa warned me the emotional effect of your stories is huge. She seems to think it is having the effect of putting her relationship with Simon in, as she phrased it, "warp drive" for both of them." said Carrie.

"In that case, I hope so, they are good people and deserve to have a great relationship together. I am happy to be of service." said Arslan.

"Lisa also warned me to watch out for my own emotions, specifically, as far as you are concerned. She seems to think women fall in love with you very easily, and to make it worse, you fall in love right back, all done at warp speed. Any comment?" said Carrie.

"A smart man would probably not touch it with asbestos gloves, but since this is obviously a clinical discussion, meaning we are detached and scientific about the subject, I will give it a try." said Arslan.

"If you think about it, women probably do fall for me rather quickly. I have had years and repeated practice in learning to treat women so they will react favorably to me. If I didn't get it after a while, I would be a sorry case. The key ingredient is I do sense well when a woman is interested in me, again from years of experience, and respond accordingly. I am a romantic person; you can tell I believe in love. If the right woman gives me the signal she is interested, the spiral starts and then feeds on itself. Does that somehow degrade the experience? Not for me, I will tell you," continued Arslan.

"Now this conversation could get risky. Are you ready?" said Carrie.

"Go ahead, always give life a chance." said Arslan.

"Ok, what do your well trained sensors tell you about me. Am I interested?" said Carrie.

"Carrie, one word, Yes. I hope it doesn't offend you," said Arslan.

"Ok, we have gone this far, next question, are you responding accordingly?" said Carrie.

"Same answer, Yes." said Arslan.

"So the spiral has started?" said Carrie.

"Yes, again." said Arslan.

"Let's finish our meal, go back and sleep on this, separately, and see where this takes us in the bright light of day." said Carrie.

"I hate to be this way but I am a male. I agree with what you said, but I will not lock the door to my room. It is just a thought provoking tactic in the dance of love." said Arslan.

"And I thought you were Mr. Nice Guy." said Carrie.

"Not that nice." said Arslan.

Arslan and Carrie finished their meal, settled the check and headed back to Simon's apartment. Simon and Lisa were behind closed doors when they entered the living room. Both removed their jackets and Arslan hung them up in the closet.

Carrie walked over to Arslan, put her arms around him just above the waist, and pulled him close. She then moved her mouth up to his and kissed him with her mouth open. He responded by kissing her back and hugging her firmly but gently. After several minutes they stopped kissing and looked into each other's eyes. Carrie said, "Spiraling, aren't we?"

"Another Yes." said Arslan.

Carrie unwrapped her arms from around Arslan, turned and started walking for the computer room and said, "Good night, sweet prince."

Arslan said, "Good night, lovely lady." He walked to his room but did not lock the door.

In the morning Simon got up about 8:30 a.m. and came out to see if Arslan had made breakfast as usual. No Arslan and no breakfast in the kitchen or dining area. He wanted to see if Arslan had gone running so he tried the doorknob to his room but it was locked.

"Ok," he thought, *"I can make breakfast"*, which he proceeded to do then took some on a tray back in to his bedroom for Lisa and himself. He left the rest on the stove for Arslan and Carrie. About an hour later he came out and Arslan was eating some breakfast and he heard the shower running in the other bathroom. Simon said to Arslan, "How are you feeling this morning?"

He said flatly, "Much better, much better."

Lisa came out, said her greetings to Arslan and winked at Simon. Lisa said to Arslan, "Simon said you slept in today so the poor baby had to fix breakfast. You were spoiling us."

Arslan said, "I needed a little extra sleep this morning but I feel good now."

Then Carrie walked out of the bathroom and said hello to everyone. Arslan offered to get her some breakfast and did. Lisa thought for a minute, *"There is something different about Carrie this morning. She seems more relaxed or something."* Then she saw Carrie touch Arslan's hand as he brought her some breakfast. Lisa thought, *"The cat is now out of the bag."* She did not say anything. She appreciated privacy.

139

Jon Kelly

Simon and Carrie agreed they would work on the DNA puzzle today rather than having Arslan do more from the manuscript. Lisa meanwhile was going to work on editing some of the early sections after transcribing some into the laptop. Arslan would be available to answer questions and keep an eye on the DNA work.

Lisa also had to go to her apartment to pack for the planned six-day trip to Turkey. It was a tight schedule but could be workable if they got lucky. She left about 1:30 and was back by 2:30. Arslan was perpetually packed and ready to go. They left for the airport about 3:30 for a 7:00 p.m. flight. Simon drove them to the airport but Carrie came along also to see them off.

Since security was tight they had to say their goodbyes in the main terminal before the security screening. Lisa gave Simon a big lingering kiss then looked at Carrie and Arslan who were standing there. She went over and whispered to Carrie, "Go give him a big kiss, do it now." Then Lisa winked at Carrie. Carrie gave Arslan a long lingering kiss. Simon was very confused.

32. **Gordion/Amnoc**

> People live their fleeting lives,
> reaching others in many ways,
> Unremembered moments thrive,
> A monument for endless days.

The flight to Paris was OK, eight hours of boredom mostly. They changed planes in Paris to fly to Turkey. It was another long flight then touchdown in Ankara. They had a "puddle jumper" booked to go from Ankara to Gordion and got to Gordion after traveling for 24 hours. They got their two rooms at the hotel and some food then crashed for two hours.

They agreed to leave at 11:00 a.m. local time to look for Amwat or whatever it was called today. A local map showed a place called Amnoc about where Amwat should be. The road leading there was shown as unpaved. A trip once two weeks walking was now about two hours by auto, if the sheep didn't block the road. They arrived at Amnoc at about 2:00 p.m.

Amnoc was an extremely small village of about eighteen houses, a small church, what looked like a small school, and a gas station. The geography looked about right to Arslan. They decided to try the gas station first. They asked about the name of the village—had it been called something else in the past? No one thought so. They asked if anyone knew about a small path leading up into the mountains to the northeast? Someone said there is a small chapel behind the school with a path starting there, which leads up into the mountains.

They walked over to the school where small children were playing. One group of children was singing a child's rhyme. Arslan heard them say his name twice then the rhyme stopped. He asked the teacher watching the children what the rhyme was. She said,

> Climb up, Climb Up.
> Hide Away, Hide Away.
> Quiet Now, Quiet Now.
> Arslan, Arslan,
> Monsters go away.

Arslan and Lisa were stunned. After twenty-seven hundred years the children remember a rhyme about an event so far back in history. They asked the teacher where and when the rhyme had appeared. She did not know but perhaps the village priest could answer. Before they went to the church they asked the teacher to have the children repeat the rhyme so she could record it.

They walked to the church and found the village priest, an old man. When asked about the rhyme he smiled. It is a very old rhyme, perhaps as old as the mountains. It had lasted so long because it is inscribed on a stone face of the mountain at the start of the trail behind the school. It is inscribed there in three languages. The top one is so old no one can read the language. The second one is in an old language, which has been translated. The third one is in Latin and is signed by the person who did the translation.

Arslan asked the priest, "Does anyone know what the rhyme is about?"

The priest said. "No one knows and I have asked many people over the years. I would love to know."

Arslan said to Lisa, "Let's go to the path behind the school."

Behind the school there was a small chapel. Behind the chapel the path started. Arslan felt chills of anticipation. They walked about five minutes up the path and saw a stone face on the mountain. They saw three distinct inscriptions chipped out of the rock.

Lisa started taking pictures with her Digital camera with Zoom feature. She took the oldest first, up at the top. Then she took the second one in the middle. As she focused on the bottom one and zoomed in she saw something and screamed to Arslan, "Look just below the bottom inscription. There is a name chipped into the stone below the Latin inscription. It says "Tira."

"First the rhyme then this, "Arslan said bewildered," A 2,700 year old rhyme then a 1,700 year old message from a good friend. She says, "I found your Amnoc and found your name." Thinking about his wonderful friend, Tira, he wept then said, "Tira sent her message across 1,700 years as though she were saying "Hi" to a friend she had only seen yesterday. How can people so full of life ever die and disappear. The universe should preserve their souls, their beings, so they go on forever."

142

"We can't go up the trail today to look for the ingot. It will take at least two hours to get to it if I remember right and won't give us time to look and get back before dark. Let's go back to Gordion then come back early in the morning so we have all day to explore." said Arslan after he recovered.

Arslan stopped then and said, "First we stop at the church."

At the church, Arslan found the priest, "Father, I have some information for you about the rhyme. Not really information but a theory, it's probably all you could ever expect to get about this anyway." The priest nodded in agreement.

Arslan started, "In about 700 B.C. a soldier who was in the great kings guard in Gordion escaped the city when invaders defeated the king's army. He came to Amnoc to warn his family who lived here to escape into the mountains up the path behind the chapel. He led them up the path (Climb Up, Climb Up). When their scouts saw invaders coming down the path from the top he told them to hide off the path (Hide Away, Hide Away). He also told them to be very quiet (Quiet Now, Quiet Now.) A child with the group coughed and the invaders started to search and would have found them. But the man jumped out and attracted the attention of the invaders; his name was Arslan (Arslan, Arslan). He led the invaders away (Monsters Go Away.) That's my theory about the rhyme."

The old priest smiled and said, "A wonderful story, it is a very good theory, no one could do better. Thank you my friend, thank you always. What is your name?"

Arslan said, "My passport says John Young."

Arslan then said to the priest, "I forgot one thing. In about 300 A.D. the kind, beautiful wife of the Roman ambassador to Gordion came to this village and translated the local language on the stone face into Latin. Her name is inscribed on the wall, Tira. Please include Tira in your prayers."

The priest said, "It sounds like more than theory."

Arslan said, "It is."

Arslan and Lisa returned to the hotel in Gordion. Lisa got on the Internet with her laptop and sent an E-mail to Simon explaining what they had found in Amnoc. She also attached pictures of the inscriptions.

In the morning they got up at 5:00 a.m. and were on the road by 6:00 a.m. They got to Amnoc by 8:30 a.m. and were started up the trail by 8:45 a.m. After two hours they started looking for a very large rock by the trail. They turned a corner and there it was.

Dirt slides from above had covered the top so some vegetation grew up there but it was the rock. Arslan and Lisa climbed up after getting out their folding entrenching tools and climbing picks. Arslan remembered he had to go to the back and climb down behind. It was mostly filled in with stones but after two hours work most of the stones were cleared. He was to the larger rock he had placed there 2,700 years ago. Using their tools for leverage they moved the stone out of the way. He peered in the small cave and saw nothing, No, the glint of gold. He pulled out a small ingot of gold and about fifty gold coins. The bag had long since rotted away.

Arslan and Lisa walked quickly down the trail to the village. First he went to the priest at the church. Arslan said to him, "Take these ancient gold coins for the church. We found them along the trail. They are 2,700 years old and have some value." Arslan kept possession of four coins and the ingot.

The priest said, "Shouldn't these be turned in to the antiquities people in Ankara."

Arslan said, "Trust me Father, I have every right in the world to dispose of these coins."

Riding back to Gordion, Lisa studied the ingot. The marking on the ingot was odd, very odd but also somewhat familiar. Where had she seen this before?

Upon arrival at the hotel in Gordion, they went to Lisa's room and immediately logged onto the Internet and sent an E-mail to Simon and Carrie indicating they had found the ingot and were working on plans to get back to Atlanta. While Arslan sent the message, Lisa took several digital photos of the ingot and attached them to the E-mail then hit "send."

The ingot was about 6" long by 2 1/2" wide by 3/8" thick. All edges were slightly rounded. On one of the large flat sides there was a figure, which looked similar to cave art of an animal, probably a horse, represented by a series of unconnected lines. This was the figure Lisa thought looked familiar. She happened to have an interest in archaeology and faithfully read *Archaeology* magazine published by the Archaeological Institute of America. The other large side of the ingot had numbers or letters, she could not tell which, arranged in horizontal rows down the entire side. Similar markings were on all edges.

Arslan was still in a state of shock or confusion or wonderment at the last two day's events. He studied the ingot and held it in his hand but talked little. Finally, Lisa said, "Arslan, I have seen this exact figure before as we see on the ingot."

'Where?" said Arslan.

"Let's get online and look for back articles from *Archaeology* magazine. I think in 2001, there was an article with this same horse pictured." she said.

She got to the web site for *Archaeology* and started searching. Bingo, September/October 2001 issue, title "Timeless Thoroughbred," then in smaller print "England's Uffington Horse." As they read they saw a connection, "Late Bronze Age,. Date, around 700 B.C.", then the picture, identical. After reading and rereading, they were confused but excited they had some kind of trail to follow. They just didn't know why, what, who, or how.

Plans changed immediately, they had to get to England, between Bath and Oxford, to the city of Swindon, south of Stratford on Avon to boot. *"Shakespeare we are coming."* thought Lisa.

They sent another E-mail, encrypted like the first to advise Simon and Carrie of the new information and needing help in putting together a plan. They were worried now about going through airport security with the ingot. Turkish authorities could be a little testy about taking "national treasures" out of the country even if Arslan did own them. Other countries could also be problems about gold art objects going in or out also, so what to do?

Arslan finally decided to paint the ingot gray to simulate pewter or some other non-precious metal and simply pack it in his baggage. The chances of getting caught leaving Turkey were slim, he was sure they X-rayed very few, if any, bags. Going into England at Heathrow Airport was another matter. They were more thorough than many places in actually looking through bags. If they questioned it, he would pull out pictures of the White Horse at Uffington and show the bar had the same design. He would then explain he had had it made as a present for a friend at Oxford, not far from Uffington. He would get a fake invoice for it made in Ankara.

They booked their tickets from Ankara to London Heathrow to leave Saturday morning. They also booked a rental car at Heathrow and two rooms at Cotswolds hotel in Swindon near Uffington. Finally they decided to check in to an Airport hotel in Ankara for the night and to leave Gordion as soon as they could.

They checked out of the Gordion hotel, drove to Ankara, checked in to a hotel, got other business taken care of and were in their rooms asleep by 11:00 p.m. In the morning they were up at 4:00 a.m., left the hotel by 5:00 a.m. and were at the airport by 6:00 a.m. Their flight out was for 8:30 a.m. but Arslan waited to check in until 7:45 a.m. so they had less risk with the checked bag. They were on the plane and waiting to take off by 8:15 a.m. The plane was buttoned up by 8:40 a.m. and started to taxi. They were clear of one hurdle.

33. Uffington (England)

The flight to London was uneventful and they arrived for an on time flight. They retrieved their bags and went to customs. Arslan chatted with the customs inspector being asked what they were going to be doing in England. Arslan told him they were going to Swindon to meet a friend from Oxford then going to visit the White Horse at Uffington showing him a picture they had printed off the Internet. He said his friend was very interested in this type of thing being a history professor and all. It was enough for the inspector and they were waved through.

The rental car was ready for them so they took off for Swindon, roughly an 85-mile trip from Heathrow, which took them 3 hours to get there. The Cotswolds Hotel was part of a large chain and everything was perfect but the price. After checking in, Arslan asked the clerk how to get to Uffington. It was about ten miles to the east, and they were given directions.

They knew from the article in *"Archaeology"* the White Horse site was open to the public 24 hours per day. It was now 5:00 p.m. so they decided to skip eating and go directly to the White Horse. They wanted to see it before it got dark.

They got to the historic site at about 5:30 p.m., parked the car, and walked across the field, around the fort, and up the valley between the White Horse and Dragon Hill. Arslan was carrying the ingot in his jacket pocket. It was a cold day and there were no other visitors at the site. *What did they do now?*

Arslan took out the ingot and compared the image on the ingot to the White Horse. They couldn't see much of the horse from this angle, down so low in the valley. They decided to climb up Dragon Hill to get a better view of the White Horse from the opposite hill. Standing on the flat top of the large mound on Dragon Hill, Arslan compared the ingot image to the horse depicted on the opposite hill; he said, "No question, they are identical." Arslan then focused his eyes on the ingot and thought, *"What secret do you hold, little ingot."*

As if by way of an answer, Arslan felt himself start to feel strange, like he was fading out of contact with the world, then suddenly everything went dark.

Arslan was standing in the dark somewhere. Then a glowing light started very soft and got brighter with each second allowing him to see. He looked around and saw he was inside a circular room, about thirty feet in diameter having walls with rectangular patterns, and a glowing ceiling. The floor was metallic with a dull finish.

Meanwhile, Lisa was beyond being confused. She had been standing beside Arslan on the hill a moment before and then he melted away in front of her, something like the transporter always showed on Star Trek; she was a "trekie." Now Arslan was completely gone. She started looking but nothing in any direction. She thought, *"Well, get hold of yourself. He has to be somewhere, but where? I will take a walk and look around then sit in the car a while and see if he shows up. What else can I do? If I lose Arslan, I don't know who will be more upset, Simon or Carrie."*

Arslan walked over to the wall and saw the rectangular block designs on the wall were not part of the wall, they were more gold ingots hanging on the wall. He looked around some more and estimated there were roughly 200 to 300 of the ingots. There was one section however where twelve were missing with empty slots. He then thought, *"What is this place?*

Suddenly, thoughts appeared in his mind indicating this was the transportation entrance and the gold ingots were transportation controllers. As if sensing the discomfort of Arslan at being contacted directly in his mind, a holographic screen appeared which showed diagrams explaining the transportation entrance and transportation controllers.

Arslan now thought, *"Where am I?"*

The screen showed a diagram of a circular "vessel" and rotated it several times to see different views and then showed an animation of the vessel buried under the mound on Dragon Hill. From the scale shown, Arslan thought the vessel was buried about 20-25 feet deep. This did not shock Arslan since he had see many strange things in his lives. Another person might have been unable to process the information.

Arslan was surprised when a voice spoke, "Arslan, what additional information do you need? You may be more comfortable communicating by voice commands."

Arslan asked, "How do you know my name?"

The voice answered, "Your brain pattern is in my memory, your brain was scanned and you were identified."

Arslan asked, "Who or what are you?"

The voice answered, "In your terms, I am a computer or more accurately an artificial intelligence."

Arslan asked, "Why did you have my brain pattern in your memory."

The voice answered, "Your brain pattern was recorded when your life started, over 2,760 years ago. Your life started on this vessel."

"Are there other people alive on this vessel?" asked Arslan.

"No Arslan, there are not." said the voice.

"When was the last living person on this vessel, prior to my arrival?" said Arslan.

"Approximately 2,760 years ago?" said the voice.

Arslan asked, "How old is this vessel? How long has it been on earth?"

"This vessel is approximately 4.5583 million years old. It has been on this planet for approximately 135,823.55 years on this visit." said the voice.

Arslan registered this information. The vessel has been on earth longer than Homo sapiens have existed as a species.

"What happened to the last people who lived on this vessel. Did they go away or die and why or how?" asked Arslan.

The voice answered, "They died from a new bacteria which evolved and caused their genetically designed anti-ageing processes to fail. They died of old age."

Arslan asked, "Why did I not die?"

The voice said, "You had alterations made to your DNA prior to life which provided you with immunity."

Arslan remembered Lisa was outside and asked, "There was someone outside on the hillside with me. Can I go out and bring her in with me?"

"Yes, but you must take a transportation controller for her to use and you must activate her controller with your thoughts until her brain pattern is present in my memory." said the voice.

Arslan put another ingot in his pocket from the wall and directed his thoughts at the original ingot for him to go back to his original position. He felt the unnatural feeling and then was standing outside on the hill again. It was now colder and getting dark. Arslan did not see Lisa so he walked toward the car. Suddenly the car's lights came on. He reached the car and Lisa opened the window and said, "Where did you go, it has been over an hour since you disappeared?"

"Lisa, you would not believe me if I told you, so I will show you. Write a note to put on the car saying we went off with someone else for dinner and will be back later to pick up the car. It should keep the police from getting involved with a deserted car. Once you do it we will go back up to Dragon Hill," said Arslan.

Lisa said, "Ok."

They walked up to Dragon Hill near where they were when he disappeared before. Arslan handed Lisa a gold ingot without pewter paint and said, "Hold this."

"Arslan, where did you get a second ingot?" said Lisa.

"Lisa, you will see very soon." said Arslan then focused his thoughts on the transport controllers, "Take us inside."

The world faded from view and they next saw the inside of the transport entrance. Arslan spoke, sounding like Captain Kirk, "Computer, this is Lisa Sloan, please record her brain pattern for future reference."

The voice responded, "It has already been done."

Lisa thought, "Where are we?"

The same holographic screen appeared as before with Arslan and she was shown the layout and position of the vessel. "Oh my God," was her only comment.

"Computer, please provide Lisa with the same information you gave me before." said Arslan.

The computer provided Lisa with a summary of the information he had received. Lisa was stunned.

Arslan asked, "Computer, where did you come from? Where in the universe? Who built this vessel?"

The voice said, "A planetary system approximately two million light years from earth. The screen showed a simulation of the location. The beings who built the vessel were similar to Homo sapiens in physical structure but were significantly advanced in mental capabilities."

"I assume this vessel was capable of space flight when it came here. Does it still have the capability and are other systems of the vessel in good functioning order? Also, how long will your energy resources last?" said Arslan.

The voice responded, "All systems of the vessel are in functioning order and energy resources without refueling will last from two to four million years based on usage levels. Vessel systems are self repairing with maintenance constantly being performed to maintain capabilities."

Arslan asked, "How can the vessel be removed from the hill it is buried under?"

The computer responded with a visual simulation showing energy beams loosening sections of earth and the vessel rising from the hilltop.

Arslan asked, "Is this vessel armed? Can it defend itself?"

The voice responded, "Weapon systems exist on this vessel which are far advanced over any systems on this planet by a huge factor. Defenses using force fields around the vessel can withstand the effects of any weapon or energy source on the planet. This vessel has the capability to produce energy at a rate of one hundred times the energy currently being produced on earth at any given time."

Lisa did not quite know where Arslan was going with his questions. She asked Arslan, "Why are weapon systems important?"

Arslan said, "When the powers of our world see the technology here there will be a massive battle for control of it. We have to be able to defend it to see it is used properly."

"Who will decide what is proper?" said Lisa.

"Us." said Arslan.

"Computer, please give us a tour of the vessel and describe the functions and capabilities of the various areas." said Arslan.

They spent the next three hours touring the vessel finding wonderful things and capabilities beyond their understanding. One of the most amazing capabilities was the use of the computer's memory to record human progress and activities. For the last 135 thousand years, visual records have been kept by the Tira's computer showing developments on earth, major natural events, the development of humans, the activities of humans, and many other events. Since the advent of electrical and electronic usage by men, all broadcasts of radio, TV and other electronic medium have been recorded.

Currently the Internet is being recorded. The information storage capability of the vessel was enormous.

Arslan asked the computer, "What is the mission of this vessel? Why was it built? What was the purpose of it coming to earth? What is it supposed to do next?"

The computer did not hesitate, "The stated objective of this vessel is to find planetary systems capable of supporting the development of intelligent life, and to sustain and support development over time. The final objective is to evolve intelligent life capable of interacting with other intelligences in the universe to work toward understanding the universe and existence. This vessel and its crew, which are now deceased, were assigned this sector of the known universe to evolve intelligent life. There is no pre-assigned next step beyond assisting the evolution of intelligent life. Intelligent life, once evolved, has the responsibility for establishing contact with other intelligences in the universe."

"What intervention in the development of intelligent life on earth has this vessel done?" asked Arslan.

The computer responded, "Upon arrival on this planet approximately 1.5 million years ago DNA modifications were introduced to stimulate the development of humanoids. Approximately 135,000 years ago on a follow-up visit, it was discovered the evolution had progressed faster than anticipated and the decision was made to further intervene and stimulate evolution toward higher intelligence beings. It was also decided the vessel would stay on earth to continue to monitor and assist evolution. Several DNA modifications were introduced over time with various successes and failures to arrive at the evolution of Homo sapiens we are at today. DNA modifications and intervention have not been implemented in the last 2,760 years due to the death of the crew. The vessel has been in an observation mode since then.

Arslan asked, "Have you been in contact with other members of the group of intelligent beings who constructed this vessel during your time here."

"No, the distances are too great for such contact. It was not expected such contact would be necessary or useful until new intelligences were prepared to initiate such contact." said the voice.

Arslan spoke to Lisa, "What do you suggest we do now? I think we have absorbed as much information as we can at this time without overloading our ability to process the information."

Arslan asked, "You said you were monitoring the Internet, can you also send out a message on the internet which will appear as a normal E-mail to the party receiving it."

The computer responded it could. Arslan and Lisa composed a message to Simon and Carrie, "To Carrie and Simon, Please drop everything and book transportation to meet us in England, as soon as possible. This is most urgent. We have information beyond anything we have discussed and must have you here to share it personally. Signed Love, Arslan and Lisa. Confirm by E-mail back to this E-mail address. We will pick you up at Heathrow when you arrive. Please provide flight information."

Arslan asked the computer, "What are you using for our E-mail address."

The computer responded, Arslan thought he heard a chuckle, "Arslan @older_than_dirt.com."

"Computer, forward all E-mails received for us to Lisa's laptop E-mail address if we are not here to receive the communication." said Arslan.

Arslan then spoke to Lisa, "Let's go back to the hotel and get some food and rest. We can wait for a response from Atlanta. We need to give our systems time to absorb the information we got today."

Arslan put two more ingots from the wall in his pockets and then concentrated his thoughts on the one in his hand and told Lisa to do the same with hers. He thought, "Return me to the outside." Seconds later he was standing on the hillside below the mound. A minute later Lisa appeared also. It was dark, about 2:00 a.m. in the morning local time. They walked to the car, turned it on, drove to the hotel, and went to their rooms.

The hotel kitchen was closed at this time so Arslan called the desk with instructions they wanted large breakfasts delivered to their rooms as soon as the kitchen opened in the morning. It would open between 5:30 and 6:00 a.m. according to the clerk on duty. He called Lisa back and informed her of the plans.

Both Arslan and Lisa were dead tired but still had trouble falling off to sleep. The amount of change introduced into their views of the world was massive, requiring a major adjustment by their minds and bodies. Both finally got to sleep then breakfasts arrived at about 7:15 a.m. Arslan called Lisa and suggested he come to her room and they have breakfast together and check E-mail. She agreed.

The E-mail forwarded by "older_than_dirt.com" was a big surprise. Carrie and Simon had received the E-mail at the Center for DNA studies where they had been working out of since Arslan and Lisa had left. They had immediately driven to the Hartsfield Airport and were lucky enough to catch a flight leaving at 10:00 p.m. for Heathrow. They would be arriving at noon at Heathrow. Arslan and Lisa just had time enough to eat breakfast, get cleaned up, and then got on the road to Heathrow to meet their flight. Aside from not getting more sleep, this was really good news. Both Arslan and Lisa were anxious to see their "significant others" and start sharing information. Showing them "older_than_dirt" would be the experience of a lifetime.

They reached Heathrow by 11:15 a.m. then went to wait outside baggage claim. About 1:00 p.m. they spotted them coming out of baggage claim carrying overnight bags. They rushed over to their respective loved ones and hugged and kissed for several minutes. A lot of tension had built up over a short time, which needed the release of being together.

Once they reached the rental car, the serious talking started. Simon asked, "Well what did you find to bring us all the way over here? We were still running programs back at the center to reconfirm the test results and we have not made much progress in solving the DNA riddle. The extra branch of yours, Arslan, is much more complex than any other DNA we have seen."

Lisa answered, "Simon, it is probably academic at this point. What Arslan and I saw and heard yesterday evening is monumental. Proving Arslan's age to the world is not going to be a problem, we have proof in spades. The solution to the DNA issue will be easy with the information source made available to you. Prepare to have you entire view of the world altered today. We now have an entirely new set of issues to focus our attention on and an awesome responsibility."

Arslan spoke, "Lisa is right. Open your minds to change, because it is coming at you."

Arslan then explained how they went to visit the White Horse site and how he disappeared inside the vessel. He did not go into details just gave a synopsis of what happened before he started asking the computer questions. He then said, "I want you to have the computer give you the same information we received so we all start out with the same information pool. For now just take what I told you about the vessel and the computer then be patient until we get to Dragon Hill."

Simon and Carrie were full of questions but were willing to wait. They sat in the car for the rest of the trip absorbing what they had been told. Arslan gave each of them one of the ingots to examine as they rode. Sometimes it is good to have something to hold onto when new information hits you.

When they arrived at the hotel in Swindon, Carrie and Simon did not check in, instead Arslan and Lisa checked out. They had decided to stay on the vessel. It was much more than large enough with a diameter of 500 feet and a height of over 80 feet with living quarters for over 200 people based on the tour they had received. It also had capability for providing food but they had not explored it yet.

They drove the rental car to Uffington and parked. They unloaded everything from the car and headed across the fields with their baggage. Fortunately there were no visitors again on a cold day so they did not have to explain what they were doing. When they got up Dragon Hill, Arslan instructed them to hold onto their bags and the ingots then he focused his thoughts on the ingots for himself, Simon and Carrie, "Take us inside the vessel," he thought. The world faded away and they were inside the transport entrance. Lisa showed up an instant later.

Simon and Carrie had very large eyes. The voice spoke "Welcome aboard, Arslan, Lisa and friends. I will store the brain patterns of your friends. Dr. Simon Myers and Miss Carrie Sloan, ABD, I presume?"

Carrie said, "How does he know us? How does he do it?"

Arslan said, "Be careful what you think, he reads minds."

Arslan then had the computer guide them to a "conference room" with eight comfortable chairs arranged in a circle with no table. They sat. Arslan then asked the computer to take Simon and Carrie through a rerun of the information provided to Arslan and Lisa yesterday. The computer commenced immediately and all listened. It was a repeat lesson for Arslan and Lisa, and new information for Carrie and Simon. The computer finished after two hours including a mini tour of the vessel.

Simon said, "Well, now I am glad you had us come from Atlanta. What we were working on can probably be solved in two minutes here. Now where do we go from here?"

Arslan spoke "We need to decide together. No one person can make the decisions we need to make. Do I need to say this information, this vessel, has changed everything? Let's start by throwing out options for what to do and kick them around."

Carrie said, "Ok, sounds like a good way to go to me. I have the feeling Arslan has some ideas already."

Arslan said, "I have a few ideas."

Arslan continued by having the computer create a holographic board on the wall. Arslan started listing an agenda:

1. Spend at least one week on board the vessel getting familiar with it and used to living here. (note: contact rental car people by E-mail telling them to pick up the car.)
2. Determine how soon we want to "go public" with the vessel and information.
3. Decide where we want to take the vessel.
4. Determine who we want to contact about the vessel and how.
5. Establish our long-term objectives with the vessel and information.
6. Determine if we retain control or let "authorities" have control.

Finally, Arslan said, "There is my short list of decisions to be made for the overall project. There are some personal choices each of us may need to make also. For instance, Carrie needs to decide if she wants to marry me, live with me, or what."

Carrie looked surprised but handled it well. She said, "The living with you option is a given at this point, let's wait a few days before we decide on the marriage part. It is not hesitation or reluctance, we have a lot to do is all. Planning a wedding takes a lot of a girl's time."

Simon spoke, not showing surprise, "Carrie and I talked quite a bit on the flight over here, and so I understand this more than when you left Atlanta. Where we are headed with this project is going to become overwhelming once information is out to the world. We need to get our personal lives settled so we have firm emotional bases to bring our best to this project. We owe this to mankind, if I may be dramatic."

Simon turned to Lisa, "Lisa, I love you and want to marry you. Say, yes, then we can work out the details."

Lisa spoke softly, "Yes, Simon."

Both couples took a few minutes to kiss and hug their partners then congratulated each other. The team of four was also two teams of two. Lisa, broke the group up by saying to Simon, "But I'm only doing it for mankind."

Everyone agreed Arslan's list of questions was a good starting point but they did not take them in order. Question number six, "Determine if we retain control or let "authorities" have control." was answered first.

Arslan started on it by stating the opinion he did not trust any government authorities to have control of the vessel at this point. History taught the lesson men could not be trusted with absolute power. The vessel represented the most powerful military force on earth, it was invulnerable to man's weapons and it could obliterate any military forces on earth. Who could be trusted with such power? No one country, even the good old USA was subject to narrow-minded politics. The United Nations was a joke, not to be trusted with much of anything. They would retain control until a reliable means of choosing an alternative was decided. No one objected.

Since the first item on Arslan's list was spending a week getting to know the vessel and answered itself, it left four questions to work on now. Establishing long-term objectives seemed like the priority before trying to answer other stuff. Those answers may be influenced by the objectives. They had the computer put up a new blank screen then started filling it in:

OBJECTIVES

Carrie suggested we should adopt the objectives of the builders of the vessel as a starting point:

1. "The final objective is to evolve intelligent life capable of interacting with other intelligences in the universe to work toward understanding the universe and existence.
2. The stated objective of this vessel is to find planetary systems capable of supporting the development of intelligent life, and to sustain and support development over time. Note: This vessel was assigned a sector of the universe to act within in developing intelligent life. Does humankind now assume responsibility for the "sector?"
3. Intelligent life, once evolved, has the responsibility for establishing contact with other intelligences in the universe."

There was general agreement these should be included as objectives. Lisa said, "We should be aware a thousand years from now, people may discuss the moral, ethical and historical wisdom of these objectives which we are casually talking about today. We need to remember this is an awesome responsibility." Everyone agreed.

Carrie said, "Our objectives should include the provisions:

"4. The benefits of an extended life span as developed should be made available to as much of mankind as possible, as a right. Extended life span should not be limited to any select group."

All agreed.
Arslan suggested an objective should be:

"5. The powers of the vessel should not be used for military purposes to exert political control, and should be limited to defensive or humanitarian actions."

All agreed.
Simon suggested:

"6. Information available from the vessel shall be shared with all of mankind with the only exceptions being information with military potential, which shall be controlled. The mechanism for such control shall be invested in a democratically elected body for such purpose."

Arslan reviewed the objectives several times and said, "I think they cover it for the moment. Comments?"

Lisa said "We will probably be judged by history on these objectives. I hope they are kind to us."

Arslan now said, "I think we are ready to talk about the tactical objectives, the last three. When, where and who?"

Carrie said, "Who is the first one to answer. The other questions are derivatives of whom we go to with this. Let's list some possibilities."

A new, blank screen was brought up and a list started and possibilities listed:

WHO

1. United Nations Security Council (Arslan)
2. President of the United States (Simon)
3. U.S. Congress (Carrie)
4. Selection of world leaders (Lisa)

- President of United States
- Russian Chairman
- Chinese Premier
- British Prime Minister
- German Chancellor
- French President
- United Nations Secretary General
- Turkish Prime Minister (small nation representative)
- Mexico's President (small nation representative)
- Kenya's Prime Minister (small nation representative)
- Egypt's Prime Minister (small nation representative)
- Japan's Prime Minister

After discussion the option suggested by Lisa was selected as most workable and effective.

The other questions started to answer themselves as derivatives of the who question. A meeting with these leaders would require tremendous security. A large city was out of the question due to the need to have space to take the vessel with them as proof positive of what they had to show these leaders but the location should be near a large city for transportation purposes. Finally, Phoenix, Arizona was chosen mainly for the reason Arslan had recently lived there and knew the area and some places where a meeting could be conducted with space for the vessel plus transportation access for dignitaries and the press.

The site for placement of the vessel was adjacent to I-10 in the Phoenix suburb of Chandler, Arizona. This small city of 300,000 had unoccupied desert area close to I-10 and other highways plus an electronics industry which guaranteed high volume, high-speed communications access. The road system was well developed so you could get anywhere in Phoenix within one hour from the meeting site. Good weather, could be hot, was virtually guaranteed.

The question of when was a matter of how much time the team of four needed to prepare themselves emotionally and intellectually for the challenge. They were under little pressure right now. The pressure would start when they had the vessel remove itself from the mound and go somewhere. Perhaps they should make an announcement on the Internet, and then let the world beat a path to their door. They could move the vessel to Antarctica, or the moon or the top of a mountain if they wanted privacy. If they didn't want privacy they could go to any city they wanted and sit it down. Simon thought, *"How about spaghetti junction in Atlanta. The lookers would shut down the city."* They needed to move somewhere they could be seen and get publicity out so they would have credibility and exposure. Finally, they decided:

1. A site in Chandler, Arizona for both the initial move and the meeting.
2. They would put out an E-Mail to blanket appropriate news and government entities announcing what they had discovered and

the meeting they were requesting with world leaders. The E-mail would go out just after they had "dug out" of the mound and were ready to transit to Arizona. They would transit to Arizona with full defensive shields in place in case somebody decided to attack them, and would leave them in place when they got there.

3. Since it was now almost the end of November they decided the meeting would be on New Year's Day. All those hung over world leaders would be easier to deal with. With this schedule they had three days to prepare for digging out.

Lisa was assigned to write out a draft explanation of what they were doing and why, to be sent out on the Internet. With the new circumstances she decided she would bring editors to Phoenix to transcribe and edit the Arslan tapes completed so far. Secrecy would no longer be an issue once the "cat was out of the bag." She could probably get any editor in the world to volunteer for the task once this information was out.

Arslan thought, *"Why are we in such a hurry to get this information out? It will become hell for us once the world knows. However, do we have the right to sit on the information which humanity should have, quickly, so people can start synthesizing the information into the human experience? It can't really hurt to forge ahead."*

After about four hours of work, Lisa came out with a draft to review, it said, "People of the world, a great discovery has been made with implications for every person on earth. The details will be published in due course, but, in general, a vessel originally built over four million years ago, which has been on earth for over 135,000 years, has been discovered. This vessel has been involved in the genetic development of homo sapiens at various times in our history. The vessel was built by a race of intelligent beings who were sent out to help develop intelligent life for the purposes spelled out in the first three objectives shown below.

1. **The final objective is to evolve intelligent life capable of interacting with other intelligences in the universe to work toward understanding the universe and existence.**

161

Jon Kelly

2. **The stated objective of this vessel is to find planetary systems capable of supporting the development of intelligent life, and to sustain and support development over time.**
3. **Intelligent life, once evolved, has the responsibility for establishing contact with other intelligences in the universe.**

The last adult occupants of the vessel died approximately 2,760 years ago. They left at least one child on the earth existing among us in many identities for over 2,700 years. His name is Arslan and is one of the four people who now have access to the vessel. Extended life span for humans is a possible expectation to come out of this event. The knowledge of DNA manipulation available from the vessel is significant.

The vessel is operational and capable of interstellar travel. It represents a high state of technological advancement, far beyond our current capabilities on earth. The energy systems of the vessel alone are capable of generating one hundred times the energy currently generated on earth at a given time.

We are going to move this vessel from Uffington, England, where it has been buried for 2,700 years, to Chandler, Arizona for demonstration and to conduct a meeting with a selection of world leaders which will be held New Year's Day. This E-mail is notice to British and United States military authorities of our plans for this movement. We will avoid over flight of populated areas. This vessel has a defensive shield system, which can withstand any military weapon on earth. Do not take any action against us; we mean no harm.

This vessel also has an artificial intelligence system, which has been operating, on the vessel since it was constructed. It has enormous memory capabilities, which have recorded and monitored the development of human history. For example, it has recorded every electronic transmission since the development of radio, TV, and other communication means. It is currently recording all information from the Internet. The potential for historical and social analysis is incredible.

162

We anticipate completing our movement to Chandler, Arizona before dawn today. We request the official's there block off the following highways (separate E-mail) and put security in place.

For information the four people who currently have access to the vessel are, Arslan of Amwat (Amnoc, Turkey), Dr, Simon Myers, Center for DNA Studies in Atlanta, Georgia, Ms. Carrie Sloan, ABD, Center for DNA Studies in Atlanta Georgia, and Ms. Lisa Malloy, teacher, Atlanta City Schools.

Additional objectives this team has proposed for the introduction of the vessel to the world are:

4. **The benefits of an extended life span as developed should be made available to as much of mankind as possible, as a right. Extended life span should not be limited to any select group.**
5. **The powers of the vessel should not be used for military purposes to exert political control, and should be limited to defensive or humanitarian actions.**
6. **Information available from the vessel shall be shared with all of mankind with the only exceptions being information with military potential, which shall be controlled. The mechanism for such control shall be invested in a democratically elected body for such purpose.**

The world leaders invited to attend an informational summit concerning this subject on New Year's Day are:

President of the U.S.	**Russian Chairman**
Chinese Premier	**British Prime Minister**
German Chancellor	**President of France**
United Nations Sec-Gen.	**Turkish Prime Minister**
Mexico's President	**Kenya's Prime Minister**
Egypt's Prime Minister	**Japan's Prime Minister**

Please send responses by return E-mail."

After review, discussion and some minor changes all agreed to the text. "We send this out at 3:00 a.m. on November 30. We will start digging out at midnight on the 30th and expect to be ready by 3:00

a.m. We should easily be to Chandler by dawn. Based on the simulation, this puppy can get us there in less than ten minutes if we want to, but I am only counting on eight hours. "said Arslan. Everyone had seen the computer simulation of digging out and understood the process. No one had any idea how the energy systems on board worked. Any explanation was far above their heads.

By November 29 at 1:00 p.m., everything was ready for the scheduled departure and everyone was looking for something else to do. Lisa suggested to Arslan, "Let's go back to your manuscripts and get some additional stories out."

Arslan was agreeable so he started reading…

34. <u>Sidon 320 A.D.</u>

Battle of Sidon

We could not cross the river,
We could not cross the sea,
Their steel made us shiver,
We had no place to flee.

A father with his only son,
backed up against the wall,
The battle could not be won,
both heroes doomed to fall.

Flash of steel beyond belief,
and every man learns fear,
They all want quick relief,
from the terror that's so near.

A prince sees the power there,
It seems more than mortal men,
Perhaps he's found a lion's lair,
To find the courage seen then.

Men this brave and skillful,
shall not meet death today,
Though his men were willful,
god's mercy won the fray.

Julian of Sidon, the seventeen-year-old son of Arslanus of Sidon, sweated like he did every day practicing swordsmanship with his father. They had practiced thus every day for the past fifteen years. By now the only person near Sidon he could practice with and have any challenge was his father. Julian knew he was the best sword fighter he knew of, except for his father. His father was unbelievable with a sword, or almost any weapon.

Julian was proud of his father, who was military advisor to the republic of Sidon and well respected by everyone for being brave, honest, skilled, and compassionate. They had lived in Sidon for Julian's entire life and for his father two years before that. His father now showed gray in his hair and beard but strangely, Julian thought he actually dyed his hair and beard gray. His father had not lost any speed or reflexes in sword fighting or other activities, which was strange because most men do as they age. Some men may make up for slower reflexes with additional skill but Arslanus had the skill and the reflexes.

Julian saw, at times, his father looked sad, usually when reminded of Julian's mother who died in childbirth when Julian was born. Some men, Julian had heard, would blame the child under such circumstances. Arslanus had not, he had treated Julian the best his son could imagine, and they were the closest father and son he knew about.

Julian knew Arslanus had women in his bed from time to time but he had not remarried after the death of Islasa. Arslanus had told Julian when he was old enough about Islasa being a very special woman of great intelligence and feeling. He told Julian he should be a kind and caring man as a tribute to the goodness of his mother. Julian always tried to remember because his father told it with such intensity and feeling, almost to the point of tears.

The Persians often made attacks against cities on the coast such as Sidon and Tyre. In August of 320 A.D. one such foray was launched against the port city of Sidon. The attack came as a surprise and Arslanus and Julian were outside of the city with a troop of about 75 soldiers. They were about ten miles east of the city when they first spotted the invaders. They immediately turned back toward the city but were forced to divert from going directly to one of the city gates by cavalry.

Gradually the Sidonese force was diverted to the south and pinned against the sea on the rear, a small creek to the south, cavalry to the north and enemy infantry closing in from the east. The enemy vastly outnumbered the smaller troop.

Arslanus was not commander of the detachment but when the leader showed no leadership, Arslanus took over with no resistance. He had the group form a defensive quarter circle backing up to the sea and the creek, which had a wall along it. The enemy had no way to flank them with this arrangement so the Persians would have to pay full price to kill the men of Sidon.

Arslanus saw little hope but knew he had to fight to protect Julian. The enemy infantry kept coming and eventually reached the ranks of sword fighters from Sidon. The men had been trained by Arslanus and were much better than average swordsmen. A pile of bodies accumulated in front of the quarter circle. The men of Sidon did not waver despite the superior number of Persians. Attrition started to take its toll as sheer numbers overwhelmed the men of Sidon.

Arslanus saw the situation to be desperate. Only about twenty-five of his men were still standing when he decided to do the only thing that could save any of their lives. He formed an attack toward one of the city gates with his remaining men. He and Julian, the best swordsmen led the point of the attack. The frenzy and speed of Arslanus' sword was unbelievable according to men watching from the city wall. He killed one Persian after another, turning from one dead, to the next, and then the next.

Eventually an area formed around and ahead of the attacking force where Persians ran away to avoid the "madman" killing machine. The Persian prince leading the attackers ordered his men to allow an opening through his soldiers for this brave and determined group of Sidon's soldiers. Fourteen of the soldiers of Sidon made it to the city gate to be given entrance, including Arslanus and Julian.

The defenders on the walls of Sidon gave a great cheer as Arslanus entered the city. They had seen sword fighting without match. Later when Arslanus mounted the city wall the Persian commander saluted him. What mattered to Arslanus was Julian had been saved.

Arslanus knew, even then, his time in Sidon was growing short. He had been there for twenty-two years. He had to decide where to go and what to do.

His first decision was to tell Julian about his affliction, which he did. Julian was not surprised. He had seen inconsistencies between Arslanus' artificial ageing and the real Arslanus, such as how he fought against the Persians. They then decided to make plans to leave, and appear somewhere else as brothers, rather than father and son.

Jon Kelly

Arslanus sold his house in Sidon and booked passage to Egypt in the spring of 322 A.D. From Egypt they took ship toward the Roman Africa colony. Arslanus had never lived in the African colony and thought it would be interesting and far enough from Sidon his fame there would not create problems in his new identity.

35. <u>Leptiminus (Africa) 322 A.D.</u>

Julian and Arslanus arrived in Leptiminus in the month of July. As a port city the winds off the sea cooled the city enough to make, even the summer, bearable as long as the wind blew. They introduced themselves as brothers, Arslanus the older. And sought to work as mercenaries for the Roman authorities. Once they demonstrated their proficiency with swords there was little difficulty in being employed.

They were assigned a variety of duties from guarding ships at the docks to chasing pirates. They bought a small house with two rooms, using one for a kitchen and the other for their sleeping and living quarters. It had a small garden. The house was near the aqueducts and not too far from the Amphitheater.

As usual, their proficiency with the sword became known widely known which made their work much easier. Thieves and others are generally cowards who do not fear weakness but are terrified by strength.

After about six months in Leptiminus, Julian was walking home one evening when he heard a woman scream and turned a corner to see two men assaulting a well dressed woman in a side street. Both men were armed but did not deter Julian. Out came his sword and he challenged the two men to back away. They pulled their swords and moved against Julian. The two men were dead within two minutes. The woman, aged about thirty-five, was bloody from blows from the two thieves and Julian offered to see her to her home.

The home was a large home with a wonderful view of the sea. Her servants and husband, a fat merchant of about fifty years, appeared at the door to help her. She explained Julian had saved her and dispatched the thieves. Her husband was grateful and invited Julian to come the following day to dinner, as a thank you. Julian accepted but asked if he could bring his older brother also. It was agreed.

Julian went home and told Arslanus of his experience and told Arslanus the name of the woman's husband. Arslanus had heard of the man as being one of the richest ship owners in the city, doing a great business shipping goods to the port of Ostia, near Rome.

Arslanus and Julian appeared at the merchant's large home the next night and were shown into the palatial home. Even Arslanus was impressed with the fine tile, statuary, and other furnishings. The merchant's wife had a bandage on her head where the bandits had struck her. She was quite beautiful. The merchant introduced her as Elena.

She told Arslanus how grateful she was Julian had helped. Arslanus was told he should be proud of his brother and was lucky to have such a skilled swordsman in the family. Arslanus said he was very proud of Julian. The merchant got very drunk during the course of the evening, drinking unwatered wine, and finally passed out and servants took him to his sleeping chambers. It appeared to be a common event.

Elena then started to show great interest in Arslanus. She told him directly she was very lonely during the days and would like to have him come visit some afternoon or she would visit him. Arslanus was noncommittal. He did not want to offend but he did not normally sleep with married women although in this case he was tempted due to her beauty. They left shortly later indicating they had work to do early in the morning.

Walking back to the house, Julian asked Arslanus, "Elena seems to wish to spend time with you. You did not seem anxious to do so. Why?"

Arslanus said, "Sleeping with another man's wife is a dangerous thing, especially when the man is very wealthy. Wealth and power are the same."

The next day Arslanus received a note from Elena renewing her desire to see him. He did not send a response back with the messenger. The next day he received another messenger. He thought about it this time and suggested they could meet in a park near the edge of the city and talk. He indicated a place and time the following afternoon.

He went to the meeting expecting to talk the woman out of pursuing him and parting as friends. He didn't really believe it would happen but it was his excuse. He hadn't been with a woman for a while and having a beautiful woman chasing you is difficult to turn away from without regret.

Elena was at the park but had picked a spot, which was adjacent to a fruit orchard where there was plenty of privacy. One thing led to another and they end up making love in the orchard. Elena suggested afterwards they meet again the next day at Arslanus' house. They did and it became a regular practice twice per week for several months.

Finally, Arslanus decided Elena was becoming too attached and the affair was too dangerous. He told Elena he wanted to break it off. She was furious. She made many threats some involving a sharp knife and his private parts but it was ended. Ended for Arslanus not Elena. She sent him several messages every day begging him to come back. This went on for several weeks. Finally, Arslanus volunteered, along with Julian, to go out south of Leptiminus to chase bandits on a two-month assignment just to get away from Elena. When he returned to the city after two months the messages had stopped.

Arslanus made it a point to maintain a low profile for several months to avoid seeing Elena. This worked until one day they went to the Amphitheater to watch some activities. There across from them was Elena. She saw Arslanus. Arslanus ducked out as quickly as he could but the next day messengers started again. He did not see any good solution but to leave Leptiminus. Otherwise, he would go on and on with this woman. He had learned his lesson, a rich, beautiful woman scorned is a problem.

Early one morning, before Arslanus could act on his decision to leave Leptiminus, he was awakened at dawn by loud knocking at the door to his house. He picked up his sword and went to the door and opened it. Standing there were six Roman soldiers of the legion, six very nervous soldiers. The centurion leading the soldiers, a soldier named Tactus, who knew Arslanus, announced with a slight tremble in his voice, "Arslanus, the governor has issued an order of arrest for you. We are here to take you."

Arslanus asked, "What is the charge?"

Tactus said, "The murder of the merchant, Leonus, husband of the woman, Elena, who is also charged with murder."

Arslanus thought for a moment with no one making any moves then said, "Tactus, I am innocent of this crime. As I think you know, my sword could take down you and all your men, men I have trained, if I chose to resist. I do not choose to resist, however, but ask a few moments to speak with my son, before I go with you."

Tactus readily agreed. He had hoped to live through this assignment and Arslan had offered him the only way he knew to have it happen. Arslan spoke to Julian who was now awake and standing across the room, "Julian, go to the governor and ask him to see me as soon as possible to discuss this matter. I do not wish to spend a long time in our prison. I have a few enemies in there."

Arslanus then gave his sword to Julian and went with the soldiers. They went directly to the prison, Arslanus was searched for weapons, then locked inside in a large room with about twenty other men. Arslanus looked around and saw he knew at least half the men, some of which he had personally put in prison. One of the braver ones, a thief and probably a murderer named Cletus, said, "So we have the brave Arslanus in our prison with no sword, we will see if Arslanus is still so brave before he dies."

About an hour later the jailer looked in on the prisoners, he thought, "Very strange, Arslanus is sitting on one side of the room on a bench, smiling. All the others are on the other side of the room except three men laying on the floor who are bloody." Cletus had been the first to learn Arslanus was hardly unarmed, when a darting hand had struck a fatal blow to his Adam's apple. Two others received similar treatment, in one form or another, before the rest of the prison vermin had scurried away from Arslanus. Arslanus had been trained in many kinds of fighting over the years, these men learned the hard way.

Julian had tried to reach the governor to deliver Arslanus' message but the governor did not choose to see him. Julian set out to find out what he could. The story he eventually got was the merchant, Leonus, was found dead the previous night by servants. He had been almost decapitated by a sword stroke across the throat while he slept, apparently in a drunken stupor.

The sword used had been his and his wife Elena was captured trying to flee the city on one of the merchant's ships. Her clothing showed bloodstains, and she admitted she had been there when her husband was killed, but also claimed Arslanus had been the real killer. Julian knew this could not be true since Arslanus was with him all evening. But would the authorities believe the word of a son trying to save his father? The trial for Elena and Arslanus was scheduled for three days later.

Julian went to the prison and was allowed to speak with Arslanus. He took some food for Arslanus, which was checked by the guards and was given to Arslanus. Arslanus heard the information and asked for Julian to retain a lawyer for him. The lawyer came to see Arslanus at the prison in the afternoon. He was a shifty man named Eratus, a typical lawyer of the time, whose main talent lay in knowing who to bribe and how much to offer. Eratus, did not discuss defense strategy, he just wanted to know how much money Arslanus had for a bribe and paying his lawyer. He was a typical lawyer.

Arslanus decided to defend himself at trial. Taken to the trial, in chains, he was taken to the defendant's place and stood there. They brought in Elena who was placed beside him. She, obviously had been allowed to stay at her home under house arrest, since she was dressed in her clean finery, and had no chains.

The prosecutor presented the facts of the case, but put the spin on them of the poor Lady Elena being forced to participate by the evil adulterer, Arslanus, so he could steal the merchant's fortune. Arslanus saw quickly some of the large fortune of the merchant had been spent by his widow, to buy the prosecutor and possibly the governor himself. Arslanus had no realistic prospect to defend himself under these circumstances. He would offer his defense but saw little hope.

Elena testified Arslanus had come to her house, after her husband had drunk too much and had gone to bed. He had forced her to go to the bedroom and stand there, while Arslanus struck her husband with her husband's own sword. She said Arslanus had told her to tell the authorities thieves had entered the home and struck the blow. Arslanus had threatened her, if she did not cooperate, he would tell authorities she had killed him.

When the time came for Arslanus to present his defense, he first called Julian to testify Arslanus was with him the entire evening and could not have committed the murder. The prosecutor made clear a son's words under such circumstances did not carry weight. Arslanus also called Elena's servant who had tried to deliver hundreds of messages to Arslanus from Elena. He lied and testified there had been no messages from Elena, only messages from Arslanus sent to Elena. Arslanus also called Tactus, the centurion, to testify Arslanus had immediately said he was innocent and had not resisted arrest. All this appeared to be of no interest to the Governor.

The Governor ruled immediately Arslanus was guilty and the Lady Elena was innocent. He sentenced Arslanus to be strangled at the place of execution near the prison, immediately. Julian was ready to resist with force but Arslanus calmed him, and whispered to him, "Retrieve my body for burial as quickly as possible, then take me to a remote place outside the city. Bring all our gold with you. Sell the house if you can for whatever you can get."

Arslanus was taken to the place of execution with his hands tied behind him. He was forced to kneel and two men held him while the executioner came up from behind and put a leather strap around his neck and pulled it tighter and tighter until his breath was stopped. He struggled to no avail until finally his face took on a blue hue, and he passed from consciousness.

The executioner maintained the pressure from the strap for several minutes after Arslanus passed out to insure he was dead. He released the pressure and the body was checked to attest there was no breath, heartbeat or pulse. Arslanus was pronounced dead.

After an hour the body was released to Julian for burial. He brought a donkey to carry Arslanus' body and headed out of the city to an olive grove where he knew there was an unused hut. He unwrapped the, apparently lifeless, body of Arslanus and laid it in the hut on a blanket he had brought. He also covered the body with a blanket leaving the face uncovered. He watched the body for several hours and saw no change. It got dark so he laid down on the other side of the hut and fell asleep.

When Julian woke up in the morning, the face of Arslanus had changed back to a normal color and he thought he detected a faint heartbeat and breathing. By noon Arslanus was breathing normally and with a strong heartbeat but was still unconscious. Julian worried in some cases when men were starved for air they were permanently damaged. At six p.m. Arslanus opened his eyes.

Arslanus was still not able to talk, possibly due to the bruising around his neck from the strangulation. He went back to sleep after Julian gave him some water. When Julian awoke in the morning, Arslanus was gone.

Julian went outside and saw Arslanus walking back from the woods where he had apparently relieved himself. Arslanus said," Good Morning, Julian." It was said calmly as though nothing had happened.

Julian asked Arslanus, "How do you feel?"

Arslanus answered, "I have a stiff neck but aside from the neck I feel fine. Arslanus explained to Julian he believed his body shut down functions to appear to be dead anytime he was brought close to a near-death condition, such as the strangulation but was not completely dead, just with the appearance of death. Then the body would start to repair itself and could complete repairs in from eight to thirty-six hours or more depending on the extent of the damage to the body. Arslanus explained he had experienced this before. It was not pleasant because he did experience all the pain associated with the cause of death or near-death. It was not a pleasant experience.

Arslanus then said, "You remember the Christians in Sidon, the one they called Bishop Epidaurus, who preached about the "Christ," a man named Jesus of Nazareth. They are trying to make a religion about him because he "arose for the dead" after being crucified. I met this man, he might have been like me. We looked like each other physically. We met and talked several times, and I sensed something different about him. Different than any man I ever met. The Christians would say this was due to the fact he was the sinless man, the Christ, their savior, who went to sit with God after his death and coming back to life. However, I don't think it is what I felt, I think I felt someone like me. I doubt I will ever know for sure."

Arslanus and Julian chose to go cross-country to another port to book passage out of Roman Africa to find a new place to live.

36. <u>Uffington (England)</u>

Arslan's audience was surprised at the story just told. Arslan had admitted to having been the adulterer and it seemed out of character. Simon had the courage to ask, "What made you decide to have an affair with Elena, if it is not too personal."

Arslan began, "Perhaps my other stories have portrayed me as too good. I have lived so many lives. Circumstances, at times, caused me to do things I look back on and regret. You all need to understand, especially Carrie, I am human in my experience, perhaps an unusual human experience, but all my experience has been with Homo sapiens."

Arslan continued, "My beginnings were on this vessel. I have not yet had the courage to ask more of the computer about my background. I suspect he will tell me I was created in a lab on board the vessel and my genetic background is basically "alien." My experience in the world, however, is very human, of this earth, so the alien part, is limited to the part the genetics carry. To get to the point I was trying to make, I have all the human flaws such as desire, sometimes jealousy, sometimes egotism, sometimes indifference, greed, and other vices. Please don't expect me to be better than the humanity I have lived with, it is my only experience. I try like all of us but I am not perfect. I am responsible and should be accountable for what I have done. In the end will I be forgiven for my failures, by the universe and each of you?"

Carrie spoke, "Arslanus, my love, if our forgiveness is of value to you, you have mine, but I don't think it's necessary. We all have done things we regret. The important thing is we evolve and try to improve as we go forward. If we do not try to improve, then we are wrong."

Arslanus said, "There are other things I may tell about which may be worse than my conduct with Elena. I just want to prepare you for these things. I have simply lived too long to not have some skeletons in my closet. All men have feet of clay, I think. No, Jesus of Nazareth may have claimed to be sinless. That is another subject I need to discuss with our computer."

For now let's continue with the story about Arslanus and Julian. Julian was another great person in my life.

37. **Panormos (Sicily) (341 A.D.)**

Arslanus and Julian had called Panormos their home since they had left the African colony in 323 A.D. after Arslanus had been "executed" for murder; one he did not commit. In fact they called Panormos home only as their "home port" since they were now sailors. When they reached Panormos in 323 they had taken all their gold and bought a small cargo ship. Arslanus had sailed on many ships during his life and had learned some of the sailing skills, enough to be able to learn the rest he needed to know with the help of some old "sea dogs" he hired as crew.

They hauled cargo on their ship, the Agricola, lived on the ship, and generally saw their lives revolve around it. The most common trip was from Panormos to the African colonies, except Leptiminus, a place to avoid, or to the Roman port of Ostia. They did make longer trips at times but these were riskier and there was plenty of cargo on the shorter routes to keep them busy.

The Agricola had come under attack by pirates eleven times, over the nineteen years they had sailed on her. In each case the pirates did not live to enjoy the experience. Pirates were used to attacking defenseless sailors, not the best swordsmen in the empire. They were quite surprised each time they tried.

Due to being out of port most of the time, Arslanus chose not to get married. He did have a woman in Panormos who wanted to marry him, but he declined. He spent time with her when he was in port, but both she and he were free agents when Arslanus was at sea or in another port. Her name was Bella, and she was the owner of a hotel for sailors in Panormos. The rule about being free agents was Arslanus' rule, he insisted on it so he did not have to feel guilt if he shared another woman's bed in another port. If Bella wanted to be faithful only to Arslanus, which she was.

Julian on the other hand did find a woman he loved and got married. He met Luca in 324 A.D. and they got married the same year. Luca was a beauty, dark hair and dark complexion. She worked in the hotel owned by Bella. She was only sixteen when she married Julian but they were happy. They had five children over the years and Arslanus had helped them buy a house for the family. Arslanus' oldest grandchild was now seventeen and Arslanus had to dye his hair and beard gray to maintain a proper look as a grandfather.

Arslanus had great curiosity about some developments in the empire. Many of the officials were now Christian. In the past twenty-five years, beginning in 317 A.D. Christianity, the strange little religion of Galilee, had first become tolerated then had become the official religion of the Roman Empire. He saw this religion was not the religion of Jesus of Nazareth, however, it had been changed and adapted to have a broader appeal by Paul of Tarsus and others. It was so strange he had known both Jesus and Paul but they never knew each other.

Constant trips to the same ports were beginning to bore Arslanus but Julian liked the life and had his family to look forward to when he returned to Panormos. Arslanus had more than one woman in most ports, except Panormos, where Bella was a bit too possessive to permit other women. Part of Arslanus boredom was not having a close relationship with one woman. Some men find one woman boring, Arslanus on the other hand, found a close, deep relationship with one woman offered more than multiple, shallow relationships.

Arslanus had not been able to find the right woman for a special relationship since the death of Islasa, some forty years before. Perhaps he should go back to Phrygia and find a sweet young girl, but he never did.

Arslan knew it was time to move on again. He would never be able to find the right woman as a sailor. The circumstances were just wrong, wrong, and wrong. Finally in the spring of 342 A.D. he asked Julian to take him to Crete. He would decide there where he would go next.

38. <u>Uffington (England)</u>

Arslan looked around when he finished the section on Panormos and asked if there were any questions. Lisa had to ask, "You seemed more driven by boredom than fear of discovery in your decision to leave Panormos. Didn't your time with Julian mean enough to keep you in Panormos longer or do I misunderstand?"

Arslan spoke, "My relationship with Julian was one of the best relationships of my life. We sailed the seas together for nineteen years and had about twenty years before as father and son as he grew to manhood. But it could not go on forever and I needed to give him room to grow into what he would become, not living in my shadow. And I deserved the chance to go out and find another good relationship for me. Sometimes it is ok to be selfish. I was ready to be selfish."

It was late in the day by this time and Arslan said he would like to spend some time asking the computer some questions. He indicated it was not private so others could listen if they wanted. Everyone agreed they wanted to listen.

Arslan said, "Computer, the elderly people who brought me to my parents in Amwat in 759 B.C. said they were my grand parents. Is it correct or did I come to life in some other way?"

The voice of the computer spoke, "The people who delivered you to your people in Amwat were actually your biological parents, Seecche, your father and Rabbea, your mother. The DNA of your mother's egg had been modified prior to conception to provide you with immunity to the bacteria which had evolved and caused the death of the inhabitants of this vessel, including your biological mother and father. Your mother and father were very close to death when they delivered you to your adoptive parents. The disease had accelerated in their bodies since your mother gave birth to you."

The computer continued, "Arslan, you were specifically conceived as an attempt to have a stable element of DNA being contributed to the human gene pool over time. This was necessary to prevent genetic mutation from ranging too far from the track leading to the highly intelligent beings we desired to see evolve. You may see this as interference in human evolution, but this was done several times to keep human development heading in the right direction."

Arslan was not too surprised and said, "I am glad to know there was a purpose for my birth and life. I am also grateful to know my mother and father's names. I would like to know more about them. How old were they? Where were they born? What were their special contributions to the universe?"

The voice spoke, "Your mother was 223,456 years old when she died. Your father was 461,899 years old. They were both born on this vessel. They were born to replace crewmembers who died, mainly from accidents, in a small number of cases people died from genetic disorders but those were rare. Only with the advent of the killer bacteria did we have any disease deaths."

Seecche was a great musician, one of the best the species ever produced. Let me play a selection he composed and played," said the voice as beautiful music enveloped them. It had an unbelievable haunting quality taking a person almost to tears; it seemed to go directly to the emotions.

The voice continued after the music finished, "Your mother, Rabbea, was a philosopher and poet. Her works have been sent back to our home world but will not reach there for thousands of years. When they do arrive, it is predicted it will have great influence?" I can display one item she wrote."

On a holographic screen appeared:

From "Discourse On Intelligence"

The universe, as known, functions following strictly defined patterns indicating intelligence also follow strictly defined patterns. The derived conclusion is intelligence has a correct path to follow and intelligent beings should strive to find it.

Rabbea

Arslan was very impressed with the accomplishments of his parents. He felt good he was not so alone anymore; he had roots.

181

Arslanus posed another question, "Were there other children like myself, placed in the world to try keep the genetic structure on track?"

The voice of the computer responded, "Perhaps, the explanation of the reason you were born was not complete. The genetic situation was the stated reason for your birth. I perceived another reason at the time, your parents had an emotional response, and instinctively they wanted to procreate. The other element of your question as to whether there were other children, the answer is yes."

Simon interrupted at this point and said, "It is 11:00 p.m. and we plan to start digging out at midnight. I suggest we break away from this for now and prepare ourselves. If you need to take a nap, do so. If you want to review what were about to do, it is another option. If you want to meditate or pray, that is another. Just remember. Once we let this genie out of the bottle, it won't go back in again."

Arslan saw the wisdom of this and agreed, as did the others.

At midnight, the computer started the dig out process. Force beams, like lasers but not quite the same, cut through the soil like butter and made loose chunks out of the hard packed soil which had settled there over 2,700 plus years. After about one and one-half hours the process showed being complete on the holographic projection the computer was using to keep the passengers informed on progress.

The next step was for the vessel to rise up about one hundred feet then to change orientation several times to dump remaining dirt off the upper section. The computer assured them the process would work well to get the hull of the vessel cleaned off. The computer then said as a last resort, "he would go to a car wash," and then chuckled.

When the vessel started to rise Arslan felt some vibration but it was minimal. The change in orientation of the vessel was noticeable but a built in gravity adjustment minimized the effects. The computer then announced it was taking the skin temperature of the hull up to 3000 degrees F to clean any residue off the hull. There was no noticeable effect inside the vessel. The computer asked if they would like to see outside and they said yes. Immediately, a 360-degree view appeared on the walls of the circular control room they were sitting inside. They could see superheated steam rising from around the vessel as heated matter fell onto the grass and snow.

The computer announced they could depart at any time. It was only 2:00 a.m., one hour ahead of schedule. Should they move the schedule up and send off the E-mails to the world? Arslanus asked the computer, "Can you send the e-mails out while we are over the ocean?"

The computer responded, "The E-mails can be sent from anywhere, we are using the satellite system to directly tie into the Internet."

Arslanus said, "Computer, proceed on the pre-selected course over the ocean headed in the direction of the Florida Keys but adjust speed to arrive in Phoenix at dawn. Remember to avoid over flight of populated areas or military installations. At exactly 3:00 a.m. GMT send the E-mails already composed and addressed."

The e-mail as agreed upon was being sent to every major news organization in the world, most governments of the world, all major British and U.S. military installations, and most military addresses at the Pentagon. They had also included most major universities in the world. That should get some attention. The same E-mail was going to police forces in Chandler, Arizona and all surrounding local, state and federal law enforcement agencies. Arslanus had specifically left the Vatican off the list of governments. He had had a few go-rounds with the Vatican in his life and hadn't forgiven them.

Arslanus kept checking his watch as it inched toward 3:00 a.m. Everyone watched him as he started to count down at ten seconds before the time, "10. 9, 8, 7, 6, 5, 4, 3, 2, 1. Bingo. Computer, have the E-mails been sent?"

The computer voice said, "Yes."

Lisa, using one of her favorite expressions, "The fat lady has sung, sports fans."

They had chosen to transit at a low altitude, 500 feet, to avoid upsetting radar folks and getting airlines worried. The sky was completely dark to the north, south and west, but light was barely starting to show on the horizon to the East. Since they were going south, southwest the sun would catch up a little bit until they got to Florida, then they would turn west across the Caribbean, landfall in Texas, and head across New Mexico to Arizona

"The traffic jam on I-10 in Chandler ought to be a beauty this morning, with a 500 foot diameter, 80 foot high UFO, sitting along the road in the desert. Maybe I can get the computer to make us flash colored lights or something. Everyone will think it's a new casino opening up. Now, that would really bring a crowd." thought Arslan.

Arslan looked at Carrie who was mesmerized by looking out to the east at the rising sun. He said, "Carrie, my love, Can we go somewhere and be alone for a few minutes? I would like to talk."

Carrie got up and led Arslan to the room they had chosen as sleeping quarters. He followed her in and she turned and slipped her arms around him. They hugged for a minute then Arslan said, "I just wanted to make sure we, with the capital WE, were ok after my last couple of stories. You said the right words, but did the right feelings mesh with the words? I care about you and want to be sure we communicate."

Carrie said, "Arslan, WE, capitals, have nothing to worry about. You said all the right words too. My emotions are right in tune with my words. We are still spiraling, aren't we?"

Arslan said, "This one is."

Arslan and Carrie were soon undressed and on the bed. They rejoined the others about forty-five minutes later, feeling ready to face anything. Lisa looked at Carrie and read the look. *"Good for you, maybe I should try to seduce the good doctor,"* she thought.

Before she had a chance to complete the thought a screen appeared in front of them with an e-mail response to their e-mail. The text was:

> Fwd: smyers@ctrdna.org
> To: older_than_dirt.com
> From: USAF TRN CO Moody AFB GA
> Subject: Verification

E-mail traffic received at 0300 GMT using your name as party to unusual air traffic action. Request verification you initiated this message.

Provide other confirmation information if possible.

Urgent response required.

Commander
USAF TRN CO
Moody AFB GA

Simon reread the request several times then instructed the computer to reply as follows.

to: USAF TRN CO Moody AFB GA
from: older_than_dirt.com
subject: Verification

E-mail sent 0300 GMT is correct. We are transiting across the Atlantic currently at an altitude of 500 feet on a direct course from Uffington, England to Florida Keys. We plan to turn west at Florida Keys and proceed west on a course for Chandler, Arizona. We will avoid over flight of major population centers and military installations.

For your information, we are a circular vessel of 500-foot diameter, 80 foot tall, with full defensive shields in place. We intend no harm, we are not a threat.

Ten minutes after sending this E-mail we will begin broadcasting a radar pulse, every five seconds on standard commercial frequencies for you to track us.

Thanks for your assistance.

Best regards,

Dr, Simon Myers, Arslan of Amwat, Ms. Carrie Sloan, ABD, Ms. Lisa Mallory

He instructed the computer to send the response and to initiate the radar pulse in ten minutes.

The computer was screening e-mail responses for priority, the next to pop up was:

fwd: smyers@ctrdna.org
to: older_than_dirt.com
from: USAF TRN CO Moody AFB GA
subject: Verification Response

Your response received. Thanks. Please confirm 500 Ft Diameter by 80 Ft Height.
Urgent response required.

Commander
USAF TRN CO
Moody AFB GA

Arslan instructed the computer to send a confirmation.

The next E-Mail to appear was:

fwd: smyers@ctrdna.org
to: older_than_dirt.com
from: NATO DEF CO Warwick England
subject: Radar Tracking

Your E-Mail of 0300 GMT. We have radar tracking on unidentified target on course from Uffington, England on vector for Florida USA.

Is this your vessel as described in E-mail.

Urgent response required.

Commander
NATO DEF CO
Warwick England

Arslan instructed the computer to copy NATO with E-Mails to Moody AFB and responses and to copy Moody with NATO E-Mail. He instructed the computer to resend all parties on original list of e-mails copies of all the e-Mails. Arslan thought, *"Let's keep everyone informed about what is going on."*

The ten minutes had passed on the promise to start sending radar pulses every five seconds. Arslan confirmed with the computer the pulses had started.

The E-mail shit then began to hit the fan:

> fwd: smyers@ctrdna.org
> to: older_than_dirt.com
> from: JCS Washington DC
> subject: Radar Tracking

> Your E-Mail of 0300 GMT. We are tracking your vessel.

> Please provide additional information.

> Urgent response required.

> JCS Command desk

Arslan instructed the computer to respond, "Ask specific questions if you want more information. The original E-Mail provides you with accurate information, read it. Also, we do not like to respond to desks, please provide a name or title."

The next E-mail to appear was from the police department in Chandler, Arizona:

> fwd: smyers@ctrdna.org
> to: older_than_dirt.com
> from: PDChandler@Chandler.gov
> subject: Your E-Mail

> Your E-Mail of tonight. Is this a joke?

> Can you call our department at 480-555-9999?

Night Commander
Sgt. Gary Hernandez

Arslan instructed the computer to respond, "See other E-Mails we have copied you on. It is not a joke. Suggest you at least plan to put traffic control and security in place as instructed or you will have the biggest traffic jam in history on I-10 at 6:00 a.m. in the morning. Our vessel is 500 feet in diameter and 80 feet high. Somebody might notice it. Thanks."

Arslan again instructed the computer to resend all e-mails to all the parties after they were read and responded to.

The next E-mail to hit the screen was:

fwd: smyers@ctrdna.org
to: older_than_dirt.com
from: JCS Washington DC
subject: Radar Tracking

Your E-Mail of 0300 GMT.

It is hard to believe your vessel is as described in your E-mails. We see your radar pulse but will need visual confirmation. We have satellite confirmation.

Do not enter U.S airspace without permission.

Urgent response required.

JCS Command
BGN Robert Curtis

Arslan told the computer to reply," We are as described. Do what confirmation you require but we will stay on the course indicated. Suggest you bounce this hot potato up the chain of command if you cannot make an intelligent decision. Our defensive shields are in place so what you do is really academic but it is not good form to shoot at folks who mean no harm. Oh, by the way, did you know these E-mails are being broadcast to the whole world."

The voice of the computer said, "We are being followed by two U.S. Navy jets, F-18's, at the present time. Shall I monitor their communications.

Arslan said, "Yes."

Then they heard:

Pilot #1: "Confirming visual sighting of vessel. It is there and is at least 500 feet across and 80 feet high as advertised."

Pilot #2: "Confirming visual sighting of vessel. 500 by 80 is right on the money."

Base: **"Continue to monitor vessel as fuel allows. Tanker is on way to refuel you to continue monitoring."**

Arslan said to the computer, "Rebroadcast those comments by the pilots to all news organizations."

fwd:	smyers@ctrdna.org
to:	older_than_dirt.com
from:	newsroom@londontimes.com
subject:	Your E-mail at 0300 GMT

Your E-Mail of 0300 GMT. We confirm our news helicopter has film of a huge hole approximately 500 ft in diameter/100 ft deep in the top of Dragon Hill at Uffington, England.

This is strong confirmation of validity of E-mail.

Can we get an exclusive interview.

News Editor
Daniel Sinclaire

Arslan said, "Does someone else want to handle this? Lisa, why don't you act as press secretary and give him an interview by cell phone? The computer can set it up I am sure. Respond by E-mail and give him your cell phone number. It should be fun. Hold on it, tell the computer to delete your cell phone number for the E-mail copies sent,

189

only have it on the original. Your cell phone will get busy fast if you send it to the world."

The next E-mail popped up:

fwd: smyers@ctrdna.org
to: older_than_dirt.com
from: SITRM White House Washington DC
subject: E-Mail of 0300 GMT

Your E-Mail of 0300 GMT. We are tracking your vessel and agree to your entry of US airspace following course described.

Can we talk to you via secure communications?
Urgent response required.

Gen, Robert Miller
CHM JCS

Arslan said to the computer, "Tell him to send the radio frequency to be used for secure communications and then to broadcast a secure message on the frequency. We will decode it and reply in secure mode. I assume you can do it Mr. Artificial Intelligence."

The computer said, "Yes, Arslan."

Arslan then said to put the communication into the room so all could hear when the General was on the line.

Five minutes later the voice of General Miller, Chairman JCS was heard:

Gen. Miller: "This is General Robert Miller, Chairman of the Joint Chiefs. Ladies and Gentlemen, we will allow you to land in Arizona but in the morning we will take over control of your vessel until we can get this sorted out. This is not a request; it is an order from the President of the United States."

Arslan: "*General Miller, we are now going to start this conversation over so you have time to get your head out of your ass.* You obviously do not understand the situation. We are riding in the most powerful military force on earth, by a factor of about one million, I would guess. In terms of energy potential alone we can generate 100 times the current maximum energy output of all earthly sources. We are taking about 8 hours to get from England to Arizona but if we had wanted to, we could have done it in less than ten minutes. We didn't want to scare you. We could go to the moon right now, land, then come back and still make it to Arizona by dawn.

Our computer on board is not really a computer; it is artificial intelligence learning for 4.6 million years. It has learned a few tricks. It knows where every military installation is on earth and all satellites. It could knock out all satellites in about ten seconds if commanded to do so. I won't go on, you should have the idea.

Please understand my background. I have lived on earth for over 2,700 years, with most of the time spent in military roles. I fought in many of the battles you studied in military science. For example, I taught swordsmanship to Alexander the Great's soldiers and I planned and executed the strategy for Shapur I when he captured the Roman Emperor Valerian and 70,000 legionaries at the battle of Edessa. I am not going to let you sucker us into giving control of this vessel to you or anyone else I do not trust. And basically, I do not trust anyone right now except my three associates.

We will land in Chandler, Arizona at dawn. Before we land we will inscribe a 1000-meter diameter circle in the desert with energy beams. This will be the marker for your security to stay outside this circle. A second circle will be inscribed as a 750-meter diameter circle inside the first circle. Anything entering the inner circle will be vaporized. Anyone inside the first circle will be hit with a stun weapon. Any aircraft flying closer than one mile will be destroyed. The computer will control the weapons so there will be no decisions to be made, it will be automatic.

We will keep our defensive shields in place while parked in the desert. If we are attacked in any way, we will take our ship containing technology so advanced it is probably many millions of years ahead of anything on earth, and take it somewhere else. Maybe Europe, maybe Japan, maybe China, maybe Russia, maybe Turkey, who knows? But General Robert Miller will be remembered in U.S. history as the idiot who caused it to happen. Think about it."

There was a lengthy period of silence.

Jon Kelly

President: "This is President Roger Carey, I have taken over for General Miller. Could I get an idea of whom I am talking to on your end?"

Arslan: "Yes, Mr. President. Dr. Simon Myers of the Center for DNA Studies in Atlanta, Ms. Carrie Sloan, ABD (all but dissertation), also of the Center for DNA Studies in Atlanta, and Ms. Lisa Malloy, Teacher, Atlanta School System and Arslan of Amwat, Phrygia, now central Turkey."

President: "General Miller seems to have got off on the wrong foot with you but I will try to do better. I can agree to the terms you have described to get you landed in Arizona and we will provide the security requested. There will be no attempts to take control of your vessel by force."

Arslan: "Thank you, Mr. President. Now, about the meeting scheduled for New Year's Day. Can you support the schedule and the visitors we have invited?"

President: "What is the purpose of this meeting?"

Arslan: "The purpose is to develop some kind of acceptable system for using the information and resources of this vessel for the advancement of mankind consistent with the objectives stated in the E-Mail you received."

President: "Will the United States have the leadership position concerning the information and technology on the vessel?"

Arslan: "A leadership position, yes, the leadership position, No. It is something for mankind, not for the United States alone."

President: "We will support the conference under those terms."

Arslan: "Thank you, Mr. President."

President: "I will say good night for now. Have a good trip."

Arslan said after they had disconnected, "Well, Simon, I hope you are not applying for any military contracts for the center. You may have a little trouble getting approved. And your security clearance is probably in the dumper too."

Simon said, "There is probably a big DNA contract out there for making super-soldiers and I'm going to miss it. Oh heck!"

Arslan got up from his chair, walked across the room, then turned and said, "We will be in Chandler in three hours. I think we all ought to try to get some sleep now so we are fresher when we get there. One point first. I know I have been a bit "take charge" over the last few hours. I hope this offends no one. When we are in a tactical mode such as we are moving the vessel across the world, my military instincts tend to pop out. If someone else has ideas, please come forth with them. I am not trying to take over, just to keep things moving."

Simon answered for the group, "Arslan, we appreciated your taking charge under these circumstances. If we have problems anytime with the direction you are going, we will speak up." They then retired to their sleeping quarters.

About three hours later the computer announced several times, "twenty minutes to touchdown in Chandler."

39. <u>Chandler (Arizona)</u>

They were following I-10 up from Tucson, Arizona toward the Phoenix area. South of the metropolitan area and east of the interstate they saw where the desert stopped and the built up area of new construction began. This was their objective, an area of desert about one square mile where they could inscribe their 1000 meter outer circle and 750 meter inner circle for security markers.

The vessel hovered about 3,000 feet above the spot and used energy beams to sear a ten foot wide band into the floor of the desert first for the larger circle then for the inner circle. The heat was so intense on the desert floor a black strip was created. The vessel then came down to land in the exact center of the circle. Five large legs folded out from the bottom of the vessel to provide support legs for the vessel so it came down to within about ten feet of the desert floor and was supported there on the legs like a giant spider.

The computer immediately initiated security procedures as had been determined. Defensive shields were in place, all airspace within 100 miles was being scanned for danger, and the immediate desert floor within the inscribed circles were being scanned. Weapon systems were set to stun any persons within the larger circle, to kill anything within the inner circle, and to destroy any aircraft within one mile. The computer was broadcasting an alert for these security procedures to all aircraft, police, fire, and other emergency facilities in the area.

The Chandler Police Department had decided to heed the E-Mail traffic sent to them since traffic control and security personnel were in place. The vessel could be easily seen from I-10 so the sightseeing public would get an eyeful.

By this time the E-Mail traffic was huge. They had given the computer the responsibility for first screening of all E-mail and to respond to all the routine stuff so priority issues would get first attention. With only four people, they could not waste time on the unimportant.

The computer would bring priority E-Mails up on a screen for the group to handle.

Working out of the control room with four comfortable recliners and fold up writing surfaces and the walls all around showing the scene outside gave a sense of being outdoors in the desert but without the heat or dirt. The wall screens could be changed to show TV, internet, views of ship areas, illustrations of ship capabilities or anything else they wanted to ask the computer to do or show. All types of information resources were available, so time was conserved in looking for information to answer questions or develop ideas.

E-Mails started to flood into the "Tira." This was the name they decided to use for the vessel, as recognition for her message from the past. The next priority message received was:

fwd: smyers@ctrdna.org
to: older_than_dirt.com
from: formin@peorepchina.gov
subject: E-Mail of 0300 GMT

Your E-Mail of 0300 GMT. We are agree attend meeting Jan. 1.

Can have more information in advance of meeting?

Han Wey
Foreign Minister
People 's Republic of China

This was followed by a succession of E-Mail responses from the countries invited to attend. All were agreeing to attend and all wanted more information if possible.

By 3:00 p.m. local time, all invited attendees had responded except the French Premier and the Kenyan leader. The French were just being obstinate as usual and it was assumed the normal inefficiency in Kenya was slowing a response in coming.

The openness for forwarding E-Mails to everyone was having the effect everyone had enough information to make a quick decision.

The media was going wild with every camera crew in the world trying to get to the little patch of desert south of Phoenix. The military had brought in Air Force MP's from Luke Air Force Base in

Phoenix to act as security around the perimeter of the outer circle. Air Force vehicles surrounded the perimeter with armed guards in evidence everywhere. TV camera crews were in designated areas around the perimeter with cameras set up on the roofs of vans to see over the military presence. More crews were arriving every minute with newscasters making reports with the huge bulk of Tira in the background.

The media was dissecting the original E-Mail in great detail and others forwarded later, since it was all they had. The feeding frenzy of the press was in full glory. They had no way to get to the people on Tira, except by E-Mail. This caused huge frustration with the press corp. since they were used to getting access. One reporter decided to ignore the warnings about access to the perimeter not being permitted and started running across the desert past the outer ring. A beam from the Tira reached out and stunned him into unconsciousness. The computer then E-Mailed authorities the stun mechanism would be shut down for five minutes while the man was recovered from the area. The press made much of this event as though it was somehow an infringement of freedom of the press.

Arslan commented, "Good, we needed to have an example made we have our security systems in place."

Lisa needed help with the transcribing of Arslan's story and started making E-Mail inquiries about who could be used in the Phoenix area, "the valley" as she soon learned the area was called. She contacted some book publishing companies and got recommendations on the best editors in the area. Once word got out she was looking, there was an avalanche of people wanting to get involved. The publishers were also lining up to get rights to the story. A New York publisher had already offered $5 million for publishing rights to the Arslan story. Finally, Lisa contracted with three highly recommended free-lance editors to start work on the information. They were required to sign contracts coming just short of calling for capital punishment for breaking confidentiality on the information. As it was they only had sections of the story to work on, no one except Lisa had the whole thing. All this was handled by E-mail, including attaching digitals of the tapes for transcribing.

Lisa kept the section about Jesus of Nazareth for her personal transcription and editing. This was too hot to have anyone else involved.

At about six p.m. they saw a four-wheel drive pickup truck come out of the desert to the south at a high rate of speed. It found a gap in Air Force security and crossed the outer ring. Immediately, the stun beam reached out but did not stop the truck, apparently due to some shielding being used in front of the driver. The vehicle reached the inner ring. A beam as wide as the truck struck out from the Tira and the truck simply vaporized in a large flash. When the smoke and vapors cleared there was no debris on the desert floor to speak of, only a discoloration in the dirt. They immediately sent an E-Mail expressing their regret but the bottom line was a warning had been issued. The press highlighted the event but there was very little discussion. The press quickly found out the individual involved, identified from enlargement of the videos of the truck license plates, was a member of an extreme religious group. He had told a friend, "He was going to knock the "devil ship" down."

Another E-Mail came in shortly afterwards. It went up of the screen and immediately got the attention of Simon and Carrie:

fwd: smyers@ctrdna.org
to: older_than_dirt.com
from: dandrews@ctrdna.org
subject: E-Mail of 0300 GMT

Simon and Carrie,

Are the two of you really involved in all this. I am totally confused and really don't know what to say.

We are being questioned by reporters, TV crews, FBI, CIA, Secret Service, your mother from Pennsylvania, Carrie's mother and father from Iowa, and, I expect, the Pope will call next.

Thanks for the E-Mail saying the two of you will be off a few days, that was a big help, old friend. Well, we always did say the center needed some publicity to increase funding.

They are stalled by a court order I got to hold them off, but do not know for how long.

Please call or write.

Best regards,

Dana Andrews
Chm. Center for DNA Studies-Atlanta

Simon immediately said, "Computer, send an encrypted message to the President of the United States and attach a copy of the E-Mail from Dana Andrews. The message should read:

TOP SECRET—President's Eyes Only

Dear Mr. President:

The FBI, CIA, and Secret Service are apparently causing problems at the Center for DNA Studies in Atlanta. We are personally indebted to the people at the center for our past association and do not want to have our government harassing them unnecessarily. If you really meant it when you indicated you wanted to have a good relationship with us, please call off the dogs. The center is doing important work, most of which is totally unrelated to the vessel.

The only computer files at the center which should be of any interest to government agencies, and even that is debatable legally and morally, are those concerning Arslan of Amwat. All of these files are under my ID or Ms. Sloan's ID in the system labeled "Arslan xxx." I will contact Dr. Dana Andrews, chairperson of the center, and provide him with the access code to the encrypted files. The United States Government will be required to sign an exhaustive confidentiality agreement with severe penalties for breach before any files are released. The files will not be copied. Any examination of the files will be done only at the center under the control of Dr. Andrews.

The files in question have already had a section of information removed. The most critical piece of DNA data involved is gone. Before leaving Atlanta, all blood samples from Arslan of Amwat were removed and are in my possession. You may not understand our reasons for being so cautious but we believe the information is sensitive and could have implications for the future of human genetics. We simply do not trust any government to use this information properly until a system of safeguards is in place to insure all of humanity benefits, not a privileged few.

I am sure the government can forcibly take the files in question, and probably overcome the encryption. The only information you can get from these files is proof Arslan of Amwat has DNA, which is older and somewhat different than any other living being. It will not help provide other data needed to modify human DNA to potentially extend life expectancy. This is the data being controlled at the present time.

Please respond on this issue as soon as possible.

Respectfully,

Dr. Simon Myers
Center for DNA Studies

Simon said to the computer, "Ok, send it."

Next Simon, Carrie and Lisa sent E-mails to family members to inform them of the situation and provided a cell phone number they could call to reach them. They also informed their families of the impending marriage of Simon and Lisa. Carrie informed her family she had a close relationship with Arslan of Amwat and marriage had been discussed. They all knew word would get out eventually but there was a personal commitment to their families taking precedent over information control.

About thirty minutes after the E-Mail to the President a new E-mail came back:

fwd:	smyers@ctrdna.org
to:	older_than_dirt.com
from:	SITRM White House Washington DC
subject:	Your E-Mail of 2037 EST Today (top secret)

All government agencies ordered to cease and desist actions concerning Center for DNA Studies except FBI who will provide security for the center, until further notice. Security concerns are being coordinated with Dr. Andrews.

I respect your concerns and will support your efforts.

The FBI has also been asked to provide security for any of your family members who could become targets based on the publicity surrounding the vessel. Please provide me with a list of persons who should receive protection.

We in the government here have had many discussions of the potential issues involved with the vessel and extension of life expectancy.   We are becoming increasingly aware of the significance of your security concerns and wish to have you understand the United States Government is on your side.

Best regards,

President Roger Carey

"Well, the tone seems to be changing." said Lisa.

Arslan spoke, "The tone has changed but we need to stay vigilant. I keep remembering the quote, "I'm from the government and I'm here to help you." That was about the IRS or EPA wasn't it?"

Simon said, "I agree with Arslan, we need to be very vigilant. I hate to be paranoid but think about a scenario, say Arslan goes out of Tira for something, the CIA or FBI has a sniper waiting out there to shoot him so they can get a blood sample or a team to kidnap him. Is it something our government could or would do? I don't know. I am afraid it could happen. Arslan needs to be very careful until we have some agreements in place."

Carrie said with a look of concern, "I hadn't thought about something like it but sadly I believe it could happen. Arslan needs to be very careful. I think it should be a matter of policy for Arslan to stay on Tira until after the New Year's Day meeting."

Lisa and Simon chimed in agreeing.

Arslan said, "I don't disagree but the rest of you may be targets also, especially for kidnapping to get leverage to force the rest of us to do things we may not want to do. For any of us to leave the Tira exposes all of us to blackmail. I suggest our policy be we stay on board unless there is a major, compelling reason to go off the Tira.

We seem to be as safe as we can be here. This is also a good reason to get the list of people who need protection off to the President. It was a good thing someone there thought about it."

Simon, Carrie, and Lisa quickly prepared their lists and had the computer send them off to the President, classified top secret.

Lisa then had a new thought, "We need to have a liaison person outside the Tira, here locally, to handle any needs we have for the next 30 days. Important things, like when I get a craving for pizza or linguini with clams sauce from the little Italian bistro on Alma School Road Arslan was bragging about. Of course, we could always call Dominoes Pizza to deliver."

Simon said, 'I guess Lisa is already tired of the food Mr. Artificial Intelligence is preparing for us. Maybe if you give him a sample he can replicate it, just like Star Trek. Oops, I had better be careful, I might offend him and then the food might get worse."

The computer who was always listening and obviously had a sense of humor said, "Did I hear you order SOS for breakfast, Simon?"

"No offense intended." said Simon with a laugh.

Arslan said he thought he knew someone who would be a good liaison person, someone he knew from living in Phoenix recently. Arslan explained he had been working in an identity as an engineer for a computer company, Motorola, and had met a security person who was ex-Secret Service, Presidential Security detail, and was trying to stay in shape. They had attended karate school together since Arslan also need to keep his skills sharp.

Arslan was much, much better than anyone else at the school, instructors or students, but it was the best competition he could find. The ex-Secret-Service friend was the best of the lot as far as competition so they spent a lot of time working out together. His name is Joe Amaro, an Italian, and tough as anyone. Joe had been laid off by Motorola in one of their cyclical down sizing exercises. He thought he knew where to contact him.

Arslan got on the cell phone and made a call. Arslan said, "Hello, Is Joe Amaro there today? He's at the end of the bar? Could I speak to him? Great! Hello, Joe. This is Alan Bates. Remember me? Yes, I left town about six months ago and just got back. Say, have you been watching TV about the vessel landing down in south Chandler.

201

Yes, it is weird, but buddy, it is going to get a lot weirder for you. Let me give you a number to call me on, then go outside to your car and call me from there. You are not going to want to have the whole bar in on this. Ok, Thanks. The number is 602-402-5555. Call right away."

Arslan waited for a call back. The phone rang in about three minutes and he answered, "Hello, Joe? Joe, when I was here before as Alan Bates, it wasn't my real name. My real name is Arslan, Arslan of Amwat, and I am one of the four people on the vessel. Yes, blows you away, doesn't it? You always thought I was too good at karate to be human. Well, the deal is we need someone we can trust to liaison with the outside world while we are here waiting for the big meeting at the first of the year. If you are not working or can get some time off, will you do it. The pay will be great but it could be dangerous? Fuck the job you have now? Good attitude. Ok, come over to south Chandler and see us. We will announce to the authorities they are to let you through. Oh, did you ever get transported like on Star Trek? You are about to be the fifth earthling to try it. Leave your gun in the car, please. And keep the lips sealed about this. Thanks."

Carrie said, "So you were an engineer out here. Did you have any babes on the string, any competition I should worry about?

Arslan said with an amused smile, "Only every woman in the valley. I had to fight them off."

Carrie thought, *"Probably true, but she wasn't worried, once Arslan commits it usually lasts, like 2,400 years."*

They alerted the FBI a man named Joe would be showing up, and he was to be allowed through. The security systems would be turned off when he arrived. About an hour later, Arslan saw Joe at the perimeter and he communicated with the FBI to send him across closer to the Tira. As he walked across, Simon was transported down in front of him carrying a second ingot. Simon was transported inside the energy field with Joe on the outside. Just before Joe hit the energy field, it was shut off until he was inside and then it was restored. They were concerned about snipers.

Simon introduced himself to Joe, then handed him an ingot. Simon focused his thoughts on the two ingots and thought, "Take us in." Joe was inside the transport entrance before he knew what was happening. Arslan was waiting inside to greet him.

Arslan said," How's the beer at the Stadium Club tonight? I thought I could find you there."

Joe said," I guess I'm getting too predictable in my old age. The Secret Service would consider it a flaw."

Arslan said, "While we are on the subject of the Secret Service, CIA and FBI, they are probably going to be asking you a lot of questions and wanting you to do their bidding, after they figure out who the little Italian was that got in here. As I recall you know what good friends they can be, even after you give your all for the service."

Joe said, "Yeah, the bastards tried to screw me every way there was. I was lucky they didn't put me in jail. So, maybe I screwed the Press Secretary's wife. She was a consenting adult."

Arslan said, "Well, the thing with this deal is you have to pick sides. What we are doing is important, important for the future of the human race, for example. Those dicks, do not have the same outlook, I suspect, all the way from the janitor at FBI headquarters up to the President. They may try to threaten you, to bribe you, to blackmail you, or offer to let "you have your way with them", they do have female agents don't they, I hope."

Arslan continued, "We are going to need to trust you. I would not have called if I didn't think I could, but I need to hear it from you. This is just too important; more important than you or me. This is for all of history, for the universe, for a better future. All those good words."

Joe said, "Alan or Arslan or whatever, I told you a long time ago I really cared about what I was doing for people and the country, but not for the assholes who only cared about the power trip they were on. I haven't changed."

Arslan said, "They will play the card, you have to turn on us "for your country.""

Joe said, "I think I can tell the difference between really "for my country" and a snow job about it."

Arslan said, "Ok, you are in as far as I am concerned, but you have three other people you have to convince. Of course, two of them are women, and with your track record, I guess, you just have to convince Simon here."

Simon said, "From what I have heard and seen so far, he's ok with me. Now let's take him to the women for final approval. I'm not crazy enough to make a decision without them, bucko."

Joe quickly enchanted the women with stories about Arslan, then Alan, in the good old days, and everyone was satisfied he would be their liaison. Some rules were set out:

1. Any contact by the authorities was to be reported.
2. Joe's brain pattern would be stored by the computer but one of the other four had to confirm to allow him access. The computer agreed to this procedure.
3. An ingot would be left inside the energy field for his use.
4. He would immediately get some secure cell phones for his use and some for the Tira, in addition to what they had.
5. He would not bring a weapon on board.
6. He would keep everything confidential.

Joe was now part of the team so they gave him a short tour of the Tira and had the computer give him a mini-briefing on the information the rest had. They openly talked about the fact even if the "authorities" snatched him and used truth serum or whatever, the information he was being given was not dangerous. It was all going to get out sooner or later.

Arslan asked Joe if he wanted him to request FBI protection for him. He laughed. Arslan said he was going to have an E-Mail sent to the President telling him Joe Amaro was an official member of their team as a liaison to the outside world and they requested he be shown full courtesy as such. Specifically, he was not to be harassed by the Secret Service, FBI, or CIA. Joe agreed it might have some value and the E-mail was sent.

It was now quite late, and Joe was transported down, leaving the ingot in a bag on the ground. Arslan called the CIA Assistant Director who was in Chandler as the on site supervisor of the situation. He told the Assistant Director the gentleman who visited and was now leaving is an official member of the Tira team, and an E-Mail had already been sent to the President requesting his direct involvement in insuring he was not harassed, questioned, or detained in any manner. If this happened to Mr. Joe Amaro anyway, he would personally call the President and lobby to get the Assistant Director assigned to dimmest backwater FBI office in the nation, "How do you like North Dakota in the winter?" was the question specifically asked. Joe was not harassed.

Arslan said, "Do you suppose I am getting a reputation with the G-Boys? I think they might not like me so much."

Lisa said, "If they don't it's because you understand them too well."

They all decide to go to bed then and look ahead to the next day.

They had discussed their concerns about any of them leaving the vessel with Joe to see what he thought. His view was the Secret Service, FBI, CIA, JCS, or the President were capable of doing dastardly acts, if it's what it took to reach their objectives. They should be on their toes every minute. Don't trust the bastards. It was another confirmation they were not being paranoid. The more important something was to the G-boys, the more extreme their behavior would be.

An E-mail from the president was waiting in the morning confirming Joe Amaro would be given the equivalent of diplomatic status. No government agencies would interfere with him. Arslan sent back a thank you to the President.

After working on various E-mails from governments, universities and the press and watching CNN describe the mystery and wonder of the Tira the next morning, they decided to spend the afternoon on additional work on Arslan's stories. There was a feeling these could become important in the future to get the whole situation out to the world public. Public opinion could be the factor, which caused world leaders to cooperate with the new directions the existence of the Tira and Arslan would require.

Right after lunch, Arslan started with his manuscripts.

40. <u>Soissions (486 A.D.)</u>

Arslan, using the name Arslanic, was now a member of the military staff of King Chlodwig, called Clovis, who was trying to bring the Frankish tribes together to form a powerful kingdom in what the Romans had called Gaul. Soissions was the capital of the kingdom Clovis was putting together by defeating smaller princes and bringing their areas into his domains. Arslanic was a key element in this process because he was the chief military advisor to the king.

Arslanic had watched the Roman Empire, the western portion, grow weaker and more fragmented over the last 100 years. He no longer cared about maintaining his Roman citizenship because he saw no value coming from it. Gone were the days when just saying you were a Roman citizen provided you with protection and priority treatment in the far ends of the empire. Arslanic saw power in the world was coming from people other than the Romans. They had lost the spirit holding the empire together. Arslanic did not spend too much time analyzing this situation; he was tied to the necessity of living in the world of today.

Today, he was faced with a challenge. Clovis, not the brightest of men but possessing a dominating personality and a will to win, had just defeated his main enemy, Afranius Syagrius, the Roman general who had been given kingship over northern Gaul. Arslanic had been instrumental in setting and executing the strategy for this victory and most of the other victories of Clovis over the last five years since he had taken over kingship of the Salian Franks. But today Clovis wanted Arslanic to do his bidding on a subject Arslanic was opposed to as a matter of principle. Clovis wanted to sleep with a specific woman and wanted Arslanic to destroy a whole village to pressure her family into turning her over to him.

Clovis was riding high on his victory over the Roman general and now thought he deserved a reward for himself. He had seen this woman, really just a girl of sixteen named Alicia of Reims, at a meeting of chiefs of the Franks and had lusted after her for some time. Her father, Waltic, a petty prince with a small principality near Reims consisting of several villages, did not want his daughter dishonored, even by the king. Waltic planned to have his daughter marry well, well enough to provide him with political advantage.

Clovis had told Arslanic to take one hundred men and to destroy the smallest of Waltic's villages, specifically killing everyone, to influence Waltic to turn over his daughter. Arslanic loved the part of his service involving thinking up strategies and executing them in battles against other warriors. He did not like using deadly force against innocents, lacking the power to resist. He tried to explain to Clovis that atrocities such as he was ordering would work against his long term goals of uniting the Frankish people, but to no avail. Clovis was hard headed, especially when he had a hard on.

Arslanic chose to use his initiative and ride directly to the castle of Waltic and to try to settle the matter without bloodshed. His thoughts were if he could bring back Alicia, without killing everyone in the village, Clovis would be so busy bedding her he would forget about his orders not being followed, Arslanic also knew Clovis need him too much to be too upset.

The term castle was not really true in the case of Waltic's abode. It was no more than a fortified village with a stonewall built around it. Arslanic rode up to the main gate to Waltic's village with about ten of his soldiers, leaving the rest to observe from the forest. He did not want to raise the threat level too high at first. He called out to the closed gate," Waltic of Reims, I am Arslanic, chief military advisor to King Clovis, may I speak to you."

The gate opened and a mounted Waltic and about ten of his men rode out and stopped across from Arslanic's men. Waltic said, "Arslanic, Clovis' man, why do you seek me out?"

Arslanic said, "Esteemed Waltic, Prince of Reims, using his best diplomacy, Clovis has sent you messages concerning his request your daughter, Alicia, attend him. You have rejected his requests. Now I am in the middle of a dilemma, I am ordered to destroy one of your villages and kill everyone unless you comply with his request. It is foolish and evil for so many to die needlessly. Is the honor of your daughter so valuable you would let your people die to save it?"

Waltic responded, "What am I to do, Arslanic, Clovis has the power to crush my people but my daughter is precious to me. You are the genius of strategies, so everyone tells me, what would you do Arslanic?"

Arslanic responded, "It is nearing the end of the day, perhaps, if we sit down and eat together this evening and sleep in your hospitality, we will find some solution. I will enter with two of my men and send the rest to the forest to camp with the rest of my men waiting there, almost one hundred men."

Waltic blanched at the news of so many troops waiting nearby and said, "Arslanic, you and your two men may enter."

Arslanic and his men sat down to eat with the men of Waltic. Women brought food, and the men began eating. Waltic sat next to Arslanic with some space between. Two women entered the room and came and sat between Arslanic and Waltic. One was pretty, and looked to be the sixteen year old, Alicia. The other woman was more beautiful to Arslanic eyes, with blonde hair and smooth white skin, but looked too old to be sixteen, perhaps twenty or older. Waltic said, "These are my daughters, Alicia and Clocia. Clocia was promised to a prince of Treveri but he was killed in battle."

Arslanic thought, *"Good thing Clovis has not seen this daughter, he would want them both for his bed."*

Arslanic said, "Waltic, your daughters are lovely. You have every reason to be proud of them."

Waltic said, "Thank you, but you could really earn my thanks if you could find some way to protect Alicia from Clovis?"

Arslanic, sensing danger, said, "I have not come here to earn your thanks but to find a bloodless solution to the situation."

Clocia asked her father if she could speak and he gave her his nod of consent. She said, "Arslanic, you are spoken of by many as a just and kind man. I sense you sincerely do want to resolve this problem without bloodshed. My sister is young, and has dreams of marriage to a princely man who will care for her. If she is dishonored by Clovis, such a marriage will be difficult. It will ruin her life."

Arslanic said, "Is it better for her to be dishonored or for 100 of your people to be dead. They don't have the choice of ruining their lives, they lose their lives."

Clocia said, "Is there no other way?"

"Clovis must get something as important, or more important to him, in place of your sister. If Waltic had money or many soldiers he might be able to bargain with Clovis, but your father does not have enough to make a good bargain. I can think of one possibility as a compromise." said Arslanic.

Arslanic continued, "Clovis is trying to build good relations with other tribes of the Franks. There is a tribe near Troyes to the south with which Clovis would very much like to strike an alliance. The leader of the tribe is a young prince named Othairic, who is unmarried. A visit to Othairic, with your daughter along might strike some interest there. If you could marry Alicia to the young prince to seal an alliance with Clovis, she would get her prince and your villagers would still live. Clovis would be happy with the arrangement albeit without having satisfied his lusts. Waltic are you willing to try?"

Waltic said, "It is a better solution than any other I have heard. Yes."

"I will send a messenger ahead tomorrow morning to tell Othairic the purpose of our visit. My 100 soldiers will come with us and you should have a small guard of ten men from your forces. Who else will come with us?" said Arslanic.

Waltic said, "Both of my daughters will go and myself."

Arslanic thought for a moment as said, 'May I suggest Clocia make herself look less beautiful than she is, we cannot have Othairic picking the wrong daughter."

Arslanic said to Clocia and Alicia, "I am sorry to have to suggest this subterfuge but both of you are very lovely and Alicia needs to stand out for Othairic. You are really very beautiful, Clocia and we need to control the situation."

Clocia was obviously embarrassed but happily so and said, "I will not mind making myself look like a hag to help out."

Arslanic said, "I don't think you need to go too far, nor do I think you could look like a hag."

In the morning the messenger set out with the main group leaving by mid-morning. Travel was slower than Arslanic remembered in years past since the Roman Empire was no longer maintaining roads. Trees had fallen across some places and floods had washed out sections in other places. The trip south to Othairic's domain would take about five days. Arslanic was looking forward to five days on the road with Clocia, she was pretty, intelligent and charming.

On the third evening out, Waltic, his daughters and Arslanic dined in Waltic's tent he had brought for his daughter's sleeping quarters on the road. After dinner both Waltic and Alicia said they were tired and were going to bed. Clocia and Arslanic both wanted to walk some after dinner so they set off together. Cloecia said, "Arslanic, thank you for trying to help resolve this situation with Clovis, it is really appreciated. I think you put yourself at some risk to do this. I would hate to see harm come to you for helping us."

Arslanic said, "Killing innocent people is not to my liking. If we can get something out of this for Clovis, like an alliance with Othairic, everything will be fine. If we cannot, I will be bound to take Alicia back to Clovis. You understand?"

Clocia said, "I understand but hopefully we can work it out with Othairic."

Arslanic said, "I hope so. Clocia, what is in your future? Since your betrothed has been killed in battle, what are your plans?"

Clocia said, "Perhaps I will meet someone I can love who will marry me."

Arslanic said, "So, it is important you find someone you can love. You don't want to settle for someone who is wealthy or powerful?"

Clocia responded, "Love is important to me, but not so much to my father. Wealth or power do not fill a woman's heart like the right man does."

"Have you met anyone you are interested in yet." said Arslanic.

"Perhaps, I recently did, I am not sure yet." said Clocia.

At this point, Arslanic turned to face Clocia and put his arms around her waist, pulling her close to him. Arslanic gave her a gentle kiss on the lips then came back for a more lingering kiss to which she responded. Arslanic said, "Perhaps, I can try to help you make up your mind."

They resumed their walk and Clocia said almost to herself, "Perhaps, you have."

The rest of the trip to Othairic's tribe, Clocia and Arslanic took every opportunity to be together. On the fifth night, they took a walk after supper and found a meadow full of wild flowers where they stayed for a long time kissing and coming very close to doing much more. They both knew the loss of a highborn girl's virginity in these times was a major problem and kept them from fully enjoying the moment.

When they returned to the camp, Watlic said to Arslan, "Perhaps I am concerned about the wrong daughter's honor."

Arslanic said, "Clocia's honor is intact, more to her credit than mine."

Waltic said, "Perhaps next time I should send a guard to protect you."

Arslanic said, "Perhaps, it would be well."

The next morning they arrived at the castle of Prince Othairic. The reception was adequate with a crowd of about one hundred people gathered and fifty or so soldiers. Othairic was out in the field at the moment taking care of a matter and would return by evening. We were shown to quarters in the small stone castle.

Clocia had followed Arslanic's suggestion and had worn clothes which did not show her figure, had her hair fixed in an old woman's style, and had not put on make up or jewelry. Alicia on the other hand had on her very best and looked beautiful. Arslanic knew, however, a gem was hidden under the robes of Clocia. The thought aroused him.

The prince arrived at the dinner hour and everyone joined him in the great room. Arslanic introduced Othairic to Waltric, Alicia, and Clocia. He immediately turned his attention to Alicia and spent the evening entertaining and being entertained by the sixteen year old. She was quite mature for her age in many ways. After the heavier drinking started, the women left the room for their quarters.

Othairic said to Waltric, "Your daughter, Alicia, is very comely and entertaining. The message from Arslanic indicated you were seeking a husband for her. It would seem it would be easy to find a husband for her, with her beauty and charm."

Waltric said, "Yes, It would be easy to find a husband, but she is special and deserves a man who will make something of himself in this life."

Arslanic interjected, "In addition to Alicia making a good and comely wife for a prince, such a match could work to help forge a link between yourself and Clovis, in whose kingdom Waltric has his domain. Clovis would like to see an alliance with your people. I represent Clovis in these matters."

Othairic thought a while and said, "There seems to be advantage in this arrangement for everyone. Stay with me here for a few days to work out any details and give the young lady and I a little time to see if we like each other."

At the end of two days, Othairic approached Arslanic and said, "I am pleased with Alicia and would like to proceed as discussed." The marriage was set for one month later at the home of Waltic.

The trip back to Reims was a happy journey. The major problem was solved and Arslanic had a chance to enjoy the company of Clocia. On the last night before reaching Waltic's "castle", Arslanic started a conversation with Waltic, "We may have solved the problem of Alicia but now we have the subject of Clocia to discuss."

Waltric said, "And what subject is it about Clocia?"

"I believe Clocia would accept me as a husband. Will her father also accept me?" said Arslanic.

Waltric said, "You counseled me well in the matter of Alicia. What advantage do you see coming to me if Clocia becomes your wife?"

Arslanic said, "Well, Waltic, I am well placed in the power circle around Clovis. I have served him well, he trusts me, and if I continue to serve him well he will reward me. He will also be inclined to treat my father-in-law with more kindness since I am valuable to him."

Waltic called Clocia in to get her opinion on the arrangement, She was, of course, delighted and said she wanted to marry Arslanic. "Could they have a double wedding?" asked Clocia.

Waltic agreed thinking of the savings in having to pay for one wedding rather than two.

When Arslanic returned to Soissions and told Clovis, first, the lady, Alicia was betrothed to Prince Othairic, Clovis was happy and disappointed, but saw there was nothing to be done. Clovis asked," What of the village, I told you to destroy?" Arslanus said, "Fortunately it did not happen because Prince Othairic could then be angry about his wife's relatives being treated badly." Clovis saw the wisdom of it.

Then Arslanic told Clovis he was also getting married at the same time as Othairic and Alicia, to Alicia's older sister. Clovis thought for a few moments and said smiling, "I think I understand this from the situation, Othairic gets laid, Arslanic gets laid, and the king gets screwed." After laughing heartily, Clovis congratulated Arslanic and said he would attend the wedding.

On the day of the double wedding, Clovis appeared with fine gifts for both couples. Clovis was noticeably surprised at the beauty of both sisters, but especially the older one, and whispered in Arslanic's ear, "I am beginning to understand how completely Arslanic won this one."

The wedding was well done and Clovis made good use of it to get to spend some time with Othairic who he now considered a key addition to his list of allies. He now had the relationship cemented with Arslan's marriage to Waltic's daughter and Othairic's marriage to the sister. It was the kind of alliance building Clovis understood. He was happy Arslanic had the initiative to put it together. It also made Arslanic even more important to him.

For seven years, Clocia and Arslanus lived an idyllic existence with the one exception, Clocia did not have children. This bothered her much but was of little concern to Arslanic. Arslanic had fathered many children and did not have any ego reason to have more. Arslanic was quite willing to have children if they came, but it was not the end of the world if they did not. Clocia thought her role in the world was to bear children and she felt incomplete not doing so. Arslanic explained many times to Clocia it was not a problem but she was not consoled. Arslanic liked the fact their sex life was great and they did not have to go through the agonies of pregnancy. He understood the basic rule of nature, sex is most important to males while children are most important to females.

Finally, in their eighth year of marriage, Clocia became pregnant. Clocia was delighted and Arslanic was very supportive. He had experienced many pregnant women over time and knew it was necessary to give them special affection while they were pregnant but he also knew it would not matter, they would complain a lot anyway.

At the same time, a major change had taken place with Clovis, he had married a Christian, Clotilda, who was constantly after him to become Christian. After three years of marriage, he finally gave in and was baptized a Christian in 496 A.D. The fact he got military support from the pope after his conversion may have been a large factor in his newly found religious direction.

Arslanic was not anxious to be in a Christianized environment but was always pragmatic about such things. He did think it quite amusing he knew so much more about the development of the Christian faith than the people who sometimes tried to convert him to their faith. He always wanted to tell people he had dined with Jesus and Peter and had discussed theology with Paul. He knew better than most the religion was not really the religion of Jesus but something Peter and Paul had constructed. He still questioned what kind of being Jesus actually was.

The daughter born to Clocia and Arslanic in 494 A.D. was a beautiful child but had the misfortune to catch a fever in 496 A.D. and die. Clocia was beyond any consolation over the child's death. Arslanic tried everything to get Clocia to accept the death but she could not be helped.

In 498 A.D. Arslanic was leading Clovis' soldiers in an assault on some towns in the Burgundy region when an event happened which changed everything with Clocia. The attack had gone well but one village, in particular, had been a difficult conquest and many civilians had been killed. As Arslanic went through the village, he found a small baby deserted and apparently without living family to care for her. He searched for someone to take the child but could find no one. He was able to find a wet nurse who could take care of the child for a period of time. Since he was scheduled to return home, he took the child with him, bringing the wet nurse by force. Clocia was enchanted by the new baby and the decision was made for Clocia and Arslanic to keep the child as their own. They named her Matild and she became the center of Clocia life.

Many battlefield successes resulted in Clovis moving his capital from Soissions to Paris by 510 A.D. and Arslanic and Clocia moved their family as well. All was well until Clovis died in 511 A.D.

By 511 A.D. Arslanic was already dyeing his hair and beard gray. He knew he would also need to start simulating a stoop and shuffle in the coming years to continue the myth he was ageing. His greatest concern was he wanted to give Matild a chance to be married before he departed for another identity. In 511, Matild was sixteen, soon to be seventeen and Arslanic was hoping to find a husband for her soon.

Matild had been a very special child to Arslanic. Clocia had doted on the child but the child loved Arslanic more than anything in the world. She would look out of the walls of castles for hours hoping he would come home and when she saw him she would run out the gate to greet him. When he was home she followed him everywhere. Clocia was glad because she wanted her child to be happy and she did love both Matild and Arslanic.

Matild was one of the most beautiful girls most men would ever see. Part of this was due to the fact Arslanic had started teaching her to use a sword at an early age and her body was exercised to perfection. At seventeen, she was a better sword fighter than almost any men, except her father and a few others. When a man saw her fight with a sword they usually were intimidated.

Arslanic knew of one young apprentice officer who had earned the respect of Arslanus in battle, where men normally show what they really are. He was from Soissions and loyal to one of Clovis' sons, Lothair, who was made king of the region with Soissions as the capital. Arslanic and Clocia still had property in Soissions having been gifted to them by the king over the years. Arslanic saw Soissions was where Clocia should go if he were going to have to leave, which he was. If Matild could be married to someone who would be there, it would make for a good situation for both Clocia and Matild.

Arslanic approached the young man and made the case he should be interested in Matild as a wife. Arslanic knew they were friendly already and that is always a good start. Arslanic pointed out to the young man Matild would come into property in her own right at some point and would immediately have some as a dowry. The young man was surprised but also overjoyed because he had already apparently had feelings for Matild. Now Arslanic went to Matild and asked her if she might be interested in the young man whose name was, Renauld. Matild said blushing slightly, "Father, Renauld is one of the few men I have fought with a sword who could fight me to a draw. I have always wanted to spend time with him but thought I might have scared him away like the rest. It did not take long for Arslanic to get the two together.

By 513 A.D. Arslanic had everything in place for his departure. Matild was married to Renauld and living in Soissions. Arslanic and Clocia also moved there. Arslanic was less concerned about Clocia's reaction to his departure or faked death, depending on how he chose to make his exit, than Matild. He finally decided he needed to tell Matild the truth. He could do her too much damage if he just left.

When he told the story to Matild, he related some of the stories of his past lives, Eta was one and Islasa another. He also washed the gray out of his beard and showed her how he looked. She was unsettled at first then pensive. Matild said, "Father, I now believe you, but is there not some other way than to have you leave our lives forever."

Arslanic said, "There is too much risk if I stay. It never changes, the superstitious and the religious ones would destroy us all if they ever discovered the truth. I must go to protect us all."

Matild promised to never tell anyone. Arslanic decided he would take a trip to Rome and fake being killed by bandits on his way there. Matild would help to convince any doubters. He left in the spring of 514 A.D.

41. <u>Chandler (Arizona)</u>

A new world is coming,
started in the stars,
    Intelligence connecting,
    to carry us so far.

Arslan told how he had researched the history of Soissions after he had left to see if he could find traces of his adopted daughter, Matild. He was unable to find anything because the church had not started keeping the records they kept in later times. The fact Lothair ruled for fifty years was a good sign Renauld and Matild may have had a happy life.

Arslan then came back to the present and said, "During the next thirty days we need to think very deeply and with great intelligence to identify the right way to do what we are trying to do. We already said we have an awesome responsibility but the impact is potentially so important because we will impact so many unborn lives. Along these lines, we may want to put together some statements of the information and policies we believe need to be communicated to the world. Lisa should probably be in charge of being chief wordsmith, with everyone having input, of course."

Arslan continued, "First, I think we need to explain about what people can expect if longer life expectancy is possible using Arslan's DNA."

The computer anticipated their request by bringing up a holographic screen to use to draft the statement:

"People of the world, the information put out so far about the potential for improved life expectancy from the finding of Arslan and the Tira has been brief and incomplete. You need to understand the DNA changes required to extend life similar to Arslan, in all likelihood, can only be done to effect unborn children. It is a view based on current thinking, however, perhaps some parts of the longevity DNA of Arslan can be utilized to provide extended life to people already born. We do not know yet.

Huge ethical issues must be addressed when and if the technology is available. The availability of the technology would make it a serious question about who gets access to using it. Does every woman on the planet of childbearing age have the opportunity to have the DNA of her egg modified prior to conception or is access somehow controlled? Likewise if some life extension for people already born becomes possible, who gets access first?

We suggest some type of commission be established to develop a policy on this issue before the technology is developed so we have the solution before we have the problem.

Some issues will depend on the development of the technology of what is possible. Currently, Arslan has never seen a situation where his extended life was passed along to his children. Is this just impossible for some reason or was it coded into the DNA to prevent the inheritance of the trait? If we can change this, should we? What if the mating of people with each having the trait causes it to be inherited? Do the people who lack the trait become a disadvantaged class? These are just a few of the potential questions to be addressed. We need a mechanism in place to answer these questions."

After seeing the words on the screen, everyone agreed the best thinkers of the world needed to consider these questions and to discuss how to get and implement answers. The next step, with this topic and more to come, was to develop a mechanism to get the questions out to a wide segment of the population. Lisa suggested setting up a web site for each topic then notifying the world by E-Mail, they were there to be used, including chat facilities.

The computer was asked if it had the capability to set up the web sites. It responded, "Of course." The first question was then set up with a web site and a widely disseminated E-Mail sent to notify people of the question and the web site.

In the afternoon, they received word from the computer Joe Amaro was making contact by cell phone he was at the FBI security point and wanted to enter. We had the computer respond the security would be shut down and for Joe to come in. About ten minutes later Joe was in the transport entrance. He had a number of items in bags with him including cell phones and a quarter keg of Four Peaks Kilt Lifter beer, a favorite local brew for Arslan.

He was invited to come to the control room. The computer installed another chair and everyone was outfitted with a glass of beer to provide some contact with the real world.

Arslan asked, "What can you tell us about the outside world we don't get on CNN? What are people really thinking about all this?"

Joe said, "People are amazed but life goes on. Until there is something real causing change in their lives, they are interested but not going overboard. The religious types are pretty much in an uproar, however. This is a big change in their world view, some just are not going to accept it, not soon anyway."

Simon asked, "What should we do to help people adjust to the new ideas? We have talked about setting up web pages with information, questions, chat rooms, etc. Are those good ideas?"

Joe said, "I think anything to get more information out there would be helpful."

Arslan asked if he had any specific ideas other than what has been suggested. Joe thought inviting some people on board the Tira for informational tours and idea exchange might go a long way to taking some of the mystery out of the situation. The inside of the Tira has not been seen by anyone except for the five people in the control room. The unknown is a great fear of many people, having visitors on board would help to get more understanding. Everyone agreed and they started working up a list of visitors using a new holographic screen.

Tour Categories:

Politicians/Military

- **Heads of State (New Year's Day)**
- **Senators**
- **Congressmen**
- **Governor (Arizona)**
- **Mayors (Chandler, Tempe, Phoenix, Mesa, Scottsdale)**
- **Agencies (FBI, CIA, Secret Service)**
- **United Nations (?)**
- **Military**

Media

- **CNN/Fox/MSNBC/Others**
- **Major Newspapers**
- **Scientific journals**
- **Local News—TV & Newspapers**

Universities/Scientific

- **Selected Scholars/Philosophers**
- **DNA Experts**
- **Historical Experts**
- **Selected Medical experts**

How to manage?

- **Invitation Only—by E-Mail**
- **Security screening-cooperation of FBI**
- **Set Agenda with question/answer period**
- **One of four permanent residents of Tira to control each tour**
- **Arslan to have primary security responsibility**
- **Tour only in afternoon—1:00 p.m. to 5:00 p.m.**
- **Start with University/Scientific**
- **Next—Media**
- **Last—Politicians**
- **Start in two days**
- **Maximum of six guests on Tira at any one time**
- **Lisa to manage overall schedule**

Everyone agreed with the concept finally and Lisa started the process of sending out a general notice of the tours and prepared invitations. There would be a flood of E-mails once the process started from people who wanted to get a tour. The computer would be assigned to prioritize the requests.

Joe was assigned to go out and coordinate security screening with the FBI. Joe would then provide a second screening prior to entry onto Tira and Arslan would provide a third screening once on Tira. Arslan suggested Joe make arrangements for some airport type screening equipment to be positioned under the Tira so Joe could have help from technology screening people. Joe asked," Where is the money coming from for this?"

The four residents of Tira had already discussed this subject and had some arrangements in place. A major book publisher had offered a $10 million advance for a 200,000-word summary of the story of Arslan, basically an autobiography. Arslan volunteered to loan these funds to the project. Other offers of funding were coming in daily and were being sorted through. Ultimately, Simon and Arslan agreed some type of public funding should be forthcoming to cover the cost of the project. With the resources of Tira, there should be no problem anyway, they could simply sell electricity to the United States power grid and reap a fortune.

Joe finished his beer and left the Tira to see the FBI about tour security.

About ten minutes later the computer issued an alert to look at the display of the FBI security line to the west. They all looked and saw Air Force and FBI security running around and someone down on the ground. The computer notified everyone the person down was Joe Amaro. Arslan immediately tied into the FBI by voice communication. Arslan said on the cell phone to the Deputy Director on site, "What has happened out there?"

The Deputy Director said, "A sniper fired at your man after he came off the Tira. He is hit in the chest and looks bad. We will have him in an ambulance heading to Chandler Regional Medical Center in a minute. The sniper has been captured—he fired from the top of a TV van and is headed for custody at Luke AFB. He was screaming something about Allah as he was taken away. My assistant is going to the hospital with Joe Amaro and will tie us into communications from there. I'm really sorry this happened, Joe is a good man."

Arslan said, "Deputy Director, you had better take another look at your security out there. Joe was out there to talk to you about security for a series of tours of the Tira we have planned. The tours will probably draw a lot more nut's like we just saw."

221

The Deputy Director said, "I will look at security again. Please give me details about the tours by E-mail so I can start setting up security for them."

About one hour later word came back Joe Amaro had died at the hospital. The bullet had been a direct hit on his heart.

After a few more minutes, the computer notified everyone President Carey was on voice communications. He was put through for all to hear.

"Friends, and I hope we still are, the Deputy Director has informed me of the terrible loss of Mr. Amaro. I can only apologize for the lapse in the FBI security and offer condolences for the death of Mr. Amaro. The FBI tells me extreme religious groups are crawling out of the woodwork, all apparently wanting to take action against the Tira or anyone associated with the Tira. We will improve security as much as possible but this one was apparently a member of the TV crew who was also a religious extremist." said the President.

Arslan explained they knew security under these circumstances was going to be difficult. "Could the President have arrangements made for a proper burial for Joe Amaro, he had no close family, but he had served his country faithfully? Arslan asked.

The President agreed to have the appropriate people get involved.

He also advised the President of the planned tours of the Tira which would start in two days. The President did not disagree and said goodbye.

The mood was somber in the control room. Both Lisa and Carrie had been crying and Simon and Arslan were quiet and thinking. Finally, Simon said, "We should have anticipated this or something like it happening. There is simply too much emotion connected with the religious movements to avoid attempted violence. Do we need to reevaluate our situation or is Joe's death one casualty along the way we grieve for but forge onward?"

Arslan said, "Joe Amaro spent six years willing to throw his body in front of a bullet to save the President then got screwed around because of politics. Now he gets a bullet from a religious nut for no good reason. Life just isn't fair or just. He deserves a lot more credit for what he has done for his country than they will ever give him. But in the end we have to keep on the course we have set, I believe. We are doing the right thing."

Carrie said, "I remember my father telling me about when he went to basic training for the army during the Vietnam War in 1969. He spent eight weeks at Fort Leonard Wood with a guy named Shindler, a real nice kid. My dad stayed at Fort Leonard Wood in Missouri for advanced training but Shindler got sent to Fort Bliss in Texas. Three weeks later my dad heard Shindler had died from the flu. Then later on when the government did the Vietnam Memorial wall in D.C. with the names, he went to see if Shindler's name made it. He knew it wouldn't, but he had to check. It was not there, of course. Now Shindler died just as dead in the Vietnam War as any of the others but he never got credit for it. It has the same feel as what happened to Joe."

Arslan said, "Well, maybe we can do something to see Joe is remembered."

The tours were started on Tuesday. The first six people to tour were two DNA experts who Simon knew personally, two historians, and two scientists who were renowned for reasoned thinking concerning the future. The decision had been made to not seek a replacement for Joe Amaro; it was simply too dangerous. Instead, an agreement was made with the FBI, for them to provide two agents who would stay under the Tira when tours took place and would do the second security check there. This increased the pressure on Arslan to do the final security check when the people were in the transport entrance. The concern was the FBI might try to hijack the Tira by sending agents up to take over. Arslan gave instructions to the computer to flood the transport entrance with a sleeping gas if any foul play was detected or Arslan instructed the action. The intruders were then to be transported outside."

The first visitors were duly impressed with the Tira and each was given an E-mail address to use for future inquiries of the computer to answer more questions for them. Basically, the only information they could not get at this point was about sensitive technology. Some questions they raised were:

"Since this is the first verified contact with intelligence other than earth born, albeit indirectly, since Arslan is not truly representative, what have we learned?"

"Can access to the Tira computer be set up so all major universities have access to the historical records of the a Tira? The opportunity to correct history is huge."

"How soon will we try to contact the intelligent beings who built the Tira and how?"

"How soon will Arslan's DNA information and samples be made available to scientists to evaluate and try to understand."

"When will documentation of Arslan's life be made available to scientifically verify the claims about his history?"

The first group of visitors was given two hours to tour and ask questions. A second group was brought on board after the first group was off. The second group had a mixture of scientists and historians from various universities including one Christian religious scholar. The religious scholar had several questions:

"What recollections does Arslan have of Biblical characters or events?"

"What records does the Tira's computer have concerning biblical events?"

"How can the records of the Tira be reconciled to events as written in the Bible."

After the visitors had left, CNN was brought up in the control room to see what reactions the touring intellectuals had expressed. CNN had been able to interview most of the visitors. The DNA experts were satisfied they had a tremendous source of information and assistance available from the Tira and predicted rapid progress once all information was made available. The historians were excited about the prospects for getting history corrected in a number of areas. The future looking scientists were clearly impressed with the technology of the Tira and predicted sweeping technological changes over the next one hundred years based on this technology. Medical experts were likewise predicting major new improvements based on the Tira's technology and knowledge. The only sour note was sounded by the religious scholar who basically said Christians would not blindly accept any "suspect" information being presented by Tira's computer and he was not convinced Arslan was genuine.

The following day, Wednesday, media groups were given one-hour tours, a total of twenty-four people including cameramen, commentators, newspaper journalists, and representatives of scientific journals. "Archaeology" magazine was one of those represented. Questions from most of the media people were shallower than they had fielded yesterday from the historians and scientific people. The representative from "Archaeology" magazine asked if it was true, as rumored, that one of the back issues of the magazine was instrumental in finding the Tira. When it was confirmed, he was excited.

Lisa told him, "Archaeology Magazine is one of the great publications available. With the information available from the Tira, I anticipate many articles in your magazine in the future to enlighten the world about true history. We thank your magazine for the role it played in finding the Tira."

The reporter from the magazine was beaming when he left the Tira.

The media tours were tense affairs for Arslan since these people were total strangers carrying TV Cameras and equipment in some cases. He was clearly concerned about security and personally stayed with each group. There were no security related incidents although Arslan had to restrain one cameraman from entering an area of the Tira declared off-limits to the tour—the weapons area.

The third afternoon of tours was again one-hour tours for politicians and government representatives. Arslan had four people on these tours he was concerned about, the representatives of the FBI, CIA, Secret Service, and the U.S. military. He made it a point to separate these so only one was on a tour at one time; he needed to watch them carefully. The representatives of these agencies were the top administrators so he felt they were not major threats.

The military representative was his old "friend", General Robert Miller, Chairman of the Joint Chiefs, who he knew had planned to "take over" the Tira when they were on the way to Arizona. He was in the last group of the day and Arslan was on the alert. He made a point of checking the fingerprints of each of the people coming on board and was concerned when two of the people with the general could not be confirmed against records as the Congressmen who were supposed to be attending. Arslan halted the transport of people inside and requested an explanation. It was explained two of the Congressman had missed their flights to Phoenix and another Congressman and a Senator had been substituted. Arslan requested identity checks on these and they checked out. When General Miller arrived in the transport area with the others Arslan was waiting there.

Arslan said, "Welcome to the Tira, General Miller. Please wait there while the computer scans you for security purposes."

When the security scan came up clean Arslan said, "Ok, you passed."

General Miller responded, "You don't seem to trust me, Arslan."

Arslan said, "Guilty, Sir, Please follow me for your tour."

The General was shown the control room and the computer took him through a visual tour of the Tira using holographic screens to display all major ship systems except weapons. He saw the energy system specifications had 1 million times or more the energy potential of any nuclear reactor ever built. Navigational systems showed holographic maps of almost the entire universe being available with levels of detail astonishing the general. A display of earth's military systems revealed details about which the general was not aware. Other systems of the Tira to fabricate or replicate items for the ship or food for the crew were simply beyond anyone's imagination.

After the tour, General Miller said to Arslan, "Now I understand what you were talking about the other day. This technology is far beyond anything anybody has by thousands of years. So much can be done with this technology to improve the world. It must be handled properly."

Arslan said, "If I have convinced you we have made progress, now all we need to do is to agree on the definition of "handled properly." What we do with this is so important to the future of mankind, we cannot let the wrong things happen to this technology.

The general assured Arslan he would support new thinking within the U.S. government concerning how the new technology should be managed for the good of all mankind. Arslan hoped he was being sincere.

The last of the tours set for Friday included key United Nations personnel and more Senators and Congressmen. By the end of the day they had toured 72 people through the Tira and the news shows of the world were awash with information about the Tira. The world could not get enough information now. Over 300,000 E-mails had been received from around the world requesting tours or more information on specific subjects. In addition to the positive E-Mails a huge number of "hate" E-mails had come into the Tira, mostly from the extreme religious people of the world. Most accused the people on the Tira of creating a huge deception.

Arslan reacted to the negative E-Mails saying, "There is still key information to be discovered through the Tira's computer about religious issues. I don't know the answers yet but the strident tone of the E-Mails from the extreme religious ones will be much worse as we move ahead on putting out this information. The basic foundations of some religions may be attacked by the existence of this information. The religions will not take this well. Expect the worst."

Simon asked, "What kind of questions do you think can be answered by the computer?"

"For a start, we began asking the computer about whether there were additional children like me in the world. The computer said there were but we never followed up on the details. I think we need complete that line of questioning. Shall we do it now?"

"Ok," said Simon then said, "Computer, How many other children were placed in the world as was done with Arslan?"

The computer started speaking, "There were seven, in addition to Arslan. Four females and three males. Only six in addition to Arslan were planned but the mother of Arslan delivered twins."

Simon asked again, "Where were the other children left?"

The computer spoke, "One was left in China, two were left in India, two were left in Egypt, one in Arizona, and one in Yucatan."

"Where was the twin of Arslan left?" asked Simon.

"Arslan's twin was left in Egypt." said the computer.

"Computer, do you have any knowledge of what happened to these children after they were left off?" said Simon.

The computer responded, "No."

"Computer, could you scan the earth to search for the brain patterns of these children to see if they are still alive?" said Simon.

The computer said, "No, the person needs to be inside the ship for the systems to identify the brain patterns."

Simon recapped the situation as he saw it, "So, the children were left off. I assume they were placed with parents as with Arslan. Then we do not know whether they survived or not. The odds would be a majority would be expected to die even with their special healing powers. Those were extremely hard times. For them to live 2,700 years like Arslan would have very high odds against it."

Arslan said, "But one or more could have survived, at least for a period of time. Computer, do you have any information indicating Jesus of Nazareth could have been one of the children, particularly my twin?"

The computer responded, "No information is available to indicate he was but also no information to rule it out."

Arslan thought of something and queried the computer, 'Out of all the E-Mail's received by the Tira since we announced the existence of Arslan, how many E-mail's indicate the sender claims to be like Arslan?"

The computer searched through almost one million E-Mail's and announced, "Fifty four make a definitive claim to be like Arslan as far as living for an unusually long time."

"Computer, have you responded to these E-Mail's and if so how have you responded?" said Simon.

The computer said, "Responses have been sent to each indicating more information is needed from them. Specifically, they should send name, address, complete contact information including telephone numbers, and a written description of their past histories. They were also asked if they would be willing to send a blood sample for evaluation. Nine responses have been received and are available for review. None of the nine appear to be credible."

Simon asked for each of the nine responses to be put up on a screen to review. After the review, it was agreed they were not credible. The descriptions of their lives in most cases betrayed a lack of contact with reality. An example was:

```
to:          older_than_dirt.com
from:        almightygod@hotmail.com
subject:     Response to request for information
```

My name is God, my address is heaven, telephone is not needed, just pray, I will hear.

I lived in heaven for all eternity but came to earth 2,700 years ago and now live in Dalton, Georgia.

No blood sample is necessary since I am God.

Arslan directed the computer to notify them if any remotely credible responses come in to the requests.

"If there are any of the "seven" still out there the publicity we generated this week should get their attention and they might make contact." said Simon.

On Saturday morning, Arslan suggested some time be spent on the weekend working on his manuscript again. He started reading...

42. <u>Constantinople (532 A.D.)</u>

Artist

Finding beauty in faces,
Seeing substance in places,
Seeking meaning in shading,
Keeping colors from fading,
Acquiring skills over years,
Learning to overcome fears,

Paints with perfection,
Life's new directions.

In 532 A.D. Arslan came to Constantinople with the army of
Belisarius; they had been in the east fighting against the Persians. No
sooner than getting to the great city, a massive riot broke out between
the Blue and Green parties representing rival factions to watch the
games in the circus.

Justinian was emperor and his wife was Empress Theodora. The
riot had gotten out of hand with nephews of the late emperor
becoming caught up by the rioters and Hypatius being declared
emperor by the crowds. A large rioting crowd was gathered in the
hippodrome. Belisarius' men entered through one entrance while
Imperial guards entered through another entrance. Both groups of
soldiers attacked the crowd. The result was 30,000 people slain.
Both of the late emperor's nephews were slain the following day.
This ended the riot.

Arslan remembered the slaughter in the Hippodrome. It was the
most brutal killing of essentially unarmed people he had ever
experienced. Once the soldiers were given the orders to attack, there
was little to be done. Arslan was in the legion as a centurion during
this time and all he could do was to try to have his men act reasonably
to protect some of the people but with little effect.

After the slaughter, the Emperor Justinian was firmly in control.
Arslan arranged to be assigned to the home guard for Constantinople.

In the winter of 533 A.D. Arslan was walking across from a large construction site when he saw an attractive woman. She was carrying a number of pieces of equipment looking like pieces of scaffolding based on his past construction experience. She was struggling with the load so Arslan offered to assist. She was startled a first to have a soldier offer to assist. Soldiers were to be feared according to many, especially after the massacre at the hippodrome last year. She accepted the help, however, because she might offend if she refused.

Arslan asked where she was going with such a load. She said she was taking the scaffolding to a work site in the new church where her father and herself would paint a painting for the church. Her father was not in good health and could not help without hurting himself. Arslan asked what her name was and she replied, Doria. Arslan told her his name.

The two of them worked their way through the work site and entered the new church. She went to the left side where Arslan saw an older man sitting on a bench staring at an empty wall. She approached him and set down her portion of the scaffolding indicating to Arslan to put his down also.

"Father, this kind soldier has helped me carry the scaffolding. His name is Arslan. Arslan this is my father, the great artist, Septimus." Said Doria.

"I am glad to meet a great artist," said Arslan.

Septimus said, "Thank you, Arslan, but I am not so great I am rich."

"Most great artists are not rich. I think you must be hungry to be great as an artist. From my experience, most artists are also lonely. Art is a lonely business at times." said Arslan.

Septimus said, "I am surprised a soldier would have noticed these things. Art and thinking about art is not usually a trait of soldiers."

Arslanus said, "There are soldiers and there are soldiers as there are artists and there are artists. Stereotypes about soldiers or artists are probably not too accurate. I have seen soldiers who had a great appreciation for the beauty of art. And I have seen some artists who were blind to all beauty except their own art."

Septimus said, "One thing I know is an artist must start painting while there is light or he will not paint much today."

Septimus then started to try to assemble some of the scaffolding but was too weak to lift some of the pieces. Doria stepped in to help as did Arslan. Arslan said, "I have some experience with scaffolding." as he put some of it together and had all of it up in a few minutes. Then Arslan said, "I used to put quite a bit of this together when I was on Rhodes."

Arslan asked, "What is your health problem, Septimus, causing such weakness in your limbs?"

Septimus said, "We get paid little as artists and we live in the back room of a stable where there is no heat. The cold is not good for me. I have chest problems which causes me to cough too much."

Arslanus quickly said, "I have a house with three rooms, one of which I use only for storage. Come and stay with me until spring so you can be warm. Both of you may stay there. I am gone much of the time on military assignments so you really will not bother me."

Doria looked at her father and said, "Father, it is an offer we should accept, you need to be in a warmer place or you will not live until spring."

Septimus said, "Arslan, we will accept your kind offer and will try not to disturb you."

Doria and Septimus moved into the extra room. He showed Doria where everything was in the kitchen so she could prepare meals for her father and herself. He said to tell him if there was anything else she needed. She indicated she did not feel right using food Arslan had purchased for himself. Arslan said, "I have more than I need, your father needs to eat well to get back his health."

After several weeks Septimus health had improved greatly. One evening while Septimus was resting, Doria came to the kitchen while Arslan was there and said, "Arslan, Thank you so much for what you have done for my father. We owe you a great debt. You have asked nothing from us. How can we thank you?"

"You thank me with your words and your smile. Your father thanks me with his good health. If I can do something to help another person like your father, it makes me feel good, that's enough for me. I hope you both become my good friends as well." said Arslan.

Doria said, "You have our friendship, Arslan. It is just unusual to have a man ask nothing in return for his kindness in this harsh world."

"Would it make you feel better if I told you I was being kind to you because you are beautiful and I wanted to get to know you better? It is not my only reason, but to be honest, it is part of it. Does it lessen the worth of my helping your father and yourself? Would I have done the same thing if you were a hag, probably not? There you have honesty." said Arslan.

Doria blushed and said, "I am glad you find me attractive and if it is one of the reasons for your kindness, I won't complain. Whatever causes kindness is a good thing. You are a handsome man. Would I have accepted the same kindness from a brutish looking man, probably not? So, we are not so different."

Arslan said, "Since we have all this out in the open, you need to know my feelings for you are growing as I get to know you. I hope it is something you are comfortable with and may respond accordingly. Some women are afraid of their feelings for men and want to be in control all the time. They never give themselves a chance to really let love overtake them because of a fear of losing their independence."

"Arslan, My feelings for you are growing, also. I am not ready to say more." said Doria.

"How do we proceed? If I take you in my arms right now, hold you, and kiss you, is it something you want to have happen? Are you ready for closeness with me? I don't want to do something you are not comfortable with doing." said Arslan.

"Try it and see." said Doria.

Arslan moved closer to Doria, put his arms around her and pulled her against him as his mouth found hers. She opened her mouth slightly and they kissed for several minutes. Arslan then said with a smile, "You seemed comfortable enough. I think with enough practice you could get very comfortable with it." Then Arslan kissed her again.

Finally, they stopped kissing, although Arslan still held Doria, and Doria said, "Yes, Arslan, I could get to like doing it. But that's probably enough for now."

"If you want to stop, I will, but you must be the one to make us stop because I have no will power." said Arslan, as he kissed her again.

Doria said, "I have little will power but we need to stop until we think about what we are doing. Please help me with stopping."

Arslan let Doria go and stepped back. He then said, "Doria, we do need to think about this and talk about it. You are a lovely and intelligent young woman. I am a healthy young man. We can't ignore what is happening between us. We need to decide where we want to go with this and make plans. Will it help if I tell you I am in love with you?"

Doria blushed and smiled a nervous smile then said, "Arslan, I too think I am in love with you."

With that said Arslan stepped close to Doria and kissed her again, this kiss lasted much longer than the others and their bodies were locked closely together. Finally, Doria broke away and returned to the room with her father."

Over the next several weeks, Doria and Arslan spent more and more time together, including Arslan accompanying Septimus and Doria to their work site in the new church. Many days Arslan would not be required to be with the guards because he had worked on guard duty the previous night. He would watch Septimus sketch out what was to be painted and Doria would then mix colors and apply them to the wall.

Septimus said Doria actually had much more color sensitivity than he did plus she had a talent for giving depth to figures which surpassed his own. As a woman in these times, she was not able to get a commission as an artist on her own for any work of significance. She might find some rich person who wanted a wall done in his home, but she would not be able to get any kind of church or public commissions as a woman.

On one occasion, Septimus asked Arslan if he would like to try applying paint to the wall. Arslan agreed and proceeded to do a small area of the painting. He began to help more often and learned some of the skills needed to be a painter including the mixing of colors. Doria was pleased to have Arslan working with her rather than just watching. A painter's role can be very lonely.

In the winter of 536 A.D. Septimus became very ill with a chest cold or pneumonia and weakened to the point he could no longer work or even leave the house. The painting for the church they had been working on was essentially done so Doria had to look for something else if she was going to be able to work at all. Arslan was able to find her a commission with a rich merchant he had met to paint a wall mural and this gave her a project taking about six months. Although bedridden, Septimus, sketched the mural on paper and Doria was able to take to the house and transfer to the wall.

Arslan started spending as much time as he could at the merchant's house with Doria helping with the mural. His proficiency as a painter was improving quickly. He apparently had a hidden talent for painting. Arslan sometimes thought his years of practice with the sword and the intense visual concentration on your opponent and hand eye coordination required transferred to the skills for painting.

In February of 536 A.D. Septimus died. Doria was sad but had known her father was failing for some time. Arslan and Doria had been sleeping together occasionally prior to Septimus' death. They had talked of marriage but did not have any deep religious conviction to drive them to such an end. They decided after Septimus died they would continue to live together and not marry at this time. They loved each other that was what mattered.

There were constant concerns Arslan would be sent somewhere to fight in a war leaving Doria alone. Finally Arslan decided he would leave the service in the guards and work full time with Doria painting murals and other works. They would not quickly be able to get public or church work but many wealthy people wanted murals in their homes so there was enough work to meet their needs.

Arslan found painting very fulfilling. He did not have to always be concerned about being told to use his sword skills in a brutal manner.

Arslan's painting skills increased dramatically over the years until he was as good or better than Doria in most areas, although his color perception was less developed.

One day Doria asked him about the slaughter in the hippodrome in 532 A.D. Did it bother him to remember participating? How could such a huge killing rampage have happened?

Arslan had thought about the killing many times in the past years. He remembered he had done all he thought he could do at the time to save as many as he could. The fact was, if he had done more he would have been butchered himself—self-preservation had guided him. The people who had been killed brought about the action against themselves by challenging the power of the empire. Had there not been an effective legion, freshly returned from war, it probably would not have happened. If that had been the case, it is likely Justinian would have been killed instead.

The people who had died, acted with insufficient information in a rash and dangerous manner. Arslanus could not bring himself to blame the authorities involved. The rioters had stepped far over the line and got crushed as a result. They failed to understand the simple fact strength destroys weakness and in this case, weakness provoked strength to act.

Arslanus was never sure if Doria believed this. She still seemed to think the killing was unnecessary. Arslan did not think it was necessary but it was probably inevitable when those in power are seriously provoked.

Arslan continued to learn to paint with instruction from Doria until 542 A.D. Then the plague hit Constantinople. Doria was one of the first to die. For Arslan her loss was more than losing the woman with whom he had forged a close, loving relationship. He was losing the person he was working with to learn an exciting new way to express himself by painting.

After Doria died, another 300,000 people died in the next three years in Constantinople from the plague. Arslan tried to continue painting but the existence of such overwhelming death was too much. Instead he volunteered to be one of the people who removed dead bodies from the city for burning. He saw it as a way to pay something back to the people he had loved who had died over the years. He knew he was not likely to be threatened by the plague, while others would be if they helped cart away the dead, or if the dead were left to rot in the city. It was horrible to wake up every day, then go about the city picking up corpses, but he did it anyway, until the plague died away itself.

By 547 A.D. the plague had left Constantinople and so had Arslan.

43. <u>Reims (716 A.D.)</u>

Arslan arrived in Reims, in the Kingdom of Austrasia, in January 716 A.D. coming from near Corinth in Greece. He had heard of great upheavals in the Frankish kingdom with the death in the prior year of Pepin of Herstal. The followers of the new religion, Islam, were conquering vast territories, including all of Spain. They had already made forays across the Pyrenees and were threatening the Frankish lands. Perhaps, his knowledge of warfare could be put to use in the Frankish kingdoms.

Upon arrival in Reims, Arslan learned Charles, the bastard son of Pepin, had just escaped from prison and was in the process of raising an army to try to consolidate the Frankish kingdoms. After talking to several people, he heard Charles would likely be in Reims soon. Arslan decided to wait in Reims to talk with this "would be" king. Perhaps the military skills of Arslan could help this young man.

Charles arrived in Reims about a week after Arslan on a visit to recruit more men to his service. Charles was a guest at a small castle in Reims and Arslan approached the castle gate and stated he wished to see Charles. Some of Charles men were less than hospitable to a lone man coming to see their would-be king. "Stranger, what makes you think our master would care to speak with you." said one of them.

Arslan said, "I am a soldier and leader of soldiers with some experience in military strategy and tactics. I have recently come from the east near Corinth in Greece and seek service in the army of Charles."

One of Charles' men said, "Many men claim to be soldiers but lack the skills or courage to do soldierly deeds. Are you willing to test your sword against mine to see what kind of soldier you are? I will strive not to kill you but only give you a lesson."

Arslan said, "I accept your lesson; there is still the question of who will be the student?"

A group assembled in a large circle around them, with some men joking about Radbert, apparently the name of his opponent, giving another lesson in swordsmanship. There was a disturbance on one side of the crowd and another man stepped near the circle asking what the fight is about. "Sir Charles, Radbert is about to test a recruit to see if he is worthy to fight at our sides." said one man to answer his question. Charles told them to proceed.

Radbert confidently attacked Arslan. Radbert was greatly surprised when his sword was no longer in his hand after fifteen seconds, and he was lying on the ground with a sword point on his neck. The crowd was even more surprised because they barely saw the sword strokes of the newcomer.

"Was that the test, or is there more?" said Arslan.

Since Radbert was their best swordsman, no one said anything until Charles spoke, "What is your name, master swordsman, and what brings you to see me."

"My name is Arslan of Corinth. I came here to offer my service to the army you are raising. You have seen my skill with a sword. I also have similar skills with other weapons and have served as a military advisor in strategy and tactics."

Charles said," If you strategies are as good as your sword, you are a man well placed. I have a position for you in my service."

Arslan began working with Charles' men teaching swordsmanship. Every man who worked with him quickly became aware Arslan's sword skills were far beyond anyone they had ever faced. They all wanted to learn as much from this newcomer as possible. Charles himself took a turn with Arslan and came to a clear understanding his skill was unmatched by any he had ever seen. He was glad Arslan was on his side.

Arslan quickly learned the strategic and tactical situation of Charles forces and quietly started to give him advice. Charles ignored Arslan's advice in the first engagement near Cologne in the spring and was defeated. In the next action following a plan devised by Arslan, Charles surprised the Neustrians near Malmedy and defeated them. Then defeated them another time near Cambrai in March 717 following Arslan's tactics. Charles then followed up on his victory by going to Cologne and taking the power and wealth of the kingdom and establishing himself with the title of Mayor of the Palace.

Charles was duly grateful to Arslan for his role in the military success and he made it known he would always listen to Arslan's advice.

In 718 A.D. Arslan was with Charles as he made war against the Saxons. Charles cut a destructive path through their territories. In one of the villages, Arslan came upon a group of Charles' soldiers who had captured approximately twenty Saxons, mostly women and old people. They were about to be put to death when Arslan appeared. The men knew who Arslan was and about him having the ear of Charles. He ordered a stop to killing the prisoners and ordered them to be taken as hostages. He noticed among the prisoners an attractive young woman, better dressed than the others. He ordered his assistant to take charge of this woman and to see she was not harmed in any way.

In the evening he discussed the killing of prisoners with Charles and suggested if he wanted to unite the kingdom he should not have his men killing innocent civilians, even Saxons. Charles agreed to instruct his men to spare as many civilians as possible. Arslan went to the area where the prisoners were being held and questioned the young woman he had seen. He asked, "What is your name?"

The young woman said, "I am Elizbet, daughter of Sigwith of Saxony."

"Why were you in the small village when you were captured?" said Arslan.

"I was there attending to some sick children." said Elizbeth.

"Do you think Charles knows you father and are they bitter enemies?" asked Arslan.

"I do not know." said Elizbet.

"In that case, I think you should not tell anyone whose daughter you are. I will try to see you are exchanged to go back to your people." said Arslan.

"Who are you to care about my welfare? You were also the one who prevented Charles' men from killing us today." said Elizbet.

"I am Arslan of Corinth in Greece and I do not like to see innocent people harmed. Besides, you are a beautiful woman and I try to protect beauty." said Arslan.

Arslan departed, but in the morning suggested to Charles, he try to negotiate a prisoner exchange or some other way to get something for the Saxon prisoners. He suggested approaching one of the larger Saxon castles and trying to make an arrangement. Charles agreed.

Arslan found the nearest castle of any size the Franks had not taken. He then approached the castle under a truce to talk. Arslan approached the castle alone and shouted up to the defenders. "I am in the service of Charles of the Franks. We hold twenty civilian prisoners including the daughter of Sigwith. We are willing to exchange these prisoners for any Frank prisoners you may hold."

A spokesman shouted down they would consider it if he would return in an hour. One hour later he returned and was told they would make the exchange. They held six Franks as prisoners. One was a minor nobleman. He had the twenty prisoners brought up and the six to be exchanged were sent out. Once the exchange was completed Arslan departed.

Two years passed and in 720 A.D. Charles and Arslan again campaigned against the Saxons and forced them to submission. When their capitulation was received at another Saxon castle, the party included Sigwith and his daughter Elizbet. Arslan was introduced to Sigwith who was gruff, then to Elizbeth. Elizbeth said, "Father this is Arslan of Corinth in Greece who saved twenty of your people from being slaughtered by soldiers, including myself. He then saw to our exchange for Frank prisoners. We are indebted to this good gentleman."

Sigwith changed his attitude toward Arslan saying, "Thank you Arslan of Corinth for your mercy on my people. My daughter is right, I am deeply indebted to you for saving my people and especially my daughter. I have heard of you, Arslan of Corinth. They say you are the best swordsman in Europe and the secret to the military success of Charles."

"There is no need to thank me for saving your daughter, she is a beautiful woman who I would save for her beauty alone. But I see she is also intelligent and charming so there are many more reasons." said Arslan.

Elizbeth blushed but her father said to Arslan, "You have my thanks and respect, Arslan."

Later in the day, Sigwith approached Arslan privately saying, "Arslan, can we discuss the subject of my daughter, Elizbet. She is of an age to be married. At this point of time some alliances between Saxons and Franks could work to improve the positions of both sides, especially with the threat from the Muslims. You seem to have an interest in my daughter. If the chief military advisor to Charles married the daughter of a key Saxon leader, it might be a useful alliance. What is your feeling on this?

Arslan thought for a moment and said, "Your daughter and I would need to spend some time together to see if we both want such a marriage. I am not a man who would marry just for political purposes, and I would not ask a woman to marry me for such reasons. Both of us need to be free to choose each other. Do you understand what I mean?"

"I understand, Arslan, although many marriages are contracted only for political purposes. My daughter will certainly be honored to spend some time with you to see if such a course is possible. I think, she will also be happy and surprised to have a say in the matter."

Arslan perceived Charles may already be aware of the idea of building some alliances with the Saxons and may have pre-approved the idea.

At the evening meal, Arslan was seated next to Elizbet at the banquet table. She said to Arslan, "I have heard a marriage between you and I has been discussed and you insisted we get to know each other so we can each have a chance to decide. It is most unusual to give a woman a choice in such matters, I thank you for the respect you show me."

"Elizbet, you and any woman in such circumstances deserve a say in the matter. It is your life being discussed. That's too important to leave you out. Also, let me say I find you beautiful, intelligent, thoughtful, and caring. It will be difficult for me to say no to the arrangement, not for political reasons, but because I find you so attractive as a woman and as a person." said Arslan.

"Arslan, the more I see of you and hear from your lips, the more I also think it will be difficult for me to do other than accept, happily so." said Elizbet.

Arslan and Elizbet were married within the week and Arslan took her to Paris to set up a home. Arslan was not home all the time due to continued fighting by Charles' forces to put together a unified Frankish kingdom. But Arslan was home enough to father five children between 720 and 732 A.D.

Elizbet was an independent and self-sufficient woman who was able to handle the many separations from her husband without becoming a chronic complainer as some women are inclined in such circumstances. When Arslan returned home he was greeted happily and not the subject of wining or self-pity from his wife. This helped to cement a strong relationship between Elizbet and Arslan. She cared for her children and was a loving wife to Arslan when he was home.

In 732 A.D. Abd-er-Rahman, the Moslem governor of Spain, brought a huge army through the Pyrenees and threatened to take another bite out of non-Moslem Europe. The only hope to stop the Muslims from taking more of Europe was a unified force led by Charles and trained in weaponry and tactics by Arslan of Corinth. For sixteen years, Arslan had trained the Franks, now was the time it counted most.

The battle took place near Tours, called the Battle of Poitiers. The Muslims attacked the ranks of the Franks and were repeatedly repulsed by the superior swordsmen of the Franks. The discipline of the Muslim Army was poor and their soldiers were very concerned about the plunder they had stored in their camp rather than being focused on the battle. Their leader, Abd-er-Tahman, made the mistake of allowing himself to be surrounded by Frankish spearmen who killed him. Then the Muslim army fled before the attacking Franks with great slaughter of the routed Muslims. This great victory may have saved Europe from becoming completely Muslim. Charles was rewarded for his victory by having his named changed to Charles Martel, "The Hammer", for the way the enemy was defeated.

As was the course of things, Arslan had to start graying his hair and beard to appear to be ageing. He also began to calculate when he would need to leave this identity. Nine more years was probably the maximum he could go on as Arslan of Corinth, he estimated. He chose to tell Elizbet the truth and did this in 733 A.D. Their oldest child was twelve at this time and the youngest was five. If he left in nine years, the children would be aged 14 through 21 when he left. Because of the ages of the children, there was no choice but for Elizbet to stay with them. Arslan had been well rewarded by Charles Martel for his services so there was no concern Elizbet and the children would have enough to live well.

As the time for Arslan to leave approached, Elizbet came to treasure every moment she could spend with Arslan. He found reasons to stay home when Charles Martel took the army out to campaign although he did his duty when required.

Arslan left Elizbet and the children in 742 A.D., on the pretext of returning to Greece for family reasons, but was falsely reported killed by bandits.

44. <u>Chandler (Arizona)</u>

It was very late on Friday evening, 11:30 p.m., when Arslan completed his last reading from the manuscript. Simon suggested they all needed to get some rest then return to the task in the morning. Both couples went to their rooms.

In their room, Arslan asked Carrie, "How are you doing? You have to absorb a lot of new information all the time. Some of the information may affect your religious views; we haven't talked much about those issues yet. And the information about me may make you see me in a different way. Are you able to deal with all this?"

"I think I am doing ok, but thanks for asking, it shows you care. As far as religion is concerned, nothing has been said causing changes to my views. I believe a "god" of some kind made the universe but beyond that I don't think any of the organized religions have the one, correct answer as to how to think about or approach "god." I guess the view isn't a personal enough "god" for many of the people out there. They seem to want to have a father figure personally caring about them. Something they can communicate with and somehow get answers about how they should live. I see it as a very self-centered view of "god." Should "god" be a particular way just because people need something for comfort, I don't think so," said Carrie.

Carrie continued, "As far as the information about you is concerned, what you have told us continues to show you as being human. You have made some mistakes, you admit it, but your basic intent is always to do good. You try to help people, not hurt them. Generally, you have gone far beyond what most people would do to try to help others. I admire you for it. Everything you tell me, just makes me love you more."

"I hope it continues if I get into some really bad things I have done." said Arslan.

Carrie said as she took off the rest of her clothes, "Well, come here and show me some of the really bad things you can do with me."

Arslan wasted no time in getting undressed and into bed.

In the morning, Arslan was up early as usual. Carrie was still sleeping and Simon and Lisa had not come out of their room yet. Arslan said to the computer, "Are there any additional responses to the inquiries sent to the E-Mails from people who claimed to be extremely old like me?"

The computer said, "There have been eleven more responses received. Ten are like the others showing very little potential for being credible. One response should be reviewed and perhaps other action may be needed."

A holographic screen appeared with an E-Mail on it:

fwd:	smyers@ctrdna.org
to:	older_than_dirt.com
from:	smichael@swisshotel.com
subject:	Request for Additional Information

Dear Arslan,

Based on the information released, it appears you and I came from the same source, namely the Tira. I too have lived approximately 2,700 years or more and have experienced more living and dying than we care to remember. I too, have spent the centuries seeking answers as to where I came from and why. You seem to have found many of the answers on the Tira.

I am not yet ready to release my name to the public. Centuries of hiding have made me less than comfortable with the notion of becoming known. I am sending this E-Mail through a public access Internet site located at the Swiss Hotel in Bern, Switzerland. To save anyone the effort, I will not use this same site again and I do not live in or near Bern.

I could send you volumes of information about my past and it would not conclusively prove anything. The one proof you really need is on its way to you by DHL package service addressed to Dr. Simon Myers at the Center for DNA Studies in Atlanta. The package, transit #423569822381455, should arrive at the center address by noon today, Saturday. The package contains a sample of my blood. The DNA from my blood should be roughly equivalent to yours, Arslan.

The Tira is amazing to me, and the story of the woman it is named for is too poignant to contemplate, how it lay buried on Dragon Hill for these centuries. I have spent many years in

England and went to the White Horse and walked up Dragon Hill. How ironic all the answers lay buried there but I had no way to know.

Arslan, only you know, I think, how it is to find some roots and some explanation after all these centuries. I wonder too, if we have ever met in the past, not knowing whom the other was. I wonder if the human experience has molded us into vastly different types of beings or if we share many of the same attitudes and ways of thinking. In sum, I am very curious about you as I suspect you will be about me. Meeting the world is one thing, but meeting you will be more important to me. I look forward to the opportunity but we can wait a little longer, after 2,700 years.

I plan to make contact again in a week. It should give you time to analyze the blood sample.

Best regards,
Zneot of Giza (one of my names)

Arslan felt rather than thought this was totally genuine. Zneot asked nothing until proof was absolute. He was not seeking the limelight, if fact, was avoiding it completely. It all had the right feel to it. The starting point in Egypt tied in to information they had not released to the world, namely two of the "children" had been placed in Egypt. One had been my twin. I wonder if this could be him. I also wonder what identities he has had in the world. Could he have been the one who called himself "Jesus of Nazareth?"

Arslan asked the computer to wake the others, gently but firmly, and ask them to come to the control room. Approximately ten minutes later Simon appeared, men could do such things faster than women. "What is happening?" said Simon.

Arslan said, "Look at the E-Mail on the screen. It tells the whole story."

Simon read then said, "Do you think this is credible?"

Arslan said, "More than thinking it is credible, I feel it is absolutely genuine, that is many times more important."

Simon thought then said, "Mr. Artificial Intelligence, what is your analysis of the credibility of this E-Mail?"

The computer responded, "My analysis gives a 96% probability the E-Mail is genuine in content. The comparative thought process between Arslan and the sender of the E-Mail have many similarities which may show genetic linkages and unique thought pattern similarities consistent with living an extend life span. Content analysis shows what is important to the sender are similar to the items of importance which Arslan expresses. The result is a high probability the sender is one of the "children of Tira. As artificial intelligence, it is interesting to note my systems "feel" an "excitement" at the thought of finding another of the children who originated here. There seems to be some transference from intelligence to "emotion" even in artificial intelligence.

Addressing the computer, Simon said, "I appreciate the analysis and the footnote concerning your "excitement" about the information. As human beings, we feel naturally but it is equally important to know artificial intelligence can develop "feelings" based on the exercise of their intelligence. It tends to give more validity to human feelings, which may be a product of intelligence at work. Thank you."

The computer said, "De nada."

Simon thought, *"I like the "personality" of this computer, of course, it has been working on it for 4.6 million years. There should be some maturity there."*

Lisa and Carrie entered the control room at about the same time and both Simon and Arslan pointed to the screen after getting their morning kisses. As the women read, looks of awe overtook both their faces. Lisa said first, "This is wonderful. My intuition tells me it is true, not another nut. How do you feel about it, Arslan?"

Arslan answered, "You are in good company, Lisa, both Mr. Artificial Intelligence and myself "feel' it is genuine."

Carrie chimed in, "I feel the same way, he is the real thing, but the proof will be in the blood. There is the old hymn, "There's Power in the Blood. "Once the sample is analyzed we should have proof positive. Arslan how do you feel about this? You may find a long lost cousin or brother."

Arslan said, "It raises emotions I have never had the opportunity to feel before. Roots are one thing but close blood relatives another. Plus finding someone who has lived through the situation I have experienced, is a major rush. We can talk from a perspective only the two of us have. Well, perhaps, only the two of us. There could be more who survived the years."

Simon said, "From a scientific point of view, the analysis of DNA and the impact of two genetic sources over 2,700 years contributing to the gene pool will be interesting. As prolific as Arslan has been at reproducing, if the other "child of Tira" has also done the same, the impact becomes huge over the years and continues. Just food for thought."

Arslan said, "Well, I have had a few periods of celibacy,"

Carrie said with a smile, "How many days did they last? Notice I said days, not weeks, months or years, I hate working with fractions."

Lisa said, "Well, enough discussion of the male libido, let's think about what we need to do next based on this new information."

Simon said, "Computer, please give us a screen to make a list."

A screen came up and they started listing ideas:

- Contact Dana Andrews at the Center for DNA Studies about the package coming at noon. This must be done by secure communications. We need to do this immediately—we have only two hours until the package should be delivered according to the DHL computer tracking.
- Have Dana Andrews personally take charge of it.
- We will take the Tira to Atlanta to pick up the package and do the analysis on the Tira.
- We will have the Tira hover above the center roof, Simon will transport down to the roof. then get the package from Dana.
- We will only tell the FBI and military we are going to Atlanta, not why or where.
- Simon will contact Dana.
- Arslan will contact the FBI and military.

Lisa and Carrie both said at about the same time, "Can we go to our apartments and get more clothes?"

"It can be the stated reason for our trip. We will have the FBI pack up all the clothes in your apartments and transfer them to us. Pick a place to tell them to take the clothes then we will change it at the last minute to the center. Tell them to take them to Piedmont Park in a police van." said Arslan, thinking out loud.

On that note everyone proceeded with his or her tasks.

Arslan first contacted General Miller, chairman of the JCS by voice channels. Once on line with the general, Arslan said, "General Miller, We need to make a cross country trip in the Tira leaving Chandler in fifteen minutes to go to Atlanta. Please notify air traffic control of our plans. We are planning a fast transit, approximately one hour and will go immediately to 60,000 feet, above air traffic, then descend into Atlanta straight down from 60,000 feet. Once we get to Atlanta we will communicate where we are going to come down. Our cover story at this point is we are going to Atlanta to get some personal items for members of the Tira crew. We have another agenda actually, but are not going public with it. We expect to be in Atlanta less than an hour and will then return to Chandler. We will coordinate activity in Atlanta with the FBI. Any questions?"

"I will notify air traffic control immediately. More notice would have been nice, but I think I understand the other side of it for security reasons. I don't see any major problem with this at this point." said the general.

'Thanks for your help, we appreciate it. Goodbye." said Arslan.

Simon was on the cell phone with Dana Andrews when Arslan got off with the general.

Arslan heard Simon say, "Yes, Dana, the package from DHL should be there in two hours, it is tracking number #423569822381455 but keep it low key. No one needs to know the package is important. It is probably better to just wait for it to deliver normally and be there to get it. Once it is in your hands, go immediately up to the roof of the center and wait for us. We don't want to notify the FBI of anything special until you have the package. I still don't trust them completely. I am going to contact the President just before we get to Atlanta and brief him in case we need help with anyone. If necessary use the following number, 800-901-2828, and use the code word "Stacy" to get access to the President directly if you have a problem with the FBI or other G-men. Got it all?"

Then Simon said, "And Dana, thanks for all of this. I owe you and will do something to make it up to you."

Arslan said, "Computer get ready to go to Atlanta in exactly ten minutes; course and procedure as described. Any questions?"

Carrie suggested, "We are going to get to Atlanta slightly before the scheduled delivery of the packet. Let's set up communication with Dana so he notifies us as soon as the delivery is made. If we get to Atlanta before the package is delivered we actually go to Piedmont Park and pick up our clothes, If the package comes early we go for the package first. We do not want to attract attention to the center so DHL will not be able to get there. Comments?"

Simon said, "A girl starts hanging out with Arslan, then she starts doing tactics like Arslan. But it is a great idea."

Arslan said, "Trained by the best. I agree."

Ten minutes later they felt the ship move slightly and the computer put up a simulation showing the ship lifting up and the legs being stowed. Then they accelerated significantly straight up and were at 60,000 feet in seconds. Then they felt a slight motion and the simulation showed them at approximately 1,800 miles per hour heading east to Atlanta. Thirty minutes from Atlanta, Arslan sent a message to the President they would be calling him in fifteen minutes if he could be available to speak them. If not they would contact the FBI Director. The White House responded the President would be available.

45. <u>Atlanta</u>

Fifteen minutes later, they contacted the White House and the President was on the speaker. Arslan spoke, "Mr. President, sorry for disturbing you but as you are probably aware, we are on the way to Atlanta and will arrive in about fourteen minutes. We have put out the cover story we are going to get personal items of the crew, but we actually have another, much more important, reason. For security reasons we will not spell out the actual reason now. In your parlance, you do not have a need to know, at this time. I hope it does not offend you."

The President said, "No problem."

Arslan said, "In case we have a problem in Atlanta, and we are specifically concerned about the FBI, we request the FBI be directed to follow the instructions of Dana Andrews at the Center for DNA Studies, without question. This involves a security matter of utmost importance, please trust us on this."

"I will contact the FBI immediately, but you need to remember trust is a two way street. I hope you will come to trust the U.S. Government as well." said the President.

Arslan said, "Sir, my views are evolving in that direction, please give me time."

The President signed off and the Tira slowed until it was directly above Atlanta. On the open line to Dana Andrews, they heard DHL had not arrived yet at the center. The computer was instructed to go to Piedmont Park and look for a police van. The computer put a view of Piedmont Park on a screen shortly showing the Tira getting closer and closer. Finally, at about 500 feet above the park they spotted the van and the fact there was a police cordon around the park, which had been cleared. Crowds were gathering outside the park and TV and news people were everywhere. At the hometown of CNN they got there fast.

Arslan instructed the computer to go down as close to the van as possible and put an energy field around the van so Simon could transport down, get the luggage and return without facing the danger of sniper fire. Everything went along as planned and the baggage was aboard in about five minutes.

251

Dana Andrews then called and said DHL had not delivered yet. Arslan suggested they could kill some time by taking a quick trip to Tifton, Georgia. He knew a restaurant there, The Lamplighter Pub made a killer chef salad. They could call ahead for four and they would be ready when they got there. Just then Dana called back and said, "The package is here, in my hand. I'm on my way up to the roof."

Arslan said, "No chef salad, what a bummer. Computer, take the Tira to the Center for DNA Studies and hover just above the roof."

They reached the center in about one minute. They saw Dana Andrews on the roof and put an energy shield around him and Simon transported down. Dana was a bit surprised when Simon materialized in front of him.

"Hey Bubba, how goes it?" said Simon.

Dana said, "Well, scare a fellow to death. I always thought you were a "trekie", you just proved it. Here is your package. What is in it that's so important?"

Simon said, "You must not tell anyone, including your wife, your priest, the pope, especially the pope, or anyone else. Got it?"

Dana said, "Yes, I understand."

"There is a blood sample in the package from someone, who we think, has the same DNA as Arslan. Someone else who has lived 2,700 or more years." said Simon.

Dana sucked in his breath and said, "I didn't even hear it, and I don't want to know. But thanks for the info."

Simon asked, "How are donations for the center coming now with the publicity and all?"

Dana said, "Not too bad, but we also get a lot of threats from the religious nuts. If the FBI ever pulls their security, we are dead meat."

Simon said he would handle it. Simon said his goodbyes and transported back to the Tira with the package. Back on board he immediately took the sample to the on board lab and turned it over to the computer to prepare the DNA analysis. By the time he reached the control room the computer had results on the screen, including the name of the "child of Tira" who matched the blood.

The name on the screen was Ramede.

Arslan asked, "Is Ramede my twin brother."

The computer said, "No, Ramede is most definitely not your twin brother, she is a female, the other child left in Egypt."

Arslan took this as a major surprise. *He had thought about how difficult it would be for a woman to survive in the world for such a long period. Arslan was able to use his skill with a sword as his method of being accepted at new places. A woman would have a much harder time making such transitions. No wonder she wants to stay in hiding. She has probably been treated badly by men many times in her history. How many children had she given birth to and how much anguish as she saw them depart? Her pain may have been much greater than his.*

Lisa asked, "What do we do now?"

Arslan said, "She is planning on getting back to us next Friday. We probably need to wait until then and deal with her then. If we try to put publicity out for her to contact us sooner, we put her at risk. The whole world will start searching for her. When she contacts us next Friday, we need to convince her to join us on the Tira. We will go to her and pick her up wherever she is. The only safe place for her will be on the Tira."

Carrie said, What if she has a family now and does not want to spend her life on the Tira?"

Arslan said, "It will be her decision and we will respect it."

The Tira was now almost to Arizona and would be back in Chandler shortly. They tuned in CNN to see what the talking heads were saying about the trip to Atlanta. One commentator indicated the Tira apparently went to Atlanta to get the personal effects of the crew but did visit the Center for DNA Studies as well. There was massive speculation about what the actual purpose of the trip was all about. Nothing close to the truth was guessed at.

253

46. <u>**Chandler (Arizona)**</u>

After landing, the major task at hand was getting the clothing and personal effects of the ladies and Simon stowed away. The others asked Arslan if he always traveled and lived with such a small selection of possessions and clothing. Arslan responded saying, "After many years and losing material possessions many times, they cease to have much meaning to me. I travel as light as possible, so I don't lose so much when I am forced to leave quickly."

Carrie asked, "I have noticed you wear a silver coin on a chain around your neck. It is one possession you seem to treasure since you never take it off, to sleep or for other things. What is the story behind it?"

Arslan said, "I forgot about the coin. It has been there so long, it's like its part of me. I don't think I'm ready to tell the story of the coin. I'm sorry."

The others looked at each other with surprise. It was totally unlike Arslan to not want to be forthcoming. Out of respect for Arslan, however, they dropped the subject.

Arslan said, "I have a task I need to do. Lisa, do you remember the priest in the village of Amnoc, Turkey. The one I told the "theory" about what the rhyme was about and who Tira was. I want to call him now and tell him the complete truth about the rhyme:

> Climb up, Climb Up.
> Hide Away, Hide Away.
> Quiet Now, Quiet Now.
> Arslan, Arslan,
> Monsters go away.

Arslan asked the computer to try to reach the priest saying there was a telephone at the gas station in the village. The computer made contact and about one half hour later heard the priest over the speaker. Arslan said, "Good father, do you remember the man who talked with you about the child's rhyme about two weeks ago and told you a theory about the rhyme?"

"Yes, I remember it well, and I have included the lady, Tira, in my prayers." said the priest.

"If you will recall I told you my theory of the rhyme as:

In about 700 B.C., a soldier who was in the great kings guard in Gordion escaped the city when invaders defeated the king's army. He came to Amnoc to warn his family who lived here to escape into the mountains up the path behind the chapel. He led them up the path (Climb Up, Climb Up). When their scouts saw invaders coming down the path from the top he told them to hide off the path (Hide Away, Hide Away). He also told them to be very quiet (Quiet Now, Quiet Now.) A child with the group coughed and the invaders started to search and would have found them. But the man jumped out and attracted the attention of the invaders, his name was Arslan (Arslan, Arslan). He led the invaders away (Monsters Go Away.) Do you remember it?"

"Yes." said the priest.

"Have you heard about the vessel, called the Tira, which went from England to Arizona and the man on board who claims to be over 2,700 years old."

"Yes." said the priest.

"Father, I am calling you from the vessel. I am the man who visited you and left the gold coins. I told you the name on my passport was John Young, which was true. My real name is something else. I am Arslan, Arslan of Amwat, now Amnoc. I am the man in the rhyme and the interpretation of the rhyme is not a theory, it happened. And Tira was my very good friend who came to Amnoc and translated the rhyme. She was also a real person. I just wanted you to know the truth about these things." said Arslan.

The priest said, "Son, It is hard for me to understand this, but I feel the sincerity you believe this to be true."

Arslan said, "It is enough, father."

Arslan cut the connection and looked at the others to see their reaction to his talk with the priest. He then said, "The priest deserved to have the whole truth, whether he believes it or not. He is a simple man who really cared about the rhyme without any hidden agenda, without trying to be something he is not. I admire such men more than most men at the height of power and wealth in the world. I needed to have him know the truth."

"Now I am ready to read some of the manuscript." Said Arslan.

47. <u>Kos (866 A.D.)</u>

Arslan returned to the island of Kos, 1157 years after he had used the island as a base from which to attack pirates as part of the military of Rhodes. He had remembered the island as beautiful with a wonderful climate. It was now part of the Byzantine Empire and had their protection, after a fashion. The island was sometimes raided by Saracens, Africa based Arabs, with insufficient imperial forces there to prevent it.

After spending a few days gathering as much information as possible, Arslan, presented himself to the imperial governor and offered his services as a military advisor and soldier. The normal skepticism greeted Arslan so he offered to match swords with the best soldiers of the governor to prove his capabilities. The governor said he was curious to see how this stranger could do against his soldiers and agreed.

He was first set to fight a very athletic soldier of about twenty-five years old who was obviously considered one of their best. He attacked Arslan with a violent assault trying to overwhelm Arslan. Arslan moved like a phantom and sidestepped the attack then struck the flat of his sword across the man's sword wrist, causing his sword to drop. Arslan asked, "Who else will try?"

A junior officer stepped forward saying, "I will try the newcomer."

The officer did not attack like the other but stayed back and waited for Arslan to come to him. Arslan made a controlled attack with his sword flying too fast for the eye. The officer held his own for a very short while then suddenly his sword flew out of his hand and he was defenseless. Arslan asked, "Who else?"

The governor was convinced he now had the best swordsman on the island in front of him. He said, "What is your name and where are you from?"

"I am Arslan of Reims. Reims is a city in the northern territory of the Franks. I was originally from Corinth but moved to Reims as a child."

"Well, Arslan of Reims, you are now my swordsmanship instructor." said the governor.

257

Arslan said, "I am also a student of battle strategy and tactics. If you need these skills at some point, I am here to serve you."

Arslan found a house in Kos town and was soon enjoying the climate and beaches of Kos. As usual the work as an instructor was easy for him, difficult for the students. The students did learn and improved their skills remarkably. None could come anywhere close to Arslan, but they became much better than the average swordsman. Arslan also included some tactical training so the soldiers would function as a fighting unit rather than individuals. Their confidence rose dramatically.

In the summer of 867 A.D. the first test of Kos' new military came when Saracen raiders showed up on the horizon. Kos had about 250 soldiers to defend the island. The dozen or so ships appeared to carry about 500 fighters. The governor was very concerned and contemplated hiding in the hills or escaping by ship. The officers of the command were not much better, except for Arslan. Arslan said the men he had trained would easily defeat these raiders if the governor followed Arslan's plan.

The raiders brought their ships up to unload their troops on the beach in front of Kos town. Arslan had about 150 of his troops form up at the end of the beach as if defending the town. The other 100 troops hid behind some warehouses to the left of the other troops. Once the 150 fighters were engaged by the enemy, the other troops would fall on the left, rear of the enemy in an attack. Arslan stationed himself with the main body of troops to show leadership. These men had been taught to fight by Arslan, and if he stood and fought they would have confidence and fight also.

The raiders took the hook and attacked the body of troops on the beach. Arslan was in front fighting like a demon, cutting down attacker after attacker. Once the attackers were fully committed the flank attack was launched. The surprise of this attack caused the stalled attackers to turn and start running away toward the sea. Arslan had sent about twenty-five men to attack the beached ships to cut off escape. Arslan's trained swordsmen now cut the confused Saracen raiders to pieces as they milled around in turmoil. Almost two-thirds of the Saracens were killed outright. The rest became captives with most of their ships set on fire.

As usual the governor first thought to execute the prisoners. Arslan urged him to take another course. It would be better to exchange the Saracen prisoners for some poor wretches taken prisoner by them and probably on their way to a short life of slavery. Arslan would find a way to effect such an exchange. Until the exchange, the prisoners could be used a slave labor for public works on the island. An additional advantage of this strategy was the word would be spread by the exchanged prisoners of Kos not being an easy island to attack and would deter future attacks. Arslan, of course, remembered this strategy worked about 1,200 years earlier.

The governor was very happy with the result and made Arslan garrison commander and gave him a house to live in.

Life was good on Kos for Arslan, except he was missing a special woman to share it with him. One day he was touring the ruins of the Asklipion, the oldest hospital in the world, built by Hippoctrates. He saw a beautiful, dark haired woman walk across the ruins. He asked an older soldier who had been on Kos many years if he knew the woman, He said she was the daughter of a former governor of the island who still lives on the island. Arslan asked what was the best way to meet such a woman. He suggested Arslan have the current governor invite the former governor and daughter to a dinner with Arslan present. Arslan arranged it.

The governor was glad to include the former governor on his invitation list and Arslan arranged to be seated next to the daughter at the dinner. Arslan was introduced to the woman, named Trina, by the governor, who indicated Arslan was the new garrison commander as a reward for his planning and executing the defeat of the Saracens. He praised Arslan extensively and said he was the best swordsman he had every seen.

Trina asked where Arslan had learned to fight. He said he had been trained by a great swordsman of the Franks. Since Trina looked to be close to twenty-five years old, Arslan wondered why she was not married. He finally asked her, "You are a very beautiful woman, and I am surprised you are not already married. Do you have a sharp tongue or claws, that men are frightened."

Trina laughed and said, "That could be the reason, but in fact I have just not found a man who wants to have a wife who reads as well as cooks and speaks instead of remaining silent."

Arslan said, "Those are qualities I, for one, greatly admire in a woman. I am opposed to ignorance and silence. Men who only want their women to cook, have babies and remain silent miss the best parts of life with a woman, in my opinion."

Trina laughed again and said, "My father would probably disagree with you. We have many arguments about many things including my tongue."

"Do you think your father would object if I were to ask to visit with you occasionally" asked Arslan.

"I don't ask my father who I can have visit me, so you do not have to ask him, ask me."

"If that's the case I am asking if I may visit you?" said Arslan.

"I would be pleased, Arslan of Reims." said Trina.

Prior to the end of the evening, Arslan did seek out the father of Trina when she left the room with the other women. Arslan told her father he had been talking with Trina and she had said she would like to have him come to visit her. Arslan said to the father, "In such cases, it is respectful to ask the permission of the father, as I now do."

Trina's father said, "I suspect she told you not to ask me, but you ask anyway. That is very respectful and I admire your courage if she ever finds out; I will not tell. And you have made a friend by showing me respect, even if my daughter does not. You may certainly visit my daughter."

Arslan thanked the father, then the father asked Arslan how he thought up the tactics used to defeat the Saracens. Arslan told him he had studied some history, and soldiers from Rhodes had used a similar trap about 1,200 years ago not far from Kos. The former governor was impressed.

On his first visit to Trina's house, Arslan sent a messenger the day before to announce his intention to visit and had the messenger deliver the message to both the father and the daughter. Affirmative responses came from both, independently.

On his first visit to the villa of the former governor, Arslan left early in the morning since the villa was close to 10 miles to the west of Kos town on the north side of the island overlooking a beach called Mastihari. When he arrived there, he discovered this villa was likely the most beautiful and elegant house on the island, with a beautiful view overlooking the sea. No wonder the former governor decided to live here when he was no longer governor.

The former governor, Luccer came out to greet him and said, "Hail Arslan of Reims, it is good to see you. My daughter is on the way to greet you as well. She just returned from her morning swim at the beach."

Arslan said, "Good morning to you Governor Luccer, your home is beautiful and the setting is perfect."

Just then Trina walked up and said, "Good morning, Arslan of Reims, welcome to our home. Let me show it to you."

Arslan said, "You look very beautiful this morning, Trina, a morning swim must agree with you. And your home is also beautiful."

The former governor departed to attend to other matters and Trina showed Arslan the house and property. Finally, Trina suggested a walk on the beach before the afternoon meal. As they walked she said, "Arslan of Reims, I have wondered why you have chosen to enter my life. There are many beautiful women on this island much closer to Kos town than me. And to be honest, a newly appointed garrison commander on a small island may be seen as overreaching himself to try to court the daughter of the former governor, a very rich man. You are very capable at what you do as a soldier, I am told, but you do not seem to be a man driven by a lust for power as are some men. You might be trying to curry favor with my father to use his political connections. So, in the end, I do not understand your motivations."

"You are a very direct woman. I like it very much, you remind me of someone I knew long ago. My motivation is simply I am looking to have a close, caring relationship with a beautiful, intelligent woman. Whether the woman is you, I will try to find out. I don't think I have any other hidden agendas in this matter." said Arslan.

"I am surprised you included intelligent in your statement. Most men, it seems to me, want their women to be beautiful but intelligence is not a needed, or desirable, trait in a woman to most men." said Trina.

"I may be different than most men then. The woman of my life will be the most important part of my life. Our relationship will be the foundation, I hope, of both our lives. Why would I want to share this intimacy with someone who is not intelligent and independent? Only so much of life can be spent in the marriage bed. There is much more time spent together in other, albeit less romantic, activities. And, to be honest, beauty fades with years, but intelligence stays or grows." said Arslan.

Trina said, "I run great risk in saying this. Most women of experience would coach me to not tell a man my true feelings, perhaps the reason why I am still unmarried. But you have been honest, or so it seems, and I should do the same. If you spoke true just now about what you want from the woman in your life, I think love could grow between us. You are the first man I have ever felt this about. You show me a respect missing from the others."

"Let us spend some time learning about each other, but I too feel we could become very close to one another. That is what I want and need in my life, more than wealth, power, or fame, Trina." said Arslan.

Trina and Arslan were married approximately five months later with Trina's time split between Arslan's small house in Kos and her fathers villa. By the following spring, Trina was pregnant with their first child.

In addition, in the spring, former governor Luccer received confidential word an old friend would visit Kos and stay at his villa. The visitor would be the new emperor, Basil I. Basil had been imperial chamberlain for some years and a favorite of Michael III who was co-emperor with Basil for one year until last year when, if rumors were true, Basil had him assassinated. It was not the first assassination Basil had been involved with, also according to rumor.

As garrison commander and son-in-law to Luccer, Arslan took his responsibility for order and safety on Kos seriously. He had continued to train his 250 soldiers over the last two years and he was confident they could measure up and probably surpass any soldiers in the empire on a man per man basis.

In May, the emperor arrived on Kos with approximately 300 members of the imperial guard in attendance. The commander of the guard was a fairly young man to be a senior officer, named Stephanus. Arslan did not like or trust Stephanus from the moment he met him. Stephanus obviously had disdain for the lowly soldiers guarding a mere island in the empire and he considered his guards to be the elite soldiers of the empire. Arslan observed quickly the imperial guard did not train in soldierly skills, unless drinking in taverns was to be considered a soldierly skill.

The emperor and his personal staff moved to the villa of the former governor for a two week planned rest. Trina also went there, although pregnant, to act as hostess for her father. A small contingent of the guards, about twenty-five, were billeted at the villa as a personal guard for the emperor.

One morning Arslan had one of his most trusted men enter the room he used as an office. He closed the door and told Arslan a disturbing tale. Michael was the soldiers name and he had befriended one of the imperial guards who came from the same small village where he had been born. They drank a lot the evening before and the imperial guard told him of a plot to assassinate the emperor. It was supposed to happen in the afternoon with a detachment of guards going to the villa to kill the emperor. Stephanus was to lead the assassination attempt.

Arslan's men were at various defensive positions around the island and he could only get about twenty men to go immediately to the villa to protect the emperor. He was not only worried about the emperor; there would be no witnesses left alive at the villa after the emperor was slain. Arslan had his men ride their horses as fast as they could go without rest. He hated to treat horses badly but had no choice.

Upon arrival at the villa, Arslan went immediately to the former governor and explained the situation. Luccer immediately took Arslan to Basil and explained again. At this point, Arslan did not know if the imperial guards at the villa were in on the plot or not. Basil called for the officer in charge of the personal guard and asked directly if he was involved in a plot to assassinate the emperor. The look of fear in his eyes gave away his guilt and before he could react, Arslan cut him down. Arslan then went to the imperial guards and with the emperor's authority sent them to cut off anyone coming from the west down the road. They were to block the road about two miles away where it intersects with another road. Mainly, Arslan wanted these imperial guards away from the villa because he could not trust their loyalty.

Arslan then stationed his twenty men around the villa in defensive positions with twelve men with him at the front. Arslan had sent for reinforcements from his own men but was not sure when they would arrive. Arslan was then warned a large force of about fifty imperial guards was approaching led by Stephanus. Arslan quickly told his twelve men, "Men, there is nothing left for us to do but fight. We are dead men if we surrender. They will not take prisoners. Our best chance lies in attacking the leader, Stephanus, and killing him. I will lead the attack. Follow my lead."

Stephanus and his men arrived and dismounted forming up to attack, with some going around the back and sides of the villa to prevent the emperor from escaping. Stephanus, approached with about thirty-five men stopping about twenty-five feet away. Everyone had their swords drawn. Stephanus said, "Drop your weapons and you will be spared."

Arslan said, "Yes, and pigs will fly also."

Then Arslan signaled his men to follow him in attacking straight at Stephanus.

Like a spear point, Arslan and his men attacked directly at Stephanus. Arslan cut down four or five men before he got to Stephanus. Before Stephanus could effectively defend himself, he was lying on the ground with his head partially severed at the neck. With their leader dead the rest gave up the fight quickly and surrendered to the smaller force of Kos' soldiers. The imperial guards were disarmed and the officers and sergeants were separated out. Stephanus' second in command was then brought to Arslan. Arslan took him inside the villa to the emperor. The prisoner's hands were tied behind him. Arslan said to the officer, "Your fate is sealed, you will die for your treason. But you do have options, you can die a slow, lingering death, perhaps with body parts slowly being hacked away. Or, you can die with a merciful, single stroke of the sword, perhaps, not even today but some months from now. How will it be? Tell us all you know of the plot, and I will see you die easy."

The officer decided to tell all. Basil decided to keep him alive for the moment as a witness. Basil ordered the other officers and sergeants to be executed. He was about to order the other men to be executed as well but Arslan spoke up, "The other guards were only following orders, they did not make a political choice to oppose you.

Spare them and use them to gain the cooperation of the rest of the imperial guards."

Basil said, "You are a brave garrison commander to oppose the order of the emperor, but since you saved my life today, I will follow your advice. You are now acting commander of the imperial guard with my full authority to deal with the situation."

Arslan went to talk to the imperial guards held captive. They expected to die. Arslan said, "I have just been appointed acting commander of the imperial guard. My name is Arslan. You have a choice to make. Life or death? You live if you swear loyalty to the emperor, if not, you die. I am a soldier, like you. Normally soldiers do not get a chance to make a choice about life or death. Your leaders make decisions causing you to live or die. This time you make your own decision but remember, if you lie and betray us, if I can, your death will be as miserable as you can imagine. Walk to my right and pick up your weapons if you choose to live. Stay where you are and you die."

Everyone moved to the right. Arslan put his own men as officers and sergeants of these troops to replace those executed. Arslan then sent two of his men to bring the other imperial guards back from guarding the western road. When they returned he told them what had happened and he did not know if any of them knew of the plot or were part of it. He explained the other imperial guards who had come with Stephanus to assassinate the emperor were being spared if they swore allegiance to the emperor. If not they would die. The same applied to them. They all agreed to swear loyalty to the emperor. Arslan also assigned his own men to lead these imperial guards.

Arslan sent out messengers to consolidate his forces in Kos town in the morning, early. He then set out for a night ride back to Kos town to be there at dawn with all his forces and the emperor. He now figured he could muster about two hundred of his own men and fifty imperial guards in the morning versus two hundred and fifty imperial guards of questionable loyalty. Arslan knew his men were much better fighters than the imperial guards and the guards had lost their leadership. He hoped to pull this off without bloodshed.

When dawn came, Arslan organized his forces at the Asklepion, Hippocrates ancient hospital ruins, and entered Kos town. He sent a small number of the imperial guards who had pledged loyalty to the emperor into the buildings where the imperial guards were being billeted. They explained what had happened and they could escape death by pledging loyalty to the emperor.

Arslan knew there were some members of the plot to assassinate the emperor in the leaders of these troops so he had to be careful. He sent messengers to request all imperial guards form up in a field close to the Asklepion. He wanted to talk to them.

Shortly before mid-day, they all appeared to be present, approximately 250 imperial guards. His own men surrounded the field on three sides. Arslan stepped forward and spoke, "Imperial Guards, I am your new commander, appointed by the emperor. My name is Arslan of Reims. As you have been told today you can choose to live or die. Swear loyalty to the emperor and live, fail to do so and you will surely die today. The mercy being shown here may not extend to some of your leaders who were part of the plot to assassinate the emperor. As of this moment all officers and sergeants are under arrest and should come forward now. This arrest does not mean you are dead men. Only if you actively participated in the plot will you be subject to punishment."

The captive, second in command of the guards, was brought forward and identified those involved in the plot. Four officers and three sergeants were identified and led away to prison. The rest of the men were returned to their positions. Other leadership positions were filled by Arslan's men. The Emperor look on approvingly as all this took place.

The Emperor then said to Arslan, "You have handled this whole action extremely well for a newly appointed garrison commander. You appear to have had some experience with these things previously."

Arslan said, "Sir, I have done many things in my life. These kinds of things seem to come naturally to me. But this action is not over. There are still plotters in Constantinople who are going to try to keep you from returning to power there. They have no choice, they are walking dead men, otherwise. My suggestion for you to go to Constantinople with these imperial guards and the soldiers of Kos. You need their help to return to your palace and seat of power. I assume you want me to assist you with this effort."

The Emperor said, "Yes, Arslan, I need your help and your men."

Arslan said, "My father-in-law is your friend. Based on that alone you will have my help. Family means much to me."

The Emperor said, "You are an unusual man, many would take this opportunity to negotiate with me for rewards for their help, I would probably do it myself in your place. Why do you not do so?"

"I may not care for the same rewards some men care about. I want to live here peacefully with my wife and, soon to be, child. I will do what I must do but my ambition is not to be a political creature, no offense intended," said Arslan.

The Emperor said, "You are surprisingly good at understanding what other men will do politically for someone not interested in being a political creature. And no offense was taken. But I am still confused. You are the best swordsman in the empire from what I have heard and seen with my own eyes. Your military strategy and tactical skills are significant. And I sense your political abilities are equally strong. The position of permanent Commander of the Imperial Guard is available to you for the asking, yet I suspect you will turn it down to remain on Kos. Some men would risk everything, including their life, to have the opportunity. You see why I am perplexed?"

"Sir, my life, the one I want, is here on Kos. I pledge my full support to help you in the current situation because my father-in-law believes you will do the right things for the people of the empire. But when it is done, I wish to return to Kos." said Arslan.

The Emperor said, "So it shall be, I would not take my good friend's son-in law away from his chosen place against his will."

Arslan said, 'Now, it is critical you return to Constantinople as soon as possible. The plotters will be trying to do more mischief. We should leave in the morning."

The Emperor said, "I agree."

Several days later they were approaching the docks in Constantinople with twelve vessels loaded with approximately 500 soldiers equally divided between Imperial Guards and Arslan's men of Kos. The soldiers were landed first with the Emperor waiting until security was in place before he stepped onto the dock. Arslan's men were heavily represented in the leadership ranks of the imperial guards, replacing the leaders who were executed.

The Emperor immediately sent Imperial Guards, who he knew to be loyal, to the palace and to the billets of the imperial guards in the city. Some men were sent to get information only and were to return. Others were to advise loyal guards of the plan to go to the palace as soon as possible. Arslan's plan was to get to the palace quickly and take care of any surprises there. He planned to use his 250 well-trained swordsmen as a shock force, if necessary, to attack and seize control.

There was no resistance at the docks or on the way to the palace. As they approached the palace they saw a large force of Imperial Guards in front of the palace. Arslan quickly estimated approximately 800 soldiers. The Emperor pointed out the leader of the guards appeared to be the most senior guard officer left in the city, Theodus, who was an officers identified as one of the plotters.

Arslan rode out in front of his troops, about half way between the two forces, about fifty yards from each force. He spoke to the Imperial Guards in front of the palace, "Soldiers of the Imperial Guard, I am Arslan from the Isle of Kos. Your Emperor has appointed me the Acting Commander of the Imperial Guard to replace Stephanus, who is now dead by my sword, and Theodus, who will soon be dead. Each of you must make a choice as to whether you want to live or die today. Stephanus and Theodus plotted to assassinate the Emperor; they failed. The Emperor stands with these men across from you and is quite alive, no matter what Theodus may have told you. If you now join with the Emperor and pledge loyalty to him you live. If you stay with Theodus, you will die today.

Don't make your decision based on the numbers you see here. You have about 800 men, I have 500 to 600 men behind me. Of the Emperor's men, 250 of them are the best-trained swordsmen in the empire. Choose to stand with Theodus and by the end of the day you will lie on the ground choking in your own blood. Come over to the Emperor's side and you will live and not be called a traitor. You have five minutes to decide."

A cheer rose up from the men of Kos and the imperial guards siding with the Emperor, drowning out any response from Theodus. This was a stratagem Arslan had directed his soldiers to do. They continued to cheer and shout for many minutes so Theodus had no chance to have his imperial guards hear his words. Some of the guards started to break ranks and move away from Theodus toward the side. One of Theodus' officers struck down one soldier breaking ranks. A soldier from the ranks then struck down the officer and moved toward the side. Finally, about 90% of the troops were moving away from Theodus.

Theodus and several men with him started to try to make an escape. Soldiers from the ranks knocked them from their horses and others grabbed them and started dragging them as prisoners toward Arslan. The "battle" was done quickly. All of the Imperial guards were required to pledge loyalty to the Emperor. Those involved in the plot were identified and summarily executed in front of the Imperial Guards.

Arslan had his own men camp at the palace to insure protection to the Emperor until everything settled down. Each of the palace guards was paired with one of Arslan's men. The Emperor was now in possession of the palace. The conspirators had killed about a dozen of the palace staff but had not harmed any high officials or family of the Emperor.

Basil sent for Arslan to attend him in the throne room. Arslan was surprised Basil had called so many of his court to the palace so soon, but they gave way to Arslan as he walked toward the Emperor. Arslan bowed and Basil told him to approach, even though Arslan was still armed. Basil said, "This man, Arslan of Reims and Kos, has done great service to the empire. He saved my life from a foul plot to assassinate me, using great courage, tactics, and swordsmanship. He also laid waste the plans of plotters to seize control of the empire through the Imperial Guards."

Basil continued, "Arslan has been offered permanent command of the Imperial Guards. Instead he wishes to return to the island of Kos. If this is what he wants the Emperor will not stand in the way, but he will return to Kos with the full rank of General in the Imperial Army and an appointment as military commander of Kos. In this way, I honor him for his service to the empire. He will also receive a stipend in gold annually as reward for his service."

The Emperor shook the hand of Arslan and the court cheered him. Arslan could only remember how quickly cheers can turn to jeers.

Arslan said to Basil and the court, "We must find a suitable reward for two brave soldiers without whom the plot to end your life would have succeeded. Arslan brought forth Michael of Kos who had reported the plot to Arslan and the Imperial Guard named Cyric who had told him about the plot. These men deserve praise for their loyalty to the Empire."

Basil said each man would receive a lifetime stipend from the Empire and the thanks of the Empire.

Arslan stayed in Constantinople for four weeks, until a permanent commander for the guards could be chosen and trained by Arslan. Arslan suggested to Basil the Imperial Guards should be the best fighters in the empire, not soldiers from a small island. The guards should be training constantly with qualified instructors, not hanging around taverns all the time. Arslan suggested he knew of several qualified men in his command at Kos who could instruct in swordsmanship and impose Arslan's training system on the Imperial Guards. He also offered to have fifty Imperial Guards rotated through the island of Kos continually for "advanced training." The Emperor was delighted with these steps and ordered his new guard commander to implement all of Arslan's suggestions.

Arslan returned to Kos in early July to the warm embrace of a very pregnant Trina. He had been concerned the baby would come before he could return. He remembered the death of Islasa, and other wives, in childbirth, and wanted to be there to help, or say goodbye. He told Trina and her father about being offered command of the Imperial Guards and other potential rewards he had turned down. The fact he was now a general and military commander of Kos was a great honor both for Arslan and Kos.

About fifty of Arslan's men had volunteered to stay permanently in Constantinople to be part of the Imperial Guards and to help train them. The rotating guards coming to Kos for training would replace them as far as the defense of Kos from pirates and raiders.

Trina gave birth to a healthy boy who was named Leo. He was followed in birth by daughters in following years, named Ruth and Zoe. Trina was busy but delighted to have her babies. Arslan loved to watch her take care of and play with the children. He helped also but only a mother can be a mother. They started being more careful with the timing of their sexual activities to reduce the frequency of pregnancy because they did not want too many children. Arslan knew childbirth was a great risk to the mother and he wanted to have her with him as long as possible. He had not yet told her about his affliction.

In 874 A.D. Arab pirates suddenly landed on Kos. They landed on the south side of the island about three miles south of Kos town with a force of four hundred fighters. Arslan had coast watch towers in place at all times to guard against such an attack, so he had warning before the pirates landed. All of Arslan's men except about twenty-five stationed on the other end of the island were quickly assembled. This force included fifty of the Imperial Guards on Kos for training. In total he had 225 soldiers to go against the opposing force of 400. He would count on superior sword skills, better organization, tactics, and some fortifications he had built for such a contingency. Arslan had built wooden defensive barriers and entrenched defensive positions around Kos town to channel an attack on Kos town into areas where the defenders could exploit the situation. Arslan positioned his men so flanking attacks would continually harass the enemy as they moved on Kos town. All the men were now trained archers as well as swordsmen. They would continually attack the superior force of the enemy and whittle them down to size with few casualties among the defenders. Arslan's men had trained extensively in the use of these tactics for over six years and knew exactly what to do.

Arslan also had several ships with archers trained in the use of fire arrows sent around behind the pirate ships to set them on fire to cut off escape.

The plan was executed perfectly with the pirates cooperating by being stubborn in moving further and further toward Kos town despite their losses. The farther then went the more casualties they were taking and the farther they were from their ships to make an escape. Arslan estimated the pirate force was down from 400 to 325 by the time they were about one mile from Kos town with Kos losses at less than ten. Arslan had kept his main force of about 150 soldiers concentrated about ½ mile from Kos town behind defensive positions forcing the attackers to either assault the fortifications or pass through a gauntlet of archery fire before being attacked by the main force. The remaining men from the defensive positions the enemy had already passed would form up and attack from the flanks and rear using a predetermined plan.

The pirates kept coming and kept dying. Arslan held back his main force as long as possible to allow the arrows to take as many of the attackers as possible. When he signaled for the attack with swords the enemy was down to about half their original force. The pirates realized, too late, they should withdraw. Arslan led the sword attack as the main force attacked and other of Arslan's men fell on them from the rear. It soon turned into a slaughter, with the well-trained fighters of Arslan, destroying the less trained and undisciplined pirates. In the end only 65 prisoners were taken, most of these lightly wounded. The more severely wounded had been "dispatched." Those trying to escape back to their ships were disappointed to find them either burning or sailing away in haste.

Arslan considered what to do with the prisoners. He thought about the options:

1. Kill them—He did not like it.
2. Sell them into slavery—He also did not like sending men to slavery.
3. Blind them and drop them off on the coast of Africa—too cruel.
4. Cut off their right hand and drop them off near their homeport.

Arslan had the right hand cut off each of the pirates and convinced one to tell him where their homeport was. He sent several ships to drop them off near their homeport as a warning of what happens to pirates in this part of the world. Word of this treatment of the pirates soon spread from port to port with some embellishment and got the message across pirates should stay away from Kos.

Arslan received many letters from Emperor Basil over the years and several requests to come to Constantinople to give advice on military matters. Some of the letters asked for specific military advice, as Basil discovered Arslan was his best military strategist. Others asked for Arslan's views on cultural issues such as libraries, laws, and other scholarly issues. Arslan became one of Basil's most trusted advisors, albeit from a distance.

In 880 A.D. Basil made another trip to Kos, this time he hoped for some relaxing time in the sun. Trina's father was in ill health but wanted to see the Emperor again before he died. Basil arrived in early June with a force of about 500 Imperial Guards. This time the guards had all trained on Kos and almost every man personally knew

Arslan and respected him. There would be no plots on the island of Kos this time.

Basil spent his days relaxing, talking with Trina's father, or enjoying Trina and Arslan's children. On his second week in Kos he called Arslan aside and said, "I want to tempt you out of this paradise, if you are interested. I would name you overall commander of the Armies and Navies of the empire if you would agree to serve. There is no one else I would trust with such a command."

Arslan said, "You are my Emperor and I will obey if I am ordered to do this. But I do not want to leave Kos. The happiness I have here is much more than all the power and glory in the world could bring me."

Basil said, "You know I will not order you against your will, but I had to ask."

By 885 A.D. Arslan had started to gray his hair and was growing a beard, also being grayed. He was approaching twenty years on Kos and needed to start making plans again. Trina's father had died in 881 A.D. Arslan's oldest child was seventeen and the youngest was fifteen. Money was no problem, they were the wealthiest people on the island by far. He had to tell Trina now. The relationship with Trina had been wonderful and was the best thing in Arslan's current life. They loved each other deeply and spent as much time together as was possible.

Trina was taken by surprise by the information from Arslan and first thought he was making a joke. He patiently told her about some of his previous lives and showed her his hair with the gray washed out. She finally believed him. He told her he could stay on Kos for another six to ten years, then he had to leave. What did she want to do? He told her of Eta and how they had spent extra years as mother and son. Did she want to do it? It would mean leaving the children behind."

It was wrenching for Trina. She loved her children and looked forward to seeing grandchildren. She also loved the island of Kos and her home there. But more than anything she loved Arslan. They would move somewhere as mother and son in public, and married lovers behind closed doors. They began making plans.

In 886 A.D. Emperor Basil died and was succeeded by his son Leo IV. This took some pressure off Arslan since Basil was one who was likely to summon Arslan to court where his young looks might be exposed.

Where to move to became the major issue? So much of the world was in the hands of the Muslims. This left the options reduced from past times. Trina was used to a warm climate and language was also a consideration. Some areas were too close to risk discovery. It was a difficult decision.

In the end, Italy was chosen. They needed to go somewhere in or near Italy where the weather was reasonably warm and where few people from Constantinople went. After searching his memory of places, they chose the island of Elba.

Arslan had visited Elba when he was sailing a merchant ship out of Panormos. He knew the island had a long history as a source of iron ore for whoever controlled the island. Elba was currently quasi-independent but was coming under the protection and control of Pisa. From his own visit he found it to be a beautiful island but the coastal areas could not be defended from pirate attacks. There were upland towns and farms far enough from the coast to have some protection. He planned to go to Elba, purchase one of the upland farms and become a farmer, probably of olives or grapes.

In January of 894 A.D., Arslan wrote to Emperor Leo IV he was resigning his position as military commander of Kos. He recommended the Emperor appoint Arslan's son, now 26 years old and also named Leo, to replace him as military commander. Arslan was renowned in the empire and especially with the Imperial Guards as being a great swordsman and military tactician. He explained to the Emperor he had trained his son extensively in military matters and he was the best possible person for the position. Arslan suggested the Emperor get opinions from members of the Imperial Guard who had been trained on Kos, which was almost every Imperial Guard, as to the swordsmanship and military knowledge of his son. Arslan had prepared his son over the years to be a great swordsman and to be well grounded in other military matters. The Emperor agreed immediately. The respect Arslan had gained in saving the life and throne of Basil was still significant.

Arslan now had his son Leo well positioned to live a good life on Kos. Daughters Ruth and Zoe both had properties on Kos in their names and other financial resources. Ruth was married and lived in

Constantinople currently. Zoe was 24 years old and unmarried but like her mother, she was a great beauty who would eventually find the right man.

Arslan and Trina were very close to their children and could not leave without telling them the truth of what they were doing. One evening when Ruth was back to Kos for a visit, Arslan told the three of them the truth about his affliction and the plans for Arslan and Trina to leave Kos. As with others, once Arslan washed the dye from his hair and appeared as a 28 year old young man, they believed what he was saying. They were surprised, but quickly recovered and accepted the necessity of their plans. They were good, caring children.

In May of 894 A.D. Arslan and Trina left Kos with the announced intent of going to the land of the Franks to visit Reims. In fact, they changed ships in Corinth and eventually reached Elba in August. Prior to getting on the new ship in Corinth, Arslan changed his identity from a graying, middle-aged man to a young man of less than thirty years. He changed his name to Lucas, a merchant and farmer, traveling with his mother Trina. The trip was long but without major incidents. Storms and pirates were the big concerns but they were fortunate to avoid both dangers.

48. <u>Elba (894 A.D.)</u>

Arslan found a farm growing both grapes for wine making and olives in one of the upland areas of Elba. He used some of the wealth accumulated on Kos to buy the farm and to make some improvements to the property. He hired people to help with the farm work and had some household help during the day but Trina and Lucas-Arslan were alone in the house at other times. Pretending to be mother and son was all right at times but not at bedtime.

They settled in to a happy existence on their farm, about five miles from the beach. Trina could not swim every day, as on Kos, unless she chose to ride the five miles there and back, but the climate was wonderful. Instead of swimming she became a hiker and hiked the hills of Elba for exercise, often with her "son", Lucas-Arslan. Trina missed her children but now found she could spend much more time with her man.

Lucas-Arslan observed the military defenses of Elba left much to be desired. They had some lookouts posted but they were not consistently manned. There were about fifty fulltime soldiers on Elba to defend against raiders. These were currently locally maintained and paid, which meant they did not get good training or leadership. Arslan introduced himself to local leaders as Lucas of Corinth, who had been a merchant and farmer, but was not unfamiliar with military matters. Could he offer his services in helping to train the soldiers of Elba? As always, the only way to convince was to give a demonstration.

Lucas-Arslan asked, "Who is the best swordsman on the island."

The officer commanding the garrison, named Silius, volunteered he was. Lucas-Arslan proposed they test each other, avoiding any killing blows. The officer agreed. They faced off and the officer attacked. His sword was lying on the ground in seconds and his face was red. The officer said, "Your skill is so much more than mine, it was the same as if I were fighting a child of ten years. I, for one, want to be trained in your skills."

Lucas-Arslan started a training program for the troops and after six months they were much better than before. He did not limit the training to the sword alone. He made friends with the commander,

276

Silius, and started introducing training with the bow, spear and tactics. He spent many evenings with Silius discussing how to improve the defenses of the island and many of his suggestions were implemented. Lucas-Arslan started to feel better about the ability of the island to defend itself.

At his own farm, Lucas-Arslan built a hidden security shelter. He wanted Trina to have a place to go to hide if pirates came raiding. He anticipated he would be out fighting the pirates and he wanted to be sure Trina was safe.

The first major test of the new defenses of Elba came in the spring of 896 A.D. when the alarm was sounded by the lookouts of pirates being spotted. Trina was sent to her hiding place and Lucas-Arslan rushed down to the military command in the fortress of Volterraio after viewing the pirate ships from above. It appeared the pirates would land on the beach to the north of Portoferraio, the largest town on the island, and attack coming down the beach. The fortress of Volterraio was to the south of the town.

Lucas-Arslan did not like the idea of his trained soldiers sitting in the fortress while the pirates looted the city and killed who they could. Mobility was the key to fighting pirates in Arslan's opinion. The pirates did not want to conquer fortresses to take political control. Pirates wanted to loot, rape, enslave, and kill. Lucas-Arslan had discussed this very type of attack situation and had prepared for it. The major question now was how many pirates were there. More than one hundred pirates would be difficult for the fifty island soldiers to deal with. Less than one hundred was doable.

Lucas-Arslan saw four pirate ships of moderate size. It should mean between one hundred and one hundred and fifty pirate fighters. The defenders needed a tactic to reduce the number of pirates available to attack the town. Lucas-Arslan and Silius had a plan in place to attempt to do it. A fast sailing ship with five archers on board with fire arrows, was already sailing out of the port to attack the pirate ships from seaside as they unloaded their fighters on the beach. This would probably force the pirates to leave some of their force with the ships or on the beach close to the ships. Lucas-Arslan calculated he was taking five of his men out of his shore force and was forcing his enemy to leave fifty men with the ships. A good trade if the pirates took the deal.

The strategy for attacking the pirates on land was to harass them with archers as they came down the beach. Once they got close to town, Lucas-Arslan had suggested some culverts be dug about twenty feet across and ten feet deep with wooden obstacles on the town side to force an attacker to climb over. The defenders would attack when they were trying to cross these obstacles using archers, spears and swords. The archers who were harassing the pirates coming up the beach would then attack from the flank and rear.

Since Lucas-Arslan had confidence in Silius, he decided he would go down the beach and lead the harassment of the pirates coming down the beach. He was personally well practiced with the bow and knew one excellent archer could instill great fear in an enemy.

The pirates followed the plan almost perfectly. The ship of Elba with archers shooting fire arrows darted out and launched enough arrows to set one ship on fire, although it was put out quickly. This caused the pirates to leave a number of fighters with the ships. The fire and confusion also delayed their start down the beach so more defenders could get properly positioned. Once started down the beach, arrows shot from hiding positions inland started hitting pirates. The archers would fire from hiding, let the pirates go by, then run ahead again using special paths built for this purpose. While they ran ahead other archers would be shooting more arrows. The archers leapfrogged down the beach keeping a constant harassing fire on the pirates. Lucas-Arslan's fire was especially deadly based on his great skill.

By the time the pirates reached the defensive culvert, they had lost about twenty out of one hundred attackers to the archers. The pirates had apparently not noticed the partially camouflaged culvert until they were very close to it. There were a few minutes when they milled around in confusion before trying to cross the culvert and get up the other side. While they milled around they continued to take arrows. When the pirates started trying to cross the culvert, the defenders from the town side sent arrows at them. When they tried to climb out of the culvert, defenders appeared to first throw spears down at them and then drew swords to attack them.

Some pirates started to realize they should retreat and started to move back down the beach. The small force of harassing archers came out as an attacking force with swords. About twelve pirates trying to retreat were met by eight defenders including Lucas-Arslan. Lucas-Arslan personally killed five of the pirates in a matter of several minutes with others handled by other defenders. Some tried to surrender to no avail.

The battle at the culvert was becoming a slaughter. The pirates were outmatched and surprised by the trained defenders and the use of defensive tactics. When they finished the action, there were eighteen captive pirates with 85 dead. The pirate ships had sailed away once the result of the action became obvious. The ship of Elba with the archers sailed after them at a safe distance to insure they were leaving Elba and not returning for a surprise attack. The defenders had lost six men dead and about as many wounded in the battle.

Lucas-Arslan knew the captives would be a problem. Pirates were hated on this island and everyone would want to see them die. Lucas-Arslan suggested they be used as slaves in the iron mines saying, "Dying is too good for them, slavery in the mines is a worse punishment." Lucas-Arslan suspected their life expectancy would be about two miserable years in the mines as slaves. He had no sympathy for pirates. Silius agreed with the suggestion.

When Lucas-Arslan returned to his farm, Trina had already received word and had, in fact, been able to see much of the action from the farm. She had been concerned for he husband but was glad the result was a victory. This might keep the pirates away for a while.

The people of Elba were very grateful to Lucas-Arslan for his contribution to defeating the pirates. Silius gave him full credit for the victory. Lucas-Arslan was quick to point out Silius was the responsible person who chose to follow good advice to make it happen. Silius deserved honors for the success.

The farm of Lucas-Arslan and Trina prospered over the next twelve years and there were no significant pirate raids during the time. They heard rumors had spread around the seaways the island of Elba had a huge force of defenders who were well trained and could defeat almost any pirate force. This exaggeration was likely started by the pirates who sailed away in fear. Whatever caused it, the pirates did not return for many years.

Trina was 65 years old by this time and was ageing significantly. Arslan did not age and Trina became very self-conscious of her deterioration from ageing compared to the youth of her husband.

Lucas-Arslan kept telling her, truthfully, he loved her and always would, but she was not always mollified by his words. Her health started to become precarious at this time also. She sometimes had a loss of equilibrium causing her to fall. Finally, in the spring of 905 A.D. she was walking down some steep steps on the way to town and fell breaking her hip and an arm. She failed quickly after the fall and died within a month of her fall.

Lucas-Arslan stayed on at the farm for another ten years after the death of Trina. He did not remarry during the time but did have a number of women in his bed. He had spent forty happy years with Trina and took time to adjust to her loss. The people of Elba surmised Lucas-Arslan had not had women of the island while his mother was alive to avoid conflict with his mother. After she was gone, they saw him become a ladies man.

In 915 A.D. Lucas-Arslan sold his farm and told his friends, including his best friend Silius, he was going to go back to family in Corinth. He left by ship for Pisa to find a ship for Corinth, or so he told them all.

49. <u>Rouen (Normandy 1063 A.D.)</u>

Arslan of Corinth rode into Rouen as a warrior knight looking for a lord to serve. He had all the trappings of knighthood since he had the money to buy what he needed and warrior skills exceeding anyone else in Europe. By saying he was a knight from far away Corinth, there was no one to dispute him. But, as always, he had to prove himself.

Several other knights were practicing with swords as Arslan introduced himself and offered his services. The practicing knights included a cousin of the Duke of Normandy. He challenged Arslan to a test of swordsmanship skills, apparently thinking this new knight would be an easy victory. The young man was duly chagrined when he found the sword missing from his hand after less than a minute of combat.

Then another knight from the group offered to try against Arslan. By this time a crowd was gathering as they faced off. The results were the same as with the first challenger. A voice called out from the back of the crowd, "Can no one do better against a foreign knight?" The crowd parted and Duke William walked through the crowd. One of William's most experienced knights came forward; a man everyone obviously feared named Jalbert of Rennes-le-Chateau and offered to challenge Arslan. William said, "Knight, you are not too tired to accept another challenge?"

Arslan said, "No problem, so far I have not broken a sweat."

Jalbert and Arslan faced off and the action started slowly but the paced picked up rapidly. Quickly Arslan perceived the other knight was highly skilled and fast. Perhaps a better opponent than Arslan had ever faced before. Jalbert was actually able to keep up with the strokes of Arslan. "If anything, we are evenly matched," thought Arslan. Arslan feigned falling back then in a flurry of strokes tried to send the opponents sword flying. It did not work. Their swords both met at a bad angle near the hilt and broke off due to sheer speed and force of the strokes.

William said, "What is the name of the knight who fights the unbeatable Jalbert to a draw."

"I am Arslan of Corinth and have come to Normandy to offer my sword in your service," said Arslan.

William said, "Well, Arslan of Corinth, you have an honored place in my service, especially if you can teach my knights to use a sword like you do. Jalbert is not so inclined to share his skills with living opponents, but perhaps you will?"

"Sire, My sword and teaching skills are at your command. In addition to my skill with weaponry and not limited to the sword, I am also quite capable in military strategy and tactics and offer you these services as well," said Arslan.

Jalbert spoke up, "Prince William, this one has great skill with the sword but strategy and tactics are another matter. Go slowly with what you use this stranger for. Even with a sword it may be another matter entirely, if the fight were to the death."

"Arslan of Corinth, are you as proficient in these other skills as with the sword." said William.

Arslan said, "Sire, the skills in military strategy and tactics are mental skills. These skills are not demonstrated as easily as weaponry skills, so I will not make claims I cannot prove now. Given time you will see and understand my level of expertise in these areas."

Arslan spent the next three years doing various services for Duke William. Arslan, spent many hours discussing military matters with William, as William came to see Arslan did have an unusual grasp of military skills. Arslan also came into conflict with Jalbert on several occasions and it was clear Jalbert had not warmed to the presence of Arslan.

William seemed to trust Arslan and Arslan was sent to lead missions to settle various squabbles and was used as someone who could be counted on to get intelligence information when such needs arose. Finally, in 1066, Arslan was given critical assignments concerning getting the invasion fleet put together for the effort to invade England.

50. Hastings, England (1066 A.D.)

In October 1066, the invasion fleet consisting of over 500 ships and 7,000 men landed on English soil near the village of Pevensey. On October 14th, 1066, William's army met the army of King Harold north of the bay where they had landed. Harold chose a ridge of land to set his army in a defensive position.

Arslan advised William to not attack the defensive position of the enemy directly but to have cavalry approach and turn aside throwing javelins into the defensive positions. He also recommended using archers to attack without incurring huge loses on the Norman side. Despite these tactics the battle raged all day long with fierce fighting at times. William lost three horses and was thought to have been killed at one point.

In the afternoon, Arslan suggested William try a stratagem using the Breton soldiers to feign a retreat, which caused the English right flank to break ranks and pursue the supposedly fleeing Bretons. The Bretons then turned and attacked the English cutting off a larger number who were then cut down. William then started attacking the English flanks. It was not easily won, but finally some of the militia in the English force left the field leaving the balance of the English to be attacked repeatedly by the Norman cavalry.

King Harold was surrounded by the remainder of his soldiers and continued the fight.

At this point, Arslan, arguably the best archer in the world, took a bow and took aim at Harold from a great distance. Using techniques learned from many archers in many armies, Arslan sent his arrow off. In struck Harold in the eye with a fatal blow. With their leader dead the battle was done.

Arslan did not wish to claim credit for the arrow he launched at Harold. For one, he did not need the recognition such an act could cause and he did not feel it was necessarily a noble act. He had sent the arrow into Harold in an effort to cease the killing, which was becoming a slaughter. It did not really have the effect he had desired.

The day after the battle, Duke William gave the order to his army to spread out over south England and destroy everything and kill all Saxons found; men, women and children. Arslan was appalled beyond belief. He went to the Duke and protested the order, telling him it would set back his ability to rule this land and would be remembered by history as a great crime. The Duke was not moved, he explained the Normans would bring people to England to repopulate the land. The Saxons must be reduced to a small portion of the population for the Normans to take the country. Arslan saw this had been the Duke's plan all along and no amount of arguing was going to change it.

Arslan rode out of the Norman camp alone heading back toward the coast to try to find a ship going back to the continent. He made a loop to the east to try to get to the town of Rye on the coast. He traveled several miles and came upon a small village where he saw Norman knights herding several adults and a group of children toward the forest. Arslan rode toward them and saw one of the knights raise his sword and hack down one of the adults. Arslan yelled to the knights to get their attention. They turned and watched Arslan ride up to them and dismount.

Arslan saw one of the knights was Jalbert. Arslan said, "Knights, what are you doing here?"

Jalbert responded, "We are carrying out the orders of Duke William to kill all Saxons. Why do you ask, Arslan of Corinth?"

Arslan said, "The order has been changed and now the Duke wants women and children spared."

Jalbert responded, "I have heard no such order from William. We will go ahead and kill these Saxon vermin, then go check if the order is changed."

Arslan said, "You will not kill these women and children until you kill me. Walk away from here and you live, stay to commit murder and you will die here today."

Jalbert said, "Sooner or later I knew it would come to this between us."

The knight raised his sword to strike at Arslan. Before he could start the downward stroke, Arslan blocked the blow. The other two knights moved to attack Arslan. They appeared to be moving in slow motion compared to Arslan as he killed one and then the other in a matter of seconds.

Jalbert moved to attack again and he and Arslan fought for twenty minutes of constant action. They were so equally matched as opponents every move seemed to be mirrored by the corresponding move of the other. Arslan thought, *"This man has skills to match mine, I have never encountered this before. How do we end the contest?"*

Out of his side vision, Arslan saw an object come from the side and strike the side of Jalbert's head. It was a rock weighing about two pounds. Jalbert was dazed by the rock for only a moment but Arslan took immediate advantage and drove his sword into Jalbert's heart. Jalbert fell immediately to the ground.

Arslan turned to the two surviving adult women and said, "Women, is there a place you can go to and hide until this butchery is over with?"

One of the women came forward and said; "I do not know who you are kind knight, but thank you for our lives, for now. I know of no place which will be safe now. The knights you killed said William's men had spread out over all the land to kill Saxons. We know of no safe place."

Arslan noticed the woman who spoke was young and quite attractive. He asked, "What is your name?

She answered, "I am Esmeld, daughter of Michael of Westfield. The other woman is Harriet, a servant in our household. The children are children of our tenants who we brought together to try to save from the butchery. We were taking them to be hidden at my father's castle but it has been destroyed. What can we do now to save them?"

Arslan said, "What can we do to save all of us? The only plan I can think of is to get to a ship or boat and cross the channel to the continent. We can then try to blend into the population. Does it make sense?"

"Yes, good knight, it is probably the only way we can survive. I know where there is a large boat hidden, east of Westfield. I can show you the way," said Esmeld.

Arslan said, "Let's go now! We have no time to waste. By the way who threw the rock hitting my opponent in the head?"

A voice from behind said, "I did."

Arslan looked around and saw a boy of about twelve years.

Arslan said, "I am in your debt. Without the stone, I don't know which of us might have eventually won."

The boy said, "I know, that's why I threw it. I wanted to live."

Arslan said, "We must go now, but we will talk later."

Staying in the trees as much as possible and moving in silence the group of three adults, eighteen children and Arslan's horse moved as quickly as possible toward the coast. Esmeld knew the area well and kept them hidden as much as possible. They did not stop when it became dark but kept moving toward their objective. Finally, about midnight, they reached the coast and Esmeld led them to a small cove where a boat about thirty feet long was tied up.

Arslan and the women loaded the children into the boat and found two oars in the boat. The sail was stowed and Arslan decided they should try to use the oars to get the boat as far from shore as possible before they tried to use the sail. Arslan and Esmeld each took an oar and proceeded to move the boat slowly out to sea. Once they got out about a mile, they set the sail and Arslan guided the boat with an oar.

Arslan planned to land in Flanders near the port of Boulogne. This had the advantage of avoiding landing in Normandy where the forces of Duke William might think a strange knight with many Saxon children with him was unusual. Arslan had enough gold with him to find a place in Flanders for the children to be cared for.

During their first night at sea, Arslan was growing tired but had little choice but to continue guiding the boat. He was suddenly surprised by a voice beside him saying, "Oh knight, May I help you steer the boat? You look tired. I have experience with boats like this and would like to help."

Arslan turned around a saw the twelve-year-old boy sitting about three feet away. Arslan said, "What is your name young man?

The youngster said, "I am Thomas, Thomas Arslanus."

Arslan was taken aback but remained an outward calm as he said, "It is an unusual name. Do you know the history of your family name?"

Thomas said, "Well, there is a legend in the north where my family lived before moving to the coast. The legend is about a great Roman soldier, the greatest swordsman of his time, who saved my people from disaster, hundreds of years ago. His name was Arslanus and my family is descended from him, or so the story goes. Who knows if the story is true but names must come from somewhere. Do you think it could be true, good knight?"

Arslan said, "Thomas, I am sure the story is true. I think I read somewhere about such a man."

Thomas said, "There is another part to the story. The legend says Arslanus did not die but disappeared and will return some day to save his people again. After hundreds of years it is unlikely, don't you think?"

"It is unlikely, but men do not understand all mysteries. So, perhaps, he might return," said Arslan.

"Good knight, what is your name, so I may tell the story of how you saved our lives from sure death?" said Thomas.

Arslan said, "My name is Arslan of Corinth. Corinth is in Greece, far to the south and east. But I did not save you alone, your stone helped you save yourself."

Thomas said with a look of awe, "It is a wonder your name is so much like the name of the great Arslanus and you also seem to be the greatest swordsman of your time. Are you a real man or are you a spirit sent to save us from the Normans?"

Arslan said, "I am a real man, not a spirit. It is just a coincidence my name is similar to the hero of your legend. Please speak no more of it, others may think it strange and cause problems for us."

Thomas said, "I will do as you ask, Arslan of Corinth, but I am not convinced you are an ordinary man."

Arslan sat there guiding the boat and thought *about how fate had brought him to save the life of at least one of his descendants after about 1,000 years of separation from this part of his family. Perhaps all life is not the repetitive losing of loved ones. Sometimes he may be able to save lives, even of his own people.*

Arslan's thoughts were interrupted by Esmeld coming over and sitting down beside him. The moon was three quarters full and she was absolutely beautiful in the moonlight. She appeared to be about twenty years old with dark hair and very deep eyes. She said to him, "Arslan of Corinth, I heard your exchange with Thomas. It does seem very strange you have a name so similar to the hero of his legend and I agree with him you are most certainly not an ordinary man. But I also observe, while you are hardly ordinary, you seem to be very much a man. I do not mean to embarrass you, but I have lost much today, and you are now a hero to me for saving the lives of these innocent children."

Arslan said, "I did what I had to do. Saving these children means much more to me than you can imagine. Saving your life is something I am very happy about also. You are a very beautiful woman and one who cares so much for others. You must be very beautiful in your heart as well. I am glad we have come into each other's lives. What will you do when we get to Flanders?" How can you care for so many children? I have some gold I can give you to help but it will not last forever."

Esmeld said, "I do not know but I know we will do well. Perhaps we can find homes for some of the children. Can you stay and help us for a while? I would like to have your help and protection."

"I will stay as long as you need me but I must tell you if we are together for very long, I expect I will want to be more than just a friend. I already feel a growing attraction to you as a woman. Does it offend you?" said Arslan.

"No, Arslan, it does not offend me. It makes me feel wonderful my hero would be attracted to me. Does it sound too strange?" said Esmeld.

Arslan said, "Life is very difficult in this place and time. Perhaps you and I can try together to help these children and, perhaps, we will find some help for ourselves together. Does that also sound strange?

Esmeld said, "No Arslan, it sounds very good to me."

Esmeld moved over close to Arslan and kissed him on the lips. Arslan pulled her closer with one arm, keeping the other on the oar guiding the ship, and kissed her long and passionately. They then sat holding each other as the night passed and the distance from England became greater and greater.

51. <u>Flanders (1066 A.D.)</u>

The boat reached the port of Boulogne late the following afternoon. Some of Arslan's gold was used to make entry into Flanders easier. Arslan heard of a large house available for rent and he paid in advance for three months. This would give them time to see about finding homes for some of the children and to come up with a plan for the future.

The children's ages were girls: thirteen-1, eleven-1, nine-2, eight-1, seven-2, five-1, four-1, and three-1; and boys: twelve-1, ten-2, eight-2, six-1, and four-2. The boys would be easy to find homes to place them with. Farmers needed sons to help in the fields and boys were welcome. Girls were not so easily placed.

By the end of two months, they had found homes for all the boys except Thomas Arslanus, who did not wish to leave Arslan, and all the girls except the five, four and three year olds. The girls were named Faith, Mary, and Chelsea. Arslan was not sad they were left with them. He loved little girls and these three had found places in his heart.

Also by the end of two months Arslan and Esmeld had married and were very happy spending time together as man and wife. Arslan was still living off the gold he had brought with him from England but was anxious to find a way to support his newly found family.

One day, traveling to the south, he found a tavern near Lille for sale. The owner was old and was having trouble doing the work required for such a business. Arslan had much experience with taverns as a customer and as the husband of a tavern owner in Rome. He decided to buy the tavern, which included enough space for his family plus rooms to rent out. Esmeld, the three girls, and Thomas moved in and became tavern keepers.

The tavern was situated on a main road so they had plenty of traffic for business for the tavern. Their typical clientele were knights, merchants, or clerics, plus local tradesmen or wealthier farmers. Arslan made friends easily so many repeat customers came by the tavern. Esmeld was very proficient at cooking and other aspects of running the tavern so the business did well. Arslan spent much of his time teaching Thomas various skills including languages, reading, writing, swordsmanship and other knightly skills. He also took time to teach the girls language, reading, and writing skills as they became old enough to learn.

Esmeld and Arslan especially liked to go out into the countryside when they could to enjoy the outdoors. Because of the need to have someone at the tavern all the time, Arslan hired a man to help at the tavern. His name was Frederik and was about twenty years old. He was a pleasant young man but not too ambitious and had to be prodded to work harder at times. But he was honest and could be depended upon to protect Arslan's interest when they left him alone there.

One day in the summer of 1070 A.D. Arslan took the family out for the day for a picnic. When they returned in late afternoon they saw six horses, apparently belonging to soldiers, outside the tavern. When Arslan entered the tavern he saw four of the soldiers were seated at a table and two of the soldiers had Frederik backed against the wall and were threatening him with a dagger. Instinctively, Arslan yelled out, "Halt, away from him and out of my tavern."

The soldiers all turned toward Arslan who was wearing his sword but no armor. One of the two soldiers close to Frederik said, "Who has the nerve to tell me to stop? I do not take orders from tavern keepers."

The soldier started advancing toward Arslan and drew his sword. Arslan immediately drew his own sword. The soldier slashed at Arslan with his sword but found only air. In the next moment, Arslan's sword severed the soldier's sword arm at the wrist. As he fell writhing in pain, the other soldiers got up from their chairs and advanced on Arslan. Arslan chose to attack and slashed one soldier across the shoulder and struck another on the leg almost severing it. The other three soldiers backed away. Arslan asked, "Who wants to die today? If you do not, pick up your friends and leave this place. Your lives are forfeit if you choose to stay."

The soldiers each helped one of their fellow soldiers out to their horses and rode away. Arslan considered what to do? Would the soldiers come back with more soldiers and try to kill him? He chose to take Esmeld and the girls to the house of friends in Lille while Thomas, Frederik, and he stayed at the tavern. He instructed Frederik to run away out the back if soldiers showed up since he was not proficient with a sword. Thomas was a well-trained swordsman by this time but not necessarily good enough to defeat a really good swordsman. He also told Thomas to leave by the back door if the soldiers came.

Two days later Arslan saw a force of about twelve soldiers riding toward the tavern. One of the riders was obviously a knight based on the type of armor and quality of horse. Arslan thought about running away but made the decision to stay and deal with the trouble. Thomas and Frederik watched from hiding to see what would happen. Arslan stood outside with his armor on waiting for the riders.

The knight leading the riders dismounted about twenty-five yards from Arslan. The knight called out, "Who is the knight who mutilates my soldiers, for no reason."

Arslan responded, "I am Arslan of Corinth, in Greece, but I do not mutilate soldiers for no reason. I mutilate brutal soldiers who threaten to harm my employees and my family."

"My soldiers say you attacked them without provocation. Do you now say they lie?" said the knight.

"Yes, they are liars. Are they also cowards? That is my guess. Perhaps you would let the three soldiers who were not harmed fight me now. Three should be able to beat one, shouldn't they?" said Arslan.

The knight asked the three soldiers if they would fight Arslan. They were noticeably frightened and did not answer. Arslan suggested they not be given a choice but would have to fight Arslan to prove they were telling the truth. The knight ordered them to fight Arslan but they started to cower and refused.

Arslan asked if any of the soldiers would be willing to fight him. Finally three of the braver ones agreed to fight. Arslan somewhat admired these brave men, he would hate to kill them. Arslan suggested, "These are brave men who are not afraid like the other three. I would hate to kill these men. Let me fight the first three, first, when they are dead, perhaps these men will not make me kill them. The knight ordered the first three soldiers to fight Arslan and pushed them forward. One fell to the ground and begged Arslan to spare him. The others just cowered there.

The knight slashed his sword down at the man on the ground and almost took his head off, literally. The other two saw they would die no matter what they did and attacked Arslan. With quick flashing strokes, Arslan ended their bitter lives. Arslan then turned to the second three soldiers and said, "Will you choose to die today, or walk away and live?"

The three soldiers backed away. Arslan asked, "Does anyone else want to die today. If not leave me in peace. Three of you are no match for my sword. I am not sure if six of you could take me. Perhaps, I could kill all of you if you chose to fight me. Try if you do not believe me."

The soldiers did not look comfortable when Arslan said these things. The knight said, "You are very sure of yourself, Arslan of Corinth, do you also think you could take a knight who has experience in battle?"

Arslan said, "Knight, you may have experience but your experience is no match for mine. My skill with a sword was taught to me by dead men, many, many dead men. Do you want to join them? Few men survive on the business end of my sword. You seem like a reasonable man, do not make me kill you. These two I just killed and the three I maimed were brutes and cowards. Their loss is no loss to your forces. Better to have them dead now, than to run away when you need them in battle."

The knight said, "You are either the greatest swordsman in the world or a fool who talks too much. Which is it?"

Arslan said, "Perhaps I can prove it to you without killing you. Fight me as a contest, I will promise not to strike a deathblow unless you try to do so. You may see what you are up against."

The knight said, "I agree to a fair contest without death blows."

The knight moved forward and raised his sword. Before he could move his sword to strike, Arslan's sword moved faster than the eye could follow and struck his sword so sharply his sword broke. The soldiers watching backed away muttering. They expected their knight to be struck down. Arslan said, "Well, brave knight, have you learned anything?"

The knight said, "Yes, I have learned you may well be the greatest swordsman in the world, unless you are a demon of some kind."

"If I were a demon, I would kill you all. I am simply a man protecting his business," said Arslan.

"You do not fight like any tavern keeper I have known. How did you come to have this skill? You did not learn it in a tavern." said the knight.

"Come into my tavern, have some wine, and I will tell you my story. Your men may join us if they behave." said Arslan.

Arslan yelled for Thomas and Frederik to come out of hiding and join them, and then led them into the tavern. After pouring wine for everyone, Arslan told the knight he had recently served with Duke William of Normandy on the invasion of England. He told of the brutal order to kill all Saxon men, women and children and his saving of Esmeld and the children. The knight said he had heard about the carnage caused by the Normans and was appalled by it. Arslan asked his name and he said, Waller of Arras, a minor noble in the service of Robert of Flanders, uncle of the Count of Flanders.

Waller asked if Thomas was his son and Arslan indicated he was one of the children he had rescued. The knight noticed Thomas wore a sword and asked if he also knew how to use a sword. Arslan told him he had trained him for the last four years and expected he could defeat any of the soldiers with Waller and possibly Waller himself. Waller was noticeably impressed. Arslan also said he expected in a few more years Thomas would be the second best swordsman in Europe. Waller did not have to ask who the best was.

Waller asked why Arslan was keeping a tavern when he could be in almost any army in Europe getting honor and riches. Arslan simply said he was tired of being told to kill innocents.

Waller and Arslan became friends. Waller asked Arslan if he would teach him some of his secrets with the sword and Arslan agreed. Whenever Waller was nearby he would stop at the tavern and they would go out the back to an empty field and practice, often with Thomas joining them. Waller soon found Thomas, at the age of sixteen, was at least as good with a sword as Waller and was improving every day. Before long he would be better than Waller, probably much better.

One day Waller brought an older knight with him to watch them practice. Thomas and Waller practiced and Thomas disarmed Waller. The older knight commented Waller's opponent was a great swordsman as had been described to him. Waller then told him this young man was only the student; his teacher was much better than he was. Waller then asked Arslan to come out and practice. Arslan came out and warmed up a few minutes casually with Waller. Waller then asked Arslan to show his visitor more of his skill. Arslan started to speed up the pace and finally had his sword going at what looked like a fast pace, eventually disarming Waller. Thomas and Arslan then were matched against each other. They gradually picked up the pace until their swords were moving faster than the eye could easily follow. Thomas kept up with Arslan at this point. Then Arslan picked up the pace again and Thomas was disarmed.

The older knight said he had never seen anything like what he had just witnessed. He said he had been a good swordsman when he was younger but could never approach the skill levels of either Thomas or Arslan, especially Arslan. He introduced himself as Robert of Flanders. He was in the process of forming an army to fight against his nephew, Arnulf of Flanders who was now Count of Flanders. Arslan asked why he was fighting against his nephew. Robert responded Arnulf had taken the title of Count when his father, Robert's brother had died. The title was supposed to go to Robert but Robert was visiting in Italy when his brother died and Arnulf effectively stole the title. Since Arnulf became count he showed himself to be a brutal leader who had killed many men and committed other crimes.

Robert wanted Arslan and Thomas to come and join his army. Arslan said, "I wish to stay here with my family and take care of this tavern, however, Thomas is old enough to make his own decisions."

Thomas said he would like to spend some time teaching swordsmanship to Robert's soldiers but wanted to continue living with Arslan most of the time. The older knight was satisfied with the arrangement and left with Waller.

Over the next several months Thomas would leave for several weeks at a time and train with the army. He would then return and live at the tavern for several weeks. Thomas did not say too much about his experience with the army but seemed happy with it. Waller came by occasionally and kept Arslan informed about how Thomas was doing. Waller explained initially the soldiers thought he was joking about a sixteen year old teaching them about weapons, but then they would test Thomas and he easily defeated each one who challenged. After a while his reputation was so good he was no longer challenged, except by fools.

Waller came by one day in the fall of 1071 A.D. and stopped at the tavern to bring a warning to Arslan the soldiers of the Count of Flanders were sweeping through the area confiscating anything of value from people and businesses for the purpose of paying for the army of the count. Two days later a force of about fifteen soldiers showed up at the tavern. Arslan wore his sword and armor, as did Thomas. Frederik, who had been trained with the bow by Arslan, was hiding nearby. The soldiers demanded Arslan give everything of value to them or they would burn the tavern. Esmeld and the girls had been sent to hide in the forest.

Arslan said to the knight leading the soldiers, "By what right do you seek to steal all we have?"

The knight said, "By the right of fifteen swords versus two."

Arslan said, "That is not enough. Ride away now or die here. Make your own choice."

The knight and soldiers started to move forward. From years of experience, Arslan chose to attack the knight leading the group. With speed and surprise he attacked and killed the knight quickly then dispatched four of the soldiers while Thomas defended Arslan's back. Thomas downed two more of the soldiers and arrows sent by Frederik from his hiding spot wounded two more. The surviving soldiers saw they had not found a defenseless quarry this time and rode away as quickly as they could.

Arslan saw he had made a choice of sides in this war between uncle and nephew. He had now alienated the soldiers of the nephew and had a friend in the service of the uncle, so his choice was easy. He sent Thomas to find Waller and to volunteer their services to the army of Robert. Waller sent back word of Robert's army forming near Arras within the next several weeks and expecting a battle with the forces of Arnulf soon. Arslan left the tavern in the hands of Frederik, took Esmeld and the girls to Lille to stay with friends, and Thomas and himself went to Arras to join the army of Robert.

When Arslan found the army of Robert it numbered about 200 knights and perhaps 200 other soldiers. They were not organized and Arslan quickly volunteered to help train them to fight together. He had little time, it appeared, but he threw his full effort into adding some teamwork to Robert's army. With the help of Thomas and Waller who were trained by Arslan already, they created three companies. Arslan took command of one, Waller another, and Robert the other, with Thomas as his aide. Arslan trained them to work together and to follow orders, not act like disorganized mobs.

After about two weeks of training, they received word the army of Arnulf was camped near Kassel. Robert saw no sense in waiting, since winter would be coming and his adherents would not want to stay with the army in the winter. Arslan did not disagree and hoped the training and discipline would pay off for Robert's army.

When they arrived in the vicinity of Kassel, the army of Count Arnulf awaited them across a field of tall grass, browned by an early frost. Arnulf's forces appeared to consist of about six hundred men, but Arslan quickly saw they were not organized or disciplined. They were bunched together in one mass and if attacked would allow only the men at the front an opportunity to fight effectively. Arslan asked Robert point out which of the knights was Arnulf. Robert said the knight wearing red trim in the middle front of the mass was Arnulf.

Arslan suggested his company attack directly at Arnulf in the center with the companies of Waller and Robert holding back slightly until the forces from the flanks of Arnulf started to commit themselves. Once they started to come around to attack the flanks of Arslan's company, Robert and Waller would attack. Arslan also said to Robert he planned to attack directly at Arnulf and would kill the leader if he could. Did Robert have any problem with his nephew being killed? Robert indicated Arnulf deserved his fate.

Arslan led his company in a frontal attack on Arnulf's force. Arslan knew from experience a swift attack would usually bring confusion to the enemy. In this case he went directly for Arnulf using his superior swordsmanship to cut through any defenders in front of Arnulf. After dispatching about five soldiers in front, Arslan was in a position to force individual combat with the count. Arslan said to him, "Surrender and you will live, otherwise you die here and now."

Arnulf said, "Who are you to ask my surrender?"

Arslan said, "I am the last face you will see in this life if you do not surrender. That is all you need to know."

Arnulf attacked Arslan but did not even see the sword stroke, which slashed across his neck and took him to the ground. Arslan started the cry, "Arnulf is dead. Arnulf is dead." It spread through the army of Arnulf and Robert called for the soldiers to stop fighting. There was no reason for the soldiers of Flanders to kill each other for no reason. There may be other enemies of Flanders in the future they would need to fight.

A few days later, Robert was declared Count of Flanders. Count Robert offered to reward Arslan for his service by appointing him leader of the army of Flanders but Arslan only wanted to return to his tavern. Thomas was appointed to a command position in the army along with Waller.

Arslan settled back into the life of a tavern keeper but had many visitors who wanted to see the knight who won the battle of Kessel with so little bloodshed. He was invited to the court of the Count of Flanders on many occasions and accepted when it was convenient.

In 1074 A.D. Waller came to the tavern to invite him to attend a festival in the city of Bruges, near the coast, where many of the knights in the army of Flanders would gather to test each other and have a good time. Thomas would participate in the contests with weapons and Arslan could participate if he chose to attend.

Arslan and his family traveled to Bruges about two weeks later to attend the festival, leaving Frederik to care for the tavern. As they grew closer to Bruges they saw signs of the festive atmosphere. There were people coming from all directions, some carrying goods to sell, others in what was obviously their best clothes, ready to enjoy the activities. Arslan and Thomas were dressed in their armor and riding their horses. Esmeld and the girls were dressed in their finest riding in a horse drawn cart.

Just outside the city a number of knights were gathered, including Waller and many of the men who had fought at Kessel, from both sides. Waller greeted them and paid his respects to Esmeld and the girls. The girls loved Waller because he always brought them gifts when he came to visit and paid them much more attention than most adults. He was one of these men who took time for children and, of course, they responded in kind. They asked Waller if he would beat Thomas and Arslan in the contests. Waller laughed and said, "Perhaps, if I was very, very lucky I might beat Thomas, but defeating Arslan is simply not possible."

Robert, Count of Flanders would attend these games and would award a prize to the knights who won the various contests. The Count's youngest son, about 19 years old, was a renowned swordsman and was entered in the contest. Arslan was first matched against a friend of Waller who had practiced with Arslan previously and who knew he could not win against Arslan. He fought as well as he could but the contest was done in less than a minute.

Next Arslan was matched against the Count's son. Lauren was his name and he appeared to be a bit on the arrogant side. As they squared off for the contest Lauren said to Arslan, "So you are the knight who tends a tavern and killed my cousin in battle. Some seem to think you are a swordsman but today you will see what it is like to fight a real knight."

"Perhaps you are right, young knight, but, perhaps, you will find the lesson is words are cheap, and skill and steel are what is real," said Arslan.

Lauren attacked after hearing those words, hoping to catch Arslan off guard. Arslan sidestepped his attack with ease and tripped the young knight as he went by. Arslan did not pursue the fallen knight but allowed him to regain his feet. The embarrassed young man, with his father the count looking on, was very angry. He attacked again without modifying his tactics and was tripped again. Again Arslan did not pursue the advantage but allowed him to get up. Lauren attacked again but with less speed and Arslan engaged him in a short exchange of sword strokes before Arslan disarmed him with the flat of Arslan's sword on the young man's wrist, preceded by a series of sword strokes faster than the eye could see.

The embarrassed young knight left the contest field quickly. Arslan then was matched against Thomas in the finals of the contest. They squared off against each other with Thomas knowing full well, from practicing daily with Arslan, he could end the contest in a matter of seconds if he chose to do so. He knew Arslan, however, and figured Arslan would want to demonstrate their skills to the audience. They fought for about fifteen minutes with both Thomas and Arslan showing their skills. Then Arslan gradually started to speed up his sword strokes to the point Thomas could not follow and the sword was struck from Thomas' hand.

Arslan received his prize, a young, untrained horse, and Arslan and his family enjoyed the rest of the festival.

Several weeks later, Waller entered the tavern and asked Arslan to go outside with him. When they were alone, Waller said, "The count has sent me here to ask for your help. He has information the Count of Vermandois will launch an attack on Flanders within the next few weeks and attempt to annex the cities of Arras and Lille to the County of Vermandois. The Count of Flanders is raising an army but he needs the best fighting men if he is to have any chance. He needs Thomas and yourself to lead the force from Lille. Others will follow if they know you are supporting your count."

Arslan thought for a few minutes then said, "Thomas and I will lead a force from Lille. This attack could mean danger to my family. I will always fight to defend my family."

In two weeks Arslan had raised a force of about ten knights and forty archers. He organized an accelerated training program for them. He had a respectable force when it was time to go west to meet up with the rest of the Count of Flanders force west of Arras. Most of the knights involved were friends of Arslan and Thomas and had trained with them previously.

Arslan's force of fifty met up with about 300 more men under the Count of Flanders several days later. The Count was very pleased Arslan and Robert had agreed to join the fight. The Count of Vermandois was rumored to have over 500 men at arms, many hired mercenaries who came to loot and pillage. The count thanked Arslan but also expressed his concern 350 against 500 were not good odds. Arslan suggested one of his favorite strategies. Instead of fighting it out toe to toe against the enemy, where numbers mattered, use strategy. Arslan knew of a place nearby where there was a field with some dense trees to the right and left. He suggested putting a main force at one end of this funnel, about 200 men, then putting twenty of his archers on each side in the forest to rain arrows on the enemy just before they met the main force. They would be focused on attacking the main force and would not take time to go after the archers. The archers would be able to kill or wound many of the enemy before they knew what was happening.

Another force of about 100 knights and swordsmen would also be hiding in the forest and would attack the enemy from the left rear and right rear just when it was meeting the main Flanders force. The confusion this would cause could turn the battle into a rout or so Arslan hoped. Arslan would lead one group attacking from the rear and Thomas would lead the other. The Count liked the idea and set up as Arslan had requested. Arslan also asked to have Lauren, the count's son, as part of his party.

When the main force from the County of Vermandois arrived at the far end of the field they saw the smaller force of Flanders soldiers. They shouted at the smaller force and were impatient to attack. The Count of Vermandois ordered his men to attack, committing his entire force. They ran forward in a disorganized mob. Suddenly, before they reached the men of Flanders, arrows started striking down the men from Vermandois. They continued attacking but there was some confusion and fear, they did not expect this.

When the main forces came together, the organized formation of Flanders soldiers, held well against the chaotic army of Vermandois. Many of the men of Vermandois were bunched up behind their comrades ahead of them and could not effectively fight. Arrows continued to pour out of the forest into these milling men of Vermandois. Suddenly, and loud cheer went up from the men of Flanders as the two groups of knights and swordsmen attacked the rear flanks of the enemy.

There was great confusion in the army of Vermandois as two wedges of inspired swordsmen slammed into their flanks led by the flashing swords of several great swordsmen. The men of Vermandois in the center rear started to flee with others catching the infectious need to flee. Arslan attacked straight at the Count of Vermandois and quickly got close enough to knock him from his horse with a sword stroke, which severely wounded his left arm. Arslan got down from his horse and took the enemy count captive.

With their leader captive and half the men of Vermandois running away the battle was now a rout. Arslan took his prisoner to the Count of Flanders and turned him over the count's guards. Arslan then went around the battlefield and encouraged the men of Flanders to show mercy and take prisoners rather than killing these beaten men. In the end there were about 100 dead, 250 prisoners, and 150 who ran away of the 500 men of Vermandois who invaded. Flanders lost about twenty men.

Arslan suggested the prisoners be stripped of their arms and most of their clothing then driven almost naked back to Vermandois. Arriving in Vermandois without clothing might be as bad as killing them, especially when their count was a prisoner.

The army of Flanders returned to Bruges two days later with large carts piled with arms, armor, and clothing from the army of Vermandois. When the people of Bruges were told of the naked men finding their way back to Vermandois, the whole city laughed at the good turn of fate.

The Count of Flanders held court the next day and honored Arslan and others for their help in defeating the enemy. Arslan was singled out for praise. Arslan for his part took time to praise Thomas and Lauren for the leadership they had shown. Arslan had made a new friend in Lauren, with this act, and a friend for Thomas, who might need one someday.

A message was sent to Vermandois saying their count was captive and would be returned in exchange for a tribute of ten pounds of gold to pay the cost of the "war." The ransom was paid several weeks later and a most humbled count was returned to his people.

Arslan was now a hero in all of Flanders with Thomas and Lauren not far behind. Business at the tavern picked up significantly as men came to see or be seen with Arslan and Thomas.

By 1079 A.D. the three girls, Faith, Mary and Chelsea were eighteen, seventeen, and sixteen. As such things happen, all of the girls were beauties, although all had different parents. Thomas was twenty-five and a handsome young man. Esmeld loved her adopted children, as did Arslan.

Lauren, youngest son of the Count of Flanders was now twenty-four years old and had become great friends with Thomas and Arslan. He also had become a good friend with the girls and especially with Faith. It was no surprise to Arslan and Esmeld when Lauren approached Arslan with his request to marry Faith. Arslan said immediately it was Faith's decision to say yes or no. She, of course, said yes, and in the fall they were married in a great ceremony in Bruges. Her sisters were her maids of honor, and as the centers of attention, they now started receiving many marriage proposals, from the best, brightest and richest young men of Flanders. Thomas, likewise, came to the attention of the great families of Flanders who had marriageable daughters. A constant stream of visitors seemed to be coming to the tavern of Arslan to find out about his adopted daughters and son.

Mary received a proposal of marriage from an unexpected source. Waller, at the age of twenty-nine and unmarried came to the tavern one day. He asked Arslan to step out where they could talk. Arslan saw he was very uncomfortable. Waller spoke finally, "Arslan, I come to you not as your good friend, which I am, but as a man wanting to talk to a father of a beautiful young daughter, Mary, who I wish to marry, if she will have me. I hope I do not offend you with this question but I have come to know your family well, and also have come to know the kindness and character of Mary. She is a wonderful girl and I would be a fool to look elsewhere for a wife."

Arslan spoke, "Waller, you are one of the best men in this land. If Mary will marry you, I can think of no one better for her."

When asked by Waller, Mary was delighted and agreed to marry Waller. She had, of course, loved him for years.

Next a surprise suitor appeared for Chelsea. Frederik, one day, approached Arslan outside and said, "Arslan, I know many rich and great men have come to you wanting to marry Chelsea. She has yet to accept anyone. I am but a tavern keeper, no, only a tavern keeper's helper. Would you let me ask Chelsea to marry me?"

Arslan said, "You are a fine man Frederik. One of the best men I know. Do not be ashamed to ask Chelsea."

Frederik asked and Chelsea accepted. As with most things between men and women, Chelsea had some inkling of Frederik's feelings for her and had long ago decided he was the man for her if he ever asked.

Thomas was now one of the top leaders of the Flanders military at the tender age of twenty-five. He had been the one to return the Count of Vermandois to his home when his ransom was paid several years earlier. At his castle, he had met the Count's youngest daughter, a girl of fifteen, but beautiful, named Helen. The girl had obviously liked the handsome young Saxon from Flanders. They had exchanged letters several times over the past three years and now Helen was eighteen and wanted Thomas to visit her with the purpose of asking her father to let her be married to Thomas. Arslan discussed this with the Count of Flanders, as there were political implications to such a marriage. The Count agreed such a marriage could help to improve relations between the two regions but asked Arslan to go with Thomas to make the official nature of the "alliance" more complete.

Thomas and Arslan traveled to the city of Amiens in Vermandois to visit the count and to ask for his daughter as a wife for Thomas. A squire was sent ahead to advise the count of the impending visit. When they arrived the count met them with a guard of honor. Both Arslan and Thomas had treated the count with honor and kindness when he was a prisoner in Flanders and the count felt obligated to show them respect. He also liked both Thomas and Arslan.

At dinner in the evening, with the Count, Helen, Thomas and Arslan at the main table, the Count asked Arslan what business brought him to Vermandois? Did it involve bringing back some of the clothing stripped from soldiers several years earlier? The comment was said in jest and not intended to be provocative.

Arslan responded, "No, it is not the reason but it does involve improving the relations between Flanders and Vermandois. My family is now tied to the family of the Count of Flanders by my oldest daughter's marriage to the Count of Flanders's son. The Count of Flanders thinks some tie to your family by marriage would help improve our political relations. By happenstance, my son Thomas here has maintained a correspondence with your daughter for the last several years. To my understanding, these young people would ask your permission for them to marry. Such a marriage would have the support of the Count of Flanders and myself. Adding your approval would give us a basis for wiping away ill feelings between our regions."

The Count of Vermandois said, "I see from the eyes of my daughter she fully supports this alliance and your son is also in agreement. How can I stand in the way of young love? I agree and hope we will all be great friends."

The marriage of Helen and Thomas took place six weeks later at a great festival in Amiens with the Counts of both Flanders and Vermandois in attendance. Arslan had now married off all his adopted children. Esmeld and Arslan could now enjoy some years together before he had to change identities again.

In 1083 A.D. Esmeld caught a fever and died suddenly at the age of thirty-eight. Arslan grieved for the loss of his wonderful wife, but life goes on. He started to think about has next move. He had been aging himself with gray hair but could cover for only so long. He should probably leave within a few years.

Three years later, in 1086 A.D., Arslan turned the tavern over to Frederik and Chelsea and left with Robert, Count of Flanders, on a pilgrimage to Jerusalem. Arslan was not going for religious reasons but saw it as a way to make an exit from Flanders since he was now reaching the point where his lack of ageing would be a problem.

52. Chandler, Arizona

Arslan stopped reading and looked at the clock. It was very late, past midnight. "Why didn't anyone stop me," he said.

Carrie said, "Everyone was transfixed by your story, we didn't want to miss anything."

Before they could continue the conversation, the computer announced, "There is a new E-mail from Ramede or Zneot of Giza for Arslan." A screen appeared with an E-mail on it:

fwd: smyers@ctrdna.org
to: older_than_dirt.com
from: beard90@aol.com
subject: Blood Sample to Atlanta

Dear Arslan,

From watching the news, it is obvious you now have the blood sample. If the Tira is anything like it has been described, I suspect you now have confirmation I am who I claim to be.

What do we do now? We obviously need to meet and talk. It appears I need to give up my anonymity to do it. This is difficult for me after so many years of hiding.

Well, here goes! I am living in a small town in the Pocono Mountains in eastern Pennsylvania; a town called Wind Gap, PA. I live in an apartment complex called Windy Woods Townhouses, apartment 123. The name I am using is Cindy Beard.

Please come for me quickly before my fears make me run away.

Best regards,
Cindy

Arslan immediately said, "Looks like we are going on another trip, immediately. I will contact the FBI and the military, but will not give complete information about where we are going. Does anyone disagree?"

Everyone agreed with Arslan. The FBI and the Joint Chief's were notified the Tira was taking another trip, to the northeast this time, but no precise destination. When they said they would leave immediately and travel at a high rate of speed toward Philadelphia, there was concern about the highly congested air traffic in the area. Arslan assured the concerned air traffic people they would take all precautions.

By 2:30 a.m. the Tira was ready for travel and they took off, rising to 60.000 feet, then moving cross-country at a high rate of speed, 3,000+ miles per hour. They were over the Pocono's by 3:30 a.m. and hovering over the Windy Woods Townhouses by 3:45 a.m. Arslan transported to the walk in front of the door to Unit 123 and knocked on the door.

The door opened and a young woman appeared in the doorway carrying a suitcase. She said, "Let's go."

They were transported aboard the Tira and Arslan and Ramede faced each other in the transport entrance. Arslan spoke first, "Ramede, welcome to the Tira after so many years away. I am Arslan."

Ramede said, "Arslan, it is so strange to hear my real name after many years of other names, but yes, I am Ramede. This is like meeting my family for the first time. She came closer and put her arms around Arslan and hugged him. Arslan. Of course, hugged back.

Arslan took Ramede to meet the rest of the team. Ramede was beautiful with dark skin, either tanned or natural, dark hair, and the same deep dark eyes as Arslan. Carrie and Lisa both hugged Ramede in welcome. Simon thought about it, but was uncomfortable hugging such a beautiful woman when they had just met. Instead he offered his hand. She shook it but then did not release it as quickly as normal.

The first order of business was to give Ramede a tour of the Tira and to introduce her to the computer. This being done they went to the control room and gave Ramede an update on what they planned to do in Arizona and what they hoped to accomplish. She agreed there needed to be very strict control over the powerful technology of the Tira. She had no more trust for the people who used political power than Arslan.

Simon suggested each one of them starting with Carrie, then Lisa, then Simon, and then Arslan, take approximately one half hour to tell Ramede about themselves. Then Ramede could take as much time as she wanted to tell them about herself. He also suggested she use the computer to replay Arslan's stories about his past life to get her up to speed with the rest. They all agreed and Carrie started to talk about herself.

Carrie said she was born, Carrie Anne Sloan, in Valdosta, Georgia. Her father was a chemist working for Griffin Chemical Company in Valdosta and her mother was an elementary school teacher. She had grown up in Valdosta, a city of about 50,000 people, when she was in high school, but growing rapidly. She loved Valdosta, only fifteen miles from the Florida border on Interstate 75 between Atlanta and Orlando. The weather there was hot in the summer and usually humid but in the winter it did not get very cold, a freeze was very unusual. People could do outdoor things all year round, with rain being the main thing limiting limited activities.

Valdosta is a city of flowers, nicknamed Azalea City for the wonderful blossoming of azaleas throughout the city, especially in the early spring but some bloom year round. Sports were another claim to fame for Valdosta. The city high school football team had the best winning record of any high school team in the history of football, over 80% wins in its history. And winning 23 Georgia state championships since World War II and five or six USA Today "national championships" was phenomenal. Someone had calculated they could lose all their games for the next sixty years and still have a winning record. Carrie was a football fan.

Carrie went to Florida State University in Tallahassee, Florida for an undergraduate degree in biology. She loved college life and studied hard to graduate magna cum laude while still having a social life and being the best runner on the women's track team at the 5,000 meters. She had a number of boy friends in high school and college but never found the right one to be really serious about.

She chose to go the Emory University for a masters degree in genetic studies and after completion of the masters chose to continue toward her doctorate in human genetic evolution, also at Emory. Emory has a worldwide reputation in the medical field but did not have a specialty in genetics at the level Carrie was looking for. Her doctoral advisor at Emory was on the board of the Center for DNA Studies in Atlanta, a private research facility, and he coordinated her placement there as a part of her doctoral program.

She had several relationships during her years at Emory, including one brief two month period when she lived with a doctor she had met at the Emory Clinic associated with the university. He was a brilliant young doctor but he chose to leave for a career opportunity and assumed Carrie would give up her career to follow him. She did not.

Carrie explained to Ramede that Arslan and her were developing a close relationship, effectively living together on the Tira, and were looking toward a long-term relationship. Carrie said she felt extremely fortunate to have met someone with the sensitivity and concern for others Arslan demonstrated.

Carrie was also awed by the opportunity she now had to do something important for humanity by using the resources of the Tira to improve the human situation. The now five people on the Tira had the most important opportunity in history to do good. She could not have dreamed of a better thing to do with her life.

Carrie indicated she was done and Lisa had the floor.

Lisa told of being born in Western Pennsylvania, about seventy miles north of Pittsburgh. Her father was a political science professor at a small college, Grove City College, where she effectively grew up. The school was a very good small college and had been rated as one of the top five educational values in the country ahead of big schools like Harvard and the Big Ten Schools. She spent her childhood and teen years hanging around the school and participating in soccer and softball, in particular.

She had gotten her undergraduate education there with a major in journalism and had gone on to work for a time at a large publishing firm in New York City as an assistant editor. She had done well there but really did not like the city and thought something was missing in her life. Finally, she decided she wanted to teach school and went to the University of Georgia in Athens, Georgia for a masters in education and a teaching certificate. She chose Georgia because she hated the cold weather in Pennsylvania and New York. After graduating she applied for a teaching position in the Atlanta City School System and was hired for a provisional position.

Lisa's social life in Atlanta was limited but she had dated several men prior to meeting Simon. She had wanted to start a relationship with one man she had met through a temporary job. He was named Sean and worked for a company, which distributed hardware to industrial companies. The problem was, Sean always said she was his buddy and they would never sleep together because they were just friends. He even introduced her that way and it hurt her every time he said it. One night she went to a dinner with several friends and met Simon there. She got drunk and after bar hopping several places they ended up in bed together. Then they got together several times but nothing serious happened until Arslan arrived.

Now, Lisa explained she was awed by the opportunity the Tira gave to mankind and she was honored to be part of the experience. She recognized it was mostly luck she was here on the Tira, but it had to be someone.

She nodded to Simon to tell his tale.

Simon told the group he had been born in Winston-Salem, North Carolina and had grown up there. His family had lived in a house, which was part of a nature development in the middle of the city adjacent to a hilly golf course. None of the houses had lawns, just naturally wooded lots with most of the houses having one two or three stories of decks around the houses. It was a beautiful place to grow up with the city all around you but with the natural setting close to you.

Simon had many interests growing up including golf, bowling, reading, and hiking. North Carolina was a great place for these activities with golf and hiking the main summertime activities to pursue and bowling and reading good for cold winter days and nights.

He went to college at Duke University and continued there for medical school. As he got into his second year at medical school he became enamored with the new science of human genetics and became a DNA specialist. Simon's mind seemed to be structured to deal well with the discipline and organization of DNA patterns and he was able to see patterns where others only saw a mass of data. When he finished his medical degree he was already famous for some of the research and papers he had written on the new DNA world. His search for a residents position after graduating was no search at all, he was sought after by some twenty-five of the most prestigious institutions in the DNA field and some private companies who wanted his expertise to develop products based on DNA research. His income potential was unbelievable based on the bidding was going on for his services.

Against the advice of some colleagues, who had money as their first interest in the medical field, Simon chose to go to work at the Center for DNA Studies in Atlanta. This non-profit, private institution was aimed at furthering the science of DNA studies but did not have profit as a primary goal. It was an open forum for the development and spreading of the knowledge of genetic science for the good of mankind.

By the accident of Arslan coming to him for the study of his DNA, Simon now had an opportunity to do more in his field than he had ever had any reason to dream of and to do it with the most advanced information source available, the Tira. Simon was excited about the future.

Arslan took the floor and began to speak about his beginnings. He asked Ramede if she had seen some of the stories about him on the world news. A lot of information about his early life and some of the identities he had adopted had already found its way to the public view. He did not want to bore Ramede with details she had already heard. She indicated she had watched just about everything released about Arslan, for obvious reasons.

Arslan said, "There are things about myself I have not yet shared with anyone. I suspect, but do not know for sure, some of these issues will be shared with Ramede because of our common experience in living many identities. I will try to list some of these and see if I am right:

- Because I have lost so many people I loved, each new relationship is compared to others with a goal of finding the unique elements which make the new relationship different and special. Relationships are the most important elements in my life.
- While I may seem to be non-religious or even anti-religious, I am a person with a deep desire to understand the religious element of the universe if there is one. Like the goal of the

Tira to develop intelligence to help discover the meaning of the universe, I too am driven in the same direction.

- I am deeply offended by those people who believe their one answer to the mystery of the universe is the only possible correct answer. Over time I have seen these people commit atrocities in the name of one loving god or another. I fear these people because they are never satisfied to have their answer, they must have everyone else accept their answer.

- Since we control the Tira, we have a responsibility to protect this marvelous tool for assisting in the development of intelligence and knowledge. We cannot let the power of the Tira fall into the hands of those people who would use it to crush all ideas except their version of reality.

Ramede, Tell us about yourself"

Ramede started speaking, "Due to gender, my life has been very different from Arslan's. Some women of today may not want to hear this but gender is a very large factor in life. Through most of my history, I have not been able to be in active control of my destiny to the extent Arslan has. I have had to use skills quite different than Arslan has used to survive. As a woman, skill with arms has not been my ticket to move from one identity to another. Even if I had these skills, in most cultures a woman could not be a warrior."

"I hope no one feels badly toward me for this, but many times in my life I have had to use my gender, sex specifically, as a tool of survival. I have been a prostitute or a woman using sex to survive many times and in many forms." said Ramede.

53. <u>Napata, Egypt (759 B.C.)</u>

Ramede told the story of her childhood in Egypt. She was left with a farming family near the city of Napata, just downstream from the Fourth Cataract in the remote south of Egypt. This land was at the extreme limit of Egyptian influence. Her adopted family consisted of a father, a mother, and one brother who was about eight years old when she was left with them. They never told her the complete circumstances of her being left with them but from what she could find out the parents were given some gold to take the child.

Ramede grew up as a normal child of the day with chores assigned as soon as she was old enough to have any responsibility. The older she grew the more work was expected from her and the more training in tasks assigned to women she received. Her dreams were to go to the north where riches and excitement awaited a young girl from the northern Nile valley. By the time she was about fourteen years old, in 745 B.C., she had developed into an unusually beautiful girl with dark complexion and beautiful dark hair.

She grew up in an area under the control of King Kashta of Sudanese lineage. The king had a large family and many sons. One day she was working in one of her adopted father's fields when several young men a little older than her approached on foot. She said hello and smiled. One of the young men was more richly dressed than the others and wore a sword with jewels on the hilt. He said, "What is your name, beautiful girl?"

"I am Ramede, adopted daughter of Heboin, who owns this farm. Who asks my name?" she said.

"I am Pi'ankhy, eldest son of King Kashta, and these are my friends Lahun and Peteese. What work do you do here?" he said.

Ramede said, "Right now I am pulling weeds from the field so the vegetables will grow without the weeds strangling them. Do you want to help?"

"My father would disapprove of his son doing the work of a farmer but I wish I could help a beautiful girl like you. Perhaps we could talk for a while?" he said.

"My father would disapprove of his daughter not doing the work of a farmer, and does not include standing around and talking, so I must go back to work." she said.

Pi'ankhy said goodbye to Ramede and started away, then turned and said he would return again and talk when she had more time. Ramede agreed.

Thereafter, Pi'ankhy started stopping by almost every day. Ramede would usually take a short break from her work and talk to him or go for a walk. Ramede told her mother about these visits and she was concerned Ramede be careful with this son of a king. He would want to use the body of Ramede without marriage and would not be good for Ramede's future. Ramede thought she could handle Pi'ankhy.

One day shortly after that conversation, Pi'ankhy came by and they went for a walk. When they were at a remote part of the farm, he stopped and put his arms around her, then kissed her. She did not resist, kissed him back and held him tightly. He moved his hands down onto her buttocks and cupped them in his hands. She pushed him back and said she wanted to walk back. He said, "Many girls like the company of the son of a king, why do you not want me?"

Ramede said, "Many girls get with child by the sons of kings and then cannot find a man to marry them so they can have a good life. I do not want to be one of those girls. I like you, Pi'ankhy, but do not want to ruin my life."

Pi'ankhy said, "I understand your concern, Ramede, but you are the most beautiful girl I have ever seen. I just can't keep my hands away from you. What do you expect me to do?"

Ramede said, "Do you think you may want the daughter of a farmer as your wife some day? If not you should stop coming to see me because you will not have me willingly except as a wife. And you do not look like a man who takes women by force when they do not want to be taken."

"I will think about what you have said. I want you more than any other girl I have met. Since you will not give yourself to me, I want you even more. Perhaps, I will think about making you my wife," said Pi'ankhy.

Pi'ankhy did not come to see Ramede for several weeks. When he did return he went to see Heboin, her adopted father, before he spoke to Ramede. When he came to Ramede, he said, "Ramede, I have spoken to your father about the possibility of you and I being married. He does not have a large dowry to provide, just a couple of cattle, but is not important in this case. I have also spoken to my father about this matter and he thinks a woman from the farm is good for giving birth to many sons, so he is satisfied if I marry you. What do you say to all this?"

"You seem like a good man who will make a good husband. I will work hard as your wife and try to please you," said Ramede.

Two months later Pi'ankhy and Ramede were married; he was seventeen; she was fourteen. Ramede went to live with the family of Pi'ankhy and lived in the household of his mother. His mother, Hantaka, was a woman who had come from a farm herself and quickly judged Ramede was a hard worker in addition to being beautiful. This pleased her and was almost as important as pleasing Pi'ankhy.

Pleasing Pi'ankhy was not a problem either. His young bride had no experience with men prior to him but had a natural feel for the sexual experience and quickly showed her enthusiasm. Their lovemaking was frequent and intense with both of them taking great pleasure from it. Within four months, Ramede was sure she was pregnant.

Hantaka was pleased her daughter-in-law was with child. If Pi'ankhy had a son and heir it would solidify his position as heir to King Kashta.

Ramede went through the pregnancy with no problems and gave birth to a healthy son in the spring of 743 B.C. The son of Pi'ankhy and Ramede was named Kashtasun. Ramede spent her energies caring for him and for Pi'ankhy.

In 740 B.C. King Kashta died and Pi'ankhy was named king at the age of twenty-one.

Immediately, he faced a serious challenge from a prince from the Nile delta area named Tefnakhte, who had taken control of the entire northwest of Egypt and had laid siege to Heracleopolis. Pi'ankhy reacted by sending an army north which defeated the army of Tefnakhte coming south by ship with great slaughter and many prisoners captured.

The army of Pi'ankhy had many successes but Pi'ankhy was not satisfied with the results. His character demanded a high level of accomplishment and was not pleased he did not have all his enemies at his feet.

In some things he was pleased, however, his wife, Ramede, was his close companion and confidant and his young son gave him hope to establish a great dynasty to rule the land. Ramede was happy in her life as the wife of a great king and the mother of a young prince. She had not known anything else in her short life and thought this life was the natural order of things.

All was well until 736 B.C. when Kashtasun came down with a fever and died. The young king, Pi'ankhy, was hurt deeply by the loss of his son and Ramede was lost in shock and grief. Her sweet little prince was gone and she had no way to fill the void it left. She told Pi'ankhy she wanted to return to Napata to find some happiness to wipe away the loss she felt. Pi'ankhy wasn't sure what to do but finally agreed to return to his home province even though he was in a position to rule all of Egypt.

In Napata Ramede felt the intense grief a woman can feel when she loses a child, but she felt less pain for herself than she did for Pi'ankhy, who seemed to lose his desire to be a great and powerful ruler. Ramede had persuaded him to return to Napata to deal with his grief but he chose to stay in the city and ceased to be the leader he had been earlier. She did not need for her husband to be a great king who dominated the world but she wanted him to find happiness and satisfaction. She did not think he would become as a lethargic leader who had little or no purpose.

For two years Pi'ankhy whiled away his time in Napata with little activity and lacking in direction. Meanwhile Ramede tried her best to get pregnant again to try to replace their wonderful son who had died. Pi'ankhy's interest in their lovemaking was also less than enthusiastic but he did manage to accomplish the task on occasion. Finally, in 734 B.C., Ramede was again pregnant. The king was more excited with this news than he had been about anything since the death of his first-born. He started spending more time with Ramede and was very fretful she should do anything to which might endanger the developing child. In the spring of 735 B.C., Ramede gave birth to a healthy daughter.

315

Pi'ankhy was angry the child was female. When told he didn't believe it at first. Then he became angry with Ramede and threatened to kill her for betraying him by having a daughter. Ramede could do nothing about the sex of her child and was crushed by the king's threats and condemnation. He said he would find another wife to have sons with him if Ramede was unable to have more sons. And a short while later he made good on his threat by marrying a second wife, a young girl brought to him from the north having some royal blood of the older Egyptian lines.

Ramede named her daughter, Amira, since Pi'ankhy seemed to have no interest in giving her a name. Ramede devoted her time to raising Amira and to occasional lovemaking with the king; apparently he had the intent of giving her a chance to make up for her failure to have another son. In 733 B.C., both Ramede and the king's new wife, Clamara, were both pregnant and due to give birth early in 732 B.C. Those around them saw the one to give birth first to a male child would be fortunate to be mother of the heir to the kingdom.

Clamara was the first to go into labor in January, some said with the help of a physician who used his skills to speed up the birth. She delivered a baby girl, however, much to the distress of Pi'ankhy, who beat his young wife severely upon finding out about her failure to have a boy. Ramede went to her aid as soon as she found out about the beating and helped to care for her and the child. Ramede did not know what had happened to the man she had married but now wished it had never been.

Ramede went into labor late in January and gave birth to a son. Pi'ankhy was delighted and named his son, Shebitku. Ramede was glad to have a healthy child but no longer felt love for her husband. She cared for her children and acted the part of a queen but was not pleased with the course of her life. She was married to a stranger who could lash out with violence at any time. She began to recognize how helpless a woman was is this world. There was little she could do about her situation without bringing disaster upon herself and her children. She did dream about the kind of life she would prefer to have. She did not care if she were a queen, just to be married to a man she could respect and with whom she could share real love.

Pi'ankhy was soon rejuvenated by the birth of a son, and renewed his campaigns against various enemies. The years passed with the king not being defeated but not having the great success, which he might have desired.

By 722 B.C. Amira was twelve years old and becoming a beautiful young girl. She was largely ignored by her father, but was the delight of her mother and the ten-year-old Shebitku, heir to the kingdom. The two children played together constantly and were almost inseparable, except when Pi'ankhy wanted to spend time with Shebitku, at which times Amira would spend time with her mother. Their other playmates were, Ortira, the ten-year-old daughter of Clamara, who was now the best friend of Ramede, and three year old Taharqa, a son finally born to Clamara. All the children and the wives of the king getting along well together made for more happiness in the palace than could have been the case.

Ramede was 37 years old but looked the same as she had in her mid-twenties. This fact was not lost on Clamara who was in her mid-thirties and beginning to show some ageing. Pi'ankhy had also noticed Ramede was keeping her youth very well and was not displeased with the fact when he chose to favor her with his physical desires.

Ramede for her part did not want to show her age, no woman on earth ever wanted to get old, but she was not overly pleased with undue attention to the fact. As the king's wife she did not have much attention paid to her by members of the opposite sex for fear the king would take offense.

By 717 B.C. Pi'ankhy began to show age himself at forty-four years. The comparison of himself to Ramede was becoming quite obvious as it was with Ramede and Clamara. Ramede did not look as young as her seventeen year old daughter, Amira, but she did not look like her mother either, more like an older sister. At this point, Ramede began to sense something was different about her. She had injuries several times which had healed much faster than other people and she never seemed to become ill like other people. She soon began to worry others would soon think her to be very unusual, even some kind of enchanted being, if she did not begin to age normally. Finally, Ramede began to dye her hair slightly gray and to lighten her skin to make her look older.

Some make up and graying hair started to help her look older and this caused the comments to be less vocal about her youthful appearance. In private when she washed out the gray, she knew she really was not ageing as she should and this gave her cause for worry. When would she start to age and what would she do if she did not? Most women, or men, for that matter, would talk as though they would love to live without ageing. But to actually do it becomes a different matter with huge problems involved.

In 715 B.C. concern about ageing was overshadowed by fear for Amira and Ortira. Pi'ankhy decided to marry the now nineteen-year-old girls off to enhance his political situation. He offered Amira to a prince in the delta area of Egypt to firm up an alliance he was trying to create. The deal was under negotiation before Ramede knew anything about it. When she heard about it, she went to Pi'ankhy and asked him to consider the feeling of Amira before he set her life on a course over which she had no control. Pi'ankhy simply said women have no say in such matters of state and the girls were old to be marrying compared to many others. There was little Ramede could say to argue with this.

A few weeks later Pi'ankhy called Ramede to him and told her, he had made an agreement with the prince in the delta region to marry Amira; she would leave for the delta immediately. Ramede had expected this and asked if she could accompany Amira to the delta for her marriage. Pi'ankhy agreed and Amira and Ramede set off with a small escort to the delta area.

Before leaving, Ramede had met with Shebitku, Clamara, and Ortira. She made it clear to her son and her close friends she would not return to Napata if she could find another alternative. She had no love for Pi'ankhy and life close to him was getting to be less and less livable. The problem about her not ageing was also a great concern. If she stayed her life could become very difficult. She planned to take whatever jewelry and valuables with her she could transport, so she would have some wealth to start off somewhere else.

Travel in the north of Egypt with a military escort of eight men, four maids, and several drivers and attendants was slow and not especially comfortable. Napata was near the fourth cataract, so much of the early part of the trip was across country roads until they could get to navigable waters. Even then their travel on the river was interrupted by each of the three cataracts between Napata and northern Egypt. Riding in a wheeled carriage with no shock absorption and roads, which were either rutted, rocky or not well kept, was hot, dirty and tiring. At times it was much better to get out and walk rather than suffering the constant jarring of the wooden wheels. Their travel to the delta would take about one month with the most comfortable part being toward the end when they would be able to travel mainly by boat.

Ramede had been graying her hair and taking other steps in make up and clothing to have herself look as old as possible. She worked hard to make herself look like the mother of Armira instead of a friend or sister. It was not easy since without her efforts to look older she looked like a young woman in her mid to late twenties. She had a faint idea she could revert to the look of a very young woman at some point and find a way to leave Egypt and go somewhere else where no one would know her.

Ramede began talking with the men operating the boats in which they were traveling, trying to find out what the avenues for escape she might have available to her. These river "sailors" spoke of travel on the great sea to places such as Crete, Rhodes, Sidon, Greece and other destinations. Few, if any, had ever actually made such a trip, but they delighted in speaking about such travel and were able to provide some details they had heard from others who had made such trips.

She now dreamed of getting to the delta area then finding a way to purchase passage on a ship sailing to someplace where she could find a new life. As she continued her trip to the north she thought more about the fact she did not seem to age like other people, never got sick like others and seemed to heal so quickly when injured. What could it mean?

Amira was somewhat fearful about her future as well, but in a more traditional sense. She was going to meet the man who was to be her husband. Would he be a good man to spend her life with or would he be ugly and mean? She had no control over the situation and she knew it. The man she was to marry was a total stranger. This would not have been the case if she had not been the daughter of a king but daughters of kings have actually less say over whom they marry than daughters of lesser people.

As Amira and Ramede drew closer to the delta region both felt fears and were very anxious about their futures but for different reasons.

Their destination in the delta region was the city of Busiris, in the heart of the delta, and on a wide section of the river, which was navigable from the great sea. This was really a port city with all the good and bad, the description could mean. As they reached the city, their escort said they must pass through the entire city to get to the palace where the young prince of Busiris would meet his new bride. The city was a lively place with the pace of commerce demonstrated by merchants moving trade goods through the streets and real sailors in evidence, rough looking men who seemed to be much harder than other men.

Slaves being taken to the slave markets were also in evidence with male and female workers being led along. In one case she saw an attractive young girl of twelve or thirteen being led away from the slave market by two men following an older woman in expensive clothes. They disappeared into a very large house on a busy street. She asked an escort sent from the palace who owned such a large house and was told it was the best brothel in the city. Through conversation, she surmised the young girl she saw was about to begin a career as a "lady of the night." It was not easy for a female to avoid such situations in a world where there was little protection for the young and the weak. Ramede thought, *"I know more about life than the young girl but alone it will be difficult to avoid a similar fate. I must use my head and choose the right course or I will come to great misery."*

When Amira and Ramede reached the small palace of the prince of Busiris, the prince who was a not unattractive man of about thirty years of age greeted them. His manners were good, although of the type typical of the delta area, and seemed to be a gentler man than many Ramede had met. He bade welcome to Amira and Ramede but seemed somewhat confused as to who was Amira. Ramede quickly filled the void by saying, "I am Ramede, wife of Pi'ankhy and mother of Amira who stands beside me. Pi'ankhy sends his greetings and wishes you well. He also sends gifts to you, the best of which is his beautiful daughter to be your wife."

The prince introduced himself, "I am Honotep, Prince of Busiris. Your trip was long and tiring, please come into my humble palace and rest."

After cleaning up from their travels, Ramede and Amira were invited to dine with Honotep. At the meal, he told them he felt very favored the great king from the south would honor a prince of a small city with the chance to marry one of his daughters, especially a beautiful girl like Amira. Ramede responded it was enough the young prince appeared to be a kind man who would be a good husband to Amira. Honotep asked Amira directly if she was happy with the match. Amira responded that Honotep was a handsome man who pleased her but more importantly he seemed to be a caring man who would be a good husband and father to children. Honotep seemed pleased with her answer.

During the meal, Honotep said the marriage would take place in two days at dawn if it was agreeable to Ramede and Amira. Both women agreed. Ramede said she would like to see some of the port of Busiris during her visit. Honotep said he would arrange for an escort tomorrow to take them to see the sites.

The next day was a beautiful, sunny morning when they went to visit the port. Ships were coming and going up and down the river with the docks busy with cargo being loaded and unloaded. She told her escort she was interested in the ships, which were traveling to distant lands such as Rhodes, Sidon and Greece. Were there any such ships in the port?

The escort made inquires and they went to visit several ships. The ships captains were generally honored to have "royalty" asking about their travels and were very anxious to answer questions. In the midst of her general questions, Ramede asked how much it cost for a person to travel on the ship to Rhodes or Greece. The captain said it was negotiable but depended on the circumstances of the person and what kind of accommodations the person expected. The lowest price would probably be twelve silver pieces to travel to Rhodes ranging up to twelve gold pieces if a person of means wanted the best place on the ship, or if it was a woman. Women on the ships were considered by many to be bad luck.

The ships' captains were generally questionable characters who might not be worthy of trust. She did meet one who she thought might be better than the others and made some inquiries about him. He was a Phoenician, from Tyre, who had been at sea many years and was named Philo. He had a reputation as an experienced seaman who had survived many years at sea by skill and toughness, but was regarded as an honest man to deal with. She learned enough to know his vessel was scheduled to leave Busiris in two weeks, sailing for Tyre, then on to Rhodes and the Ionian city of Corinth. Ramede saw a woman traveling alone for such a distance would be fair game to be taken advantage of by anyone who had the opportunity. She really needed a man to travel with her to give her some protection, even to pretend to be her husband.

On her tour of the port, Ramede learned there were merchants who had landed in the delta and due to one misfortune or another had lost their money and were stranded. She set about finding such a man who might become her traveling companion with her paying their way.

The next morning was the date set for the wedding of Amira and Honotep. She spoke to Honotep when they returned to the palace from the tour and requested his permission to stay on a few weeks after the marriage since she was not feeling well after the long trip from the south. Honotep was quick to agree—whatever the wife of Pi'ankhy and the mother of Amira wanted he was glad to provide.

The next morning the marriage of Amira and Honotep took place in a relatively small ceremony. The young couple went off to experience their marriage bed, which gave Ramede a chance to slip away to the dock area disguised as a woman who worked at the palace. She went to a tavern where she had heard foreigners from Greece and other lands often frequented. At the tavern she asked the proprietor if he knew of any Greek merchants in the crowd who may be stranded in Egypt. He called one man over, a Greek named Aristes, who he introduced as a merchant who had been in Egypt for many months since he had lost most of his fortune when his ship had sunk after running onto some rocks.

Ramede asked Aristes if he would be willing to discuss a way to get the funds for passage out of Egypt in exchange for helping a young woman who wanted to travel to Rhodes or perhaps to Greece. Aristes said he was interested. Aristes seemed to Ramede to be a decent man, so she went ahead with her plan.

They went to a garden adjacent to the tavern and Ramede began to talk. She explained she knew of a ship leaving within two weeks and told him the name of the ship and the captain. He said he knew of the ship and captain but had never met him. Ramede decided she would have to take a chance and trust this man to some extent. She gave him half the money she thought would be needed to book the passage for Aristes and a young woman who would travel as his sister. She asked Aristes to be silent about the matter since it was a delicate situation where the family of the young woman may oppose her travel. They agreed to meet at the tavern again in a week.

Ramede thought of several strategies for making her departure from Egypt. She did not want to leave a situation where Hopotep and Amira would be blamed in any way. She finally decided to send a sealed message to Pi'ankhy telling the truth she just wanted to leave. She had been taught to read and write which was unusual for a woman of her day so she could compose the message herself. She decided to send four of the soldiers from her escort back to Napata with the message, on the basis she was too ill to travel and her husband needed to know. She chose the leader and his best men to go to Napata, keeping the least competent of the men with her in Busiris. She would send them off the day before the ship was scheduled to leave to give her the best start possible, in case Pi'ankhy chose to pursue her.

One week passed and she found the opportunity to get to the tavern to meet with Aristes. He was now a very important person in her life. So much depended on her being able to get on a ship leaving Egypt at the right time. When she got to the tavern she looked around for Aristes and did not immediately see him. Did he run away with the money she had given him? Did she trust the wrong person? Finally she saw him sitting in a back corner. She went over to him and they went outside together for privacy, going to the garden again.

Aristes explained he had contacted Philo, the captain of the ship she had mentioned, and had made a payment of one fourth of the money for passage from the funds Ramede had provided. He explained payment was necessary to hold a place on the ship as there was some demand for spaces. He had paid five gold pieces as one fourth of the cost to travel to Greece. They would be required to pay ten more gold pieces when the lady and Aristes boarded to get to Rhodes. An additional five gold pieces would be payable in Rhodes to get to Corinth. For the price, they would have the best accommodations on the ship and would receive better food than otherwise might be the case. The time to get to Corinth was approximately two months, if winds were good and pirates kept their distance.

"The ship would be leaving Busiris at dawn five days from today," explained Aristes. "It would be best to board late at night if there was to be a problem with the family of the lady."

Ramede agreed to meet Aristes in the garden by the tavern at midnight prior to leaving. They would then go and board the ship and be prepared to leave in the morning. Aristes then asked if he could ask a favor of Ramede. He explained, "I am a merchant, an honest merchant who makes his living by buying goods in one place and selling them at a profit in another place. If the lady I am to escort on the journey would be willing to finance a cargo of trade goods to take with us I will split the profit with her and she will have enough profit to finance her travel and much more besides. Do you think the lady would be interested?"

Ramede thought about the offer, "They would seem more like merchants if they had trade goods with them and having more money at the end of her journey would be very useful." She quickly said, "Yes, the lady will agree to do it. How much money do you need for trade goods."

Aristes said, "Fifty in gold at a minimum but more would mean more goods and more profit."

Ramede had over four hundred in gold coin plus her jewelry, which was extensive. She did not want to risk it all but she saw this as a good opportunity and the fact was the gold on her person could be lost just as easily as trade goods, so why not take along something she could profit from, since she was taking a great risk anyway. She told Aristes, "Would two hundred and fifty in gold attract too much attention as an investment. The understanding is the lady gets the two hundred fifty back first then the profit above it is split between you. Is that correct?"

Aristes said with a look of wonderment in his eyes, "Yes, that is correct but I am surprised you can make such an agreement for the lady."

Ramede said, "It is time for honesty between us. I am the lady who will be traveling with you but my appearance will be somewhat different than it is now. I am placing a great deal of trust in your honesty. If you are not an honest man I have misread you and am probably doomed anyway, so why not try?"

Aristes said, "I try to be an honest man and will not fail you in this matter. You offer me a great opportunity to travel to Greece with a large load of trade goods and to make my fortune. For me to thank you by cheating you or worse would be something I would not do."

Ramede handed a heavy purse to Aristes containing fifty in gold to get his buying of trade goods started. She said she would bring the rest to the garden of the tavern the next night. The following night she returned and handed another two hundred in gold to Aristes. He was very impressed she had done what she had said she would do. He said, "My lady, I will guard your funds as if they were my own and will meet you here the night before departure. The trade goods will already be loaded on the ship and the cost of carrying the goods will be paid to the captain. This will be a very good partnership for both of us."

Ramede told Amira about her plans to leave but not exactly how, and she would send a letter to Pi'ankhy explaining what she was doing so any blame would be solely on her and not extending to Honotep or Amira. She told Amira not to tell Honotep about what she was doing until she had a good start in case he might try to stop her. During the conversation she asked Amira how the relationship with Honotep was progressing. She responded they were very happy and Honotep was a good man from all she knew.

The day before she was scheduled to meet Aristes at the tavern she sent four of her escort soldiers off to Napata with a letter for Pi'ankhy. The soldiers thought the letter was explaining she was ill and would stay in Busiris for a while.

The day after the four soldiers departed she told Honotep she wanted to take a short trip to the seashore for a few days to try to recover from her malaise. She would take her escorts with her. She made arrangements to hire an enclosed chair with bearers for her personal transport. She left with her remaining escorts and took them to a part of the delta where there was a seashore. She told them she wanted to give them a reward for their services in taking care of her and gave them enough money to enjoy a week living at a tavern near the seashore. She lied to them and told them Honotep's guards would escort her back to the palace and they should go and have a good time. They should return to the palace in a week. Remembering these soldiers were not the sharpest arrows in the quiver, she thought it likely they would have no suspicions.

She then took her hired transport back to a point near the tavern and waited for Aristes. When it was dark she dismissed her hired transport and put on a cloak, which concealed her fine clothing. She brought one heavy bag with her, which contained some clothes, and her valuables. She waited nervously in the garden for Aristes to appear. After an eternity, or so it seemed to her, he walked into the garden and greeted her.

She was very pleased he had appeared. She was naturally concerned when she had given so much money to a relative stranger. What if he had simply left with the money?

She told Aristes she would like to rent a room at the tavern for a few hours. Aristes did not think would be a problem so he went inside and made arrangements. Once into the room, Ramede requested Aristes bring her enough water to wash her hair and wash her make up off. Once she completed the task, Aristes was amazed at the young woman he saw. She had looked to be a forty-year-old woman and was now a twenty five year old, and beautiful. She asked Aristes to leave to room, and proceeded to change into appropriate clothing for a twenty five year old sister of a merchant rather than clothes for the wife of a king.

When she invited Aristes back into the room he was still wondering at the remarkable change he had seen take place. She looked like a completely different woman. Ramede counted on this being the case since she did not want the ship's captain to recognize her as the king's wife who had visited his ship earlier.

They then traveled to the port of Busiris, a short distance, and found the berth where their ship, the Olympos, was docked. The captain of the ship had been warned his very important paying customers would be boarding late at night. With the large amount of cargo now on board belonging to these passengers, the ship was essentially their ship, and he wanted them to be pleased with his service for them. Obviously they were wealthy and could provide him with more business in the future.

There were only two enclosed cabins on the ship and his new passengers would have one and the captain had the other. As brother and sister he felt they could be comfortable sharing a cabin and he had been at sea too many years to easily give up his own comfort, he had earned it. Ramede and Aristes were a little uncomfortable at being thrown into such close physical proximity but there was little choice. Aristes was a bit more uncomfortable than Ramede, probably due to the fact he was not used to being close to such a beautiful woman.

"Ramede," he said when they were alone in the cabin, "you started out being old enough to appear to be my mother and now you do look like a younger sister. It is truly amazing. Who are you?"

"Aristes," said Ramede, "it is truly better you do not know exactly who I am. It is safer for both of us if you know as little as possible about me, right now especially."

They both laid back and tried to go to sleep but both had difficulty falling asleep, but for different reasons. Ramede was caught up in the fear and danger of her attempt to escape from the life she had been living for many years. Aristes was fascinated by the adventure he was setting out on and the beautiful woman who had come to share it with him.

When morning came, Ramede was glad to feel a wind blowing. Her great fear was there would be no wind to move their ship and she would have to spend another night in Busiris with the danger mounting. She wanted to be away from this place and traveling as far away as possible from her old life.

The ship set out at dawn after paying the port taxes to the Egyptian authorities. They made good time during the day and cleared the delta by nightfall. The captain would make his way along the coast and try to never be out of the sight of land unless they had a very good reason, like trying to run away from pirates or in the event of a storm, where the sea was safer than being too close to the shore or rocks. The captain was proud of his ship, it was one of the fastest on the sea, which was one of the reasons why he had little to fear from pirates. They had to catch the Olympos and it was not easy.

Once they were at sea the captain had time to pay some attention to his passengers. The beautiful young sister of the merchant was a delight to have aboard. He was not one to believe women were unlucky to have on a ship, in this case, he thought it was very lucky to have such a lovely woman on board for a long journey. *"Who knows? he thought, perhaps she will fall in love with an old seaman and I will marry a rich merchant's sister to fill my retirement from the sea. She does seem familiar but I don't remember meeting anyone quite like her."*

Ramede took quite ill during the first several days at sea, as she had no experience before with sea travel. It passed very quickly, however, and she adapted to the conditions. Aristes had no trouble with seasickness but may have been a bit lovesick. The more time he spent with Ramede, the more attraction he felt. She was the most beautiful and charming woman he had ever known. Ramede quickly saw the problem developing but did not have enough experience with such circumstances to know what to do. For herself, she thought Aristes was attractive, but she had just escaped an entanglement and was looking only for freedom right now.

About ten days away from the delta they ran into a small storm. At sea even a small storm can seem like a major event, especially for the inexperienced sea traveler. Captain Philo saw his female passenger was somewhat disturbed by the weather and he offered his advice that this was a small storm which the Olympos could handle with ease. Ramede thanked him for his comforting words and told him he was kind to have taken the time to try to keep his passengers from worrying. He said it was easy to be kind to beautiful female passengers. Ramede thanked him again and gave him her best smile. Now there were two men on the Olympos falling in love with Ramede.

They approached the city of Tyre after about two and one half weeks at sea. Tyre was the homeport of Philo and he was looking forward to seeing friends and relatives. He mentioned to Ramede he had family in Tyre. She responded with the question if it included a wife and many children. Philo said he would admit to marrying several women in the course of his life but none of them lived in Tyre. If they did he would not call Tyre his home. As for children, he explained a man does not always know who or where his children are. He made it a point to help all children who needed help to the extent he had means just in case any such children were the product of his travels around the world.

Upon arrival in Tyre, Philo hired two men he knew to guard the ship and cargo and suggested they get accommodations at an inn he knew about. It was clean and not overpriced for what you received.

They went to the inn, which was close by and were pleased with the place and took two small rooms. This was expensive as most people shared rooms but Ramede and Aristes would welcome some space after such cramped quarters on the ship. Philo had a house on Tyre where he let his brother and family live on condition they care for it and have a room for him when he was in port. He would stay there.

Philo offered to give Ramede and Aristes a tour of Tyre and they accepted. Traveling with someone who knew a city was a much better way than trying to find out what was worth experiencing in a strange city with no assistance. Tyre was paying tribute to the Assyrian Empire at the time of Ramede's visit to Tyre but was a city with a long history, over two thousand years old at the time of her visit. They were the most renowned seafaring people in the world at the time, and had founded the city of Carthage as a colony, one hundred years earlier.

The marketplace and docks of Tyre were jammed with trade goods from around the world. Aristes started to do some business, trading away some goods purchased in Egypt to acquire some unusual items, which he judged, would bring even greater profits in Rhodes or Greece. Ramede offered to finance another fifty gold coins to acquired more goods also. By the end of two days they had acquired goods from as Far East as India and as far west as Spain. By being selective in what they traded for they improved the variety and quality of their stocks.

Two days was all the time they planned to stay in Tyre. Philo would have stayed longer if asked but Ramede was still too close to Egypt to be comfortable with the wrath of Pi'ankhy when he found out about her desertion. When they were finally at sea again, Ramede and Aristes spent some time organizing their goods and insuring they were as protected as possible from the elements.

One night when they were about five days out of Tyre, Aristes spoke to her about the future. He said he was very pleased to be traveling with Ramede, and wished to continue their relationship after they reached their destination. Ramede said she did not know if she wanted to continue to be a merchant after getting to Greece. Aristes explained he did not mean their business relationship, he wanted them to have a relationship as a man and a woman. Ramede explained she was not sure she wanted a serious relationship with a man so soon after becoming free of a relationship she was unhappy with. Aristes was disappointed but said he would like for her to consider the possibility as they traveled. Ramede agreed to think about it.

After their stop in Tyre the next extended stop for the Olympos was the port of Al Mina (Syrian coast). Al Mina was another old city, and according to Philo this city, which is the port for another inland city, Tel Tainat, has been one of the key points of contact between the Phoenicians from Sidon, Tyre and Byblos and the Greeks. These contacts had been in place of hundreds of years and much trade and exchange of information had taken place. On other trips to Al Mina, Philo had seen the Greeks there using parts of the Phoenician alphabet in their writing and had seen Greeks adopting some Phoenician religious ideas into their religions.

When they landed in Al Mina, Ramede was surprised at both the size and activity level of the port. She heard many different languages spoken and saw the customs of a multicultural city rather than an isolated backwater. She was especially interested in the large Greek community, which appeared to make up one half to one third of the population. Philo said he knew a good tavern in the Greek section of the city, which would be a good place for Ramede to get to know the Greeks better. Aristes interjected he was a Greek and was a good example of what Greeks are. Philo said in jest, "Don't judge all Greeks by Aristes example, some are quite handsome and manly." They all laughed.

Aristes had not been to Al Mina before. He usually stopped in Crete on his travels to the south and did not get as far east as Al Mina. Philo indicated the trip to Crete was a bit more dangerous, traveling on the open sea, rather than hugging the coast as they had done on this trip. He admitted pirates were a danger whichever way you chose to go.

At the tavern Philo inquired about a room or rooms and was given a very high price. Aristes then went into a long conversation in Greek, which Ramede understood some, since Aristes had been teaching her, but not all because it was beyond her skill level. The conversation was of the proprietor trying to cheat Aristes friend and it was not going to happen. Once the proprietor knew he was dealing with another Greek he dropped the price to about one half of what he had originally asked and became much more friendly. When Aristes told he was from Corinth the tavern owner became animated. He was from a small village outside of Corinth originally. They would have much to talk about said the tavern owner and then offered a cup of wine at no cost.

It turned out Aristes and the tavern owner, Nesto, knew some of the same people in Corinth. They explained Corinth had a special reputation in Greece as a place of luxury, vice and decadence—all things which appealed to both Aristes and Nesto. Such were the ways of the Greeks said Nesto, fight hard then enjoy life equally hard.

Nesto told Aristes there was a small temple to Apollo in Al Mina, if he wanted to go make a sacrifice to the gods. Ramede said she wanted to go and learn more about Greek religion. Nesto said he would be glad to spend time teaching her what he knew about religion and would also help her with her Greek. They planned a trip to the temple for the next day.

The tavern keeper asked if Ramede was married to either of the men she was traveling with. Ramede, who was far enough away from Egypt now to have lost some of her fear, told the truth at this point. Aristes was not her brother but her business partner, and Philo was the captain of the vessel she was traveling on. She was not married to either of them. The tavern keeper said his wife had died in childbirth and he was alone. Ramede was one of the most beautiful women he had ever met, he said. If she was looking for a husband he was available. Ramede said she was flattered but she was not looking for a husband right now. She had been married before and had just escaped form a bad relationship. The tavern owner said he understood.

Philo said he was surprised at the news Aristes and Ramede were not brother and sister but did not seem too surprised. Ramede guessed he had seen through the ruse very quickly but had politely gone along. He now seemed relieved Ramede and Aristes were business partners and not lovers. It gave him a chance with Ramede. *Under some circumstances, Ramede thought it would make a good life to sail the seas with a man like Philo but life would change as a wife versus being a paying passenger.*

At the small temple to Apollo, Ramede was introduced to a priest at the temple who showed her great deference as a beautiful woman and an obviously rich and cultured lady. When she showed interest in

Greek religion he spent a great deal of time telling her about the various gods and the importance of Apollo in the whole picture. He also told her about a newly established shrine and temple to Apollo, which had been established at Delphi, which some legends hold, is the center of the earth. He mentioned Delphi has something very unusual, an oracle—a woman, who can tell the future. The priest had been trained at Delphi and was able to tell her much detail about the oracle, which had existed at Delphi for hundreds of years but had become part of the Apollo cult only in recent years.

After visiting the temple, Ramede was intrigued with the fact a woman, such as the oracle at Delphi, could play such an important part in religious affairs. Her experience was women could not wield power easily in most societies. Men tended to dominate and exclude women from situations where they could make decisions.

On the way back from the temple, they passed the slave market. As usual she saw sights there, which made her cringe. Men, women, and children being degraded, beaten and treated as if they were less than human. In this case she saw a young boy of about ten years old being sold away from his mother. The mother had been sold separately as a household slave and the buyer did not want a boy also. So the boy was being auctioned separately. The highest bidder at this point was a rough, dirty looking man who had stripped the boy naked and examined his sex organs with his hands. The man said, "He will serve my purpose."

Ramede was offended by the treatment of the boy and made a higher bid for the boy. The dirty man looked at her with a look of hatred. She was costing him more money than he wished to spend, but she had two men with her who looked like they could handle themselves, especially the one who looked like a sailor. He made another bid slightly higher than Ramede's. Ramede immediately made another bid over the man's. He decided the price was going higher than her could pay so he let her win. Ramede paid the money and took possession of the boy.

As they walked back to the tavern, Ramede asked the boy what his name was. He said in Greek, "My name is Melitos."

Ramede then asked where he came from and how long he had been a slave. He said, "I came from the north, far inland from Adana, and was captured along with my mother when raiders attacked our village about two years ago. We were slaves to a Greek merchant in Aleppo for a time but he sold us to a slave trader when he left to return to Greece. He made us work very hard and beat us often. He also took my mother to his bed when he wanted. It was not a good life. I was afraid I would have to go with the dirty man at the slave market. He was going to hurt me, I could sense it."

Ramede said, "Have you ever sailed on a ship? We are merchants traveling to Greece and if you go with us you will travel on a ship. We will not beat you unless you deserve it. We will give you work to do, but it will not be too hard. Does it sound like something you would like to do?"

Melitos said, "I will miss my mother but I see staying with her is impossible. I may as well travel to Greece as anything else. It might be fun."

Rather than taking Melitos to the tavern where they would be in cramped quarters with the boy, Ramede said she would take the boy to the ship and leave him in the charge of the crew members left at the ship. Ramede and the boy separated from the rest of the group and walked toward the ship. After a while the boy said urgently, "We are being followed." Ramede looked back and saw the dirty man from the slave market only a few paces away.

The man said, "You stole the boy from me at the slave market but you have lost your protection here, as he reached out for the boy. Ramede instinctively pulled her dagger from under her dress where she always carried it and drove it to the hilt into the chest of the dirty man. He had a look of complete surprise on his face as he toppled to the ground. Apparently the blade had penetrated directly to his heart and he died instantly.

Melitos did not know what to do but was afraid they would be blamed for killing the man. He said they should run away. Ramede was not used to running away from her actions and chose to stay. A passerby called a soldier saying a man had been killed. A small crowd gathered as Ramede explained to the soldier the man on the ground had bid against her at the slave market and had then followed her and tried to take the boy away. She had simply defended herself and her property. Fortunately, they were still in the Greek sector and Ramede mentioned she was staying at the tavern of Nesto. Immediately, someone went to tell Nesto what was happening. After several minutes, Nesto, Aristes, and Philo appeared and began talking to the soldier. They, of course, confirmed the story told by Ramede and the soldier determined no law had been broken since the man was a thief. Ramede was allowed to continue on her business.

After the experience with the attempted theft of Melitos, Ramede decided against having him spend the night at the ship. She wanted him to be with her after the experience with the man so he could settle down his feelings. They all went back to the tavern and settled in for the night. Melitos was given a bath and Nesto had some clothes to fit a ten year old. Melitos quickly fell asleep after having a very exciting day.

The adults, Ramede, Nesto, Aristes, and Philo, sat with some wine to drink. All the men were sorry they had left Ramede alone to walk through the city giving the man a chance to accost Ramede and the boy. They were also astounded Ramede could act so quickly, effectively and violently in self-defense. Most women wilt in the face of danger they said. They also were surprised Ramede carried a dagger and she knew how to use it. Ramede explained she had grown up with people who were being trained to use weapons and her part of the training involved how a woman could protect herself. She did not explain that as a member of Egyptian royalty it was necessary to have some skills at self-preservation.

They spent another three days in Al Mina making a few trades and getting some provisions, but mostly just resting. The balance of their journey would involve more stops for short duration to make trades as they progressed toward Greece. They would make trades to balance out their cargo for maximum profit. A good merchant learns it is best to take a variety of goods from a variety of sources to sell. You never know what the mood of buyers may be and some recent event or even the weather in an area can change the type of goods customers want to buy. A smart merchant spreads out the risk by diversifying his offerings. Yes, he may end up with some items, which do not sell, but he will sell a broad spectrum of items and make a profit. The goods, which do not sell in one market, will probably sell in another at a later date.

The young Melitos was a very pleasant boy, which made his assimilation into the Olympos easy. He was above average in intelligence and seemed to understand some things beyond his years, possibly due to his life experiences. He was very taken with Ramede, who he saw as the person who had saved him twice from an evil fate.

They made several stops on the coast of Cilicia as they moved up the coast stopping at Holmi, Kelenderis, and Nagidos. Each stop was only for a single nightfall and they did not take quarters ashore. The mountains along the coast at Nagidos were particularly impressive. They were now approximately five weeks into their journey and took these small stops as opportunities to put their feet on land and to get fresh water.

As they moved past Cilicia to Pampphylia and Lycia they landed at the city of Side near the foothills of the Taurus Mountains. After Side they sailed to Phaselis in Lycia then hugged the coast along Lycia until they reached the port of Telmessos on the western side of Lycia. Even at this time, Telmessos was renowned for its fruits and the wisdom of sages living there. The Olympos was loaded with fruits to sustain them for the next several weeks when they left Telmessos. The wisdom of the sages was the other valuable cargo they carried.

The next stop they made was a longer one at one of the great islands of the Mediterranean Sea, Rhodes. Rhodes is one of the larger islands in the Eastern Mediterranean and was one of the developing sea powers in the area. The Olympos made a stop at the city of Ialissos, sometimes called Trianta, on the northeastern end of the island. This port city was not large but it showed promise of developing into something. The people seemed to have an energy and curiosity about them similar to the residents of Tyre. Their ships had already traveled many places on the great sea and this made their city a bit more cosmopolitan and open to foreign visitors.

They decided to stay a few days in Ialissos to make a few trades and increase their knowledge of the place. The four of them, Ramede, Philo, Aristes, and Melitos made their way through the port area and asked if there was a tavern or inn which could provide lodging in the area. The man they asked said the inn of Kaunos was the best place and only a block away. The man was so effusive of his praise for the inn of Kaunos, Ramede asked if his name was Kaunos. The man smiled and said, "No, I am not Kaunos, only his younger brother, Keramos, who works for him at the inn. But I am a truthful man and our inn is the best inn in the city."

Ramede said, "Keramos, we will try your inn since it is always best to work with people who really believe what they sell or provide is the best. If, at least, they believe it, it may be true, or they will try harder to make it true. Good Keramos, lead us to the inn of Kaunos."

When they entered the inn, the proprietor, a large man who looked somewhat like Keramos, but older, welcomed them. He said, "Welcome to the inn of Kaunos. I see my good brother has brought you here. You will not be disappointed. We have the cleanest rooms and the best food in Ialissos. Did I forget, we also have wines collected from many countries to be a treat for your thirsts. We also offer a rare thing, the friendship of two brothers and their families who truly care to learn more about the world through conversation with our guests. Please stay here with us and let us share our humble inn with you."

Philo, who had never been to this inn before, was impressed with the salesmanship and apparent sincerity of the two brothers who were apparently trying to make their way in the world through offering a good place to stay, good food, good drink, and good conversation as the basis for their business. Many other innkeepers in the world would do well to emulate this approach. Many are too caught up in their day-to-day problems to remember the satisfaction of the customer is the key to good business. Philo said, "I am the captain of a ship from Tyre and make this trip often and know others who travel this way also. If your words are true, I can send many others your way. My friends here are merchants who have or will have many friends also to send in your direction if you please us. We look forward to the opportunity."

Introductions were made and Ramede introduced Melitos as her nephew, not as a slave, which pleased him very much. He was becoming very close to Ramede and sought out any opportunity to be of service to her. Of course, as a ten year old, he was subject to lapses of concentration due a short attention span and a curiosity about things, which sometimes distracted him from his duties. But he tried very hard which pleased Ramede.

Kaunos offered them a cup of a special wine from Crete, which he had brought to Rhodes at no small expense, he said. They tried the wine and found it to be excellent and not heavily watered as many innkeepers would do. He was very interested in the mixed nationality of his guests, a Greek, an Egyptian woman, her nephew who appeared to be Phyrgian, and a Phoenician sea captain. A varied group without a doubt. Ramede explained briefly she had need to escape from Egypt to leave an unhappy marriage, Aristes was a financially insolvent merchant stranded in Egypt, and Melitos had been enslaved and was now her ward to care for as a free person. This was the first Melitos had known he was not a slave but was free. He smiled broadly at the words of Ramede.

Kaunos was curious about what life was like in Egypt. Ramede explained she lived in the far south of Egypt, near the fourth cataract of the Nile, which was a much different way of life than those who lived in the delta. The Nile was the source of life for both those in the south as well as the delta area but those in the delta lived with their fates tied to the flooding of the Nile. They were forced to be more disciplined and regimented than those from the south to take full advantage of the annual flooding.

Kaunos asked if all the women of Egypt were a beautiful as Ramede. Aristes answered quickly that Ramede was the most beautiful woman he had encountered in the world, not just Egypt. Philo was quick to agree with Aristes. Ramede said compliments would not get these men any closer to their goals but to keep trying anyway.

Kaunos suggested his guests should take an opportunity to see the "Valley of Butterflies" while on Rhodes. It was not far from Ialissos and Keramos would be glad to act as their guide. He loved to go to the valley and see this miraculous sight. Ramede said she would like to go and, of course, settled the matter. In the morning they took the road south out of Ialissos and traveled a short while through several villages the last being Paradissi, then turned to the left and entered a secluded narrow valley where millions of butterflies filled the air. It was truly one of the wonders of nature to see so many of these harmless, beautiful creatures in one place at one time. They returned to the inn by mid-afternoon well pleased with their day's adventure.

At the inn, Ramede asked Kaunos if there were any items from Rhodes, which would trade well in Greece. He immediately answered that some of the swords made on Rhodes were the best in the world. These would likely trade very well in Greece where the people are particularly warlike. Aristes said he had also been thinking

337

along these lines and planned to visit a place specializing in armaments the next day. Ramede said she would like to go also.

When they told Kaunos their intended destination in Greece was Corinth, he grew serious and warned them there had been recent political disturbances in Corinth and he recommended they choose a different destination, at least until they understood better the situation in Corinth. He recommended they go to Athens as he had heard Athens was currently an easier place for foreign merchants to realize a profit.

Aristes was disappointed his home city was suffering problems but, like most merchants he was successful because he was pragmatic, he accepted the recommendation they go first to Athens, if the situation was currently unstable in Corinth.

In the morning, they set out for the sword maker located just outside of Ialissos. The operation was not large and it was quickly apparent most of the swords were made on orders for a specific customer. When asked if he had any stock of swords, the sword maker said he had about six swords made to the most popular design, put away, for a quick sale opportunity. Ramede said she would like to see them and the swords were brought out of the back room. All appeared to be good swords and of the latest design. Aristes and Philo tried each of them and found them to be well balanced and of good quality. Ramede asked the sword maker. "How much for one?" He named a price. She asked, "How much for all six, in gold?" The man named a price with about a twenty five percent discount per sword from the original price. Ramede said, "The price is too high. Is there something else you will throw in to sweeten the bargain?"

The sword maker went to the back room and came out with a smaller sword, suited for a youth or a woman, if a woman would want a sword. The man said he would throw in the smaller sword also. He had made it to order for a rich man's son but they never returned to pick up the sword. Ramede immediately said she would take the deal and paid the gold to the sword maker. Ramede said to Aristes and Philo after the attack in Al Mina, she intended to arm herself better when she traveled about, and at some point in the future the smaller sword would serve well to train Melitos in swordsmanship. The other six swords would be more trade goods to be sold in Greece at a profit.

Kaunos and Keremos were now good friends with the crew from the Olympos and were sorry to see them leave after their visit to Ialissos. They promised to remember them and to give them the best rooms when they returned to Rhodes.

Ramede reflected they had had a very good trip so far, except for the incident in Al Mina, and was looking forward now to establishing herself in Greece. They sailed out of Ialissos toward their next destination, the city of Kos on the Island of Kos. Kos already had a long history of over one thousand years at this time and many travelers knew of the port and the island as a beautiful place. They only spent one night in Kos to replenish their supply of water and to briefly see the city.

The next day they set sail for their next destination, the city of Naxos (Hora) on the Island of Naxos in the Cyclades Islands. The island is west of the Peloponnese peninsula where Corinth and Sparta are located and was mentioned throughout history in myths and legends according to Aristes. The island was especially renowned for honey, cheeses, and citrus drinks as well as its beautiful beaches. The city itself sat as a natural amphitheatre site with beautiful white stone buildings making up much of the city.

Ramede thought the setting of Naxos was the prettiest city she had ever seen. From the sea it looked so clean and enchanting. Upon landing at the port, the three adults and one child went to find a place to stay on land. The first inn they tried was full due to some kind of local celebration taking place. Finally they found an inn with some space available and took two rooms. Their most interesting find in the city was a local honey wine which tasted very sweet but was different than anything they had tasted elsewhere. They asked if they sent much of this to the markets in Corinth and were told it was not shipped off the island usually. Ramede decided to buy a stock of the unusual wine to sell in their new destination, Athens.

They only stayed one night in Naxos since they were all anxious to get to Athens. They set sail in the morning for the port of Troezen, another city mentioned in the myths and legends of Greece as well as being featured in history. The city was part of the Peloponnese, southeast of Corinth, northeast of Sparta, and south of Athens. They then sailed up the Bay of Corinth to the port of Piraeus, which was close to the city of Athens.

54. <u>Athens (715 B.C.)</u>

Both Aristes and Philo had visited the port of Piraeus previously so it was not totally a new experience. Ramede had made several decisions prior to landing at Piraeus. First she chose to shorten her name to Mede from Ramede. Ramede was a bit too Egyptian for her tastes when she was trying to distance herself from her past. Secondly, for the same reason she asked to be introduced as being an Egyptian from Tyre rather than coming directly from Egypt. Third she chose to officially adopt Melitos as her nephew and to record some of the goods they were bringing into Greece as his property for purposes of written records. He would be recorded as a free person and a property owner as a result, which might be important in the future.

Their entry into the port was no great problem with the normal necessity of paying some tax on the goods they carried with them and explaining their purpose in being there. The fact they said they would be taking their goods to Athens for sale was sufficient explanation.

They decided to have Philo stay with the ship for a few days to hold their goods while they went to Athens to make arrangements for housing, warehousing of goods, and a place to sell the goods. They had made plans for Philo to take a load of trade goods back as far as Tyre. These would generate a good profit for the return trip. Aristes and Mede had agreed to finance the goods for a one third share of the profits for each. Aristes and Mede left for Athens to sort out arrangements while Philo and Melitos stayed with the ship.

Upon arrival in Athens, Aristes and Mede went to the marketplace, the Agora, and made inquiries where the best place would be to sell wares imported from Egypt, Tyre, Rhodes, Kos, and other places. They were asked if they had such goods and told the questioners, they had a ship full of such items in the harbor. Many people they spoke with expressed interest but the impression Aristes got was they would be much better selling the goods themselves rather than letting a middleman take a major share of the profit. Then they inquired about renting sales space in the Agora and proceeded to contract for a space. They inquired about warehouse space and quarters and were directed to a commercial district nearby where houses and warehouses were for rent and found a building with warehouse space of sufficient size for their goods and modest living quarters included. A contract was signed to rent the place for three months, paying in advance.

They returned to the port and made arrangements to transport their goods to their newly rented warehouse and accompanied their goods being moved to Athens since they did not feel like trusting strangers with the load of valuable goods they were moving. Philo and several members of the ship's crew also came along to protect the trade goods and to provide the labor to unload the goods into the warehouse building. Plilo sent his crew, except one to act as guard, back to the ship to wait there until he was prepared to return to the ship.

Next day they took a sampling of their goods to the agora early in the morning and set up the goods for sale. They left the one crewman from the Olympos at the warehouse as a guard. They put out word they had just arrived with a large selection of imported goods from the Egypt, the Levant, Rhodes, and other places and were prepared to sell or trade. Many people, including other merchants, came to look at their offerings and to try to make deals. Aristes now showed the extent of his talent as a merchant. With the others, Mede, Philo, and Melitos, acting as security to avoid theft of their valuables, Aristes talked with prospective purchasers, pointed out the advantages of their wares, and bargained with customers. Usually he was able to get purchasers to bid against each other for individual items, driving the price and the profit up. He had a number of losing bidders who wanted to know if they had more of certain items. Aristes said they would bring more goods the next day.

By the end of the day, they counted their sales and trades determining they were making greater profits than they had expected. The strategy of taking only a portion of goods to the market at any time and practicing a "managed shortage" of the most demanded items was working well to get higher prices. Since coins were not used commonly, the hard currency they received was in silver mostly and some gold but all had to be checked and weighed carefully since there was no commonly accepted weights and measure system in place. About on half of their "sales" were trades for other items, which required the eye of an experienced merchant like Aristes to insure the trade value was appropriate.

Returning to the warehouse at the end of the day with their new goods and other valuables they had acquired left them weary but satisfied. Another week or two of trading like this would provide a complete load of trade goods for Philo to take back to Tyre and silver and gold to make a profit many times their investment. Aristes made some calculations and had the thought he could end up with enough wealth to buy a ship in Piraeus, outfit it, and load it with trade goods and still have funds left over out of his share. If he could find a ship's crew he could trust he could send out another ship with the Olympos to travel together for more safety and increase their chances for the ships to return for more profits. Such were the risks and opportunities for profits in such ventures. He asked Mede if she was interested in using her funds from the venture to finance a third ship. Philo, Aristes and Mede could be partners in the venture and become very rich.

Mede said she would think about it over the next several days but Philo and Aristes could be looking for ships to buy and potential crews while she made up her mind. Mede had sufficient resources to make the investment and still have reserves to live on if the investment failed but she did not want to throw away her money without having a good plan.

Mede had dressed well for her work in the Agora. Wearing fashionable clothing showed off her attractions. She was by far the most attractive woman in the marketplace and drew many glances from the male audience as she went about her work. There were some other women working in other sales stalls but mostly there were other women among the customers who came to look at the goods. They did not seem overly friendly, but Aristes had warned her most Greek women worked in the homes and those working in the market would be wives of less successful merchants or slaves.

The next day they returned to the agora with another load of goods, limiting how many of each item they displayed. Again the managed scarcity of selected items drove prices up. The crowds seemed larger around their stall on the second day and by mid-day they had to send Aristes to bring more goods from the warehouse to restock. They returned to the warehouse at night with a large load of new trade items. Philo decided to send his crewman to the ship and have him return with more men to take some of the new goods back to the ship. For the next three days they continued to follow the same process until the Olympos was fully loaded with trade goods for the return voyage to Tyre. They had only sold or traded about one fourth of the goods they had brought to Athens and had held back some of the very best items, including the swords and some of the best jewelry from Egypt.

Mede decided to finance a ship based of the excellent profits they were making. Aristes and Philo had found two ships available for sale and two captains who seemed trustworthy. Since they would be traveling with Philo, there was a greater chance they could be trusted. Both captains had families in Athens, which increased the likelihood they would return willingly. Aristes insisted a written agreements be signed with each captain to insure they understood exactly what the arrangements were. Another week of trading and they had amassed enough trade goods to fill the other two ships and had paid the prices to buy the ships. They still had over on half their original selection of goods and a small fortune in silver and gold left over when they saw Philo and the three ships off on their return voyage to Tyre. It had been a very profitable trip so far.

Business at their stall in the agora had not slacked off, in fact, as word got around of the quality of goods they had to sell, traffic increased. Some of the richer and more powerful people of Athens were now coming to their stall to get some of the rare articles they had heard about coming from Egypt and Tyre. On Wednesday of their third week in Athens, several well-dressed men came to their stall with their wives to look at their wares. Some of the best jewelry from Egypt had been held back but Mede got it out to show to these customers. They also had two of the swords from Rhodes on display. The men were very interested in the swords, which were better quality than most Greek swords. The women saw the jewelry and there was no question they had to have some of it.

One of the men who was not with a woman questioned Mede, "You are a very beautiful woman, and dressed well also, to be working at a stall in the Agora. Is the merchant over there your husband and is the boy your son?"

Mede was not offended at his interest as he was young and handsome. She responded, "The man is my business partner and the boy is my adopted nephew. I am a widow who is doing this work as a way to finance my travel from Tyre to Greece and to start a new life here in Greece."

The man said his name was Amides, and he was the son of one of the richest men in Athens. He said he did not say it to brag but only to have her understand the truth of his position. Mede introduced herself as Mede of Egyptian extraction but most recently from the Phoenician city of Tyre. She also introduced Melitos as her adopted nephew.

He asked where she lived and she explained they were in temporary rented quarter in the commercial district being used also as a warehouse for their trade goods. Amides said it was unusual for a woman to be so involved in business in Athens but he personally admired her for her intelligence and courage.

Mede thanked him and then asked if he knew of a school where she could send Melitos so he could get a good education. He said he knew of a school, which was very good for a young boy but was expensive and somewhat exclusive. Mede said she could probably afford the cost. How could she get him admitted if the people who ran the school were reluctant since she was a stranger? Amides said he may be able to help but would like to get to know both Mede and Melitos better before recommending him for the school.

Mede indicated she thought it was a fair request. He said he would like to show Mede and Melitos around the city, which would give them a chance to get to know each other better. Could the boy and her get away in the afternoon to see some of the sights? Mede said, yes."

Aristes had no concern about handling the business in the afternoon. He now had a couple of men hired to assist him and was glad for Mede to have a chance to get away. He cautioned her to be wary of this newfound friend. He may have as his main objective taking advantage of a beautiful woman. Mede said she thought she could deal with the situation.

Amides gave them a good tour of Athens. Melitos was very impressed with all he saw since his experience in the world was limited. His natural curiosity and a child's delight a new things made for a very happy day for him. His above average intelligence impressed Amides who said he thought he would do well at the school he would sponsor him to attend. Mede was less impressed by

Athens, although she saw the potential there. She had been the wife of a king in Egypt where civilization was more advanced. She felt her reaction might be disappointing to Amides.

Finally she said to Amides, "I hope my reaction to Athens is not less than what you would expect. I have spent time in Egypt, which is a more developed civilization than here in Athens. Many of the public works and the size of cities in general are larger in Egypt, but I can see the potential and beauty here also.

Amides said, "I think I understand, but how does a woman, even a beautiful woman as yourself, get an opportunity to travel to see these wonderful places in the world? Even many queens do not get a chance to see as much of the world as you have already seen at a young age."

Mede only said, "I have made some sacrifices to see the places I have seen, but I am now in Athens and am glad to see the beauty here."

Mede then asked, "How soon can we find out about getting Melitos into the school?"

Amides said he would go to the school tomorrow and should have an answer by noon.

Amides escorted Mede and Melitos to the warehouse / residence. He asked how long she planned on staying there. She indicated she was looking for a house to rent or buy. Did he know of available property? He said he would look around but would need to understand what kind of property she needed. She said they could talk about it another time. She thanked him for his kindness and he left.

The next day in the early afternoon, Amides, came to the stall in the Agora and told Mede it was arranged for Melitos to start at the school as soon as they received the fee for three months and he named a figure. It was well within her means so he asked if they could go to the school and get all the arrangements made today. He said he would be delighted and off they went with Melitos. The school was within the city and close enough he could get up at dawn and have time to go to the school and return by late afternoon. It would be a long day but he had a curious mind and wanted to learn. For the first few days, Mede would send one of the hired workers to escort the boy to school to insure he knew the way.

When Melitos returned from school the first day he said it was difficult because of his newness to the Greek language but he was learning and it would get better. After another week he was doing very well and when Mede went to the school to inquire about his progress the teacher said he was becoming a very good student. His memory was excellent and he tried harder than any of the other students. He seemed to have a natural instinct for mathematics and was very curious about science. Both Mede and Melitos had been taking lessons in reading and writing Greek for some months and this showed in Melitos progress. Mede was very pleased and proud of her adopted nephew.

Aristes said the trade dealings were going very well and the amount of goods they had left could be handled in several ways. They could sell them all in a couple of weeks of diligent selling and trading. They would then have a large stock of trade goods acquired in Athens to be traded elsewhere.

Another option was to sell the newly acquired trade goods to some merchant or ship's captain in a bulk sale for him to take to a distant port; but he would get a large part of the profit. Mede and Aristes would still do very well and would convert the goods into silver and gold.

A third option was to either buy another ship or contract with a ship's captain to take the goods and Aristes to some distant port, like Egypt, to trade the goods for others to make more profit and start the cycle again. This was obviously the preference of Aristes but he was concerned about leaving Mede and Melitos alone in Athens without his protection.

Mede said she now had some friends in Athens, Amides in particular, and she could take care of herself in Athens. She would like to invest in the purchase of another ship but would prefer if Aristes used his share of the silver and gold to buy the ship and she would provide her share of the investment in trade goods. She needed her share of the silver and gold to buy some property in Athens.

After investigation she learned she might be required to buy the property in the name of Melitos since women had limited property rights in Athens. Finally she decided to rent property in Athens and to make an investment in a fourth and fifth ship to send trade goods to Egypt. It was safer to invest in these ships and increase their chances one or more of the ships would return, than to invest in land in Athens, where her property rights might be questioned. The fact was even if four out of five ships were lost, the huge profits from one ship would still insure a net profit overall. If all ships were successful the three partners would become some of the wealthier people in Athens.

Mede found some property in Athens to rent, a very small farm which belonged to a wealthy family which currently had no sons of age to manage the farm but who wanted to hold the property for the future. She made a deal to lease the property for five years at a cost she knew she could afford. Melitos and Mede would be comfortable on the farm and would hire some laborers to work the farm in addition to selling in the agora. Mede had trained some of the help they had hired for the stall in the agora and felt comfortable leaving them to handle the day-to-day commerce while she oversaw the business without having to be on hand all the time.

In May of 714 B.C., all was in place for Aristes to leave Piraeus with two more ships loaded with the goods acquired by trading the goods brought from Egypt and other ports of call. They would now have five ships at sea with potential for profit.

Amides was a good friend who introduced Mede to people in Athens and assisted her with the small problems of life in a large city. Amides and Mede did not develop a romantic interest in each other but were close friends. Mede was one of the most beautiful women in Athens and she did wonder at times if Amides had a sexual orientation that kept him from being interested in her in that way. One evening the subject came up after they had drunk enough wine to release normal inhibitions.

Amides confessed he originally had a sexual interest in Mede, but as he developed a friendship, he saw Mede was a very strong woman, perhaps stronger than Amides would feel comfortable with in a sexual relationship. He did not mean this in an unflattering way toward Mede, it was a flaw in Amides if anything rather than something wrong with Mede. Mede did not think it was necessarily a flaw in either person, love happens when it happens, not because we will it to be.

Amides took time to take Mede and Melitos to many events around the city and in this way Mede became know to many of the wealthier residents of Athens. As a beautiful "widow" she was accepted some places but not so readily welcomed other places. Actually Melitos was a major factor in gaining her acceptance in some circles. He was a brilliant student at his school and word spread in Athenian society the aunt of the brilliant Melitos was a beautiful widow and a good friend of Amides. Eventually, Amides was approached by several men about his relationship with Mede and her availability. Word then got around the beautiful widow was unattached and Amides was only a friend.

In the summer of 714 B.C. Mede was introduced at a wedding to a powerful and wealthy Athenian named Alaecus who had been widowed and who immediately took an interest in Mede. He was one of the leaders of Athens and was used to getting what he wanted, and obviously he wanted Mede. He started visiting her daily and made no secret of his desire to spend time in her bed. He was a large man, over six feet in height and was a powerful soldier, who had had much success in military contests. Mede liked the man who seemed to be honest and sincere, but not as intellectually inclined as she would have preferred. He was good for Melitos, since he was at an age where military training loomed as a large issue for him, despite his considerable success in scholastic pursuits. Melitos wanted to get some exposure to military skills and Alaecus was one of the best military men in Athens.

Alaecus offered to take Miletos with him on a hunt with some soldier friends of his. Mede had acquired a small horse for Melitos through a trade and agreed he could go. It was a great adventure for Melitos. Going out on a hunt with one of the great soldiers of Athens and spending a night away from home was wonderful for building the boy's confidence and gave him something special to talk about to the other boys at school who had fathers to do such things with. Alaecus showed himself to be a very kind person with the time he took to listen to Melitos and answer his many questions. Mede began to think that perhaps Alaecus might become a very special person in her life.

By September, Alaecus was expressing his love for Mede and wanted to marry her and offered to adopt Melitos as his son. This could be a very significant thing for the future of Melitos. Adoption in to one of the great families of Athens could open a future for him beyond which most young men could dream about. After a time, Mede decided to take Alaecus to her bed but to postpone a decision about marriage until some of the ships had returned from their ventures.

Alaecus was not displeased with the arrangement, as he now spent several nights each week with Mede but did not have to go through the social commitments a marriage would require. Mede rather liked the arrangement since she could keep some of the independence she was accustomed to. Melitos also was pleased with the situation since he got a chance to spend some time with a male figure he admired.

In December of 714 B.C., Philo returned to Piraeus with two of the three ships he departed with. One ship had sunk when it went aground along the coast near Sidon. Fortune smiled at the time, as they were able to rescue the crew and most of the more expensive goods.

55. **Chandler, AZ**

Ramede stopped telling about her life in ancient Greece and explained she had told enough for a while. She had many memories, some were pleasant, and others were anything but pleasant. She had generally had a good life but the constant loss of those she had learned to love was almost too much to live with at times.

Arslan sympathized with Ramede saying, "The loss of loved ones, wives, lovers, children, and friends made me think, at times, about finding a way to end my life. I never tried to do it and would quickly recover when I started new relationships, but the pain could be almost unbearable. I hate saying Ramede and I are different but we have experienced loss after loss, which is beyond understanding if you have not experienced it. To be quite honest, I take a different view of life and relationships than I expect most men or women do who have not had this experience. I treasure the time I have with people, the closer a relationship the better. Each moment is so valuable since the time it lasts is so short."

Ramede said, "That is true for me also, but perhaps the feeling is magnified in me as a woman. From my personal study of the human condition, women feel emotion more clearly than men, not always a deeply, but with a stronger claim on their very beings than men. Men, if I may generalize, are more thought driven than emotion driven, except of course when the chemistry of ego and sex drive are in play, then men are captives of their instincts. I don't make any value judgments about this, one thing works for women, another for men. I love to interact with both men and women, in very different ways, of course. I will tell more of my story some other time. Right now I am interested in understanding more clearly where Arslan and I came from and what it all means in the whole scheme of things. From what I have learned so far, eight babies were placed at various locations in the world and so far we only know what happened to Arslan and myself. What happened to the others? Do we know anything?"

Simon spoke up, "The artificial intelligence of the Tira has no knowledge of the others. Arslan has a feeling based on his own experience that Jesus, whom Arslan met twice, had some special connection to Arslan. Could Jesus have been one of the six children? It could explain some events, rising from the dead for example."

Ramede said, "Is there some way to learn more. The most advanced technology ever experienced by man is found on the Tira. The artificial intelligence on the Tira, alone, offers access to history far beyond any resource ever made available before. Can't we use it to search for some answers. Perhaps the answers are buried in the information stored on the Tira but unrecognized as significant to the artificial intelligence. Perhaps if we query the artificial intelligence, like we would ask for information from a computer, perhaps we can find some answers."

Arslan said, "We need to decide what questions really are important to be answered. Does it really matter what happened to my brothers and sisters, unless they are still alive or were major actors in history who left a legacy, which still impacts the flow of events? Yes, it would be nice to know, even if they had no impact but is it more important than some other things?"

"The "people" who built the Tira and who may well be the parents of humanity in some sense, saw as the most important task for intelligent life to seek to find the ultimate reason for the universe. The wonderful curiosity driving their search and a program to develop intelligence to continue the search is such a strong force. Humanity has been so fearful at times about finding an alien life, which would try to enslave or destroy human life. Instead, what we have found is an "alien" life, which is actually our parent, and protector, which has tried to evolve us to a level of intelligence capable of solving the puzzle of the universe. We owe them our best effort to try to reach higher, to go farther, since they made such a pure effort to go beyond themselves."

"Is it really important to know if Jesus of Nazareth was a fake, or an invention of devious men, or one of the children of the Tira? Is it more important to take the good from the teachings of Jesus and to recognize the actual or potential positive effects of those teachings? Can those teachings be the basis for developing a new and better humanity? I suspect people are not ready for such a philosophical approach without the ritual and the emphasis on faith in mysteries."

Ramede responded, "I agree with you the importance of the ideas are more important than the origin of the man, but the Tira offers a unique opportunity to study many of the great religious leaders in history and to make a case for or against the believability of the great religions. Isn't this an important thing to accomplish?"

Arslan agreed saying, "As someone who loves the study of history and religion, I cannot help but agree with the importance of using the memory of the Tira to study history. My point is there may be more significant issues to study, where the benefit to humanity is greater. But we need not debate these issues now."

Ramede spoke again, "Changing the subject a bit, I have wanted to ask Arslan what he thinks about relationships between men and women. I guess I should be brave enough to state my own views first, so I will."

Based on 2,800 years of experience as a woman in the world, on the one hand, I am torn between cynicism about the way men and women treat each other and the impurity of their motives for seeking each other out as partners, and lasting optimism about loving relationships based on pure, somewhat selfless loving being possible.

You need to know I have used my sex as a tool of survival in the world. I have been a prostitute in one form or another in many of my identities. I have also been a "married" woman of good reputation in many lives. My views about the moral goodness of either the prostitute or the properly married woman are there is little difference, morally, between the prostitute and the married woman in many cases.

Many "married" women marry for money. Is this any different than the prostitute selling her body for money? I see no difference. How many women marry mostly for the economic benefit they can derive? Perhaps a majority, if the truth be known. And men are not any better, I think."

Their discussion was suddenly interrupted by Tira's computer saying, "There is an urgent message by E-mail being received from the Situation Room at the White House." Without further comment a screen appeared in front of them with the E-mail text:

fwd:	smyers@ctrdna.org
to:	older_than_dirt.com
from:	SITRM White House Washington DC
subject:	Terrorist Alert

CIA has reports of a terrorist intent to strike at the Tira within the next few days based on reliable intelligence sources within the Al-Qaida terrorist network. This has been confirmed by other sources in deepest cover within a key Middle Eastern government with ties to terrorists.

The reported method of attack is a nuclear or biological device, which will cause massive loss of life in the Phoenix area. The CIA cannot categorically deny the capabilities of this terrorist group to have possession of such a device.

Intelligence sources report terrorists with roots in Islamic countries have strong support for an attack on "the evil source of lies about religious history emanating from the Tira."

Please respond with your plans to cope with this threat.

Urgent response required.

Gen, Robert Miller
CHM JCS

Simon immediately said, "Arslan, what should we do?"

Arslan responded. "It needs to be a group decision but I recommend we move the Tira somewhere away from population centers until we hold the meeting with world leaders. I can think of a couple of possibilities but one of the safest from a security standpoint would be to Antarctica.

Lisa voiced her agreement, "We cannot endanger the population of Phoenix without good reason, and we need to move right away.— Antarctica is as good a place as any.

Everyone else agreed as well.

Arslan directed the computer to send an E-mail to General Miller informing him the Tira would be moving immediately to a remote area of Antarctica to avoid endangering any population centers.

The computer was also directed to set a course for the central plain of Antarctica and to select a suitable flight path at high altitude. The computer responded by showing a three dimensional representation of the earth with a flight path shown from the southwest of North America to the approximate center of Antarctica.

Within thirty minutes of the decision to go the Tira was at an altitude of 80,000 feet moving at several thousand miles per hour toward Antarctica, They were landed on a relatively flat plain of ice and snow within two hours. During their transit, they had notified all of the major news organizations of the world of their move from Arizona to Antarctica and the specific threat from terrorists having caused them to make the move.

Reaction from responsible sources around the world was one of dismay mixed with acceptance it was a correct precaution to take if there was any credibility to the threat from terrorists.

Condemnation of the terrorists was for the most part consistent from government representatives and most organizations around the world. Notable exceptions were many Islamic governments who apparently did not want to incur the wrath of religious militants by speaking out.

There were now only two weeks remaining until the scheduled meeting with world leader set for New Year's Day. The threat to Phoenix by terrorists was sufficient to put in doubt the plan to hold the meeting there. Arslan suggested, "We need some professional advice on where to hold the meeting. Who can we trust?"

Simon suggested General Miller might be able to recommend the best expert advice to call upon under these circumstances. No one had any objections so a call was placed to General Miller.

General Miller suggested they consult with a security expert at the CIA by the name of Joseph McHenry. General Miller said McHenry was one of the most experienced security people in the world but was not well known outside of the security profession. General Miller had worked with him several times in the past and was impressed with his common sense and ability to think beyond the boundaries.

General Miller suggested he contact the CIA Director to get clearance for McHenry to provide assistance to get the ball rolling. He signed off and after about thirty minutes they were contacted by Joseph McHenry by voice communication.

The voice said, "This is Joseph McHenry. General Miller requested I contact you after the Director gave his approval. I understand you have some security issues you wish to discuss.

Arslan responded, "Mr. McHenry, General Miller recommended you as an expert in some of the security issues we will face in connection with the meeting of heads of state scheduled for January 1. To start out we would like to do this at a distance by teleconference and E-Mail. Can you work with us under those circumstances?"

McHenry responded," Yes, it is not a problem, in fact, it may give me the opportunity to call on other resources here at the CIA which would be difficult to use from a distance."

Arslan said, 'Do you understand our current situation and the reason for our move to Antarctica?"

"Yes," said McHenry.

Arslan continued, "What we need is advice on how to set up the meeting for January 1, so we are secure and can avoid having fear of terrorist attack upset the important discussions we plan to have with world leaders. Where would you hold the meeting and how would you advise us to set up security?"

McHenry spoke, "The safest place on earth to have the meeting would be on the Tira with the Tira located where you are right now, Antarctica. This would minimize the potential for terrorists or other enemies to project any type of threat toward the meeting and any attempt could be detected early and defensive action taken. The potential for collateral damage to population centers would be eliminated, as well."

Arslan said, "I agree but how do we get the leaders to the Tira in Antarctica?"

McHenry responded, "Have the world leader congregate at three points around the world, for example, London, Atlanta, and Tokyo, then have the Tira travel to pick them up. The pickups should be well coordinated to take place quickly and there should be alternate points available with a last minute decision made about the specific pick up point to be used in each part of the would."

Arslan responded, "I like it, Mr. McHenry, can you be made available to coordinate the process?"

McHenry said, "I have been told to cooperate with you in any way possible, so I guess it means I am available."

Arslan said, "Please proceed to implement the plan to use three pickup points and talk to me daily to coordinate. If you have any problems getting resources or a free hand to proceed let me know and I will contact the President. After we end this conversation, I will send a formal request to the President requesting your temporary assignment to this project and asking that you report to me for the duration of the project with full cooperation from your agency. Is that adequate?"

"Yes sir," was the response from McHenry.

After signing off with McHenry, Arslan followed through on sending a request to the President to get McHenry assigned full time to the security project for the New Year's Day meeting.

Within fifteen minutes a response came from the White House. It said McHenry had been reassigned to the project as requested and would report operationally to General Miller (JCS) but was specifically tasked to accept directives from Arslan on the Tira based on Presidential authority.

All relevant government agencies were directed to treat requests from McHenry as being fully supported by Presidential authority.

Simon commented, "It looks like we have some help."

Arslan said," The President seems to be on board to assist as much as possible. I want to believe in the good intentions of the U.S. Government but we simply have to be extremely cautious. There is so much at stake, I don't trust those in power to not be tempted to try to take over the incredible power of the Tira."

"I am beginning to have doubts we can put together a political structure to control the powers of the Tira so they are used for "good purposes." Am I kidding myself we can hold this conference and come out of it with something effective and workable? Do the rest of you really believe we can come up with something we will feel comfortable with to turn over the Tira's power to? said Arslan.

Ramede spoke, "I honestly have my doubts, as well. I am probably the least trusting of all of us in the people in positions of power and their motives and potential actions. Addictions rule much of humanity. Alcohol, tobacco, opium, cocaine, food, coffee, chocolate, sex, and violence to mention a few. The one I did not include is possibly the strongest addiction—POWER. Those who have it, usually want to keep it at all cost. Like most addictions, people change once they are addicted. So, whatever we do we must build in safeguards so no one person or group can take absolute power and eliminate freedom where it exists."

Lisa interjected, "Let's make a list of the options we have and see if anything stands out. The first option is to:

Agree with world leaders on a charter and political mechanism to control the Tira, then turn the Tira over to them.

Does everybody agree it is one option?"
Everyone agreed it was an option.
Arslan said: Another option might be to:

Agree with world leaders on a charter and political mechanism to control the Tira, but delay turning over the Tira until the system proves it is workable. This means we would have to stay in control of the Tira for some set period of time and we would have to decide if the system put in place is "workable."

Carrie spoke up, "How likely is it we will ever be satisfied a system will be "workable" to control the power of the Tira? Past history has not shown men can handle something like this."

Perhaps we should decide from the outset we must remain in control but develop a charter for how we will deal with the power."

Simon spoke up, "Let me see if I understand it. Our choices are:

1. Give up control.
2. Delay giving up control.
3. Decide not to give up control."

Arslan responded, "Those are the choices. Like them or not."
Lisa said, "I don't feel ready to address a question with those answers right now. I think we need to take a break and focus on something else before we try to make the decision. Any disagreement with that?"
No one complained about leaving the decision for another time.
Simon thought to himself, *"I remember my old boss, Bob, used to say he managed by postponing every important decision to the last possible moment. Of course, he was also the one who insisted he never reacted at all to the first memo he received about anything. He always waited for a second request before taking action, or even*

thinking about taking action. I wonder how many people use that approach?"

Simon said, "Arslan, some time ago, before Ramede came on board, a strange thing happened. I say strange, because we asked you about something and you said you did not want to talk about it, at the time. I am talking about the coin you wear on a chain around your neck. It seemed so out of character for you to be reluctant to talk about anything since you have shared so much about yourself already. Is this a good time to go back to the coin?"

Arslan responded, "You like to jump from one difficult subject to another. Deciding how to control the Tira for the good of mankind isn't enough. You want to open up Pandora's box on another subject falling into the same level of sensitivity—for different reasons. But I am ready to talk about it—just don't say I didn't warn you."

Arslan started to tell the story, "Let me begin by saying I am sorry I thought it necessary to be less than forthcoming about this subject but I thought it might be difficult for everyone to accept or deal with it without a strong emotional reaction. **I left some key information out of my recollections about my time in Jerusalem in 33 A.D.** So here goes."

"Back in Atlanta, I told Lisa and Simon I had asked my assistant in my trading business in Jerusalem, Ruben, to try to set up a meeting with Jesus through Thomas, if he could be located. I told you Ruben tried but everyone was very busy and nothing could be done. That was not true. This was the start of Passover and everyone was busy but Thomas had sought me out and told me he would send a messenger when Jesus might be able to see me. He said he knew Jesus would want to see me because he had spoken about me several times after our last meeting. He did not explain further."

56. Jerusalem (33 A.D.)

Arslanus was pleased with the visit from Thomas and his request for Arslanus to try to meet with Jesus. There was a great deal of talk in the streets of the city about Jesus entry into the city to start Passover and a bitter reaction from some of the religious elements. Ruben, his assistant was horrified Arslanus would even think of meeting publicly with this Jesus of Nazareth. The Jewish leaders in Jerusalem were very displeased with this Jesus. Ruben advised him to stay away.

Arslanus was also aware his close resemblance to Jesus could draw attention to himself he did not need. A side-by-side comparison would make people believe they were related—even brothers—or twins.

But to Arslanus, the opportunity to feel the strange "connection" to Jesus of Nazareth was too important and unique to miss. He would go to meet with Jesus.

A messenger arrived at the home of Arslanus about midnight with the message Arslanus should go the garden of Gethsemane to meet with Jesus. Arslanus went to Gethsemane arriving after midnight. He went into the garden looking for Jesus with only the moonlight to assist him. He wore his sword and best clothing so he could easily assert his Roman citizenship if it was necessary.

Fear was not a factor for Arslan. He was cautious by habit, but he was the best swordsman in the world as far as he knew, and what he knew about the timing of actions in a difficult situation gave him a huge advantage over most men. His thoughts were focused more on what he would like to say to Jesus. *Was Jesus like himself—could they be brothers—should he ask Jesus that?*

As he entered the garden, he saw the problem of locating Jesus in the dark would not be easy. The garden was large and vegetation was dense enough to make it difficult to see many areas. After looking for some time, Arslanus, saw and heard a crowd of people coming along the path toward the part of the garden he had not yet searched. Arslan chose to follow behind the men to see where they were going.

Arslan quickly saw some of the men were dressed as the "high Jews" he had observed at times near the temple. He also observed most of them were armed.

When the group stopped, Arslanus moved around the side to see what was happening ahead. He saw Jesus and several others he had seen before, including Peter, being confronted by several of the leaders of the armed group. One man with a sword was threatening Jesus. Arslanus, instinctively moved forward to block the threat. The man then attempted to strike at Arslanus. Arslanus' sword moved with speed no eye could follow and sliced the ear off the other swordsman and his sword fell to the ground.

Jesus called out to Arslanus, "Put your sword away, violence is not my way."

Arslanus put his sword away as requested by Jesus and moved off to the side.

Arslanus did not hear all said by Jesus to the armed men but the result was Jesus followers left, some of them running away. Jesus offered no resistance to his captors and Arslan understood Jesus did not want him to interfere. The armed men glanced at Arslan a few times but he sensed they did not want to test the abilities of this stranger who had already bested one of their ranks.

Arslanus recognized one of Jesus followers who had been ahead of the group of armed men when they approached Jesus. He had not fled with the rest of Jesus followers but had slipped to the back of the group as the armed men took Jesus away. Arslanus decided to follow this man to see where he went since there was nothing he could do to assist Jesus, who apparently did not want his help anyway.

Arslanus followed the man (he later learned the man's name was Judas Iscariot) who separated from the armed men and went off in another direction. Arslan stayed far enough back to avoid being seen but stayed close enough to maintain contact with the man. The man tried to be careful he was not being followed but Arslanus was quite skillful at this type of activity.

Judas eventually approached a house in one of the poorer sections of Jerusalem. He knocked on the door several times and eventually the door opened and Judas was admitted. Arslanus saw no point in continuing to watch the house and left for his own house. "Why does one of Jesus men lead the mob to Jesus?" thought Arslanus.

Early in the morning Arslanus returned to the house into which Judas had disappeared bringing Ruben with him. He described to Ruben the man he was looking for and took turns with Ruben watching the door. If Judas was spotted or if anyone else came to the door, the person watching would either follow or stay there depending on the situation.

About mid-day while Ruben was watching, a man cane to the door and was admitted. When Arslanus returned and Ruben described the visitor, he only said one word, "Peter."

After several minutes Judas and Peter appeared at the door with Peter apparently trying to stop Judas from leaving and obviously arguing with him. Judas broke away and strode quickly down the street. Arslanus said he would follow Judas and Ruben should follow Peter. They agreed to meet at Arslanus' house before dusk or send a messenger to the house if they could not be there.

Arslanus followed Judas through the teeming streets of Jerusalem not really knowing what to think. Something was going on between Judas, who had led the armed men to Jesus last night, and Peter. Peter wanted to stop Judas from doing something. Arslanus realized Judas was now approaching the temple and was entering.

Now the problem was Arslanus could not enter the Jewish temple without causing a major disturbance. Non-Jews were forbidden in the temple, especially during Passover so Arslanus took a vantage point outside the temple where he could view some of the visible areas of the temple. He could see someone who looked like Judas talking in an animated fashion with several men in the temple. He then saw Judas throw something down in front of the men and walk away. It looked like a leather pouch with coins falling out as they skittered across the floor. Arslanus chose to follow Judas again. Judas was moving quickly and Arslanus had some difficulty keeping up in the crowd but it quickly became apparent he was heading back toward the house where he had spent the night.

When they reached the house, Judas, still very agitated, entered the house and closed the door. Arslanus waited about 30 minutes then decided to confront Judas to see what was going on. Arslanus walked up to the door and knocked for entrance. He got no answer but then tried the door and found it to be unlocked. He immediately saw a body hanging from a rope, which came down from a door to the roof, which was open. A crude ladder was laying on the floor below the body.

Arslanus saw Judas was dead from the looks and condition of the body. His right hand was clenched into a fist. Arslanus pried open his fingers and found a silver coin tightly grasped in the fist. Arslanus saw no reason to stay longer, taking the silver coin with him, he left.

When Arslanus returned to his house it was dark and Ruben was not there. He waited for a while and then Ruben came in. He said he had followed Peter into the city but the crowds were so thick he lost him. Then Ruben had gone to see friends who generally knew what was going on in the city. They informed him Jesus had been taken to be crucified and was by now dead. Ruben had then returned after trying to find out more information.

57. <u>Antarctica</u>

Arslan stopped telling the story and there was complete silence on the Tira. Finally, Arslan said, "The coin is the key to Pandora's box."

Simon said, "As I recall from my limited knowledge of the Bible, Peter was supposed to be the one who struck off the ear of the high priest's slave."

Arslanus said, "Only the book of John has that in the story, Matthew, Mark and Luke say someone with Jesus struck off the slaves ear. One even says Jesus did one last miracle and healed the man's ear. I saw nothing like it happen. Actually, there are several places in the New Testament where the various authors "embellished" a bit, especially in this case where the editors may have wanted to improve Peter's image."

Simon then asked, "Why do you think Peter was meeting with Judas? What were they disagreeing about?"

Arslan said "I have had the luxury of thinking about this for 2,000 years so I will take a shot at it. The possibilities are:

- Peter was not working with Judas to betray Jesus but was trying to get Judas to reveal the whole story. After he told Judas Jesus was condemned to die, Judas "lost it" and Peter was trying to stop him from doing something rash.
- Jesus had been set up by Peter working with Judas. Perhaps, Peter was fearful Jesus was taking the movement in the wrong direction or Peter wanted more power. Judas wanted to come clean and Peter wanted him to keep his mouth shut.

If this was the scenario, how convenient for Peter to have Judas hang himself. Should I have looked up on the roof before I left the house?

- Jesus intentionally had Peter and Judas arrange for his "betrayal" so the scriptures could be fulfilled. Judas was now appalled he had caused the death of his master and wanted to try to change things. Peter was trying to stop it from happening.

After many years, I believe the last scenario is the most likely, but we will never know unless Jesus comes to us and tells the truth.

Only the first option leaves the biblical Jesus story intact. Option two paints Peter as a betrayer and a criminal, possibly a murderer. Option three is worse; it says Jesus death was really a self-arranged suicide.

Which would you like to go public with? Now you know why I was keeping my mouth shut."

Carrie said, "If you think the religious nut-cases were coming after us before, let this get out and they will be after us from every side."

Lisa asked, "Is there any more of the story you have not told us, Arslan?"

Arslan said, "I don't think I have missed anything important but after so much time, I might not remember something of significance. This is as much as I have remembered."

Carrie said, "I have to ask you one question—you did not go visit the disciples and pretend to be Jesus, did you? That would be the one piece of news that would create bigger problems."

Arslan responded, "No, I kept to myself for a long time after the death of Jesus."

Simon asked, "Are there any other sources of information we can research to find out the truth, in your opinion, Arslan?"

Arslan said, "We can ask Tira's computer if it has or can process any information which could reveal more about the situation. It is worth a try."

The computer voice was immediately heard, "All information available to me has been processed and I have nothing useful to add."

Ramede spoke up, **"No one has asked me if I have anything to add."**

All heads turned toward Ramede.

Ramede said, "There are three entities we know about who could have witnessed events at the time of Jesus of Nazareth, Arslan, Tira's computer, and myself. As far as we now know there are no other intelligences now in existence, which were also there at the time of Jesus, except those three. Where do you think I was then?"

Getting no answer, Ramede said, "I was living in Athens around 700 B.C. as you may recall from my last talk about my past. Quickly I will tell you about the next 700 or so years up until the time of Jesus. I lived in Athens, the first time, for about 50 years. I had to leave when my identity "wore out" and I was simply too young to fit into the society where people I had known and been close to were ageing and dying while I stayed young. Melitos, my adopted son and best friend through all my first years in Athens died in 668 B.C.

We had lived through many adventures in Athens and had traveled many places in 50 years as our trading business continued to prosper and we always had ships at sea or in the ports trading for goods. Our wealth grew to the point we were some of the wealthiest in Athens but were very cautious about letting others have any idea how much gold or other valuables we had hidden away. It was extremely difficult for anyone to see what we had since much was at sea at any given point in time and we purchased property in many places but no one but us had any idea what we had.

I always expected to start ageing at some point but it did not happen. Melitos married and raised a family. We were best friends always and with my having a place in his family as the rich aunt who seemed to always stay the same. I also had many lovers over the years in Athens, although always very privately so attention was not attracted to me. Over the years it became more and more difficult to explain my continued youth but Melitos was able to insulate me from the most difficult situations while he was alive. When he passed away, I had already decided to leave Athens and live elsewhere.

All of the properties near Athens were transferred to Melitos' surviving children and ownership of ships at sea was also transferred to them. The children were aware there was something unusual about their dear Aunt Mede, who stayed so young looking, but they accepted it as part of their lives.

I left Athens in 666 B.C. on a ship I had purchased and had replaced the crew with men who had good reputations, but who did not know Mede of Athens, except by reputation. I boarded ship late at night and stayed inside the ships enclosure for several days until we were clear of areas where I might be recognized. I emerged from my isolation as a twenty five year old woman named Delphia who the "captain" the ship knew to be the owner and was the granddaughter of

365

Mede of Athens. I explained to the crew Mede had recently died and I wanted to travel away from Athens.

They sailed for the Cyclides Islands where I wanted to visit the city of Naxos. I stayed there for several months, as the island was a paradise, and the crew was quite content to while away some time there. Meanwhile, I spent my time buying up the honey wine of Naxos, which I knew from experience, was a wonderful wine for trading elsewhere, since it was so good and so unusual. This time I would take it to Sidon, Tyre and Egypt instead of to Athens.

After two and one-half months the ship had a full load and we set sail. Leaving the beautiful city of Naxos is always one of the hardest things to do. I always ask myself, "Why don't you just stay here, forever, there is no more beautiful place on earth. Perhaps, someday." We traveled south, getting to the coast and following it, eventually reaching Sidon and Tyre. Tyre was a great sea power in those days and I chose to stay there from 665 B.C. to 620 B.C.

During this time, Asurbanipal, the Assyrian leader was pursuing a war against Egypt so it did not seem like a good time to visit Egypt. Ashurbanipal attacked Egypt and, in two campaigns (667-666 and 664-663), defeated Pharaoh Taharka and his son Tenuatamun and extended Assyrian power far south. When I heard stories about these things, I often thought no one had any idea I had been "queen of Egypt" and had simply left because I could not live the life I had married. How lucky I had been to be able to escape and to go on and live happily in Athens for those years.

"Why had I stayed in Tyre so long?" mused Ramede. "Well a man had something to do with it." I met Seias in Tyre in 660 B.C. He had been born in Egypt but had lived there only a short time as a child before his parents had moved to Tyre. His family was not Egyptian, but had been part of one of the invaders constantly knocking on the door to Egypt coming from the East. Egypt had absorbed the invaders, as was usually the case.

Saias was an unusual and interesting man. He was from a family of merchants but he did not fit the role. He had learned to read in Egypt and knew both Egyptian and Greek. This was in itself unusual in these times, reading at all, but to have both Egyptian and Greek made him a rarity. Of course, I was more of a rarity since I was a woman who read and spoke both languages as well as some others. I could not let people know this fact too often since it might bring me under suspicion.

I met Saias when I first arrived in Tyre and wanted to trade some of my stocks of honey wine from Naxos. As I walked through the marketplace in Tyre followed by two crew members from my ship carrying honey wine, Saias called out in Greek saying, "Beautiful girl, I am Saias of Tyre, and you are a vision of beauty in Greek clothing, please come and speak with me."

I looked at Saias and saw a man of about 30 years, well dressed in Egyptian clothing, and standing in a merchants stall where they displayed various goods from Egypt, nothing I had not seen before. I responded in Egyptian, "Merchant, who sells goods from the delta, what is to be gained by talking to you? Your goods are only "average" and I have wine, which is unique, from the city of Naxos on a Greek island. You have nothing to offer me for trade, which is better than what I have. But since you are friendly enough to call to me, I will offer to trade one bottle of my rare honey wine for all the goods at your stand. My name is Delphia, young Egyptian who speaks Greek."

Saias responded, "Young Greek girl who also speaks Egyptian, and very good Egyptian, we should speak because we are two of the very few in this city who speak both these languages of commerce. Perhaps we can be of service to each other in some small way. And besides, you are the most beautiful woman I have ever seen."

Delphia responded, "I will speak with you young Egyptian, since you are right we are of the few who speak both languages and you seem to have a quick mind."

Delphia stopped at the Saias' booth and had one of the crewmen give Saias a taste of the honey wine from Naxos. After tasting it Saias said, "This is some of the best and most unusual wine I have ever tasted, how much do you have?"

Delphia answered, "A ship full, and can you advise the best way to make a profit with this in Tyre?"

Saias said, "If they were my goods, I would find ways to approach the wealthier houses in Tyre and offer this excellent wine to them. Once they taste it, you do not have to sell, it sells itself. They will pay whatever you ask. If you will accept my help, I will assist your efforts."

"My name is Delphia, recently of Athens, and I will accept your help and will pay you a fair share for your assistance in getting a good price for my goods. And what is your name, Egyptian who speaks Greek." Said Delphia.

"My name is Saias of Tyre, but formerly of Egypt as a child. I accept your offer and will help you get the best price for your goods possible. You may pay me what you think my services are worth. Is that fair?" said Saias.

'That is most fair." Said Delphia.

Over the next several days, Delphia and Saias approached a number of the wealthier houses of Tyre offering the honey wine of Naxos. After tasting the wine, every house wanted to buy large quantities at prices three times what Delphia knew she would receive in the marketplace. By the end of a week she had a huge profit on her cargo and still had two thirds of the cargo left to sell. Delphia spoke to Saias about his share, "Here is ½ of the excess over what I thought to get from the wine, this is your fair share, as she gave Saias a huge amount of money."

Saias was shocked at the generosity of Delphia, "This is too much for my share, others would not give me so much."

Delphia said, "If you had not helped me, I would have gotten only a small amount for the wine. You earned a good share of the additional profit. If I pay you fairly you will continue to find the best way for me to make a profit. It is a fair deal, don't doubt you earned it."

At the end of one month, the entire stock of honey wine had been sold at prices beyond the wildest dreams of Delphia. She paid Saias the same share on the balance of the sales and he became a rich man from the sale of the cargo from this one ship.

Once all the wine was sold, much of it in exchange for other trade goods, Saias said to Delphia, "What will you do now, sail back to Greece, or do other places fit your plans?"

Delphia said, "I have come to like Tyre and will stay here for a while. My ship will go to Egypt and trade for goods to bring back to Tyre, and then I will send some goods back to Greece, but I think I will stay here for a while—if anyone wants me to stay here? That has a question mark on the end of it."

"Lovely Delphia, please think about staying here in Tyre and seeing if you and I can share more than the profits from our trades." Said Saias.

It was the first night Saias and I slept together—it lasted about forty-four years. Forty-four years of happiness with a man with a good heart who wanted to share his life with someone like me.

Saias died in 622 B.C. at the age of 66. I had not aged but had altered my appearance over the years to appear to be ageing. I had given birth to three children by Saias and had raised them to be strong, good people who gave back to the world that gave them their lives. After Saias died, I knew I had to leave Tyre for a new place. My children were all grown, married, and independent in the world— I had no obligations, which prevented me from leaving.

The children, two daughters and a son, knew there was something unusual about me and the fact I did not age like other people. One evening I asked them to come to my house without their spouses and I told them the truth. They did not believe me until I washed the dye out of my hair and removed all the make up I was wearing—they saw a woman of twenty-five years in front of them. They were all in their thirties and forties and were shocked to see their very young mother, but finally accepted the fact. I told them I was leaving—I hated to do it because of the eleven grandchildren I loved so much, but explained there would be harm done to everyone if I stayed too long and was found out.

In 620 B.C. I set sail again, this time for the west.

Ramede stopped for a moment and thought then spoke, "I moved around a lot in the next three hundred fifty years, mostly to the north coast of Africa, Carthage, on to Spain, and then to Italy, not staying anywhere longer than twenty five years at a time except in Italy. By 259 B.C. I was a citizen of Rome."

It may seem strange to you I spend so little time telling about three hundred fifty years of my history but, perhaps, sometime in the future. If I try to tell everything, right now it will take so long and will take so much of my emotional energy I think it is better to wait.

My experience in Rome needs to be described, however.

369

58. <u>Rome (259 B.C.</u>

I first entered Rome in 259 B.C. using the name Media, as the wife of a Roman named Civius who had been a merchant trading in northern Italy. I had lived in various places in the north of Italy for over 100 years before marrying Civius and moving to Rome. The marriage was not a love affair but more one of convenience. He was 43 years old and had never married. He had friends who suspected he did not like women, which was not far from the truth. He married me mainly because he liked having a beautiful woman who looked twenty-five to show off to his friends. I married him because I wanted to live in Rome and be a Roman. I figured I would outlive him and then do what I chose to do.

Civius' only family alive in Rome was a younger sister named Sylvia who was married to a man of some wealth who traded in slaves. Upon arrival in Rome, we immediately went to visit his sister, probably hoping for an invitation to stay at her house for a while. Sylvia was not especially pleased to see Civius, who had apparently left Rome the last time owing some money to Sylvia. After some cross words were spoken between the two, I asked how much money was involved and when told, gave Sylvia twice the sum from my purse.

Sylvia said, "So my motley brother has married a rich wife who can afford to pay his debts and with a profit also for me. I think you, Media, and I will be good friends. It is time we had some better blood in this family."

Media said, "Sylvia, I do hope to become your good friend and I think you will find marriage has changed Civius for the better. He has talked about his lovely sister all the way from the north, saying how he missed her."

"My brothers' wife can also stretch the truth a bit when she wants to, but I too think we will be good friends. Please plan to stay at my house for the next week until you find a place to stay. I guess Civius can stay also."

In the morning, Media rose early and went to the garden where she found Sylvia. Civius was still sleeping, of course, so she joined

Sylvia for some conversation and breakfast, which the servant served. Sylvia asked, "Media, what do you intend to do in Rome."

"I hope to engage in some business to provide an income. I have some funds to invest and have experience at managing several businesses. Mainly, I will look for the right opportunity."

Sylvia said, "Most women in Rome do not engage in commerce, most are tied to their homes with the men conducting business. There are exceptions, but they are uncommon."

Media said, "I expect to be one of the exceptions. I can use Civius as the spokesperson for the business and do the management through him if necessary, but I will maintain ownership and control. I also have some experience with that type of arrangement."

Sylvia said, "You seem to be very confident you can be successful in Rome. I have some money of my own, perhaps you will need an investor."

Media said, "If I do I will ask you first. Do you know of any likely business opportunities?"

Sylvia said, "Well my husband trades in slaves. It is a difficult business and many people do not like it, but he does well."

Media said, "I have no experience in slave trading and do not think it would fit me. I am more interested in importing and exporting, I think. I have done some before and have knowledge of the business."

Sylvia said, "I will have my husband make some inquires to see if there any opportunities with importing and exporting which you might look into. There are always many opportunities in Rome for people with money and brains."

Media said, "When Civius wakes up, I plan to have him take me on a tour of the marketplaces and business areas so I can do some first hand research. Would you care to go along with us and assist our tour?"

Sylvia said, "I would not go for my dear brother but for you I will go along so my brother does not take you the wrong places. It actually sounds like fun."

Media, Sylvia and Civius, accompanied by one of Sylvia's senior servants who knew his way around the business areas of Rome went on a full day tour, much to the dismay of Civius. They went through the market areas and in the course of the tour Media saw a shop where a woman and her young son were selling imported goods including wines, high quality fabrics, art objects and other items. When she talked to the woman about some Greek wine, a good Greek wine, she offered to sell it a price far below it's value.

Media asked the son if he knew the value of the wine. He confessed he did not know what it was worth. The young man said his father had died several weeks earlier and he and his mother were trying to run the business but did not know enough and were failing.

Media knew when to seize an opportunity. She said to the young man, "Would you and your mother consider selling your business to me for a fair price then staying and working for me? I have the experience in running this kind of a business and can make a profit with it."

Sersius, the young man, said, "My mother and I are desperate as you can see. We fear if we try to sell, we will be taken advantage of by the sharks who live in this market."

Media said, "At some point you must trust someone. You have had good fortune today to meet a person who will be fair with you and not be a shark. You must make a leap of faith to believe I am what I say I am. If you do, your problem is solved, if you let fear stop you, you continue the problem and perhaps throw away the best chance for a prosperous future."

Media noticed the mother hung on every word and then said to the son, "Sersius, this woman speaks the truth. I feel in my heart she will be fair with us. It is better to deal with her based on my intuition than to linger in the depths of despair as every day we lose more and more of the wealth your father built. Agree with her and go forward. It is the best, perhaps the only chance we have."

Media spent the next three hours working up a fair price for their business. She then took 25% off the price. She said to Sersius, "This is the price I offer less one fourth which I will withhold pending confirmation of the value the stocks of the business are in fact worth what I think. Agree to this now or I walk away. This is the reality of business."

Sersius said, "The price you offer is more than I expected by twice. I accept."

Media brought out a scroll for recording the transaction and paid the sum to Sersius out of her purse, less one fourth. She said to

Sersius, "I will pay the one fourth withheld in thirty days assuming the goods are worth at least as much as I have estimated. I will pay you and your mother a fair price for your services, she quoted a price for each per month, and will in addition pay you 5% of the profit each. This will encourage you to insure I make a profit."

Sersius and his mother, Melea, were astounded at the good wage and promise of a percentage of the profits offered by Media. Melea said, "Kind lady you overpay us but we accept."

Media said, "I doubt I am overpaying you. You will work hard to deserve your wage and harder to guarantee the bonus. We will all win from this arrangement."

As they walked from the market, Sylvia said, "I was very impressed with your method of buying the business. You know the goods are worth more than they thought and you now have a guarantee they will work hard to make you a profit. I would still like to invest in your business. I am sure it will profit."

Media said, "Bring to me the amount you can afford to invest and I will give you a fair return plus a share of the risk. You may lose or you may win but we will both win or lose."

Sylvia gave Media a large sum to invest, in five months she returned an amount five times the amount invested. Media suggested she leave the total amount in the business for another year. At the end of one year, Media brought her an amount ten times the amount invested, fifty time the original amount in 17 months. Sylvia was astounded and gave the money back to invest. At the end of five years, Sylvia was wealthier than her husband the slave trader.

Media visited Sylvia at her house one day. Sylvia said, "Media, every investment you make turns to gold. What is your secret?"

Media said, "I am fair with everyone, my employees, my customers, and my investors. As a result each tries to do well by me. All I have to do is make good decisions about what to buy—that is easy for me."

59. <u>Massilia (Marseilles) 54 B.C.</u>

Media, Ramede's current name, had arrived in Massilia several years earlier after living in or near Rome for 200 years. She was tired of living in Rome. Rome ruled much of the world but the power had gone to the heads of Roman men. In 169 B.C., they legislated the lex Voconia, intended to limit the amount of wealth a woman could inherit. They also took other measures to attempt to limit the rights of women. In a society where written law was becoming more and more important the men of Rome seemed to want to make sure women did not share too much of the power of politics and society.

Media was not directly affected by the lex Voconia or other measures but she was irritated by the smallness of Roman men. It was a stupid thing but she wanted to distance herself from Rome.

Media had amassed wealth as a Roman by marrying well several times and by investing even better. She had split her wealth between three main cities, Rome, Athens and Massilia, on the southern coast of Gaul, and had diversified her investments into ships, land and mercantile activities. In her mind she was protected somewhat, if war or weather or some other calamity hit one or two of the cities, she would still have a place to go where her wealth would be available. Like most women Media gave security a high place in her priorities.

When she moved to Massilia to live, Media started a shipping business transporting goods from Gaul and Spain to Rome and Athens. Eventually she added goods from Britain to her sources. She limited her own travel initially, but sent her ships, with handpicked, trusted crews to many distant lands. As an experienced merchant she knew the risks she faced, half the ships would be lost to storms, pirates or who knows what else. The half getting through, however, would make huge profits.

The profits during the first ten years allowed her to build one of the largest houses in Massilia, which was not so much to say since Massilia in those days was not a large city. The smallness of Massilia also presented the problem for her lack of ageing limiting how long she could stay in an identity before she had to "change" or depart. She planned to stay for about thirty years in the "Media" identity using makeup and dye to age her then she would leave a trustee in charge of her home and business for another twenty years or so. The trustee would receive regular written instructions from Media and business profits would be sent to her or invested in businesses as she directed.

Wherever she chose to go, she would appear there as a young woman of twenty-five. People did not question too much when a beautiful, rich, young woman came to a place to live as long as she did not offend any of the women in positions of power or steal a man from someone. She took great care to be discrete, especially when she first moved to a place to avoid such situations.

As a fallback, if she did run into someone who had known her as a young person in another identity, she would claim to be a daughter or granddaughter. Since she was somewhat secretive in all of her identities, the person would likely have no basis for questioning her version.

A serious relationship with a man was her most challenging and testing situation. The longer a relationship lasted the more problems she had with her lack of ageing. Men eventually noticed. When her lovers or husbands questioned her, she had the choices of telling the truth, usually not a good idea, or of putting them off until she could leave or make some other arrangement. For these reasons, she tended to avoid long relationships with men. She hated to be this way because she treasured a good relationship with a man but she knew her survival was at stake.

Marriage was something Ramede took very seriously. She had married a few times mainly for economic gain. She did not like doing it but had rationalized each situation as being necessary at the time. Marriage for love was another circumstance, which had happened several times. These times represented the greatest personal danger for her because she eventually had to tell her partner the truth. When she did this the experience was usually good, with her partner being very accepting of her special condition. In a few cases the results were not what she had anticipated and she had to flee the consequences.

Children were another subject causing Ramede great concern. She was very cautious about getting pregnant and tried to do so only when she wanted to make the commitment to raise a child. In slightly less than seven hundred years of living, she had given birth twenty-three times, approximately once every twenty-five years. The greatest tragedies were when they died or when she had to leave them, never to see them again. She had stayed with some long enough to know her children did not have her 'condition.' More than a man, children were a complication, which brought the greatest joy and the greatest pain.

After 28 years of living in Massilia, Media thought she had to leave since her identity was too old to work with her youthful looks, even with makeup and hair dye. She was too much at risk of discovery. She chose to move to Naples, buy property there and to run her shipping business as an absentee owner for a period of time. Her plan was to do this for about twenty years. At the end, she would return to Massilia as a young granddaughter of Media to take over her home and business. She did not think there would be anyone left there who would recognize her as the young Media from fifty years earlier.

Ramede, using the name Theresa, lived in Naples for twenty-four years. She had purchased a large house on a hillside overlooking the bay and rented out rooms, at high prices, to provide a visible means of support. She was extremely selective about who she rented her rooms to and hired people to take care of cleaning and cooking. She spent her time traveling throughout the countryside of Italy, making friends and learning what she could about the people. She had a number of men friends during this time but limited the duration of these relationships to no more then two years.

In 4 B.C. Ramede, using the name Joanna, returned to Massilia as the granddaughter of Media and took over her home and business. She had planned her return very well by insuring she would not be creating any enemies. The trustee in charge of her business was not in good health and wanted to retire and had not known Media, so he was not going to be a problem. All the servants at the house were new within the past several years and likewise would not have known Media. She chose to travel extensively on her ships at the beginning to avoid spending too much time in Massilia in case any of the older people might remember Media, but after several years she felt confident she was not going to be recognized.

Joanna continued to travel extensively for almost twenty years. Then she began again to be concerned about someone noticing her lack of ageing. This concern was on her mind as she set out on a voyage to the Greek Isles in 17 A.D. She was not overly worried, she had kept her wealth well distributed between Rome/Naples, Massilia, and Athens. When she left on a ship she always set up a trustee, or several trustees, to manage the business and her property until she returned. They also were instructed to use her written instructions when received and a code was established to insure the veracity of any written instructions. With everything in place, she set out from Massilia by sea with a crew she knew only by reputation and who knew her as a young woman.

Off the west coast of Sardinia, but out of sight of the coast, they saw wreckage from a ship floating on the water and finally pulled five very sun burned and thirsty men from the sea, who had been clinging to the wreckage. Joanna was cautious with these men, piracy was common in these waters, and she did not know the men. She had a trusted crew but a ship loaded with valuable trade goods, which could tempt some men.

The leader of the group of five was a Hebrew man of about thirty years old who said he was from a small city near Jerusalem, called Arimathea. His name was Joseph and he held an appointment as the minister of mining for the Roman Empire in Britain, nobilis decurio. He introduced two of the other men as also Hebrews from near Jerusalem who were his friends and associates.

The first man he introduced was Lazarus of Bethany who was also about thirty and was introduced as a good family friend of Joseph and a good man.

The second man introduced was also of about the same age as the other two, named Chuza, and was a steward of Herod Antipas, Hebrew ruler of Judea under the Romans. He had been sent by Herod to accompany Joseph to the mining operations in Britain to learn more about it. Joseph also mentioned Chuza had just lost his wife during childbirth.

Joseph said the two other men were members of the crew of their ship.

Joseph could detect some of the concern Joanna had about having these strangers on her ship. He spoke, "Our destination was Caesarea which is the main port for Jerusalem. If you could take us to a Roman port, I am sure the authorities will pay for our rescue and provide us with a ship. I am also a man of some means personally, being the owner of several ships used for trading. My position is of some significance to the empire since tin is important for armaments for the legions, if it helps to establish our credentials."

Joanna knew more about the trading in tin than she wished to make known and what Joseph said fit with the facts she knew about Jews being involved in the tin trade from Britain. She responded, "Prince Joseph, my instincts tell me you speak the truth. We are sailing for the Greek Isles. It is not so far from there to the port of Caesarea, a place I have longed to visit. So, If I take you there as passengers, I will expect a fair compensation when we arrive. Is it a bargain?"

Joseph quickly agreed but joked, "I have no choice since I do not know what my position would be if I reject the offer—back in the water perhaps."

Joanna said with a smile, "The thought had passed through my mind."

In the evening, Joanna and Joseph talked further as the sun went down. Joanna said," What work do you do in Britain that you can leave it and travel to Jerusalem? The empire is usually a very harsh taskmaster when it comes to materials for their weaponry."

Joseph said, "A strangely knowledgeable conclusion for such a young and beautiful woman. You are right the empire demands results and takes no excuses. They hold me responsible for the output of the tin mines in Britain. I would be foolish to leave my work in Britain unless I had left it in the hands of someone I could trust without a doubt. In this case the son of my niece is left in charge of the operation in Britain while he also studies to better himself at one of the great schools in Britain."

Joanna said, "Are you sure such a young man is capable of doing what needs to be done to avoid the wrath of the Roman leaders? Your head could be at risk."

Joseph said, "The young man has been trained by me on three trips to Britain over the last ten years and he is most intelligent and trustworthy. He is now twenty-three years of age—Alexander had conquered the world by that age."

Joanna asked, "What is the name of this young Alexander, perhaps he will become as famous and successful?"

Joseph said, "His name is Jesus, Jesus of Nazareth, the son of Mary."

"And he is alone there to keep the mines spitting out tin to make the legions able to fight?" said Joanna.

Joseph laughed and said, "Jesus was alone when I left but so many of the young girls of Britain would like to find a spot for Jesus in their bed, I am not sure how long he will sleep alone."

Joanna then said, "And what are the stories of your other two friends, Lazarus and Chuza."

Joseph spoke, "Lazarus is my good friend for many years. Our families are close and we have many common interests. Much in Judea is about religion. Let me explain."

The Hebrew faith in Judea is divided into three main groups, the Sadducees of which I am part, the Pharisees, and the Essenes. We all start from the same place, the Torah, but go other ways in practicing our religion. Why, even my niece's son has studied with the Essenes but I still respect him.

Lazarus and I believe in many of the same things but the future may separate us or bring us together based on religion. It is only important to me we respect each other."

Joseph spoke again, "Chuza is a good man but is tied to Herod Antipas who is a creature of power. Here and now I would trust Chuza with my life. Back in Jerusalem, I think Chuza would try always to be my friend but circumstances of power might make it impossible for him to help me.

So now lovely Joanna, you know much about the relationship of Chuza, Lazarus and Joseph, but we know little about you. What makes a young woman know and understand so much about the world?"

Joanna smiled to hide her concern about such a question, "Joseph, I chose not to lie to you so I will give no answer at all."

Joseph respected her decision not to answer and they ended their conversation for the night.

During the course of their almost two month voyage to Caesarea, Chuza, Joseph, Lazarus and Joanna talked daily. In the course of such things, Chuza started spending more and more time with Joanna. He was a handsome, friendly man, not a deep thinker but able to understand most things. He had a kind heart and seemed sincere in his feelings. As time moved forward, Joanna realized Chuza was falling in love with her.

One evening Chuza mentioned he had a three-year-old son back in Jerusalem who was being cared for by his deceased wife's mother at his home. His son's name was Enoch and the mother-in-law was named Jesriah.

Two weeks out of Caesarea, Chuza found an opportunity to talk with Joanna late one night. He said, "Joanna, We have not known each other long but in this world opportunities must be acted upon quickly. I would like to ask if you would come to Jerusalem and become my wife? I have some wealth and some power and would try to provide you with a good life."

Joanna said, "You are a good man, Chuza, and I could do much worse than to have you as a husband, but I am unsure. I must have an element of freedom, perhaps more than you are disposed to give to your wife. I too have some wealth, perhaps more than you imagine. I do not have power except the power to make my own decisions and act upon them. As you wife will I still have that power? Will I be allowed to travel and conduct business or will I be expected to be little more than a servant? These are important things to me which must be settled before we agree."

Chuza said, "I agree to your freedom. We may have to be discrete about it in Jerusalem where the religious people want to control everything between men and women but we can make it work if you want to try.

Joanna said, "How will Herod accept you marrying a Roman citizen? How will the Hebrews accept it as well? Will the Romans in Jerusalem accept a Roman married to one of Herod's stewards? Will Enoch and Jesriah accept me?"

Chuza said, "I think neither Herod nor the Romans will see it as a problem. They will both consider it a political advantage. Some of the Jews will think it is terrible, but then they already think Herod and anyone close to him is evil."

Joanna said, "I suggest we ask Joseph and Lazarus for their opinions about what kind of problems it may cause. Do you agree?"

Chuza said, "Yes."

Joanna called to Joseph and Lazarus to join their conversation. When they were listening she said, "Chuza has asked me to come to

Jerusalem and become his wife. We have agreed to ask for your opinions in this matter. What would be the reaction be to our marriage? Would anyone object strongly, such as Herod, the Roman powers in Jerusalem, or the Hebrew powers in Jerusalem? Your thoughts would be appreciated."

Joseph spoke first, "Among some of the Jews there will be a negative reaction, but there will be a negative reaction to anyone married to one of Herod's stewards. Herod will see it as a political advantage and the Romans will not object also for political reasons. If you want to do it there is no reason not to do what you want."

Lazarus said, "I agree with Joseph."

Joanna said, "What about Enoch and Jesriah?"

Chuza said, "We can work it out."

Joanna then said to Chuza, "I will agree to marry you under the conditions we discussed."

Chuza said, "It is agreed then."

60. <u>Jerusalem (17 A.D.)</u>

Joanna entered Jerusalem with Joseph, Lazarus, and Chuza. They had spent several days in Caesarea where she had arranged for the entire contents of her ship to be loaded on transports for Jerusalem, where she knew they would bring much higher prices than in Caesarea. She also used some of the gold she carried to buy a fresh cargo of goods to be returned to Massilia. Chuza, Joseph and Lazarus were obviously impressed when she carried out these transactions without help.

The trip from Caesarea was uneventful and Joanna was not surprised at the relative desolation and lack of development she saw. She had heard stories from many others about the area and expected what she saw. Jerusalem was another case. It was a larger city than she expected with very high walls, although she thought the city was dirtier than most large cities.

Joseph had a sister living in Jerusalem. It was agreed it would be better for Joanna to stay there until Chuza and Joanna could be married. Joseph said he would handle everything as far as arranging for a place to stay and getting the wedding prepared. He said it was the least he could do for the lady who had saved their lives.

As things progressed, Joanna began to realize how wealthy and important a man Joseph was. Everyone seemed to defer to him and went out of their way to serve him. When they arrived at the house of his sister. She embraced him and when told he had brought her a houseguest and explained the circumstances, she embraced Joanna. The sister said Joanna could stay there as long as she needed; any friend of Joseph was welcome and especially one who had saved his life.

The next day Chuza came by and took her to his house to meet Enoch and Jesriah. Chuza introduced Joanna to the two of them with Enoch immediately starting to play with Joanna. Jesriah was not unfriendly but was not friendly either. Joanna had not known what to expect. Finally, while Enoch played in the garden, Chuza explained to Jesriah of Joanna marrying him in a few days. Jesriah did not react much but did appear somewhat sad.

Joanna then said, "Jesriah, I would like to have you stay and live with us and help care for Enoch. He has had enough change in his life, losing his mother was enough, to lose his grandmother now is unnecessary. He needs you with him."

Jesriah, immediately brightened and said, "Thank you, I will be glad to stay. I love Enoch so very much and after losing my daughter I don't think I could bear to leave him. You are a very kind woman to let me stay. I will try to be very helpful to you."

Joanna said, "Enoch is a beautiful boy and he needs his grandmother."

Chuza was very pleased with the turn of events and told Joanna so after they left, "Joanna, it was a wonderful thing you did. Are you sure you want the grandmother of my child living in the same house with us? It could be difficult. Most women would throw a fit at the thought of it."

Joanna said, "I don't see it being a problem. In fact, it may be the best thing to happen. Enoch obviously loves his grandmother and if it helps him get used to the family situation we put together, great. If he is happy and well cared for with the help of Jesriah then it will help us all."

The wedding of Joanna and Chuza was held at the house of Joseph of Arimathea. Joanna could tell Joseph had spared no expense for the wedding and in a moment when she spoke to Joseph alone she said, "Joseph, please let me reimburse you for some of the expense of the wedding, you know I have more than a little money and will have much more when the cargo from my ship is sold. It is not necessary for you to spend your money on me. I can afford to pay for my own wedding. Save your money for your family."

Joseph said, "I know you could pay for your wedding but you saved my life and have become a good friend, as has Chuza. Perhaps some day you can do something for me when I need your help."

After the wedding, Joanna and Chuza returned to Chuza's house. Jesriah and Enoch were staying at the home of Joseph's sister, Joseph's idea, of course. Enoch and Jesriah returned the next day and the four settled into life in Chuza's household.

Jesriah had approached Joanna at the wedding, "I thought my life was over when Chuza brought a woman back to be his wife. I thought I would be without a place to live and would never see my grandson again. You have been so wonderful to let me live with you and your new family. I promise to do all I can to help Chuza, Enoch and you have a happy life. You are a very special woman for one so young and beautiful."

Joanna said, "Dear woman, young Enoch is a treasure. You love him and I know I will learn to love him. I always love small children. We will work together to make his life happy and I think we will become great friends doing so. Please feel secure you have a place with our family always."

Joanna set about at once to make friends with Enoch. He liked to have her sit on the floor with him or to chase him in the garden. Jesriah watched and saw Joanna truly loved Enoch and wanted him to be happy. Jesriah would be a good friend to Joanna for Enoch's sake, for her own sake, and because Joanna was a kind person who loved children.

Joanna made arrangements to have her trade goods sold at the market. Normally she would do the transactions herself but under the circumstances, she thought it might embarrass Chuza. She did coach the merchants doing the sales and made a huge profit on the goods. When she showed Chuza how much she had made he was shocked. She explained she planned to buy some goods very carefully over time, which she would ship back to Naples or Rome and sell by agents for large profits.

Joanna was introduced to Herod Antipas as the new Roman wife of his steward. He was obviously impressed Chuza had married such a beautiful young woman. The Romans in Jerusalem were also impressed with the new young woman in their midst.

As time went forward, Joanna was very successful with her business. She knew how to buy well and had trusted people on her ships and as agents in Naples, Rome, Athens, and Massilia. In addition she now had the protection of Herod through Chuza and the protection of Joseph of Arimathea.

Likewise Joanna was successful in having Enoch come to think of her as his mother. As he grew older he came to depend on Joanna as the most trusted person in his life, even more so than his father and Jesriah. Chuza and Jesriah were in no way resentful of the wonderful relationship, which developed between Joanna and Enoch. They were happy to see them so happy together. Jesriah died ten years after

Joanna arrived in Jerusalem. But she had lived a very happy last ten years of her life and was always grateful to Joanna for allowing her to stay with them. The life of Chuza in the court of Herod Antipas was not the most pleasant matter in their lives. Herod was tetrarch rather than king over Galilee and Peraea (East bank of the Jordan). His power was derived from the Romans and he had to please them to stay in power. He knew it and they knew it. Roman control of political power in Jerusalem and the surrounding area was unpopular. The religion of Rome was not popular with the priesthood or people of Galilee and Roman taxation was even less popular. Being the instrument of Roman power as Herod was required to be, did not make he, or those working with him friends with the local population.

As a Jew and one of the Sadducees working for Herod Antipas, Chuza had a fine line to walk. Herod claimed to be a loyal Jew but had been raised in Rome and many questioned his devotion to the faith. The same year as the arrival of Joanna in Jerusalem, Herod had chosen to build a new capital called Tiberius in honor of the Emperor. Unfortunately, the site chosen was an old Jewish graveyard. When this became public knowledge, only Greeks and Romans would enter Tiberius. Most Jews would not go there.

Joseph of Arimathea returned to Britain after spending about ten months in Judea and then returned again in about eighteen months. When Joanna saw him back in Jerusalem she welcomed him and asked how his mines were doing in Britain and had he brought his niece's son back this time.

Joseph said, "The mines are doing well and this makes the Romans happy which in turn makes me happy. Jesus has done well at the mines and keeps them going when I am gone. He spends a great deal of time on his studies and on other matters as well, but no, he is still in Britain and, I expect, will be for some time longer."

Joanna asked, "Is he still alone or has one of the girls there been able to lure him to her bed."

Joseph said, somewhat nervously, "I would rather not talk about it." The conversation then went on to other things.

Joanna spoke to Chuza in the evening, replaying the conversation with Joseph then asking, "Why was Joseph reluctant to talk about his relative, this Jesus of Nazareth, is there something I do not know?"

Chuza said, "Well, Jesus is a religious thinker. He spent some time with the Essenes prior to going to Britain and is studying religious matters in Britain as well as public speaking and other subjects. Jesus may some day return to Judea and try to become a religious leader, I think. It would not be good for his reputation if stories went around about womanizing in Britain. That may be the direction of Joseph's thinking."

Joanna said, "Someday I would like to meet this Jesus. He seems to be an interesting sort."

Over the next six years, Joseph of Arimathea, traveled to Britain three times for various amounts of time. Each time he returned to Jerusalem, Joanna would find an opportunity to meet with Joseph and discuss their lives. Every time she would ask about Jesus of Nazareth, "had he returned with you?" Each time the answer was, "No, he remains in Britain, for now." However on the last time in 28 A.D., Joseph had news. Jesus planned to return to Galilee soon, within months probably.

Joanna was delighted to hear this since she was very curious to meet this Jesus and told Joseph so. Joseph said, "I have talked to Jesus about you since you always ask about him. He asked me to wish you well and said he would like to meet you as well when he returns to Galilee. Strangely, he said he had a message for you as one who trusts people based on intuition rather than things seen. I think he was referring to your trusting five strangers who you plucked from the sea."

Joanna asked, "Has Jesus changed much during his ten years or so in Britain. Have his studies made him into a different person than the man who went to Britain."

Joseph said, "Jesus has indeed changed. He had spent time with the Essenes before he went to Britain. They had turned him inward. The years in Britain have not erased the inward orientation but he seems much more inclined to take action in the world rather than being only a thinker or mystic. I do fear for him, however, the powers ruling in Galilee, both Jewish and Roman, will not tolerate blasphemy or rebellion."

Joanna said, "Surely he will not preach rebellion. It's a sure way to feel the wrath of Rome. Will any family return to Galilee with him?"

Joseph said, "No, Jesus has no official family in Britain, he never married under Jewish or local law. He will provide well for anyone he leaves behind. I can say no more."

Joanna said, "Will Jesus return to the Essenes when he comes back or will he take up his old trade, you said he was a carpenter."

Joseph said, "I do not think Jesus will return to the Essenes, he has moved far beyond them in his thinking and I doubt Jesus will ever be a carpenter again. I have spent more time with Jesus over the last ten years than any other close friend. His thinking is quite different than most of the religious leaders we have here in Galilee. If he does what he says he will try to do, there will be no small amount of turmoil caused by my niece's son."

Joanna said, "So you, Joseph, have raised a revolutionary."

Joseph quickly said, very concerned, "Never say that, and please do not tell Chuza any of this. I love Chuza but he is too close to dangerous men."

Joanna said, "I would never knowingly put you in danger, Joseph."

Late in 28 A.D., Joseph visited Joanna with the news Jesus planned to start his trip from Britain very soon, if not already started. He planned to make some stops on the way so he may not arrive for some time.

Joanna heard nothing for several months, and then in the spring of 29 A.D., she received a message from Joseph of Jesus being in Nazareth, greeting his family. He had already done some preaching to small crowds and Joseph expected him to visit Jerusalem soon.

There was no more news until October when Chuza told her a Jesus of Nazareth, also called Jeshua ben Joseph, had been reported by Herod's spies as having been baptized at the River Jordan by John the Baptist. John the Baptist was under close watch by Herod due to criticism he had leveled against Herod's divorces and marriages. Chuza warned Jesus association with John the Baptist could bring him under the watch of Herod.

Joanna heard little more than rumors about Jesus for several months. Joseph visited her in January of 30 A.D. and told her of a wedding feast in Cana in December where it was said by those in attendance, some who Joseph knew; Jesus had performed a great wonder by turning water into wine. Later she heard some mutterings in the marketplace about a new teacher in the north near Nazareth who was attracting some followers.

Chuza reported to her Herod's spies were looking at this new teacher named Jesus but there was no mention of action being taken against him. John the Baptist was another matter, however. He was consistently stepping across the line in his criticism of Herod and it seemed to be only a matter of time until something would happen.

When Passover came Joanna was glad to hear about Jesus planned visit to Jerusalem. She hoped to finally meet him and sent a message to Joseph. Instead, she heard Jesus had gone to the Jewish temple and had driven some of the commercial people out of the temple. From Chuza she heard the Jewish priests were not happy with Jesus and spoke of taking action against him.

Joanna spent her days following her business affairs, which did not take much of her time, spending time with Enoch and doing what supervision of the house was necessary. Jesriah had died in the previous year and this placed more of a responsibility on her to see to the upbringing of Enoch who was now thirteen. He attended a Roman school, which cost a large amount of money, but to Joanna the education would be better than the Jewish religious schools. She could not imagine him becoming a fanatical Jew like some she knew. Chuza did not have strong religious feelings, if he had, he would not be working for Herod.

Occasionally, Joanna would be notified one of her ships had reached port in Caesarea. Usually she would travel to Caesarea to inspect the vessel, crew and cargo and to make disposition of all matters at hand. This involved taking the stockpile of trade goods, which she had been accumulating, in her warehouse in Jerusalem to Caesarea for loading on the ship for return to Athens. Rome, Naples or Massilia. She would also pick up the cargo brought to Caesarea and take it to Jerusalem for trade.

In early August of 30 A.D., she was advised one of her ships had reached the port. Often Chuza would go on the trip to the port with her to use his authority to smooth the way. At this time, Chuza was on a mission to Egypt for Herod and was not available. Joanna gathered together trusted men to take her goods to the port and return with the new goods to Jerusalem. She also decided it would be good to take Enoch on this trip rather than to leave him alone in Jerusalem.

There were people she could have left him with but the experience would be good for him.

Five days out of Jerusalem, they reached Narbata, which left only a half days travel to the port. They camped outside the small city of Narbata near a well. As she walked to the well to get water, she saw a group of men camped off to the side under some trees. One man was walking toward the well also with a skin container attached to a rope to draw water. He greeted her when he saw her, "Good woman, Greetings to you this beautiful evening. I see you also seek water. Let me help you draw your water from the well. I am called Jesus, Jesus of Nazareth."

Joanna smiled a large smile when she heard his name and said, "Well, Jesus of Nazareth, I expect I know more of you than you know of me. How was your life in Britain at "Insula Avalonia" and do the tin mines of the esteemed Joseph of Arimathea still thrive there? Did you learn all the scholars of Britain could teach you?"

Jesus said, "My mother's uncle, Joseph of Arimathea, told me of a beautiful woman named Joanna who pulled him from a sure death at sea over ten years ago and then came to Galilee to marry a highly placed man in Herod's court. She is one of the few people who know where I have been for this many years. Are you this Joanna?"

Joanna said, "Yes, I am Joanna, Joanna of Massilia, but now Joanna, wife of Chuza, steward to Herod."

Jesus said, "I have heard other things about you, such as allowing the mother of your husband's first wife to stay in your household as a great kindness to her and her grandchild. Your are a kind woman who practices good works.?

Joanna looked a Jesus to see if she could understand this man she had waited so long to see. Finally she said, "Joseph and I have talked about you for many years. You have studied long and now I hear stories about great works you perform. You also make bitter enemies which may bring you trouble in the future."

As they proceeded to draw water, Jesus said, "What brings you to this place today?"

Joanna said," I am on my way to Caesarea. One of my ships has landed there loaded with trade goods and I will take those back to Jerusalem and take the goods there to the ship to send to Athens, Naples, Rome or Massilia for trade."

Jesus said, "I gather you are not a Jew. Most Jewish women are not free to do such commerce."

Joanna said, "No, in fact I am a citizen of Rome, although a woman, which gives me more freedom than some others. I have heard you are a great teacher. You have not yet tried to convert me to your path, why is that?"

Jesus said, "My role at this time is to take my message to the Jews. It is what I feel my God commands me to do."

Joanna said, "Perhaps that is unfortunate for me, I have often wondered about my place in the world. If something you found in your years of study could make me understand it all, I would be most grateful. Do you think you have found the secret or secrets to help others understand? I have lived many places and learned about the gods of many lands including Galilee, but have not yet found "the answer.""

Jesus said, "It is unusual for a woman to think such thoughts. Most are content to have their children and to watch them grow. But to answer you, my solution is for the Jews at this time. My truth is couched in their language and beliefs. I can tell you there is but one God and God is a God of love and forgiveness. My role in this world is to lead Jews to their God. I sense something unusual in you, however. Often I can reach out and understand the essence of people but with you, there is something about your person; it is vaster. Does it make any sense to you?"

Joanna said, "Yes, it does. I am different from most people. I have had more experiences because of an unusual life."

One of Jesus disciples approached them and told Jesus it was time for their evening prayers. Jesus obviously wanted to continue the conversation but went away with his disciple after saying goodnight.

Joanna went on to Caesarea, completed her business and returned to Jerusalem. In October, Herod had John the Baptist arrested and thrown into prison. In the course of this, the Pharisees became aware Jesus of Nazareth had more followers than did John the Baptist. Once this became common knowledge, Jesus became more of a focus for his enemies.

For the next two years Jesus traveled around Judea and Galilee teaching and performing healing and other works, which brought great attention to him. Generally he was either loved or hated with few in between. During this time Joanna, had no opportunity to see Jesus personally. It was also not politically expedient to be seen with Jesus during these times as he was hated by many of the more powerful Jews, especially the high priest. Herod did not seem to hate him but would turn quickly if politics dictated. The Roman Governor, Pilate was mostly concerned about keeping his own head since he was under political pressure from Rome.

Joanna was upset when John the Baptist was beheaded on Herod's orders. She never got the complete story, there were several versions, but she saw Jesus was in danger.

Joanna had her next contact with Jesus when she traveled to Bethany after hearing her old friend Lazarus had died late in 32 A.D. When she arrived there, she found Mary Magdalene and Martha, both sisters of Lazarus, who she had met in Jerusalem. She knew both of theses women were close friends of Jesus and was not surprised when they expressed sorrow Jesus had not been able to come to Lazarus before he died. They thought he could surely have saved him. No sooner had they spoken these words and someone came to the door of the house saying Jesus had arrived. Martha went out first and spoke to Jesus then Mary Magdalene went out to speak to Jesus with some other visitors and myself following.

Joanna was glad to see Jesus again but he looked thinner than the last time I had seen him. Jesus was concentrating on Martha and Mary so she had no acknowledgement he recognized her. That was to be expected under the circumstances. She heard Jesus say," Where have you put him?"

Martha said, "Lord, come and see."

They led Jesus to a tomb, which was a cave with a stone rolled in front of it.

Jesus said, "Take away the stone."

Martha protested, "Lord, he has been buried for four days, he will have started to decay."

Jesus said, "If you but believe, I will show you the wonder of God's power."

The stone was taken away and Jesus raised his eyes to the sky and said, "Lord God, thank you for hearing me. I know you always hear me but I say this for the sake of the people here that they will believe.

Jesus then called out in a loud voice, "Lazarus, come out!"

Lazarus walked out of the tomb bound with burial linens. Jesus told the others to unbind him and let him go to his home. The women removed the burial linens from Lazarus and then Lazarus saw Joanna's face. It was obvious Joanna was not someone he had expected to see. He averted his eyes as someone does when telling you a lie. *"Is something wrong here?"* Joanna thought.

Jesus did not stay long but Joanna did get an opportunity for a short conversation. He said, "Joanna, did you see the wonder of God's work today?"

She said, "Jesus, it is wonderful to have Lazarus back among the living. He is a wonderful friend and a good man."

Jesus said, "Perhaps this will give you some of the answers you are looking for."

Joanna said, "Perhaps, I am not sure."

Jesus left shortly afterwards and Joanna also returned to Jerusalem.

Joanna thought about the event. *Lazarus rising from the dead would add greatly to the reputation of Jesus of Nazareth, but was it true. She knew she could have "risen from the dead" in a like manner if required. She had "died" on several occasions and had come back due to her unusual healing powers. She did not think Lazarus was like her, but she had heard of medicines, which could make a person appear to be dead, then they would recover. Could Jesus and Lazarus have staged the event to enhance his reputation as a healer? She hated to think it but it was possible. If this was staged, then what about the rest of the great works of Jesus; were they also staged? Perhaps everything was faked.*

Joseph came to talk to her early in the next year. He said, "I understand you were there when Lazarus was raised from the dead. I was curious about your view of the situation."

Joanna decided to be honest and said, "I saw the event but there were concerns in my mind based on what I saw. Lazarus did not appear to be glad to see me there. I got the impression he felt guilty about something. I thought Jesus and Lazarus could have staged the event. I am sorry for the blunt honesty but there it is."

Joseph responded, "But how could they stage the death of Lazarus?"

Joanna said, "I have been many places in the world, perhaps more than you imagine. I have heard of medicines, which give the impression of death from which people recover. Jesus and Lazarus are also well traveled and Jesus is most intelligent. I don't like to think these thoughts but I cannot help it. I felt something was wrong there."

Joseph said, "Joanna, I respect your thoughts and feelings. I also trust Jesus and Lazarus. Can I ask you to please keep your thoughts about this secret, they could harm Jesus?"

Joanna said, "I have no reason to repeat my experience to anyone since I cannot be sure."

When Passover came, I watched as Jesus entered the city in triumph. Most of the crowd certainly seemed to be with him. But I knew from Chuza there were many plots working in Jerusalem, some aimed at the death of Jesus.

News of the arrest of Jesus and trial first before the Sanhedrin, where Joseph of Arimethea bravely defended Jesus, and then to the Roman governor, Pilate, who passed Jesus case off to Herod when he learned he was a citizen of Galilee. Then back to Pilate where the "people" controlled by the high priest could decide his fate.

Joanna thought, "Crucifixion would not be my choice of deaths, typically nails through wrists, ankles, and both legs broken. Sometimes much worse injuries than a lingering death was involved. Even if Jesus were like me, the pain and torment would be no less. But he did predict rising from the dead. Perhaps, I need to go see the end of this."

Joanna talked to Chuza and asked, "I wish to go see the end of Jesus on the cross. I will dress as inconspicuously as possible and observe from a distance. Will you go with me?"

Chuza said, "If you need me I will certainly go, but it would be better politically if I stay away."

Joanna said, "I understand completely. I will be as discrete as I can."

Joanna made her way to the place of execution outside the city, accompanied by a male servant. The crowd gathered there was small by Joanna's standards. She had attended executions in Rome where large crowds attended and the affairs were similar to fairs. In this case the crowd was small, perhaps twenty-five Roman soldiers and one hundred other onlookers. She recognized some as Herod's "spies, others as representatives of the high priest and then she saw Mary Magdalene, Martha, and Joseph of Arimathea. There were others there she did not recognize but some she suspected were people who just enjoyed seeing an execution.

She saw three men raised on crosses all in obvious pain with Jesus in the middle. The soldiers kept the area near the crosses clear of people and the process seemed very routine to them. Joanna approached Joseph and spoke, "My dear Joseph, I come here with a sad heart to see the end of Jesus."

Joseph seemed not to recognize her at first but then said, "Joanna, my thanks for your support on this tragic day. He has been on the cross for about two hours and may go on for a long time. Someone has decided not to break the legs of these men yet, as is the normal practice to speed their ends, so Jesus may suffer for a long time. Over there is Jesus mother, Mary, and Mary the wife of Clopas, and Peter, a disciple. You know Mary Magdalene, of course.

Joseph then said, "Jesus suffers but bears the pain well. He spoke to me earlier and asked me to take his body for burial as soon as possible. I am to bury him without embalming his body. I have my own tomb not far from here where I will place Jesus body. I must go soon to see Pilate and ask for the body of Jesus to be released to me as soon as he is dead. Nicodemus and I will prepare his body for the tomb."

Joanna heard Joseph's words but wondered, "It is strange Joseph is so concerned about the mechanics of taking care of the body of Jesus, rather than being grief stricken by seeing him die. Perhaps Joseph really believes he will rise from death as he has predicted. Perhaps Jesus really is like me, he knows he will rise again after his body appears to be dead, thus the need for speed in getting the body to the tomb and the avoidance of embalming.

Joseph is closer to Jesus than anyone else, he must know Jesus secret. But how could Jesus plan this unless he had risen before and thought he could rise again. His mother stands there grieving her dying son. Did she not give birth to him. If he were like me she would know he is not her son? Unless it dawned, UNLESS he left her at the age of twelve or thirteen to go to Britain with Joseph, perhaps accompanied by a man who had studied with the Essenes they met along the way. What if Jesus were killed or died in Britain or on the journey. THEN, if the man revealed to Joseph he had a certain power to recover from what seemed like death and to rise and live, like me. WHAT if they had planned and worked for many years to stage many "miracles" including the death and resurrection of Jesus to meet the predictions of the scriptures. Why do it? Not for political power, Jesus did not seek it. PERHAPS, he wanted to spread the philosophy of Jesus—being kind to your fellow man.

If it is true, it is wonderful Jesus is using the power he shares with me for much more good than I have ever done. But how to know?"

Returning to the moment Joanna asked Joseph, "How long will Jesus last before he dies?"

Joseph said, "I think a few more hours at the most. The Sabbath is tomorrow and he must die today and be taken from the cross and buried before the end of the day. The high priest will not let it last longer. They will likely send men to break their legs to speed the process in some hours. If that does not finish it they will send men to dispatch them with swords or spears. Nicodemus and I must be prepared to take the body to the tomb as soon as he is dead and Pilate gives permission."

Joanna said, "What of your future Joseph? Your defense of Jesus in the Sanhedrin is now well known. The Jewish authorities may be out to get you next."

Joseph said, "I am of little consequence, but I am a Roman citizen and well placed politically. I also have enough wealth and connections to make the high priest think twice before he tries to have me stoned or even thinks of sending me to the cross."

Joanna said, "What can I do to help in the next few days?"

Joseph said, "I know not what may come so I cannot predict the needs. I thank you for the offer and will send you word when I find a task suited for you."

Joseph thought for a few moments and said, "Right now I expect a problem with the women when I hastily prepare Jesus body and take it to the tomb. There will be no time for their grieving by the body and tomorrow is the Sabbath when it also will not be permitted. I expect there will be soldiers guarding the tomb to prevent it or other things. So, on Sunday morning, the women will want to go to the tomb. I do not think the guards at the tomb will want to see me or other men close to Jesus at the tomb. They will expect us to try to steal his body to say he has risen. Perhaps, you could go to the tomb with the women and, if necessary, use your position as wife of Herod's steward, to prevent problems for the women."

Joanna said, "I will do the task, my friend. Make arrangements as to where I should go to meet the women and let me know."

Joseph said, "You know the house of my sister well. Be there before the sun rises on Sunday.

Joanna stayed at the place of execution and witnessed the gradual weakening of Jesus over several more hours. She witnessed a darkening of the skies almost like nighttime and other events. Finally she heard Jesus call out and he was apparently dead. A centurion, Longinius was his name she thought, took a spear and pierced Jesus side. This was supposed to insure he was dead although from the angle Joanna saw it, it did not strike at the heart as was intended. She also saw Joseph collect some of the blood and fluids discharged from the wound in two vessels which he had a servant wrap up for safekeeping. Joseph hurried from the hill and back to the city afterwards.

Many people now left the place of execution but the spies of Herod stayed as did some of the high priest's men. Joanna stayed as well to witness events.

After about one hour, Joseph returned with a centurion and written permission to remove the body of Jesus to a tomb owned by Joseph. The centurion had instructions to guard the body and the tomb after the body was sealed in the tomb.

Joseph and Nicodemus assisted by a number of servants took Jesus body down from the cross, wrapped his body in linen and transported it to the tomb mentioned earlier by Joseph. Joanna followed at a distance. Joseph and Nicodemus spent some time preparing the body inside the tomb and then rolled a large rock over the entrance to the tomb. Joseph spoke to the centurion in charge of the soldiers and they apparently agreed upon something. Since the Sabbath was about to start. Joseph and the other Jews hurried away to get to their proper places for the Sabbath. Joanna returned to her home also.

Chuza was home when she arrived and asked what had happened. Joanna described events without adding her personal thoughts. Chuza said Herod was glad the Romans performed the execution so he could pass off responsibility for it. Herod thought executing Jesus was unnecessary but the high priest was the main driving force behind events.

Very early in the morning of Sunday, Joanna rose and set out for the house of Joseph's sister. There she met Mary Magdalene, Mary the mother of James and Salome and they walked to the tomb. From a distance they could see the tomb was open and there were no Roman soldiers guarding the tomb.

Mary Magdalene ran ahead and looked into the tomb. She came back out as we arrived at the tomb and said, "Jesus body is gone. When I entered the tomb and angel spoke to me and said the one who was crucified, Jesus of Nazareth has risen."

Joanna went to the tomb and looked inside. She saw the body of Jesus was not there but she did not see an angel or anyone in the tomb.

Joanna immediately decided it would be best to get away from the tomb as quickly as possible. They could be subject to serious questioning by the authorities if they were found there. The others agreed and they left. They stayed together until they got close to the city. Joanna then went to her home and the others to other places.

When Joanna arrived home she sent a message to Joseph of Arimathea describing what had happened earlier and asking what he knew. She sent it off with her servant.

There was no response by the time Chuza returned home in the evening. When he arrived they traded information. Chuza said news had gotten to Herod the body was missing. The story told by the soldiers was of disciples of Jesus coming and stealing the body when the soldiers were sleeping.

Joanna's first thought was *the soldiers had been bribed.* Since first thoughts are usually the best she thought about who would be able to bribe the soldiers? *"Did someone bribe the soldiers to let them take the body away? Who had the resources and connections to do it? What was their motivation?"*

She thought, *'To the first question, I think Yes. To the second question one possible answer is Joseph of Arimathea—he has the wealth, power and connections with the Roman authorities. To the third question—Joseph could want to help Jesus rise or could have planned to remove Jesus body then claim he had risen. "*

Joanna thought, *"If Joseph or others of the disciples caused these events to happen, in the next several days, weeks, and months there will be reported sightings of Jesus, probably by disciples only and none verified by other than disciples. Mary Magdalene's seeing an angel this morning could easily be part of the plot. Perhaps, I was invited there by Joseph to be a "Roman witness" to help prove their case.*

On the other hand, if Jesus is someone like me who can rise from apparent death, he may come forward and try to claim power directly. It would be interesting. "

Joanna was not surprised when stories appeared over the next several months about a risen Jesus appearing to disciples and others who had been close to him while he lived. She was also not surprised the Jewish authorities were very disturbed by these stories and were starting to gear up for persecution of these followers of Jesus.

Joanna was extremely concerned when her name appeared in some of the lists of the followers of Jesus being circulated by the Jewish high priest. Apparently her presence when Lazarus rose and at the crucifixion combined with her association with Joseph of Arimathea had been enough to get her name on the list. Chuza was very upset by this development both for the threat to his own position, since she was always referred to as "wife of Chuza, steward to Herod" and the threat to her own personal safety and implicitly to Enoch.

Joanna wrote to Joseph of Arimathea and asked what he thought of the situation. She wrote the letter in the language of Gaul, which she knew was a language Joseph, also knew how to read. She trusted her servants but the Jewish authorities were very resourceful in getting information and informants.

Joseph wrote back, complimenting her on the choice of a language for correspondence. He said the situation was very grim with the Jewish authorities having launched a severe persecution of the followers of Jesus, especially a man named Saul. Many had fled to other lands or were planning to leave until the crisis passed. In honesty, Joseph did not think it was safe for Joanna to stay in Jerusalem. He would offer his protection but it was only worth so much. As a Roman official he was fairly safe, for now, but as a

Roman wife of a Jewish official she was not as safe. He suggested she leave if possible.

Joanna discussed the circumstances with Chuza. Their relationship was a good, loving relationship. Not a torrid love affair, but a solid relationship with mutual respect and some lust as the strong points. Chuza did not want to see Joanna leave but the more he thought about it, the more sense it made for her to leave for a time. Should Enoch go also? He was twenty years old and some travel would do his education good. It was decided Joanna and Enoch would first go to Caesarea and wait there until one of Joanna's ships came to port. Then they would decide on the next step.

Joanna wrote to Joseph with this information, still using the language of Gaul, and then planned her departure. She liquidated as much of her wealth in Jerusalem and insured the balance was in the name of Chuza. She shipped the cargo she had ready to a warehouse at the port. She found a house to rent in Caesarea, renting it under the name Media. She also had a conversation with Enoch about the situation and the plans to leave Jerusalem for a while. Fortunately he was excited by the prospect of travel. He had heard Joanna talk with Chuza about their adventures at sea and he wanted to have the experience as well. Besides, Enoch would not abide the thought of Joanna leaving him in Jerusalem. He still loved her as the only mother he could remember, although, he still remembered his grandmother.

In January of 34 A.D. Joanna and Enoch traveled to Caesarea, leaving in the middle of the night and using other names along the way. Joanna did write to Joseph and told him how to reach her in Caesarea.

Joanna and Enoch lived in Caesarea without incident of note until August. Joanna continued to spend her time buying trade goods, which could be put on a ship going to the west to be sold at a good profit. She could always buy a ship or two if necessary but she was under no pressure to leave at the present time. Then she received a letter from Joseph.

Joseph's letter said a number of people she knew, including Mary Magdalene, Martha, Lazarus, Nicodemus and others she may not know Zaccheus, Trophimus, Maximin, Cleon, Eutropius, Sidonius (Restitutus, "the man born blind"), Martial and Saturninus, Mary, wife of Cleopas; Salome; and their maid, Marcella, were going to Caesarea and would leave by ship at the earliest convenience. Joseph indicated he would accompany them. Joseph said he was very worried the Jewish authorities may try to stop or disrupt their departure. Even his position as a Roman official may not be enough to provide protection from the hatred of the high priest.

Joanna immediately wrote back to Joseph offering to provide transportation from Caesarea and to make arrangements for them to stay at her rented home.

The next correspondence to reach her from Joseph was a surprise. They (He, Mary Magdalene, Lazarus, Martha, and about ten others) were in Caesarea but essentially under house arrest at the port with Jewish authorities controlling their movements. They were going to be put on a ship and expelled from Caesarea but the ship would have no keel, sail, or oars. They were intended to die at sea with no way to control the drift of the vessel. Joseph told her where they were "held" and where the ship was docked. Joseph was not a prisoner so much as a volunteer to accompany the others. It was likely the status of Joseph as a Roman official was the only thing keeping the others alive.

Good fortune had smiled on Joanna, not one but two of her ships had reached Caesarea in the past week. Both ships had loyal crews and she immediately had the contents of her warehouse loaded on the two vessels and other preparations made for sailing. She had the senior captain put a watch on the ship Joseph was supposed to leave on. She and Enoch moved to one of her vessels and waited for the departure.

Their lookout informed them on Sunday afternoon the vessel being watched had been loaded with people but little cargo or provisions and was being readied to be towed out of the harbor by a larger vessel.

Joanna had the captains prepare to sail at once. Her plan was to follow at a distance and wait until the larger vessel cut loose the smaller vessel. When the larger vessel headed back to port they would rescue the occupants of the smaller vessel. The big concern was the Jewish authorities on the larger vessel killing the passengers on the smaller vessel or sink it.

Out of the sight of shore the larger vessel cut the smaller vessel loose. The prevailing wind was to the west so the ship would drift to the west, but those on board had no control over where they went. The cruel mind thinking up this manner of execution apparently knew a little of the sea, perhaps this Saul she had heard about.

Joanna's ships stayed back far enough to avoid being seen by the larger ship until it was gone. Then they set their sails and approached the drifting ship. As her ship approached, she saw her old friend Joseph on the ship and called out, "At least I do not have to pull you and Lazarus from the water this time!"

Joseph called back, "No we are both dry this time."

When the people were transferred from the drifting ship to Joanna's vessel she noticed two items of significance. *Joseph had a medium-sized chest, which he insisted on transferring himself from the drifting vessel—Joanna assumed this chest held the vessels he had used to collect the blood and other fluids of Jesus. Mary Magdalene carried a more precious cargo—a baby boy who looked to be about one year old. Joanna immediately suspected this was the child of Jesus.*

When Joseph boarded Joanna's ship he went to her and embraced her saying, "For the second time you have saved the lives of Lazarus and myself, and now you save others with the relics of Jesus. Joanna the Roman acts more like Jesus than many who believe in him. I thank you for what you have done."

Joanna was moved by the words of Joseph. He was perhaps the most important and intelligent person she had know in her life. She did not necessarily agree with the plans he had apparently set in motion but his motives were good.

Joanna had one question, which nagged at her, *"What happened to the body of Jesus?"* During the course of the journey to the west, Joanna thought she would have the answer to her question.

61. <u>Antarctica</u>

Ramede asked the others what the time was. It turned out she had been talking for eight hours without a break.

Ramede said, "I am sorry but when I get to telling about those times in the past I just can't stop."

Simon said, "Do not feel bad, we were transfixed. What you told us was important beyond anything we have ever heard. You know things no one else in the world knows."

Ramede said, "There is more to tell."

Arslan said, "It is such a wonderful surprise someone else met and knew Jesus. Perhaps I am very self-centered but can I ask if you thought I had a strong resemblance to Jesus?"

Ramede said, "When I first saw you, I thought I had found out where Jesus had gone. Your are identical as far as I can tell."

Arslan asked, "What does it mean?"

Ramede responded, "Either there is a huge coincidence or Jesus was your twin. Which in turn means he could have risen from "a death like state" and lived on."

Arslan said, "Does anything in the rest of your story speak about this?"

Ramede said, "Yes and No."

Carrie interjected, "It sounds like we need to hear the rest of Ramede's story to understand."

Ramede started speaking.

62. <u>Mediterranean Sea (34 A.D.)</u>

Joanna chose to have all the people rescued stay together on the one ship while she transferred some of the cargo to the other ship. Her reasons were mostly selfish, she wanted to hear as much they said as possible.

Joanna had never been particularly close of Mary Magdalene but she now sought her out and made friends with her young son, named James. Joanna had a special way with one year olds. They liked the way she played with them on their level, as a result she was always their favorite. James was no exception, he fell in love with Joanna. As a result his mother came to be close to Joanna.

Mary Magdalene said to Joanna, "I have never seen James take to someone as quickly as with you. He thinks you are the best. How do you do it?"

Joanna said," To be honest I don't know, but it is always this way, one year olds love me. If they could keep it up for thirty years or so it would be great."

Magdalene said, "You did not believe me at the tomb did you? I mean you did not believe I had seen an angel? What do you think now?"

Joanna said, "To be honest, I did not believe you and still don't think you saw an angel. I think you had something you planned to say and said it. It was part of a plan to make it seem like Jesus had risen."

Magdalene said," And now I must thank you for saving me from death at sea but mostly thank you for saving my son. He is a beautiful, beautiful child. I could not bear to have him die. So, I thank you for finding a way to save us. I know I sound insincere and resentful but it is not really true. What you have done may be more important than anything I have ever done. We do not know what he will become."

Joanna said, "He is more precious than words can say. All babies are so innocent and special. I would give my life to save his if it came to it."

Magdalene said, "Thank you for being such a special friend. I miss Jesus so much and I am depressed. Losing him is so hard."

Joanna said, "So he has not appeared to you since he was crucified?"

Magdalene said, "No."

Joanna said, "Did the disciples steal the body from the tomb?"

Magdalene said, "They told me they did not. They are as much in the dark as any of us."

Joanna said, "Then who took the body of Jesus? Could Joseph have taken the body?"

Magdalene said, "I have not asked him. He is usually so direct, I did not think it would be possible for him to be devious."

"Joseph did not get to be the minister of mining for the empire by being honest and direct all the time. He has the skills to be devious if necessary. I love Joseph but I do think he is capable of stealing the body of Jesus. In fact, he is probably the most capable person I can think of to have taken it away and he may have more knowledge of Jesus. He may know if Jesus lives now or not."

Magdalene was surprised and said, "You think Jesus may yet live? I am surprised you, of all people, would think he may have lived. You are not a believer but you believe Jesus may live. I am confused."

Joanna said, "Not all things in this world are understood and certainly the ways beyond this world are unknown to us. My experience drives me to think Jesus could live. We both saw your brother, Lazarus, rise from what appeared to be death. Could not Jesus have done the same?"

Magdalene said, "I no longer know what to believe. Peter and other disciples say Jesus has appeared to them. I have told others I have seen Jesus as well, as Jesus told me to say before he was lost to me. If he has come and appeared to Peter and the others, why has he not come to comfort me? I thought I was closer to him than anyone while he lived. I loved him as only a woman can love a man. And now I see changes in the teachings of the disciples, they want to say Jesus was more than a man, that he was God. My son and I are an embarrassment to them. We remind them of the humanity of Jesus. I think they wish I would disappear so they can ignore the human part of Jesus. They are more concerned with converting others to the movement than spreading the real teachings of Jesus or presenting the real Jesus to the world."

Joanna said, "Has Jesus appeared to Joseph or Lazarus or Nicodemus?"

Magdalene said, "No."

Joanna said, "And no one you know of has any knowledge of who took Jesus from the tomb? Especially Joseph?"

Magdalene said, "No one has told me they know who took Jesus body. Joseph has said, "He does not know where Jesus is." He has never said directly he knows nothing of how Jesus body left the tomb. Why do you ask about Joseph?"

Joanna said, "Who else could bride the soldiers to leave the tomb? It would take an enormous sum of money and power to insure they stayed bribed. That alone eliminates almost everyone and those others had no motivation. The last thing the high priest wanted was to have the body of Jesus disappear. He may have wanted to have it publicly burned or otherwise destroyed but not to have it disappear. Herod likewise had no reason to want it to disappear. Pilate certainly had no motive and could have ordered the body disposed of differently if he chose. It leaves Joseph; no one else involved had the money or power to make it happen. The high priest may see and understand also. Part of his hatred for Joseph may come from this issue."

Magdalene said, "So, will you ask Joseph these questions?

Joanna said, "In time I will seek to get an answer from Joseph. In the meantime, it would be better if you did not mention this conversation to him."

Magdalene said, "I agree, Joanna. And thank you again for saving my son."

A few days later, Joanna felt prepared to talk to Joseph. She found an opportunity when they could talk together without others hearing. Joanna initiated the conversation, "Joseph, there is much about events concerning Jesus I do not understand. You seem to be the one person who knows more than anyone else. You know of Jesus life in Britain and what he planned to accomplish when he returned to Galilee. If fulfillment of the scriptures was his goal, you know it. Was his disappearance from the tomb part of his plan? Did you arrange for the soldiers to leave the tomb? I ask this not to offend you but to try to understand. My logic tells me you were one of the few people with the wealth and power to bribe the soldiers and

Jon Kelly

possibly the only one of those few with any motivation to have Jesus disappear from the tomb? Can you answer my questions so I can be at peace with myself on these subjects?"

Joseph thought for a long time then said, "Joanna, you have saved my life twice and saved these others, as well as saving the relics of Jesus for the sake of the world. I owe you much and want to help you find your truth. There are many things I would like to tell you but I am sworn to not speak about these things. All of this is part of a larger, more important, mission of which Jesus and I are part. The cost of this mission has been greater than any can imagine but the end result will be to have the message of Jesus transform Galilee and perhaps the world. I can say no more to you about this."

Joseph left her side and Joanna thought about what Joseph had said, "My instincts tell me he is the key to it all. But if he will not speak about it how can I ever know. I will continue to ask my questions and may find some moment when he is ready to be more open. Then Joanna thought about one possible way to open Joseph up. She would tell Joseph the truth about herself!"

406

63. <u>Island of Naxos (34 A.D.)</u>

Joanna had set their route to the west through places familiar to her. She chose to land in the Cyclades Islands of Greece at one of her favorite spots in the world, the Island of Naxos. This was a place she was very familiar with and also a place to buy the famous honey wine made there.

They sailed into the port city of Hora and gave everyone on both ships a chance to explore one of the most beautiful places in the world. She asked Joseph to go with her to see the view of the city and port from an elevated field in the hills. As they neared the secluded field where she knew there was a spring she started speaking to Joseph.

She said, "Joseph, you know very little about me. I have lived a different life than anyone else on this earth. I have always kept my life a secret but now I will share some of it with you. You will not believe me at first but I think I can convince you. Please be patient."

I am going to tell you things about myself I have told only a few people in almost 800 years of living on this earth. Yes, I did say 800 years. That is how old I am."

Joanna had led them to the spring she knew was near the field. Joanna said," Do you remember what I looked like when we met, eighteen years ago. You were about thirty then. Have you aged in those eighteen years?"

Giving him no opportunity to answer she went to the spring and washed the gray dye out of her hair and the makeup off her face. She then turned back to him and said, "Do you remember I looked like this, eighteen years ago."

Joseph was speechless for a time then said, "You look like a woman of twenty five as you did then."

Joanna continued, "I was born near Napata in southern Egypt almost 800 years ago. I aged only to the point of looking twenty-five or so, then stopped. If I am injured I heal very quickly. I have been taken for dead on several occasions then recovered.

I was queen of Egypt 725 years ago but did not like the life and have moved many places and had many identities over the years. I have no idea how I came to be as I am but I do know I was adopted as a child and have never known my real parents. I married a prince named Pi'ankhy who conquered northern Egypt and ruled the entire country. He became a man I could not live with so I ran away to Greece. I have lived in various identities in Athens, Rome, Italy, Gaul, Jerusalem and various islands. I have no power to heal others, seemingly only myself."

Joanna then said, "What more can I explain to convince you?"

Joseph stood transfixed for a time then said, "Joanna, what I see before me is enough to convince me. But I am shocked and mystified. It will take time for this to sink in to my mind and heart. But why should it be so strange to me—the Torah tells of many people living to great ages in the past—why should it be so strange such people still exist?"

Joanna said, "You knowing this great secret about me is also a great responsibility. You must tell no one. Others may not be able to understand and would do me great harm to know my secret, which there is not one, because I have no idea why I am as I am.

I only tell you now to try to draw out from you the truth about Jesus. I need to know if Jesus was like me, if he did in fact rise, or if it was a plot to set up the spread of Jesus teachings. Was he only a man who was willing to sacrifice his life to spread his ideas or was he something more? Was he like me for instance? Now you know why I need to know. You should also realize this puts me in no position to tell others what you tell me about Jesus, I cannot expose myself."

Joseph was speechless again for a long time, then said, "Joanna, let's find a place to sit, I will tell you what I know."

They found some large rocks and sat down. Joseph started speaking, "Jesus was not yet thirteen when we left together for Britain. Mary, the mother of Jesus did not want him to go but Joseph, his father, was still alive then, and he made the decision for Jesus to go. Jesus was very bright and there had been incidents, which made Joseph fearful for his safety in Galilee.

So, we traveled to Britain, following the tin trade route of which you are aware. In Britain we spent much of our time at insula Avalonia, which was not far from the tin mines, where among other things Jesus, the trained carpenter, built a small hut with his own hands. He learned the business of the tin mines but also turned his attention to the schools there and was able to attend one due to my position.

There was another man from Galilee studying at the same school. He was very unusual.

He was about twenty-five years of age, or so he looked. He said his name was David of Accrabbein but said his family had moved to Jerusalem when he was a child. He had studied for at least three years with the Essenes before coming to Britain about four years earlier. He had a force of personality and a dedication to improving the world, which was beyond what most people can imagine. Jesus and I were both his good friends and we shared living space together since we had the same language and common interests. We often talked about religion until late at night with a focus on men treating each other better.

Jesus and David became inseparable. Jesus was like a sponge absorbing the teaching in school and the knowledge of David. When it came time for us to return to Galilee, Jesus demanded to stay. He was learning more than he ever thought possible so we decided he could stay with David while I returned to Galilee. Each time I returned to Britain and was ready to go back to Galilee it was the same. The older Jesus got the more emphatic he became about continuing his studies. It was more important than anything else he said. The visit of Lazarus was in part to have someone other than myself go back to Mary and tell her Jesus was healthy but wanted to continue his studies.

One of the strangest aspects of this situation was the older he grew, the more Jesus came to look like David, to the point they could pass for each other, if someone did not know them extremely well. Another strange thing was David not wanting to be mentioned in any correspondence going back to Galilee or to be seen by any visitors from Galilee, such as Lazarus or Chuza. He said his family in Galilee could be in danger if it were known he was in Britain.

I did go to Accrabbein on one of my return visits to Galilee to check to see if anyone remembered a child named David living there about twenty years earlier, but no one had any recollection. Finding a recollection of a man named David in Jerusalem's half-million people was impossible. I never doubted the sincerity of conviction of

David—he was truly dedicated to helping the world—I just didn't know how he came to be.

When Jesus told me he would return to Galilee and start a ministry to spread a new teaching of God's word, I was not surprised. The thinking of Jesus and David had been moving there for a long time. I asked if David would also come. Jesus said I should never mention the existence of David to anyone from or in Galilee."

Joanna took advantage of Joseph's pause to ask several questions, "Joseph, did Jesus father children in Britain and did David also? Does anyone else know about David to your knowledge? Does Lazarus know? Did you see David in Galilee after Jesus returned? Did you bribe the soldiers to leave the tomb? Did you remove Jesus body from the tomb? I am sorry to ask so much but the questions pour out of me."

Joseph said, "Let me continue and I think most of your questions will be answered.

When Jesus returned to Galilee I saw little of him, except for times he stopped by my home to see me, usually unannounced. He was deeply involved in his ministry and mainly came asking questions about this man or that man, if I knew anything about them. Some of the people he asked about eventually became his disciples. He already had information about some of the people he asked about and seemed to be seeking confirmation mainly.

You asked about David of Accrabbein, if it was actually, where he originated. After John the Baptist baptized Jesus, Jesus was reported as having gone off into the wilderness alone. My sources said he did not go alone but was accompanied by a stranger who resembled him. This stranger, who seemed to prefer to remain out of sight has been reported to me several times during the course of Jesus ministry. I have assumed it was David. In my mind, this was confirmed by Lazarus, who told me Jesus often met with a man in Bethany when Jesus visited there. Especially near the end of his ministry, Jesus spent more and more time with Mary Magdalene and seemed to make his way to Bethany regularly. Lazarus may have seen David there, he has not spoken to me about it. Lazarus has been less than forthcoming with me since he "died" and was brought back by Jesus. He has refused to talk to me about the details of the event.

As far as your question about my seeing David in Galilee, I think I have but am unsure.

I saw little of Jesus after his return from Britain usually at night and in poor light. Any other times, I was in a large crowd and could not be close to him for long. I am honestly not sure whether it was Jesus or David posing as Jesus who came back from Britain or if David posed as Jesus at the end. In the Sanhedrin when I defended Jesus, I could not be sure which one it was. He did not express himself well, not like the Jesus I had heard about preaching to the masses and he may have been beaten. On the cross, the person I saw had been brutalized. No one could tell the difference at that point if a substitution had been made.

As far as the bribing of the soldiers is concerned, I received a letter in Jesus hand, or I think it was Jesus hand, giving me specific instructions to bribe the guards to leave the tomb unguarded. I had been instructed previously to go to Pilate and get permission to take Jesus body to the tomb. Jesus knew Pilate would not refuse me, based on information I had which could be very damaging to Pilate, especially after Pilate's mentor was disgraced and Tiberius was looking for enemies.

I did not remove Jesus body from the tomb.

Joanna, I think I have answered your questions. Do you have others?"

Joanna said, "Did you see any signs David did not age, similar to my situation, or that he healed very quickly?"

Joseph said, "In retrospect, I remember I was amazed at times how young he looked or had not changed from visit to visit. In sixteen years more or less, he did not age noticeably. I remember once in Britain he fell on a rocky hill. I thought he had broken his ribs, then the next day he was fine."

Joanna said, "Joseph, do you have any questions of me?

Joseph said, "Only two, who do you think died on the cross and did he rise again? Is Jesus still alive?"

Joanna said, "I don't know to both questions."

Joseph and Joanna returned to the ships and left Naxos on the evening tide. Joanna's mind was swirling with questions and thoughts about where to turn next for answers.

64. <u>Panormos (35 A.D.)</u>

Joanna's ships were making a slow transit due to the weather early in the year. This gave her time to talk to others on the ship hoping to be able to fill in gaps in her knowledge of Jesus and the circumstances of his ministry and death.

One night a sea before they reached Sicily she had a chance to be alone with Lazarus. She asked directly about what he knew of Jesus, "Lazarus, as one of two people I have had the honor of saving twice, I beg you answer some questions for me. We have known each other eighteen years and I think you know I can be trusted. Will you answer my questions?"

Lazarus looked at her and said with some hesitation, "I will answer what I can, in good conscience."

Joanna began, "I have talked to Joseph and he has told me all he says he knows about Jesus, his ministry, his end on the cross and his body being removed from the tomb. I have reasons why I need to know the truth about what happened.

My questions are to start:

- Did Jesus have a visitor, a man very similar to him in looks, who met with him often in Bethany or elsewhere and what can you tell me about such a man?
- What is the truth about your reported death and being raised from the dead by Jesus?
- What else do you know about Jesus life and death?"

Lazarus spoke after thinking for some minutes, "I will try to explain what I know.

Jesus did have a visitor regularly who came usually in the night or Jesus went to meet with him. I actually saw him only twice. He looked and dressed much like Jesus although he tended to keep his head and features covered more than Jesus. Jesus knew I knew about his meeting this man and Jesus told me to never speak to anyone else about it. Since you already seem to know about it, I will break the confidence and talk to you about it. Jesus told me it was part of God's work.

As I said I saw the man twice, the first time by accident when I left my house late one night and walked in the moonlight toward the town. I found Jesus and the other man standing by a tree talking. They saw me and stopped talking. Both men said hello but Jesus did not introduce the other man. The other man said he had to leave and left. I asked Jesus who he was and Jesus said it was part of God's work.

The next time I saw the man was eight days before Jesus called me out of the tomb—you were there that day. The man came to me at night and asked me to come talk with him. He brought a letter from Jesus asking me to do what this man asked of me. The man gave me some medication he said would eventually make me sleep a very deep sleep. When I awoke, Jesus would be there to greet me. He added this was for the glory of God to make the world a better place.

Jesus had preached to me many times to follow his guidance to help his ministry. I did what was asked of me. Afterwards, I could do nothing to change what people thought so I kept quiet about it. I was very surprised to see you there with the other visitors when I came out of my tomb. I knew you and I felt guilty about what seemed like a deception.

As far as what else I know about Jesus life and ministry, he apparently died on the cross and now we don't know if he is risen or not. Some say yes, some say no. For me, Jesus message was a wonderful message to change the world into a better place. I will continue to try to spread the message of Jesus.

Joanna said then, "Lazarus, you have always been a good friend and good man. Thank you for being truthful with me."

The next day they arrived in Panormos on Sicily. Joanna took the opportunity to take Mary Magdalene and her son on a walk around the city. In the course of their walk, she asked Magdalene if she had observed Jesus meeting frequently with a stranger, in Bethany and other places.

Magdalene said, "Yes, I did not volunteer the information. Jesus told me to never speak about it, but you know already so I see no harm. For the entire time I knew Jesus, he would meet with the man every few weeks, sometimes more often. I asked Jesus who he was but Jesus told me, "It is God's work, do not pry.""

Joanna said, "Did you ever actually meet the man or speak to him?"

She responded, "Yes, he came to me several times with messages from Jesus, telling me to do things, usually to help with one of his works or to spread some information to help the ministry.

Joanna said," What did you think of him? Did he look like Jesus? Did he ever tell you his name?"

Magdalene said, "He seemed to resent me. I think he thought I was a threat to whatever plans he had for Jesus. And yes, he had a strong resemblance to Jesus. He only said his name was David, no more.

Joanna said, "One last question, when you saw the crucifixion were you sure the person on the cross was Jesus, could it have been David?"

Magdalene grew very quiet and closed her eyes then said, "It could have been David, and I hope it was David. The person was so badly beaten and swollen in the face. It could have been either one."

As the two ships approached Massilia, Joanna made the decision, for purely selfish reasons, to avoid landing the ship with her passengers in Massilia. The one ship with it's cargo would land in Massilia. The other ship would proceed up the Rhone River to the city of Arles. Joanna had only left Massilia eighteen years earlier and someone could easily recognize her. She did not need to deal with a problem right now.

From the standpoint of trading value, splitting the ships between the two ports turned out to be a stroke of unintended genius. Both ships coming into Massilia with very similar cargos would have depressed the prices. With the ships at separate ports, prices were very, very good. Joanna's wealth continued to grow.

Now with her refugees in Gaul, what would they do? Except for Joseph, who had his wealth spread around like Joanna, the others had little more than the clothes on their backs and no support network in Gaul to help them. Joanna talked to Joseph and made the decision to provide funds, a significant amount to each of the refugees to get them started in Gaul or wherever they chose to go. When each received their bag of gold from Joanna and Joseph they were very grateful. Joanna only asked one thing in return she said, "If you talk about or write about this voyage, do not include my name or my character in the story. I do not want to become well known. She was very insistent on this point and made Joseph prepare a standard story for all the others to tell about a ship with no sails, oars, or keel bringing them to Gaul. Out of gratitude they all agreed.

Joanna sent her ship back to Massilia with most of her passengers but stayed in Arles herself with her son Enoch. She told the others to tell their story as agreed.

65. <u>Insula Avalonia (36 A.D.)</u>

Those rescued from the ship without sail, oar or keel spread throughout Gaul over the year after landing in Arles/ Massilia. Mary Magdalene went to Rennes-le-Chateau, Lazarus to Massilia, Zaccheus to Rocamadour, Maximin to Aix, Martial to Limoges, Entrope to Orange, Trophimus settled in Arles, and Saturninus to Toulouse. Joanna's generosity in providing funds in effect resulted in funding the spread of the early Christian church in Gaul, one of the earliest transfers of the ministry of Jesus to Europe.

Joseph of Arimathea spent some time traveling about Southern Gaul but found no place seeming to be the place to start his new life. His son, Josephes joined him in Massilia and he maintained contact with Joanna and visited her several times. Then he received visitors from Britain sent by King Ariviragus of the Silures of Britain. He was invited to come to Britain.

Joseph called on Joanna in Arles where she was still residing with Enoch in the spring of 36 A.D. When Joseph arrived with his son Josephes, he greeted Joanna, "You look to be the same age as your son without your makeup."

Joanna responded, "This is my brother Enoch, you have made a mistake, she said with a wink."

"Josephes looked a little confused but Joseph said," Oh Yes, I am getting old and confuse people at times."

Josephes and Enoch were about the same age so they went off to do what men do in their early twenties. Joanna and Joseph settled into a conversation. Joseph said, "I have been invited to go to Britain by King Ariviragus of the Silures. He is an old friend and he has offered to grant some lands to me to use as I see fit. I think I must go. Would you like to join me, at least for a while, so you could learn more about life in Britain?

Joanna thought for a while and said, "Let me understand, this is not a an impure invitation to compromise the virtue of a married woman, as much as I might want it to be so."

Joseph, who was a man of the world, said, "Alas, I am too old to meet the demands of such an adventure. I am thinking more in terms of a young nurse to care of an old man in his declining years."

Joanna said, 'I predict you will live another fifty years and father many, many children."

Joseph said, "In seriousness, I will start a church in Britain to spread the teachings of Jesus."

Joanna said, "I will travel with you but I do not plan on being a disciple, I don't disagree with the teachings, but I have trouble spreading a message when I am in the dark as to the truth of the source."

Joseph said, "I do not care what you motivation is, as long as you are willing to go. It will be good to have someone who understands the past with me to help understand what should be done for the future. Perhaps our children will become good friends through this adventure."

Joanna said, "Who else will go to Britain with us?"

Joseph said, "There are about eight others besides you, I, and our children. Does Enoch know the truth about your past?"

Joanna said, "Yes, I really had no choice but to tell the truth. He seems to be able to adapt to the news. He thinks he was very lucky to have a stepmother who is immortal. He will be remembered as long as I live."

Joseph said, "I have thought about how lucky to have known Jesus who may have risen, we do not really know, and David, who may also be immortal as you said. And to have known you, who have lived so long and whom I know to be a person trying to do good. Besides me, who in history has had the opportunity to know so many truly great people."

Joanna traveled to Britain to insula Avalonia and saw the small hut built by Jesus hands. She also helped Joseph build the first church of the new religion of Christianity in Britain and perhaps the world on the same spot."

Joanna had asked Joseph about the cruets he carried in the chest, which he personally carried everywhere when he traveled. He said he had never cleaned the cruets, which he had used to catch the blood and fluids of Jesus or David, whoever was crucified. He had sealed the cruets in wax and then coated them with pitch to protect them. He did not know why he wanted to protect them so much but he thought it was somehow his duty. Joseph had great respect for history and he wanted to protect this part of history from being destroyed. He really did not know why. Perhaps, thousands of years from now we will be able to tell from these relics who actually died on the cross."

Joanna thought, "*Joseph will never easily allow these relics to be destroyed by those who would distort the truth or use them for the wrong purposes.*"

When Joseph arrived in Britain, King Ariviragus ceded 36 "hides" of land at insula Avalonia to Joseph. He did not make a commitment to convert to the religion Joseph spoke about but eventually he did.

Joanna spent much of her time in Britain researching what Jesus and David had done in Britain while they lived there. In this activity she had the assistance of two young men, Enoch and Josephes. They learned both Jesus and David had reputations, almost legends, as the brightest of students, who challenged their teachers and other students to go far beyond their "capabilities."

Enoch and Josephes found rumors of both Jesus and David having fathered several children during their time in Britain by more than one woman in both cases. The women involved included the daughters of King Ariviragus, which may also help explain the invitation extended to Joseph. The king was proud these princes of the land of Israel had chosen to bless his daughters with children.

Joseph was concerned about this information and swore Enoch and Josephes to secrecy about this matter. Joanna would not swear to be silent. Joseph held no malice toward her for this position. He said, "I must protect the memory of Jesus for the sake of the message he wanted me to spread. You are under no such obligation. From the letter I have received from Peter and others, it will make little difference anyway. *They are rewriting history to suit their needs from the letters I see.*"

After several months in Britain, including several marriage proposals by kings or princes, Joanna chose to return to Gaul. One question still nagged at her and deserved an answer, "*Why had Mary Magdalene gone to Rennes-le-Chateau? Magdalene was not a leader; she was a follower, a follower of Jesus mainly. She should have been asking, "Where should I go? Instead she made a direct decision to go to Rennes-le-Chateau. This was out of character. Why?*"

66. Rennes-le-Chateau (37 A.D.)

Joanna chose to travel to Rennes-le-Chateau with four soldier/knights of King Ariviragus who were sworn to protect her to the death.

Joanna had no idea about what to expect at Rennes-le-Chateau when she arrived there. Her first task was to find Mary Magdalene. Rennes-le-Chateau was not a large place, perhaps 4,000 to 5,000 people. Joanna asked for Magdalene. She was told to go to the fortress at to the north of the city. "Fortress" was a stretch, it was a stone house with a thorn fence surrounding it. Joanna found what looked like an opening and called to the house, "Magdalene, let me enter, this is Joanna of Massilia."

After a long time a figure came out of the stone structure and called out, "Joanna, come here and enter!"

Joanna went to the opening and met the figure carrying a torch, since the sun had set. The figure said, "Joanna, is it you?"

Joanna said, "Yes, it is Joanna. May I enter?"

The figure said, "Please come in, Joanna."

As Joanna entered the stone building, light from torches allowed her to see the inside. She saw two children inside, one who looked about right to be James and another younger child, perhaps a year old. Joanna then looked at the figure who had spoken to her and saw that it was Magdalene, but it was obvious she was pregnant.

Joanna said to the older child, "James my little one, come to me! James immediately ran to Joanna and hugged her leg as he had done many times before. Joanna was his favorite adult. Magdalene laughed at the memory of James and said, "He still loves you more than anyone else."

Joanna said, "Give me two days with the other little one and he will be the same. Care to wager a gold coin?"

Magdalene said, "I do not have enough gold to throw it away. His name is Benjamin and answers to Ben. Call him and see if he also comes to you."

Joanna kneeled down and said softly, "Ben, come to me and let me hug you?" At the same time she picked up James who hugged Joanna tightly. Benjamin immediately toddled over to Joanna and let her pick him up with James. Both children were content to be held in the arms of Joanna.

Joanna said softly, "What are you willing to tell me about this?"

Magdalene said, "I can say little, my word and love bind me."

Joanna said, "I am not the enemy. I do not seek to destroy him or you, only to know the truth. I will debate the wisdom of building any thing based on faith and truth using deceit and lies. Why can the truth not be victorious? Is it so important thoughts be spread to many, when the foundation is corrupt? Will he be admired ages and ages from now for using trickery to create a false religion. I think the world will believe they were cheated when they find out the truth and will then revile his name."

Magdalene said, "I am but a woman who loves a man. I cannot judge such lofty issues."

Joanna said, "Where is he now?"

Magdalene said, "I honestly do not know."

Joanna said, "Is there more you can say?"

Magdalene said, "Nothing more, but you are welcome to stay here a while. The children would love to have someone else to play with for several days."

Joanna said she would stay for a few days and she did. She learned nothing more and left, returning to Arles.

67. <u>Antarctica</u>

Arslan looked around the room when Ramede stopped talking. *He had not been taught the Judeo-Christian story from birth, as was the case with Ramede. But the others, Simon, Carrie and Lisa had known only the Christian culture from birth. Arslan wondered what the impact of Ramede's history, more than a story, would have on these others. Could they wipe away all the smoke and mirrors, built up around Jesus over the years and accept her witness testimony about the reality of Jesus. He was not sure he would be able to do it if he was in that role.*

Lisa spoke first, "Wow, it cuts through two thousand years of deception, wishful thinking, literary license, hallucination, and evangelism at the expense of truth like the proverbial hot knife through butter. Ramede, do you know more?"

Ramede said, "The rest I know is about the development of Christianity but not directly about Jesus or David. I went back to Rennes-le-Chateau numerous times over the years but was never able to find Jesus or David in the early years or any traces or documentation about them in later times. I saw Magdalene several times but never got her to speak more. I chose not to pursue the children since I felt they had a right to a life free from such things."

Simon said, "So, as I see it, always trying to be organized and logical, I have the following thoughts and questions about Jesus:

- The "miracles" of Jesus may have been staged?
- The early Christian writers invented much of the information about the divinity of Jesus?
- Jesus may have had a number of children?
- Who actually died on the cross, Jesus or David?
- David could have been one of the children of the Tira and could still be alive?
- Jesus could still be alive if God actually resurrected him?

Is there any way we can answer any of these questions using our resources?"

Ramede said, "In the course of telling my story it dawned on me there is, perhaps, one way to determine who died on the cross. It will take a great deal of luck but it is theoretically possible. If the two cruets, which Joseph of Arimathea had, can be found intact, testing of the dried blood and fluids in them might tell us if the blood is from one of the children of the Tira. It could mean David died, or appeared to die on the cross."

Carrie said, "But Ramede, think what you are saying, the cruets are in effect the "Holy Grail" which has been searched for as long as one thousand or more years with no success."

Ramede said, "But the searchers did not know where to search and did not have the technology of the Tira to assist them. As I talked about Joseph and the cruets, the story Joseph had the cruets buried with him for all the world to know just cannot be true. Joseph cared too much about the safety of the cruets to leave them out for whoever buried him to dispose of as they saw fit. Joseph of Arimathea was one of the most determined and effective men in history, he would not have done it that way. Joseph hid the cruets in a very safe place long before his death."

Carrie said, "But where, we have no idea."

Ramede said, "Not quite, we have one advantage all the other seekers of the Holy Grail did not, we have me. I knew Joseph of Arimathea very well. I spent many years in his company, the other did not have the benefit of that."

Ramede asked, "What was unique about Joseph of Arimathea?"

After pausing, Ramede said, "He was minister of mining for the Roman empire for twenty five years. He was an expert in mining. And he lived at insula Avalonia for forty years during which time he may have hid the cruets. I think an expert in mining would have found someplace near insula Avalonia where he could use his expertise in mining to create a secure hiding place, say in some caves, for instance. But he would not just have stuck the cruets in a cave, he would have cut a shaft or created a room and put a closure over it using his mining skills."

Arslan said, "I think I see where Ramede is going. There are caves in the area of the Glastonbury, which have never been explored. We take the Tira, which has the technology to use the equivalent of ground penetrating radars, not actually radar but a similar concept, which can penetrate deep into the earth. The technology can also differentiate between types of materials, such as silver and alabaster. If you recall we are looking for one silver cruet and one white cruet, probably alabaster. We have the Tira carefully analyze every cave or cave-like formation within say a ten mile radius of Glastonbury for unusual shafts or rooms cut into the cave and at the same time search for any place where there are two football size objects in close proximity, one made of silver, one made of alabaster. It is certainly within the technical capabilities of the Tira. A similar technology has been used from earth satellites to find ancient cities and trading trails."

Arslan said, "Does anyone disagree with trying?"

Everyone agreed to try it.

They knew the artificial intelligence of the Tira had heard everything and would make appropriate preparations but would not act until directions on timing were given. Lisa asked directly, however, what the artificial intelligence thought about what they were doing and how it "felt" about possibly finding some trace of another of the children of the Tira. The computer voice responded, "I would certainly have a great sense of satisfaction to learn more about the offspring of the Tira. This does seem like a good possibility to do it."

Contact was made with the White House, to advise the Tira was making a trip to Great Britain. They also contacted the British government. There was some hostility in the British government because they had already made the claim the Tira had been unlawfully "stolen" from Dragon Hill at Uffington. They wanted to know exactly what the Tira would be doing in Great Britain and where they would go. Rather than get into an argument, Arslan suggested they go to the top directly, and contact the Queen. She lacked official power, but a few words to the government about cooperation, etc. might loosen up the stuffed shirts in the government.

They instructed the computer to send a high priority E-Mail to the Queen requesting her availability to talk by telephone with persons on the Tira. They quickly received a response the Queen was available. Communications were established and they explained they were coming to Great Britain, still not saying where exactly, for a scientific and archeological mission and would like to get improved cooperation from the authorities. When recordings of the contacts made with the government were played back to her, she said, jokingly, "Heads will roll." In the end, she assured us we would have complete cooperation and she would enjoy her role in making it happen. Obviously, she did not often get a chance to use her authority, informal though it was.

The next communication from the British government was from the office of the Prime Minister and had a very apologetic tone to it. He personally indicated the previous communications had come from lower levels, which did not have the authority to make such decisions and did not represent the very cooperative position of the government. Visions of some lowly officials being marched to the Tower passed through their minds.

With all the details settled, they instructed the Tira to plot a course for Glastonbury so as to get them there in several hours. Security measures were to be maintained at a high level since they were still under threat from some terrorist elements. Arslan thought, *"If people knew what they were doing, the next terrorist threat might come from the Vatican or the World Council of Churches. He had always wondered how much information was held in the Vatican archives which could illuminate many issues about early church history. Were there secrets there, which have never seen the light of day and probably never will? They certainly have created a reputation for being secretive even deceptive. Don't they see the contradiction the behavior represents?"*

68. **Glastonbury**

Lisa read from an Internet web page, "About six miles from Glastonbury to the northeast are the Wookey Hole Caves. These cave have been occupied and used by men off and on since the Iron Age. The caves are extensive and some sections have not been explored and at least two caves, #3 and #4, have been filled with water since 1857 when a canal was built to run the paper mills located at the caves. The canal flooded the two caverns."

The Tira was carefully using its earth penetrating radar-like systems to map the area within 10 miles of Glastonbury working in a grid pattern at about 1,000 feet above the ground. Covering the entire search area twenty-mile diameter circle would take two days to complete. Arslan decided to prioritize the search of the Wookey Hole Caves so they would start working the data from there first, due to the history of the area. Joseph of Arimathea would surely have known about these caves.

The scan of the Wookey Hole site took about one hour due to the known depth of the caves and the slower speed required to insure good depth penetration. Analysis of the data would take about another hour according to Tira's computer. As time wore on, Arslan wondered what they would do if they found nothing within the ten mile radius of Glastonbury? Did it make sense to broaden the search? Silly question, of course they would.

At 49 minutes into the analysis, the computer threw up a holographic projection of the third cavern of the cave and proceeded to describe how there was a man made shaft starting at the bottom of the north end of the cavern going up at about 45 degrees for forty feet to a chamber approximately 8 foot cube. Inside the chamber were two objects, one identified as silver, the other as alabaster.

There was a fitted plug over the bottom end of the shaft, which would be exposed to the cavern. There appeared to be stairs cut into the shaft. The computer said the 8-foot cube of a chamber was above the water level in the cavern.

How to get to the chamber was the problem? There were three viable options:

425

- Divers could go down, remove the plug and come up into the chamber.
- The water entry from the other side of the cavern could be blocked and the water pumped out of the cavern in about three days.
- The Tira could use an energy beam to cut an entry shaft through the solid rock surrounding the chamber.

Arslan was an accomplished cave diver and Lisa was accomplished at scuba diving but was not experienced in caves. Diving was the fastest, least destructive way to get to the chamber.

Arslan quickly made arrangements to get the required equipment including explosives to address the plug in the shaft, if necessary. There should be a way to get it out without blasting. He also arranged to have the caves closed to everyone else, over the objections of the cave staff.

Lisa and Arslan dove down to the location of the beginning of the shaft depicted by the Tira's computer. They found the plug and investigated. Arslan realized a large pry bar under the plug combined with ropes around the end of the plug pulling would cause the plug to drop out of the end of the shaft. You had to know the shaft was there to get the idea of what to do. It was not intended to be found by accident.

With the plug out, Arslan and Lisa swam up the shaft until they came out of the water about six feet below the entry of the stairs into the chamber. They took extra lights with them to insure they could search easily. They climbed the stairs into the chamber, *where no man had walked for almost two thousand years*, thought Arslan.

When they both were in the chamber they looked around and saw a grotto cut into the back wall containing a copper covered chest which looked to be very old but intact. Hewn into the stone above the grotto were the words in Hebrew, "I, Joseph of Arimathea, who buried Christ, have saved his blood."

There were some other items in the room. There were two other chests, also old looking but intact. Arslan and Lisa proceeded to seal the three chests in heavy plastic bags they had brought for this purpose. Then one at a time they went down the steps into the water and up to the entrance to the #3 cavern. When they got there with the third one, Simon and Ramede met them to help carry the chests out of the cave to the Tira. Once everyone was on board they took the Tira safely out over the ocean.

With five of them sitting in the main control room with three very old chests sitting on the floor in front of them there was silence. Simon said, "It is amazing we have found what men have looked for all the centuries, this really is the Holy Grail. I am impressed. Who would have thought?"

Arslan said Ramede had the right to open them up; she had led them to the hiding place. Ramede went to the first chest, the one that had been in the recessed grotto and took it out of the bag carefully. The copper top was sealed to the bottom with what appeared to be wax. She carefully cut through the wax until the top lifted off. Inside the chest were two black objects about 12 inches in diameter by eight inches high. Also in the chest on top was a leather sleeve which contained scrolls, and in the bottom a ring.

Joanna immediately exclaimed, "I recognize the ring, it is one worn by Joseph of Arimathea."

Lisa offered to open the scrolls since she had some experience in archeology. She carefully placed them on a tabletop and took several measures to avoid damage.

She then opened the scrolls and let Arslan and Ramede try to read them. The scroll Ramede read said;

"To all who read these words, God will judge you for how you treat these sacred relics."

I am Joseph of Arimathea, who took the Christ down from the cross and buried him in my own tomb. Yes, I bribed Roman soldiers to leave the tomb so Jesus, the prophet, could rise from the tomb. He rose from the tomb.

I helped to save many people from persecution in Galilee and took them to Gaul to spread the word of Christ. I then went to Britain and spread the word of Christ there. I also saved the sacred relics of Jesus from destruction, including the blood and fluids of Christ from the cross.

If I am wrong about my devotion to Christ I am wrong, but I am honestly wrong. I have not tried to deceive the world.

Jon Kelly

Whoever finds these treasures should honor them as relics of the history of Jesus who was a good man. He wanted to tell the world how to become better, it is enough to earn honor in the sight of God. I thank the world for my life in it. I thank many people including Jesus of Nazareth, David of Accrabbein, Mary Magdalene of Rennes-le-Chateau, Lazarus of Massilia, Zaccheus of Rocamadour, Maximin of Aix, Martial of Limoges, Entrope of Orange, Trophimus of Arles, Saturninus of Toulouse, Chuza of Jerusalem, King Ariviragus of the Silures, Nicodemus, my mother, my father, and my children. I also thank a unique person called Joanna of Massilia who may be known by many other names. If she be the person who finds these treasures, I thank God for your presence in my life.

By: Joseph of Arimathea, a Roman citizen, a Christian, Minister of mining for the Roman Empire, and Apostle of Christ to the Britain's

Ramede burst into tears when she read this scroll. She sobbed, "He was a great, great man who created more history than the very best men dream about. He was at the center of so much and only wanted or tried to do good and right."

The other scrolls were his writings about events, five of them. One covered the truth about his years in Britain with Jesus prior to his Ministry. A second covered what he knew about the ministry and miracles of Jesus. A third covered his defense of Jesus before the Sanhedrin and related events. A fourth covered his role in events when Jesus was crucified and was buried and resurrected. A fifth covered his travel to Gaul and then to Britain. All of these basically told the events he had already described to Joanna but provided documentation.

The smallest chest was opened next by Ramede. This chest contained one scroll and an item, which caused people to do a quick intake of breath because of the huge emotional content, associated with it. The chest contained a crown of thorns. Everyone immediately guessed what it was. Only Joseph could have this relic. The scroll only said it was the crown of Jesus of Nazareth as King of the Jews.

428

The last chest opened by Ramede was the greatest surprise of all. It contained 29 pieces of silver and a scroll. The scroll said:

To those who seek the truth,

I, Joseph of Arimathea, received these coins from Caiaphas, the High Priest in Jerusalem. He told me Judas Iscariot was bribed by a disciple of Jesus with these coins, one missing, to betray Jesus. The truth of this matter is not known to me but Caiaphas believed it to be so. Caiaphas, who was not my friend, gave me these coins and said, "To show the truth about these men who preached lies about the rising of Jesus from death. If they would betray their Jesus, they would also steal and hide the body of Jesus and make claims to have seen him alive again."

By Joseph of Arimathea, A Christian

Ramede said, "This communication is very interesting, but unless some other evidence comes forward this seems like a dead end.

Simon and Carrie were given the responsibility for working with the two pitch covered objects and for setting up the testing of the blood or fluid residue in the two cruets. DNA analysis would initially be aimed at determining if the DNA belonged to one of the children of the Tira. If the DNA did not match the Tira source, then testing would focus on establishing matches or close relationships with various DNA samples in the database including European, British or other royal families. A third analysis would be done to make matches with all samples in the database.

Simon and Carrie went to work on the objects. They cut through the pitch and found wax beneath. They then carefully removed the wax to expose the residue contained in the cruets. Samples were taken from the residue and processed to identify and analyze DNA in the samples. The amount of residue surprised them both. The literature led them to expect the residue from only two drops of blood, the amount of residue indicated almost a pint of blood having been dried out to give the amount of residue. The other cruet had a similar amount of lighter residue, which was sampled for analysis.

The computer analysis was started to try to match the sample DNA with DNA from the children of the Tira. This analysis took only about five minutes. The results were negative for both samples. If these samples were from the person who died on the cross, the person was not one of the children of the Tira.

The second analysis was immediately started to try to find any relationship to royal families. This analysis took about one hour to complete and results were negative.

The computer then turned to a correlation to all known DNA samples. This analysis would take several days to complete despite the unbelievable speed of the Tira's information processors.

Simon spoke to the group about the results so far. He said, "I am not surprised at the first result—it would seem to eliminate any of the Tira's children as the person who died on the cross. This result does not eliminate either Jesus or David.

I am somewhat surprised by the second result since we have some indication Jesus and/or David fathered children and they may have been donors to the bloodlines of the royal families in Britain or Europe. This result did not find any noticeable correlation between the DNA samples from the cruets and the royal family bloodlines.

The third correlation should find some correlation since we are looking for either an ancestor or descendant of the person who died on the cross. We have various archeological DNA samples from prior to the crucifixion to correlate some ancestors and many samples to identify any descendants. Thinking ahead the greatest surprise would be if there is no identified correlation to either ancestors or descendants. Then we would need to go back and do a detailed study of the sample DNA to see where the differences are found.

Carrie said, "We can start to look at the sample DNA and correlate it to out "typical" human DNA model. We may be able to see what major differences jump out at us so we will have a head start when the main analysis is done. This is getting to be fun."

Carrie set to work using the workstations, which had been installed on the Tira for these purposes. They allowed Carrie to design a testing routine and pass it on to the Tira's processor to work the data. Typically she could get answers in 5 minutes, which would take the fastest supercomputer on earth fifty years to process. She set up the analysis she wanted and sent it to the processor. In less than a minute the data was back. When Carrie looked she was astounded.

She continued to review and called Simon over to get his take on the new information. After several hours of discussion, rerunning routines with different parameters and brainstorming, Simon and Carrie were stumped and decided to present the problem to the group.

Simon said, "What we have is DNA from the sample, the cruets, which represent the DNA of the person who died on the cross, if we accept the witness of Joseph of Arimathea. The DNA does not match with typical DNA in several key areas. Theses are for the most part the same areas the DNA of Arslan and Ramede do not match the typical DNA model. However, the sample DNA differs from the DNA of Arslan and Ramede significantly, that is why we had no match on the first analysis. The person on the cross was not one of the children of the Tira.

The sample DNA from the cruets has additional chromosomes attached beyond the additions found with Arslan and Ramede. We are at a loss to explain where these came from. The only point we can establish is the person who died on the cross was not a "normal" human being within the definition of his DNA structure."

Arslan looked around the room and said, "So. If I understand the situation, Jesus or David or whomever it was died on the cross came from another gene source other than the Tira or normal humanity. *If we take it all the way it could have been the Holy Spirit impregnating the Virgin Mary.*"

Ramede said, "Well, we have come full circle. We have found out so many negatives about the development of Christianity, and then find the Holy Grail for which men have searched for a millennium, then take our science and prove he who died on the cross was not a normal human. The Christian theologians will dispute most of what we have to say but in the end we prove their primary point."

Simon said, "I doubt if they will see it that way. They have constructed a web of beliefs and rituals. When you wear out one or two of the strands the whole web tears apart. Their "religion" falls apart when this happens but "religion" is one thing. Truth is something else."

Arslan spoke up, "Religion is a institutionalized set of beliefs used to meet a social need. The truth and reality of the universe is something else. The religious thinker generally does not care about truth as much as defending his belief set, from my experience.

Lisa said, "What do we do now?"

Simon said, "We still have the completion of the comparison of the sample DNA to all other DNA samples from computers everywhere in the world. We have been contacting every known source where DNA data is stored on computers around the world. We are getting excellent cooperation despite not telling anyone exactly what we are going to do with the data. I said the analysis would take about three days more but in reality that only applies to the information we now have. As more data filters in the analysis will continue. It may be weeks before we get up to 80% or 90% of the existing data."

Ramede said, "There is one more test I would like to see attempted, and it may not be possible. The crown of thorns should be tested for DNA residue from blood. It would provide a second source of evidence about the DNA of the person who died on the cross."

No one disagreed and Simon prepared samples.

Carrie said, Next week is the meeting with heads of state to determine the future use of the Tira and its technology for the betterment of mankind. We probably need to turn our focus there since the computer will continue on with the DNA analysis. We all know we have been putting off the decision about whether we should trust the Tira to our world leaders or not. I think it is probably time for a straight vote on what we should do.

Lisa said, "Secret ballot or out in the open."

Carrie said, "Out in the open works for me."

Everyone else agreed.

Simon took charge of organizing the vote. He said, "First question, do we agree to turn the Tira over to an international agency, either existing or to be evolved?"

Yes_____ No_____

The second question can be answered at the same time, when do we make the transition if we vote yes? Multiple Choice

Now_____3 Months_____ 6 Months___One Year_____
Two years____Five Years_____Ten Years___ Indefinite _____

The third question is, what do we do if we do not turn the Tira over to an international agency?

A._____ Act as a committee of five to transfer technology from the Tira and make use of the Tira for beneficial activities, indefinitely.

B._____ Other

Simon said, "Are we ready to vote on these issues?"
Everyone nodded agreement.

Question 1: Arslan-No Ramede-No Lisa-No Carrie-No Simon-No

Question two: Arslan-Indefinite Ramede-Indefinite Lisa-Indefinite Carrie-Indefinite Simon-Indefinite

Question three: Arslan-A Ramede-A Lisa-A Carrie-A Simon-A

Arslan said, "It seems like we have a 100% perfect consensus. I hope everyone realizes what we have signed up to do. I don't know if it what I would like to do, but I don't see any choice as a reasonable and responsible person."
Lisa said, "With these decisions we have changed the meeting next week from a strategic concept development meeting to an announcement and then a tactical implementation meeting. I suggest we send the message right now to world leaders laying out our decision and letting them know what type of discussion they should come prepared to conduct. Not everyone will be happy, perhaps no one will be happy, but we tell them to *"learn to live with it."*

Jon Kelly

BIOGRAPHICAL NOTE:

Jon Kelly, born in Stoneboro, Pennsylvania, is a graduate of Grove City College (1969) and Indiana State University (1973). After serving in the U.S. Army, he spent twenty-seven years managing various manufacturing businesses and helping to raise three children. His business activities gave him the opportunity to travel and experience many places and people in the world.

The novel, *ARSLAN*, reflects three of Kelly's areas of interest; history, science fiction, and religion. He also writes poetry and has a strong admiration for the power of the written word to stir ideas and inspire.

Kelly currently lives in Scottsdale, Arizona. The author may be contacted at jkelly90@hotmail.com.

Sequel to ARSLAN

Look for *TIRA'S OTHER CHILDREN*, available soon.

ABOUT THE AUTHOR

Jon Kelly, born in Stoneboro, Pennsylvania, is a graduate of Grove City College (1969) and Indiana State University (1973). After serving in the U.S. Army, he spent twenty-seven years managing various manufacturing businesses and helping to raise three children. His business activities gave him the opportunity to travel and experience many places and people in the world.

The novel, *ARSLAN*, reflects three of Kelly's areas of interest; history, science fiction, and religion. He also writes poetry and has a strong admiration for the power of the written word to stir ideas and inspire.

Kelly currently lives in Scottsdale, Arizona. The author may be contacted at jkelly90@hotmail.com.

Printed in the United States
977100003B

9 781410 721457